Des Dillon was born and brought up in the Lanarkshire town of Coatbridge. He has written poetry and fiction, including *Me and Ma Gal*, *The Big Empty*, *Itchycooblue*, *Return of the Busby Babes* and most recently *The Big Q*, and has had several of his books adapted for film and television. He has worked as a teacher of English, a creative writing tutor and as a script-writer for *High Road*. Des Dillon lives in West Kilbride, and is currently Writer in Residence at Castlemilk.

To Alisa.

All best wishes

Des Dillon.

Also by Des Dillon

Me and Ma Gal
The Big Empty
Itchycooblue
Return of the Busby Babes
The Big Q

Duck

Des Dillon

review

First Published in 1998 by Argyll Publishing

First Published in this edition in 2001
by REVIEW

An imprint of Headline Book Publishing

10 9 8 7 6 5 4 3 2 1

ISBN 0 7472 6707 3

Typeset by
Letterpart Limited, Reigate, Surrey

Printed and bound in Great Britain by
Clays Ltd, St Ives plc

Headline Book Publishing
A division of Hodder Headline
338 Euston Road
London NW1 3BH

www.headline.co.uk
www.hodderheadline.com

For all them
that's doing it a day at a time
and to David Jago

Canal

I mind the night I flung Carmen in the canal.

We're at Stars an I've been talkin to this bird.

Outside I'm breathin in November air deep an cool in that way ye can only do when ye're pished. I smell her comin. She's starin up the sky an blowin her fringe.

Oh oh – trouble, I says, *trouble*.

I throws the arm round her.

But she spins out of the hold before I can smack the lips on her. Clip clop clip clop she goes wi folded arms an smoke smoke smokin away at a Club King Size. She sways from side to side, smoke comin out at regular intervals. Steam train. Sex.

Whit the fucks up now? I goes. But ma words zoom in the West End Park an bounce off the flats shatterin like Buckfast bottles an showers of tiny green stars fall through the clip clop smoke smoke puff puff folded arms an wigglin arse. She's fadin into darkness. I makes after her.

For fucksakes wait! I'm shoutin at her shadow.

BUMP

I'm that drunk I bumps right into her. The red light of her fag's comin at me. Right on the forehead.

Hissssssssssssssssssssssssssssssssssssssssssss
Singed flesh. Bastard. I slaps the hand on ma head.

Aaaaaaaaaaaaaaaaaaaaaaaaww *what the fuck did ye do that for?*

Go an get the wee tart puff *if ye want her.* Puff puff.

What? I'm rubbin spit on ma forehead.

That wee fuckin tart. Go an shag her. Fuckin slut.

What the fuck're you on about.

Harriet the Chariot that's who. Pressin her tits up yer arm. Thought I wasn't lookin? Thought I couldn't see?

Fuck me. Caught rotten.

Was she fuck, I goes. *You are fuckin crazy, so ye are. It's help you need – know that? The fuckin loony bin ye should be in. Hartwood. Locked up.*

She's pullin her hair wi two hands. Her voice's squeezin out gaps in gritted teeth like mashed tatties.

Don't call me mad. Don't call me mad. Don't point *call* point *me mad* point.

She's diggin her finger in her chest. Ye can hear it thumpin through the park like a mad rabbit wi a limp.

Don't thump *call* thump *me* thump *mad* thump.
Don't thump *call* thump *me* thump *mad* thump.
Don't thump *call* thump *me* thump *mad* thump.
Don't thump *call* thump *me* thump *mad* thump.

She wasn't anywhere near me, I says.

Don't thump *call* thump *me* thump *mad* thump.

She was at the other end of the table for Christsakes.

Don't thump call thump me thump fuckin thump mad thump.

She's diggin her finger in ma shoulder now.

Is there a law against talkin now?
She starts stalkin me like a cat goin,

I goes for the calm-her-down approach.

Look, I love YOU. What would I want wi slut like that?

What would ye want? What the fuck would ye want? Shag her that's what.

I wouldn't go near her wi a barge . . .

She's in sharp as a tack.

So ye'd go near other burds then?

Aw for fucksake. No . . . I . . .

Who would ye go near wi a bargepole? Eh? Who?

She's shakin me an the nails're diggin in so I rips away an starts walkin.

See. Can't face the truth. Hoormaster.

...ooooooooooRMAAAAAAAAAAAASTER!!!!!!

She's shoutin loud as fuck an shapes of punters comin out the dancin're strainin through webs of streetlight to see where the commotion is. But all they can see's the blackness of the middle of the park where disembodied voices, like ghosts that never quite found heaven're doin battle in eternal jealousy.

If I noticed she was into me I'd've got to fuck out her road.

Ya bastard ... *ye wanted to fuckin shag her ... didn't ye? Didn't ye?*

You ... are ... fuckin ... crazy, I goes pronouncin every word slow an loud.

ZIIIIIIIIIIIIIIIIIIIIIIIIIIIIIIIIIIIIIIIING!!!!!!!!!!!!!!!

She fucks the head right on me. Can see nothin. Cunts're shoutin abuse from the edge of the park an her runnin feet're crunchin in the grass. She's shoutin,

HOOOOOOOORMAAAAAAASTER!!!!!!!

over an over an its gettin smaller an smaller in the direction of the canal.

HOOOOOOOORMAAAAAAASTER!!!!!!!

HOOOOOOOORMAAAAAAASTER!!!!!!!

HOOOOOOOORMAAAAAAASTER!!!!!!!

HOOOOOOOORMAAAAAAASTER!!!!!!!

HOOOOOOOORMAAAAAAASTER!!!!!!!

HOOOOOOOORMAAAAAAASTER!!!!!!!

I drags ma eyes open an I'm speared by yella streetlights. It's like underwater. Ma head's spinnin. Ma nose's throbbin an nippin like fuck. Ever been thundered right on the beak? It's no fun. I starts runnin.

Right **sniffle** *ya fuckin* **sniffle** *bastard, that's* **sniffle** *it.*

She stays a cute step out ma reach, runnin in short bursts callin me all the wankers an hoormasters an dicks under the sun.

I want to choke the life out her – slow.

!

● I get this idea.

Ma life flashes before me. I don't like it. Ma life wi her flashes before me. I don't like that neither. This blackness floods in me. Another darkness's radiatin out ma spine. Ma inside's a fridge. It's clear what I've got to do. I've got to do maself in.

I decides to jump in the canal.

That's it – I'm in the canal. I've had enough of this. Just you watch. This's somethin you're never goin to forget. You'll be fuckin sorry so ye will.

I waited for her to run over an slobber me wi kisses but does she fuck. She starts rippin up lumps of turf an flingin them.

Jump fuckin jump ya waaaanker. Fuckin waaaanker. Waaaaaanker. WAAAAAAAANKER!!!!!

They must've heard her at The Fountain. They must've heard her in every house in The Brig.

WAAAAAAAAAAAAAAAAAAAANKER!!!!!
she's goin like a banshee. Lights in the flats're switchin an curtains're twitchin. Voices an peerin eyes on the edge of the park're submergin their heads in our black world. Duckin for danger. I marches at the canal sayin nothin. She's eggin me on.

Jump jump ya bastard I can't wait . . .

I sees the canal bridge. Stars're gettin closer all the time. Ma breath's billowin out an tornadoin up to heaven. I can smell the rancid canal banks. I lights ma last fag so's she'll know I means business.

She's hissin low an lights're goin out in the flats. Curtains stop twitchin. The murmurin edges of the park become lines of yella light on black. In distant streets voices laugh an giggle their way to cosy beds an condoms.

I'm surrounded by dark. The night's crept in me an it's cold under ma skin. Carmen's off the grass. The clip clop clip of her heels begins on the path. I steadys maself comin off the grass. It's easier walkin on grass than concrete when ye're pished.

She thinks I won't do it. She's got folded arms an puffin away darin me. I looks over the bridge an back in her eyes. No words. All or nothin. If I don't she'll clip clop away singin some stupid song nothin to do wi it – an yet everythin to do wi it. Roll out the fuckin barrel or somethin. But I've got somethin in ma favour this time. It's been lodged in ma head for weeks now – the canal. Ye think of some mental things drunk. Mibbi ye don't do them that night an ye don't do them next few times ye're out yer face.

An when ye wake up in the cold light of day ye say,

Thank fuck I never done that – jump off the flats – drive a car full steam ahead through the Polis station windie – run bollock up the Main Street smashin all the windies – run round ASDA wreckin the joint – walk along the Main Street on a Saturday wi yer hair on fire – let a pack of crocodiles out their face on acid loose in the Social – saw down all the lampposts wi a Sthill Saw . . . an millions of other stuff that comes in yer head like a good idea when ye're pished. So she knows fuck all about this jumpin in the canal bein a plan.

I struggle up on the wall like a mad monkey. Her head tilts back an her mouth's wide open. I'm tryin to balance cos it's one of them walls wi a pointy bit.

Fuck me I nearly

fell

tryin to stand up. I mean, what's the point doin yersel in if

ye're goin to look like a dick in the process. She's holdin the
fag an exact inch from her red lips. Paralysed. I need
somethin good to say, last words an all that, but all I can say
is,

You ruined ma fuckin life.

I'm just about to add

Tell the world I'm sleepin in the stars.

an recommend a song for ma funeral – 'Bridge Over
Troubled Waters', or 'My Way' (Sid Vicious version
preferred) – when I slips. I glimpse her face as I sinks
through black November air. She looks like Plug out the

Beano when he goes GULP!

So do I.

On the way down a lot of things happened. Ye'd think
nothin much could happen in twenty feet but time goes dead
slow. Ma coat flings itself back up at the wall like it never
wanted to jump, like it was taken by surprise. So was I.

Every time ye talk about suicide some cunt says –

*What if ye jumped off the flats an on the way down ye changed
yer mind?*

I mean what do ye do? Phone a fuckin taxi? I used to think
people like that were pricks but here I'm rattlin down at the
cold canal warp factor five an I've changed ma mind the
minute I slip off the wall. Yer mind works fast as fuck. I'm
thinkin all this an suckin the aul breath in so I can stay alive
till I resurface. It's an hour before Carmen lets out this big

scream.

An another hour before I surge in the water.

I nearly break ma fuckin legs. It's only four feet deep.

Crumple. I goes under for a millisecond an shoots back up
wi white water an shards of ice fallin off me like a Trident

7

missile. There's sheets of ice here an there slidin under the still water. All kinds of ducks an stuff're flappin like fuck out ma road an I suppose the sleepin fishes exploded, duntin their heads off the canal bank tryin to get away. The cold hits me like a fuckin lightnin bolt of ice. I'm some weight seein as how bein dressed for the dancin's not the best way to be dressed in a canal in the middle of winter in the middle of the night.

I'm makin for the edge takin sharp breaths when I sees her in her disco dancin gear cloppin down the stairs. I don't know where I gets the courage but under I goes for twenty seconds.

1

2

3

4

5

6

7

8

9

10

11

12

13

14

15

16

17

18
19
20

When I surface she's roarin *I'm sorry I'm sorry I'm sorry* . . .

I clear ma eyes. She's roarin. She's runnin up an down bumpin into the ASDA trolleys an rusty prams. She's searchin the water, tryin to look through its black surface wi her black eyes an shoutin, *Please please God I'll do anything, I'll do anythin.*

I'm clingin to the rushes at the edge an, even though I'm freezin, I'm lovin it. I'm lovin it for two reasons:

1. I've got her roarin an cryin.

2. She loves me.

Sometimes at a Rosary I burst out laughin. So here's me hidin in the canal. More likely to freeze to death than die from the fall an what does I do? I starts laughin that's what. She's sobbin first, then she's off again. Greetin. Ever noticed how burds use these big long vowels when they're cryin?

Ohhhhhhhhhh Gaaaaaaawd don't let him diiiiiiiiiiiiiiiiiie don't let him diiiiiiiiiiiiiiiiiiiiiiiiiiiiiiiiiie.

I starts laughin. Can't stop. I'm bendin over wi it nearly

drownin. I comes to ma senses when the water starts goin up like the *General Belgrano*.

Sploosh splosh sploosh it's goin.

She's launchin half-bricks. How's there no full bricks lyin about ever? I drags maself out like a wet Labrador, takin some on the back. I starts chasin her down the canal an every now an then she bends an lobs a Buckie bottle over her shoulder as she's runnin. So it takes me longer than usual to get her. When I do I launch her in the canal. I don't want to kill her. I only want to see her face when she hits the water.

She can't swim.

But she's not slow the bold Carmen. No sir. I'm waitin for

splash

when I feels this tuggin at ma leg. Next thing I'm howked off ma feet. She's grabbed ma leg on the way down an there's the two of us in the water. But she's out like a shot lobbin rocks, bricks an washin machine lids. I'm underwater movin SAS style. Manouverin through sunken cars an mountain bikes. Every time I comes up she's fuckin me wi bricks an shoutin abuse. I gets in the reeds. She knows I'm in there somewhere but she's aimin at the wrong bit. She stops. The water's still an these two ducks're starin in ma face wonderin what the fuck's goin on.

She strikes a match. How the fuck they're still dry I don't know. There's no understandin handbags. Defy science so they do. If there's ever a nuclear war I want to be inside a wummin's handbag cos they're in-de-fuckin-structable. The match flares a big circle round her. She looks like an angel. Or a demon. I'm breathin onto the surface so's it'll mingle wi the slab of mist. She's blowin smoke up the sky an drip . . . drip . . . water runs out her clothes. She starts scrunchin along the ash path to the yella lights. Every now an then the red glow of her fag traces a thin arc down to her thighs. It's synchronised wi a long line of forward smoke, like a strange engine.

I waits till the distant click click on the pavement disappears down Blairhill Street. I slithers out like a slimy eel. Ma fags're soaked. I chucks them.

I vaults the wall.

Other end.

Fuck ye!

Down I goes tumblin through trees an landin on the hard roots winded. I tries to get up. The stars're spinnin like The Shows. I conk out. Must've lay there hours cos when I woke up ma gear creaked. Frost. I looks at maself. I'm like the fuckin Ice Man, whoever the fuck he is. If any cunt seen me they'd've ran a mile. Me creakin out the blackness all white like a spook. I'm gaspin. Creak creak I'm goin along the path lookin for fags.

It's amazin how quiet a town can be. The odd car buzzes an fades. The aul teeth're goin chitter chatter ninety to the dozen an I can't stop them. That's when it happened. Ye'd think I'd remember that night mostly for jumpin in the canal

Des Dillon

an throwin her in but that's not it. That's not it at all. This
feelin goes right in me. Big fuckin empty feelin. Through me.
A glacier. I starts runnin to get away. How daft can ye get?
It's inside me an I'm runnin to get away. Fuckin idiot.

Anyway the last thing I believe in's God an all that shite.
But guess what I does? I'm runnin through these trees like a
maddie. Twigs're slashin ma face an stingin but I keep goin.
Ma feet're the only noise in the place.

Next thing I'm on ma knees. I'm on ma knees an lookin
up into the universe like some cunt out a bible thumpin
film.

If there is a God, I'm goin,

if there is a God ye better fuckin help me!!!

I shouts loud as fuck at the tiny stars. But all they do's
buzz across the void of a million light years. An it comes to
me. That buzz's so far away an quiet it's worse than the
biggest silence. The stars're only distant midges hummin by.
I look at the spaces between them. Nothin. Lots of nothin. I
can't find somewhere to put ma eyes. Nowhere. Then what?
I bursts out greetin like a big lassie, that's what. Thank fuck
no cunt was there. Never live that down in The Brig – the
two worst things, believin in God an cryin like a big lassie.

There's no flashes of light no voices no good feelins. I stop
cryin an creak creak to the road. The only miracle's the
taxi that draws up soon as I sticks ma hand out.

Burnside Walk mate,

I goes an jumps in. I'm thinkin about Carmen. I'm goin to
beg ma way in the house an beg ma way in the bed. Not to
shag her – it's one of them cases when ye want to hold on –
to be inside them in fact. Ma whole body inside her. Away
from the world.

Cold? Asks the driver cos he hears ma teeth. I mumbles
somethin that means I'm too drunk to talk an he shuts up. I

12

can feel water seepin onto his good seats so I gets dropped ten gates away. I hands him two wet notes an I'm offski over the gardens.

Ya fuckin bastard get back here,

he's shoutin an

Tango Tango

he's screamin in the radio to get other taxis round to kick fuck out me.

But I'm burrowin in the dark an at ma back door before ye can say boo. It's open. She usually locks the lot an I've got to sleep outside. I sneaks in an **wham** the heat hits me like a hammer. I throw all ma gear off an I hears it slappin off the linoleum. I'm warm right away. My skin's tinglin wi the heat. I sneaks bollock up the stairs an opens the room door. The windie's open an a cold wind's blowin in. The bed's untouched. Smooth an neat. I flings myself on the bed goin,

God help me God help me . . .

over an over cryin loud. Outside a commotion of taxis lights up the night an fills the air wi threats. Fuck them all.

I pushes maself into the pillow where I can smell her perfume. The sweat's runnin out me. Every now an then the

DRRRIIIIIIIING
DRRRIIIIIIIIING
DRRRIIIIIIIIIING
DRRRIIIIIIIIIING

of the phone's shovin up through cracks in the floorboards, piercin the mesh of carpet. Sometimes there's:

BANG BANG BANG BANG BANG BANG

at the door. Front then back. Later I hears this taxi drillin up the street. Half of me's terrified it's cunts round to get me an half of me wishes it's Carmen. The evil red neon of the smashed up radio alarm clock's flash flashin away on the floor. It's givin me all different times. I starts goin over how it's come to this.

Blackpool Arrival

January. Blackpool. Lytham Road. No jackets. Fuckin freezin. She's got this red kimono an I'm in a thin white T-shirt. The bus wooooooooooooooooooooooooooooooooooooooooooooooooshes off. She drags the jumper I gave her round her body. What Every Wummin Wants: £5.99.

Ye not freezin in that?

I don't feel the cold, says I, vibratin.

She flings the arm round me squeezin her shoulder under ma armpit an pressin her head in ma chest.

You're ma-aa Brown-eyed girl . . . I sings an forgets the words.

I shoves ma face in her hair. *Sniff sniff* I'm goin.

Much we got? She goes.

Well, we bought fags at Preston . . . there's fuck all left hardly. Two quid odds . . .

This fat baldy guy's wipin red Formica tables an starin out his windie.

He's got this sign up:

FULL DINNERS
97 PENCE
ALL DAY

The café's a phone box wi seats. This horse shaggin song's on the jukie. *Are you tired of my my darlin*, it goes.

Carmen looks at me kiddin I'm not listenin. But it sticks in ma head. I never heard it again but I could sing ye the words to this day.

Her back's to the windie. I can see ma T-shirt reflected in her eyes.

Ello, can ei elp you morning?

He's starin at her. She leans forward. The table's soakin. She pulls a face an fingers her damp elbow. Then his big hairy arm comes between us. She peeps under his armpit.

What we getting?

He points at a chalkboard,

Full dinners, ninety-seevin pence.

Goes the Tally giving our table extrasuperwipe wi an ancient J-cloth. Squelch, slap an brown drips fallin on the floor. An another thing, there's this wet patch like he's pished hiself.

A meal for less that a quid! Is that OK?

I says nodding so she sees the wet mark. She's tryin not to laugh. We've had nothin hardly to eat for three days.

She laughs. She's noddin clasping her hands to her tits an checkin her wet elbow. He's looking at me then her, calculating. Nosy bastard.

Thees ees your wife? Yes? No? Yes?

He's liftin her hand for a ring. He could see that just lookin. Bastard. His gorilla hand's cradlin hers. Kick fuck out him's what I want to do. He flips her hand side to side like he's inspectin a fish.

Ahh . . . he goes wavin his finger . . . *thees ees not your wife.*

Then he fuckin winks.

C'mon, let's get fuckin out here.

She stuffs her fag in the foil ashtray.

Gootbye says the Tally.

Chirio.

She waves an smiles. He looks at me like he's won somethin. Prick. Then he shouts,

Cheery, come any time, I have job for so pretty.

A job? That's magic. See, see, it's not that bad. I've got a job already.

She spins round a lamppost laughing. The Tally's grinnin through the glass.

What kind of job d'ye think **HE'LL** *give ye?*

She stops, hand on hip, an blows her fringe.

What d'ye mean?

Nothin. Nothin. C'mon.

Bad pause.

She latches ma arm. We walk on sayin nothin. I need drink.

137. We scuffle to a halt.

That's it,

It's a scabby black an white door.

Marlyn's. One three seven . . . that's it . . . Lytham Road.

She rattles the door. The Tally's strainin to see.

Silence.

Chap chap chap chap.

Somethin moves.

A million bolts an chains start rattlin at the other side. The door creaks open like a horror film an we're talkin to two hands an a face. Plug ugly – a plate of porridge flung in a bin. Marlyn. Couldn't be anybody else. Daz described her. I tries to check for a wooden leg but she's leanin round the door like she's a lizard from the neck down. She looks from me to Carmen like the Tally only quicker cos she's only got one eye . . .

Can I elp your chook?

17

*I . . . I . . . I'm l . . . l . . . looking for a mate of mine Jim
Scally . . . he . . .*

Not here.

She's shuttin the door but Carmen's got the boot in.

D'ye know where he is?

Who're you?

Marlyn draws her eye skin thegether like an accordion.
Suspicious.

I'm his mate . . . Mick Riley

The name registers. Carmen moves her leg thinkin we're
in. Marlyn closes the door an when there's a couple of inches
left she croaks,

I'll tell im yi called in.

SLAM
RATTLE RATTLE RATTLE

The chains an locks're goin like the ghosts' an ghouls'
night out. I sees this pub an shouts through the letterbox,

Tell him I'm in The Albert. I'll be there all . . .

We headed over to The Albert.

I knew Daz for years. On the milk. We used to drink at
school an rob beer lorries. He married this bird, The Horrible
we called her. Usual story . . . pregnant. His Mad-Catholic
Maw makes him get married. The Horrible dumps him for
freedom an a Monday Book. He bums about, ends up in
Blackpool.

He'd come up the road an we'd get sozzled an give it how
cool, mad, bad, tough as fuck we were in the old days . . . not
like this pussy young team that needs blades – built like
jockey's fuckin whips – couldn't beat Casey's Drum. But us?
Tough as fuck . . . on an on we'd go till we couldn't talk. Said
digs were no problem – any time. He's shaggin this thing
from Barnsley. Slinky's her name. Fuckin Slinky!

Coom from Baaaaaaaaaaaaaaaaaaaaaaaaaaaaaaaaaaaaaaaaaaaaaaaansley.

She'd go, an we'd laugh like fuck.

Drinker's paradise Blackpool, Daz said. *Sell Buckie! Drink drink drink all the time. Fuckin great.*

I mind Daz's laughin out missin teeth an swiggin a Buckie bottle between tokes. But good memories don't help us stuck in Blackpool wi fuck all money an no jackets.

The Ugliest Wummin
in the World

Marlyn's a right aul cow. Like a pile of knittin needles wi pig skin flung over them. KER-PLUNK covered in balloon skin. Her legs're fuckin horrific, stickin out the bottom of her skirt into ancient woolly socks. Well I'm sayin legs but I mean

leg cos she's only got one an a peg. Fuckin wooden leg. Like a rat's tail an a broke pencil her legs. Says she's forty but she's three hunner an six at least. Whiskers bigger than the cat's, if she had a cat, but she fed that to the coffin dodgers, Daz said. Evenin meal £2.50 extra. Meeiaw.

The Ugliest Wummin in the World.

Froggy shagged her. Can ye believe it? Daz lets it out the bag. The aul cunt goes up the Noggin wi Daz an Froggy. Froggy's kiddin her on,

Show's yer beard Marlyn,

an all this stuff. But she's serious. Wantin shagged. She's brushed the cobwebs off her dusty fanny an polished her peg wi Pledge an she's wantin Froggy to Mr Sheen her thigh. She leans an whispers in his ear. Daz says Froggy's eyes light up like bulbs an next thing they're holdin hands an she's cooin like a pigeon.

Anyhow. Midnight they're back in Marlyn's an,

I'm away to ma scratcher, says Daz. But he's not off to bed he's got his ear pressed on the floor. Listenin.

Fook me Froggy Fook me Froggy. FOOK FOOK MEEEEEEEE MEEEEEEEEEEEEEEEEEEEEEEEEEEEEEEEEEEEEEEEEEE

She's screamin. Froggy's right in there gruntin. The wooden leg's bangin off the headboard. Daz's pishin hiself. Rollin about. Marlyns whoooooooooooooooooooooin away like a murder.

Slap me, slap me, slap me,

Froggy's layin the slaps in hard.

She comes. *Fuckin air-raid siren,* says Daz. Even some of the wrinklies stop dribblin their chins an break light on the darkness of the lobby. Peekin out doors cos an orgasm's somethin they almost remember.

Silence. Mumblin.

Froggy comes in the room fixin his trousers. Daz's on the floor pointin at him an laughin. He shoves his hand on Daz's face.

Smell aul foosty drawers.

Fuck off, she's mingin. I'd rather shag you than that aul cow.

Ah! But could you give me a hunner an twenty quid?

Eh?

Hunner an twenty, would you pay me that for shaggin ye?

Fuck off Froggy brain.

That was the deal, Goes Froggy takin his trousers off again.

Show's then.

No dig money, six weeks.

Daz's wantin a shag at her now an Froggy goin on about how it's a turn on shaggin a wooden leg. Different. Even if she does smell like Pitenweem Fish Filleters Club's day out at Blackpool.

An that same aul cow slagged unemployed cunts comin down from Glasgow. Beggin the Conservative government.

That same aul cunt let ye get yer Giro delivered there. Put ye down for bed an breakfast. Hunner an twenty a fortnight. She took twenty. She was a parasite on a parasite. She had all the IDs an cashed the Giros up Waterloo Post Office. She took Daz an Froggy's rent money off an handed them the rest. Mackenzie had done a bunk owin hunners. Good on him. Serves the aul cow right. He left this note:

Hope yer wooden leg catches woodworm halfway across the road ya aul cunt.

Love Jerry XX

Friday the Giros're up Waterloo wi Bill. He's this aul cunt from Manchester. Been in Marlyn's fourteen year. Fly as a jailer. Always walks different ways back cos he's got a couple of grand on him. Thirty odd Giro's goin to her house over an above the cunts that stay there. The Social're daft as brushes. How could so many people squeeze in the one wee bit? Fuckin idiots.

Bill comes back. Froggy an Daz's got the good gear on. They've been skint for a week. Chokin. Froggy's buyin a cargo wi the twenty he's savin on rent. Marlyn starts handin out the dough. Daz folds two piles. One for the back pocket another down the sock between his heel an shoe. Emergency. Froggy's smile's disappearin as he's countin.

What the fucks this Marlyn? he goes.

She looks through straggles of greasy hair an gives him the question-mark stare.

Froggy slaps the money down. Aul Bill finds somethin interesting in the frying pan. Daz's tyin his shoe lace. Froggy's got somethin to say but can't find a good way to say it.

What about . . . what about . . . our . . . our arrangement?

What arrangement's that, Chook? Marlyn's fixin away at her hair wi mockit fingernails.

You fuckin know . . . Froggy whispers hard as he can between his teeth.

*Ooh **he's** gettin touchy. That's the usual, right Bill?*

Bill grunts. He's terrified after the night Mackenzie slashed him.

You know Pinnochio. Froggy goes. (They used to call her Pinnochio cos she was made out of wood. She hated it.)

Marlyn's face lights up. She gets the drift. *Ooh you don't mean the oother night now do you, chook?*

You know fine well what I mean, Hopalong.

Marlyn lets out this witchy laugh an her top set of falsers falls an clacks onto the bottom. Her mouth's all slabbers goin up the way an down the way like stalagmites an stalagtites.

Ooh I never thought you were daft as that Froggy. Mackenzie fell for that. Boot I though you really fancied me.

She blows him a kiss. Froggy's fuckin speechless. Daz's on the floor creasin hiself an aul Bill's shoulders're goin up an down at the greasy cooker. Marlyn opens her legs. Pulls in her belly an reaches down her knickers. That's where she keeps the money – in a clean colostomy bag cut open specially. She whips out a fiver.

There, Chook, that'll put lead back in your pencil.

Froggy's stormin off an Daz grabs the fiver laughin.

Joost tap me door any time, Chook, I'll be waitin.

An her cacklin laugh follows them onto Lytham road. Froggy'll never live it down.

Anyway that's Marlyn. 137 Lytham Road. The only clean thing's the carpets an they're stinkin. Look like tar. Feel like treacle. There's two kinds of people stayin there:

1. Aul guys bedridden about to die.
2. Cunts from Coatbridge an Edinburgh an Springburn an Possil an places like that. On the run from the Polis, the wife, or somethin.

Every toilet's plastered wi shite. These aul bastards've got runs all the time. Marlyn fries bad eggs out Waterloo market. Fuckin cow. You go somewhere else for a shite. Even pishin in the chanty I'm thinkin the germs could mibbi be fast enough to propel up ma pish to ma dick. So when I pish I move about the way wanes pee in a puddle. An I pish in spurts.

Daz got us in so long as we get Giro's delivered there. He shows us our room. The door hits the bed when it opens. It stinks of damp an pish. The carpet's all glossy. This drip

drip

drip

of water's landin on an umbrella. The umbrella's propped up so the water's runnin down it onto the wall. Daz gives us his Breville, half a pan loaf an a tub of Stork. I make the pieces an Carmen counts the twenty-two blankets. The first fourteen's soaked right through. Daz says keep them on the bed an try keepin the rest dry cos it's Siberia at night. Click click. No bulb.

The lobby bulbs're too high so I creeps in this room. There's some cunt in stripy pyjamas in the bed. I can't tell if it's a man or a wummin but it's kicked the blankets off. I stands on the bed an changes the bulb for our dud. I'm sneakin out,

Mary is that you? He goes, it's an aul guy. Belfast accent. For laugh I says,

Aye its me, Mary.

He starts cryin. He can't see me an he's sayin, *Hold me Mary, hold me. I think I'm goin. I think I'm dyin, Mary. Hold me.*

Fuck knows what comes over me. There's me stealin this aul cunts bulb an I leans over an holds his hand. The room stinks to high heavens but I'm on the edge of his bed holdin his hand. I drags damp blankets over him. He coughs.

Mary do yer still love us dear, he says.

I don't know what to do or say. I squeezes his hand an goes, *Yes . . . Aye aye I do still love ye.* I says.

There's silence an I thinks he's onto me. But he squeezes ma hand tight, *Mary I think I'm . . . pray wi me, Mary.*

I don't believe in God or fuck all but I still knows a few prayers. I gives him an Our Father an a couple of Hail Marys. All the time I'm holdin his hand.

He's fallin asleep an, fuck knows why, I leans over an kisses him light on his forehead. The bad smell in the room seems to've disappeared. The moon's comin in the small windie at the top of the wall. His faint smile appears in the dim light.

Thank yer, he says an squeezes ma hand, *thank yer, darlin.*

Weird. Never seen that aul guy again.

I pops the bulb in. The room lights up an Carmen's waitin for me to do somethin. Up wi the red kimono an we burrow under a million tons of blankets. Steam from our breath's runnin down the windie an her moans echo round the damp walls. But all these twisted faces're pressin against ma head tryin to burst it. POP I come an the faces disappear.

I wake in the middle of the night. It's the odd siren blastin its way through Blackpool. I'm shakin an I'm sweatin. I blink over an over cos I can't believe how dark it is. Carmen's breathin light an her skin's glowin soft in the terrible night.

Bedsits an Windmills

The gale's blowin in ma ears. They won't hear the door
shuttin. They're still laughing an joking up in the room.
Room, that's a fuckin joke so it is. Room? Seen bigger phone
boxes. But there's eight in there bevvyin, all sittin on the
damp single bed. They think I'm away to the bog.

I'm sittin there minutes ago, on the edge of the bed wantin to
leave, but ma arse's welded to the sheets. I want to go but
the aul legs're on strike. Can't move. I pass the message I
want to go an the muscles start respondin but depression
takes over an I'm still welded. Can't move.

D'ye know what the last straw is? Her, that Edinburghslut,
Froggy's burd. I'm half-cut. Carmen's flirtin wi Froggy.
Jealousy's rushin through ma veins like miniature Christmas
trees. Backwards. I can't say nothin cos they'll all know I'm
not hard as I make out. They'd be right in tearin me apart.
They can't do it physically, the fear game. I'm mental . . .
fight like fuck an all that, but right now, in front of them I'm
crumblin. Cryin inside. Ma heart's enormous an empty. It's a
wonder they can't hear the bells of Hell ringin inside it . . .

Red. Ma skin must be red. Look at her pressin the side of her arse into him.

I draw the feet backwards to stand but I'm stuck. There's no holes in the atmosphere for leavin so I stay. Then, the Edinburghslut, she stands up mid-sentence, nice as ye like, lifts the skirt an drops the scants. Wi both hands she jerks backwards onto the sink an starts pishin. No cunt flinches. Not a one. I can hear pish squirtin out an gurglin down the plug hole. I can even smell it. I look. I can't help it. She sees me run up the white an red of her corn-beef thighs an zero in on her dark patch. Her hands're on her legs now an they squeeze the skin, leavin white blotches. I think it's on purpose but I'm not sure.

Swear to God she parts the fuckin legs a bit an lifts the front of the skirt up wi her thumb. Her eyebrows go up too. They're all too blitzed to see it. She gives me the *come up an fuck me anytime* look. Her scants're below her knees an she's stretchin the elastic so they're bitin into her outer thighs. They're not white like I like them, her knickers. They've been white but now they're grey. She gives me the *three teeth missin* smile an bounces out the sink pullin them up, starin. She wants me bad. She turns the hot well on to wash the pish away. She sits beside me. The smell in the room's boilin pish an stale tobacco an stinkin beer an damp bedclothes an rotten wood an a greasy aul Breville breathin away under dirty washin an the bodies heavin wi BO an Buckfast an her leg, her leg up an down it's goin on ma thigh, up an fuckin down. Froggy's got the arm round Carmen.

Carmen's got the arm round Froggy now. Fuck this. I imagine them shaggin – fuck sake what am I doin? I can't help it. I imagine them shaggin again an Edinburghslut's rubbin the leg up an down an Carmen's eyes dart by an they're brown, brown an shinin. Her eyes're brown. Brown-eyed girl. Her hair's on his shoulder. I want to fuckin kill him. The bastard. She's drawin strands out an lettin them fall like a schoolgirl concentratin. But she is a fuckin schoolgirl, sixteen! Six-fuckin-teen! What the fuck am I doin here? An that's when I stand up like I'm goin to the bog.

★

Sneakin down the stairs I hear slutface skulkin about in the lobby. She's slidin along the wall cos Marlyn took the fuse out to save money. But out the door I go an still they're gyratin in ma head. Froggy's on her an she's pullin at her hair like she done wi me an moanin an liftin her hips up an wantin it, **wantin it.** Fuck sake what am I doin to ma head?

I cross the empty street. Daz gave me the anorak. The hood blows down. So fuckin what. The rain rubs ma face an I walk like a zombie. No cunt'll stand in ma way. Ma eyes're madder than night. No cunt. Not unless they want to fuckin die. Not unless they want to die.

That's was it.

Die that's the answer.

Die.

In the sea.

Jump in the sea.

I'm on the front. It's me in the middle, the sea on one side, an the fuckin madness up there in that bedsit on the other. I make it to South Pier an climb the gates. The South Pier – winter – empty as a mountain. No cunt for miles. Only the sea an it's shoutin. It's hissin its melancholy song an I'm goin in. I climb the red an yella railin at the very edge an stand.

There's two feet of board between me an oblivion. Ma hands're welded to the rail behind. I lean out. Ma head's over the darkness surgin below. Water's in big slow circles an it's waitin. They're waitin back at Marlyn's but I can't let go. Ma hands won't let go.

Let go cunts, I say but the hands won't let go – they're not respondin. The sea's heavin up.

Fuckin let go hand bastards, I shout. The sea swallows ma voice. That's the voice in, all I need's the rest of me. In I go. But the hands won't let go. The hands're in a world of their own an in the hand's world they want to stay alive. I want to jump. I really want to jump. But the fuckin hands won't let go of the yella railin. The sea's waitin but it can't wait all night. It'll need to go where it goes an come back lookin for me another day.

Let go hands, let go, but this time I'm not orderin them. I'm crying cos I can't let go an I'm beggin the hands to unclasp. But there's no fuckin way they're going down that drop to the icy sea. For hours I'm jerkin forward an can't break loose. I end up rockin back an forwards wi the motion of the waves rollin onto the great iron pillars underneath.

Back.

                                      An forth.

Back.

                                      An forth.

Back.

                                      An forth.

Back.

                                      An forth.

Back.

                                      An forth.

Back.

                                      An forth.

★

The mornin light finds me sleepin in the Windmill on the beach. I stare at ma hands an wonder how the fuck I couldn't jump. If I felt bad goin on the pier I felt even worse this mornin. The spark for suicide's gone so I decide to go back. This's Jimmy McCann's Windmill. He lives here. He's an alky. It's got no bottom. Sand. He sleeps on a ledge halfway up it. But he's back in the bedsit too.

What if Froggy's an Carmen's enmeshed in each other, the stink of sex all over the room. The Edinburghslut might be there too in the same bed. Mibbi the two of them were into her. She was like that the Edinburghslut. Froggy'd bring whoever he wanted home an she'd share.

I go to stand up but less of me wants to go back to Marlyn's than stay. I spend the day trying to leave the Windmill

    back

                                            an forth

    back

                                            an forth

    back

                                            an forth

    back

                                            an forth

    into the light
    into the dark
    into the light
    into the dark

But the black thoughts of them an me an the howlin wind stills me. I see the evenin in starin out to sea.

Hill Street Blues

Marlyn's consisted of keepin rain off the bed an makin soggy French toast in a mucky Breville. Smokin. Drinkin. Cunts stuffed in the one room all night.

A stroke of luck. We gets this flat in Hill Street. Luxury compared to Marlyn's midden. Two rooms. Fold out the wall bed, wardrobe, chest of drawers, couch. Big windie. Light light light. Cooker fridge table plates pots pans knifes forks spoons in the other room. The street's quiet. Three floors up in a white buildin. Steve an Jackie's. They're thirty odds an ye can hear them shaggin at night. They like Carmen.

This's how we got it. Daz takes us up to the Pieman's. He makes pies. Potato's his speciality. The flat next to him's empty. He puts a word in wi Steve an Jackie an we're in. Twenty-five a week. Marlyn's was seventeen each. The Pieman's got one room lookin in the back garden. Fold down bed fridge cooker all in one room. He's got his fire on two bars all the time. The padlock on the meter's rigged so ye can spring it open. Steve an Jackie don't notice when they open it every week. Pieman's been in an out jail all his life.

Anyway that's us in Hill street. Things're goin to get better.

A Nice Pot of Stew

We're all in Froggy's flat this day. It's a two-room affair. A scullery an a room for everythin else. The bed folds in the wall. The bog's in the lobby so every cunt's pishin in the sink. Even I'm doin it. Jimmy McCann's drunker than usual.

Jimmy's standin wavin from side to side an singin. No cunt's payin him a blind bit of attention. He falls backwards over the telly an lands wi a crash in the corner. Right away he gets up, picks up the hairdryer an starts singin 'Danny Boy'. He gets a laugh. He's from Springburn. Came here when The Trains shut. Eventually he falls pished on the floor. Froggy dips his pockets for a tenner an off we pop to the Noggin.

It's a week later. Edinburghslut's been goin on about a smell for days. She's nagged Froggy into submission an he goes to find it. Thinks it must be sour milk or somethin or a dead rat under the floor. They get all the cupboards empty an the smells still there. Next thing Edinburghslut screams, lookin in the big soup pot.

McCann — who else could it be — shat in the pot the last time he was here. So don't be eatin stew in Froggy's house.

Fancy a wee plate of stew? We'd shout at Jimmy across the street. He'd grin like a dog caught shaggin an shuffle on.

Jerry an Danya

It's spring. Blackpool's openin up. There's me an Daz an
Carmen in Hill Street this day. Daz's from Coatbridge.
Fucked off an left his wife too. So he says. The Horrible flung
him out. We're drinkin a couple of bottles an there's a load of
Supers on the floor. He was a boxer. Me an him's been
bare-fist boxin an Carmen's flickin her hair an chain-smokin.
We're bruised an stinkin wi sweat. So we give up an start
tellin stories about the old days to impress Carmen. All that
mind the time shite.

I boost him up, he boosts me up.

*Mind the time I came in your house Daz an ye're standin there
wi yer Maw pressed up against the wall wi a knife at her throat?*

He laughs an goes, *Aye, an ye walked right back out again.*

He laughs loud as fuck an nods the head waitin for me to
go back to the start of the story. Carmen drags the fag an
swings her head like a plastic doll to Daz – to me – to Daz.
She's goes, *You had yer mother up against the wall wi a knife?*

Her mouth's wide an her top lip's curled. Daz takes a
good swig out the bottle. *Ahhhhh*, he says, *I was a right crazy
bastard when I was young. That right?* he goes to me.

Never out the jail, I says.

Fuckin mental! he says lookin to me.

A right crackpot, says I.

Kshhh Carmen crashes another Super an puts a fag out **wshshtphutt** in the old one.

Daz's squeezin plooks. *Who do I look like? I mean who the fuck do I look like? Tell they cunts who I look like!* he'd always go.

Oliver Reid, Daz, the dead spit of Oliver Reid, ma man, we'd say, an that's him happy the rest of the night. But really he looked like ET wi plukes an spots an blackheads.

Anyway. There's the three of us well oiled. I'm about to launch into this story, when

clump

clump clump

clump

there's these big footsteps on the stairs. We thinks it's the Polis. Carmen swings the black curls nippin Daz's eye. She gives me the the big brown *Terrified of the Polis* eyes an I looks at Daz cos he's an experienced jailbird.

The door bursts open an in bounces Slinky. We all sighs an laughs. There's fags sparkin up all over the place an cunts're crashin open cans left right an centre. Slinky smiles: bleached hair, red face an clothes threatening to burst if she lets her breath out. I mind her cleavage flattened in by this tight white shirt-thing.

Hi babe, says Daz. Deft as fuck she plants a slabbery, says *hiya honey*, lights a fag, picks up a can an *kshh*, she's pourin it down her neck. I was goin to clap her for professional alcoholism when I hears

sob sob sob boo hoo

sob sob sob boo hoo sob sob sob boo hoo sob

sob sob boo hoo sob sob sob boo hoo

out in the lobby. I gives Slinky the question-mark eyes:

She shakes the head an throws a sympathetic thumb over her shoulder.

It's Danya, she says, as if she's been skelped by a car.

What about her? I asks.

That bastard Jerry.

Daz jumps up wi the fightin head on. *Has he done her in again? I telt him the last time . . .*

Sit down Daz, goes Slinky, shovin him back in the chair wi a flick of her hand. For a fat burd she's sometimes graceful.

Her big arse's scuffin ma cheek everytime she turns. Carmen can't see I'm enjoying it. You can just see the printed flowers on her knickers cos she's wearing white ski pants. I'm pickin flowers so I'm not giving two fucks about Danya greetin all over the carpet.

Slinky knows that big arse's a turn on, specially wi the wee flowery knickers diggin in. Daz's all concerned cos it's Slinky's pal greetin an Carmen's too young to notice the strokes bein pulled all round her. She's believin all this *concern for a fellow human being* shite. I know Slinky's games. This's a chance she's not missin. She rubs the thigh tight across ma shoulder.

Danya gets coaxed in the room sobbin, FLOP she goes on the couch. Carmen shuffles off all important to make *a wee cup of tea.*

There there, Danya, don't worry about it . . . says Daz squeezin her knee an pattin her shoulder. Slinky's busy facing me an stretchin so I can see front of her knickers an the old pubes lookin right at me. *Shag me*, they're sayin, *Shag me, baby.* They're about four inches away an fuck me they're pulsin . . . no kiddin.

What d' ye take in yer tea? shouts Carmen in the scullery.

What d'ye take in yer tea, Danya, luv? Says Slinky in her Barnsley accent. Danya looks in Slinky's eyes like the Madonna but can't say nothin an gives it Niagara Falls again. Slinky cuddles her shoulders an Daz gives the thigh a good squeeze.

Aw the poor darlin . . . Give her milk an two sugars then! Slinky shouts.

Anyway, in comes the tea an Slinky gives us the story. *That pig Jerree. Ee should be bloody shot. D'you know what he's gone an done?*

We nod left an right like puppets. She's walking up an down by the windie. I'm gettin the gossip an an eyeful of her body. She struttin it well.

Ee took her to the Noggin. They got their Giros today so they went to the pub after they got the food in. Everything's OK nothin amiss . . . they're getting on better that usual. Nat right, luv? She goes to Danya. *Boo HOO Hoo*, goes greetin face. Slinky taps her back an Daz's hand's further up the thigh.

So, who comes in but Jimmy The fookin Bite an Jerry's speaking wi im up the bar. But Danya thinks all the whispering's about dope. Jimmy's the Man in the Noggin. Can you imagine it . . . what a sight that skinny runt Jerry an fat Jimmy The Bite, Laurel n fookin Ardy.

Danya nearly laughs but *sob sob* she goes an drops the head back in her hands. Slinky gives her a couple of seconds.

So, The Bite vanishes an it's an all-day job: pool the lot . . . great day. She even won a couple of games, that right, Chook? They've got a good drink in them. Jerry leans over an kisses Danya an if

*that don't surprise her he asks her to go home an make one of them
apple pies he loves.*

sob sob sob boo hoo

sob sob sob boo hoo sob sob sob boo hoo

sob sob sob boo hoo sob sob sob boo hoo

*Waaaaaaaaaaaaaaaaaaaaaaaaaaaaaaaaaaaaaaaaaaaaaaa
aaaaaaaaaaaaaaaaaaaaaaaaaaaaaaaaaaaa!!!!!!!!!!!!!*

Danya cries for real this time like she was holding in
vomit an out it comes. Fuck me she could strip woodchip wi
that voice. She's no Aretha Franklin. Daz pulls her close. His
hand's still on her thigh. Slinky goes on.

Danya skips home all happy that Jerry wants one of her pies . . .

an she's bloody good at making them. **Snappy Bite**
wanted to buy them by the undred nat right doll?

sob sob sob boo hoo

sob sob sob boo hoo sob sob sob boo hoo sob

*It's a blinkin sin. Well, don't three hours pass an no Jerry.
Danya phones the Noggin an George says Jerry's left just after her
wi Jimmy the Bite . . . Scotch Git. She puts the phone down an it
rings again. It's Jerry.*

Got ma apple pie ready yet? The bastard says.

*Y . . . Y . . . Yes Jerry. Been ready for ages. I can heat it up again.
Is Jimmy The Bite comin up for some too? says the poor lass.*

sob sob sob boo hoo

Ya stupit cunt! *goes Jerry.*

Well, she can't believe her ears.

Jerry?

Want to hear what that Scotch bastard says?

We all nod.

See you ya ugly bastard . . . I wouldn't feed your pies to a pig . . . force it down yer throat wi a toilet brush an die. D'ye know where I am?

The Noggin?

The NOGGIN . . . the fuckin NOGGIN? Naw . . . I'm no in the fuckin Noggin ya daft cunt . . . I'm in ma Maw's . . . she's made me an apple pie . . . listen can you hear me eating it.

Ees got the cheek to slabber an munch down the phone, one of his moother's pies. He gives it to poor Danya:

I'm sorry I ever married you ya English slut . . . I never hit ye hard enough the last time . . . I should've kilt you.

An there he is . . . up in Glasgow an eating this other apple pie over the phone at Danya.

There's no stopping Danya now.

Waaaaaaaaaaaaaaaaaaaaaaaaaaaaaaaaaaaaaaaa
aaaaaaaaaaaaaaaaaaaaaaaaaaaaaaaaaaaaaaaa
aaaaaaaaaaaaaaaaaaaaaaaaaaaaaaaaaaaaaaaa
aaaaaaaaaaaaaaaaaaaaaaaaaaaaaaaaaaaaaaaa
aaaaaaaaaaaaaaaaaaaaaaaaaa

The tears're drippin on the roofs of Super Lagers at her feet. She doesn't want a drink. She doesn't want a fag. She doesn't want her wee cup of tea. She wants Jerry. Now that puzzles me, how she'll still take him back after all the doins an dirty tricks he's pulled.

Daz, you got petrol in yer car? Slinky asks.

What? You want me to take her all the way to Coatbridge?

Well . . . it's just bloody right ain't it?

Daz's not wantin to go. He's been drinkin all day an wants to batter on. But he's no match for the bold Slinky she goes for his soft spot. She draws in a deep breath an goes,

I want you to go up wi Danya an if that prick so much as breathes the wrong way you kick his fookin cunt in right?

Daz loves that. Out comes his chest wi the car keys. He gets up an starts loadin drink in a carrier. That's when Slinky pulls the trump card.

Carmen, she goes, *mind how you wanted to go to Glasgow an get some more clothes?*

Carmen jumps up. *Yes . . . yes.* She's clapping her hands like a twelve-year-old. Slinky's arse brushes ma face.

An it'd be better for a girl to keep Danya company. Carmen, be a doll!

Me an Slinky wave them up the street. Off ye pop. There they go, a couple of days in bonnie Scotland. Back in the flat I'm in ma chair thinking how to make The Move on Slinky. Christ, in she comes; locks the door an starts gettin the kit off right in front of me. I can still hear Daz's exhaust rattlin up Lytham Road.

I'm shaggin her an I keeps seein Jerry's skinny face munchin at this other apple pie. His eyes're mad an starin an he's eatin the pie at me.

Fuck off Jerry! I shouts.

Slinky's face uncontorts an she looks. She grabs ma arse cheeks tight an pulls. I gets the rhythm goin again an she goes back to lickin her tongue over her lips an moanin.

Razor Eddie Ted McShane

Carmen comes back an tells me things've cooled down up the road but her Da an her cousin's're still goin to blade me.

She's got a load of new clothes an she looks sexy. I'm no longer thinkin of her as The Red Kimono. I starts fallin in love wi her in a fuzzy out of focus way. She's glowin in this white woollen top an long skirt – smilin – yup! Definitely smilin. I feel guilty about Slinky.

We've settled into collectin Giros an drinkin an watchin the telly when we're skint. Things're ploddin along nicely. Daz's actin suspicious but. Never away from Carmen. Must've fell in love wi her on the way up the road. But what the fuck'd she want wi an ugly cunt like that?

Pieman an Daz're stealin motors. We're watchin the box this night. In comes Pieman wi two bottles of Buckie an six Supers.

Got a Cavalier – zoom zoom. He goes, shovin his hands about like an Egyptian dancer.

Carmen's eyes light up. She's into it. I'm stone-cold sober. No way do I want caught in a knocked car on the prom. Out he goes. We get tore in about the drink.

For a guy wi no intention of goin out, an no intention of gettin in a knocked car, I'm doin a good impersonation of someone dyin to go. I've heard them whizzin by a couple of times. Sure enough in comes this set of keys janglin on the end of a cheeky hand stickin through the door.

Want a wee drive now then? says the keys.

Carmen springs off the bed an just misses grabbin them. In comes Pieman.

Got the maddest car ye ever seen, he's sayin wi sparklin night eyes. *A fuckin mountain goat. Holes in the floor, handbrake comin out the dashboard – wild. Here's the keys – me an Daz's hotwired this Jag.*

He leans his shoulders an head back in the room as he's leavin.

By the way it's blue, the mountain goat, ye'll notice it right away there's nothin else like it in the street. We'll be over the car park racin. The car park's this big expanse that runs through Blackpool like a river wi no water.

Anyway, her eyes're lit up.

Well? she goes.

Well? I says.

Fancy?

Fuck it! *Get the booze an let's go.*

It doesn't take much to find the car. This blue Renault Four's sittin there: lights on, hazards, full beam, the lot. They've even sellotaped the horn on. In we goes – after we mastered how to open the doors. Rummmmmmmmm Rummmmmmmmmmmmmm away we go. I keeps tryin for the gearstick down the left but it's stickin out the ashtray nearly. I crunches an she's panicin cos every cunt's lookin. This draught's runnin up ma jeans. I looks down an there's her blue skirt flappin up like a flag in a gale. I sees the white lacy stockins. Great! I looks at the side of her face as the lights of Blackpool go whizzin by. Her pale skin's lightin up. Her black hair's fallin an movin now an then.

She's lookin out the windie. She looks kinda sad.

Thoughts right now – tell me. Don't wait or think or pause yer thoughts right this minute – go! I shouts.

I catches her off her guard an she says, *The Cat.*

The Cat?

Nothin.

The road below's threatenin through the holes in the car. I've got the hang of the ashtray/gearstick now. I leans over an gropes her.

Is it this wee cat ye're talkin about, this wee pussy wi the hatchet in it's head?

She tightens her legs an draws me a look. Flicks the hair. There's a faint smile.

No it isn't THIS cat. As she says THIS she drops her head quick to the one side an lifts her shoulders.

Tell me then.

We had a cat years ago.

Big WAW. Or Meeaaw.

Well our Donna had a cat.

Was it as good as yours? I says givin it another feel.

Stop that or I'm not tellin ye.

OK OK. Tell me.

Holidaymakers're whizzin by lickin stalks of rock or spinnin round lampposts wearin bright red an yella clothes an 'kiss-me-slow' hats. There's short skirts an long shiny legs. Now an then they smile in the car like we're holidaymakers an happiness is our great conspiracy. Only we're not happy. We'll never be happy again. Not really.

She starts tellin me about Donna's cat.

We were wee. About eight. She had this cat

Eight? You or her?

Me. She was five. I hated her gettin the cat, I wanted a dog an they never got me it.

Awwwwwwwwwwwwwwww poor Carmen. I pats her head like a dog.

So I killed it. I stops pattin her head like a dog.

Aye! Right!

I done the wee fucker in. She looks at me an I knows she's tellin the truth. I turn out onto The Prom. South Pier. All these mad cunts're hangin off the end to impress burds, ye know – two hands then one hand danglin over the waitin sea. One wrong move an they're dead.

Drown it? I ask. She's drawin a wee cat face on the condensation on the windscreen.

Did ye drown it? I goes again. She draws a finger across her neck makin this noise like a creakin door.

Ye did not.

Slit-its-throat. She pronounces the three words strong, drawin three quick squeaky lines through the face on the windscreen.

What about . . . what about Donna? What . . .

Though it got lost. Looked for it every night for months. I used to help. Sometimes I felt sorry for her but not for the cat. No more pets, ma Maw says, more bother than they're worth. She goes imitatin her Maw's voice.

What did ye do wi it?

Under ma Grannie's garden chair. Buried.

No way!

Every time we sit on it I feet great. Powerful.

You're sick as fuck.

Not as sick as you.

What?

Runnin away wi the baby-sitter.

Ha! Takes two to tango.

You're supposed to be an adult.

Am I?

*An that's a laugh. Every **adult** I've met here acts like wanes.*

Ye've got a lot to learn. She draws me another look an I keeps ma eyes on the road. By this time we're back in South Shore up the back of the Pleasure Beach. Fast cars go by tootin an flashin an I guess when they're by it must be Daz an Pieman racin. It's a wonder they don't kill a holidaymaker.

I goes to turn in this side street to get back to Lytham Road an this big giant cunt jumps on the bonnet. My heart's goin like fuck cos it's a knocked car an I'm thinkin this's the guy that owns it.

But that's not who it is cos this guy's dressed in a grass skirt. He's fat as fuck an he's got half-coconuts for tits – like Baloo the bear. He grabs the wipers an makes this mad grin. Me an her turn at the same time, mouths open. We know him. A million people in Blackpool, this guy jumps on our knocked-off car at random an it's Ted McShane. He's too pished to notice us so I tears up an down the road behind the Pleasure Beach. He's lovin it – the faster I go the more he laughs. All these holidaymakers're pointin an laughin.

I'm laughin. She's laughin an then I remembers the car's knocked so I stops.

Ted recognises me an Carmen. When he can talk he tells us there's a bus load down from the Brig an they've hired a pub on South Shore. Carmen's cousins're there. She looks at me.

Fuck it, I says, *c'mon.* I decides now'd be a good a time as any. I checks for ma lockblade. Got it.

Right, Ted, ma man, let's hit the pub. We jump in the car an he jumps on the bonnet an sits like Buddha. There's a big crowd outside wonderin what the fuck's happened to him. They all start leanin back an laughin an spittin their drinks on the street when Ted arrives on the bonnet of Mountain Goat.

We help Ted laughin an wobblin off the bonnet. The Coatbridge team're laughin like fuck. Some laughter changes to murmurs an I can hear mine an her names in the din.

Look who it is, says Ted loud, leanin an laughin.

45

But the rest of them's already looked who it is. Carmen's cousin, Razor Eddie, moves out the front. He's got these other less frightenin cunts behind him. The place goes silent. All ye can hear's the growlin Mountain Goat an the breeze rustlin the grass on Big Ted's skirt.

Eddie's got his hand in his jacket. I've got the lockblade opened in ma pocket. Carmen's standin behind me peekin out the side.

All right, he says.

All right, I goes.

How's things?

OK.

All the other cunts've took a step back an it's me an Carmen an Eddie an the three less frightenin cunts. Holidaytime Blackpool's goin an all around us but we're frozen in a timewarp of fear. He leans to the side so he's lookin direct at her.

An how are you?

OK . . . E . . . E . . . Eddie, I'm OK.

Treatin ye all right this cunt?

I don't flinch at that.

Aye . . . aye.

He sees I've got ma hand in ma pocket. His mouth opens, his head tilts back, his lower lip falls an he looks at me down his nose. I know he wants to at least slash me. He's told every cunt so he's in a fix now. Carmen bursts in.

I was up the road last month.

Aye yer Maw said.

Ye can tell Eddie's mind's not on the words. He's puzzlin how to blade me without me bladin him.

Ma Da said if this's what I wanted that's OK.

Good on her, she's findin him a way out.

An is it what ye want?

Aye.

She grabs ma arm an gives me this squeeze – I've never had a squeeze like that off her before. Feels great. For a split second I sees Eddie's eyes narrowin an his hand tightenin on the blade in his jacket. He makes to move but I surprise maself by makin the same moves at the same time an we end up a foot closer to each other – the crowds another foot back – stalemate.

Then, like he's decided he'd let it go he says, *Nice car, pity Big Ted's flattened it.*

Every cunt laughs. They laugh like it's the best joke in the world. I laugh. Carmen laughs. The three less frightenin cunts laugh. People walkin by laugh. Blackpool's belly's heavin up an down wi hilarity. They all filter back in the pub. Carmen kisses Eddie an he shakes ma hand, but he gives me the look when he shakes it an squeezes hard. Hard as he can.

We head up Stanley Park. She's wearin this long pale blue flowing cotton suit. We pops in the park an walk a bit. We come to a swingpark surrounded by trees – or at least that's what it looked like. We start gettin tore in about each other. On the swings – bent over the concrete tunnels – backwards an forwards on the roundabout – on the grass – on the tarmac an the benches. We're up to all sorts till the light comes up. I'm lovin the shaggin but the real reason for stayin so long is so Razor Eddie won't find us if he takes a notion to rip me to bits in the middle of the night. I figure he's well out his face now. We drive Mountain Goat home an sleep the rest of the day.

A couple of days later we're back up Stanley Park. There's this row of houses we never noticed right along the front. They cunts must've got a right eyeful. She looks at the houses – at me – at the houses – at me an we laugh an fall on the grass in a bundle.

We decide to keep Mountain Goat. Carmen says nobody'd report a wreck like that missin. So we've got a car now, a car that wi luck could get us to The Brig an back.

Capo De Monte

Me, Carmen an Daz's at the back of the shops. Daz's haulin at this door. Saturday night. Feet away the lights an whizz of Blackpool's gorgin through streets like a tinsel glacier. It's fuckin Singapore out there. But in the secret doorways an back alleys it's another town. A town for the likes of us.

Blackpool's all these redbrick houses like Belfast or Manchester. Behind them's warrens of back alleys. If we're doin a turn we use the alleys to move about. They're the arteries that take the bad blood no cunt wants to see through the heart of pumpin lights an ring a ding ding arcades. The millions've got to be made.

So here's what happened. Me an her's pished, fryin pieces on sausage. In comes Daz. He's on the drink cos his eyes bulge out an he's smilin.

I'm on a downer, is what he was never done sayin. Daz's always on a downer except when he's drunk an he's always drunk except when he's on a downer.

YOOOOOOOOO HOOOOOOOOOOO!!!

He goes.

Have I got somethin to make us a wee fortune Mickey boy, Carmen baby!!!

Oh aye?

Aye . . . a right packet. He's rubbin his hands an raisin his eyebrows over the fryin pan. He pokes a sausage.

Fuck off, I goes. Carmen's puffin away interested as fuck.

A bite?

Fuck off.

A bite or I'm not tellin ye about somethin that I know you don't.

I folds him a piece on sausage an he tells us how he's nearly got the back door pulled of this shop behind the post office.

Go down there MUNCH *pass the stuff out* MUNCH *ornaments* MUNCH *that costs a fuckin fortune* MUNCH *that snobs buy* MUNCH *wee guys playin* MUNCH *cards* MUNCH *God an all they other cunts* MUNCH *round a table* MUNCH *a fuckin grand each* MUNCH *a grand!* MUNCH MUNCH MUNCH

So we're in this alley an Daz's haulin at the door an Carmen's lookin left an right watchin for The Polis.

No alarm. Look!

He's pullin the bottom of the door out till it cracks an lettin it slap back. The crack an snap echoes out the alley but the sheer nighttime noise of Blackpool drowns it out as it presses against the streets.

RIIIIIIIIIIIIIP

SNAP

RIIIIIIIIIIIIIIIP

SNAP

Then he's got this bit of door in his hand like the corner off a Rivita. Light from the main street's comin out the back door an flickerin on the cobbles as people walk by the front windie. Daz bellyflops in. I'm behind him.

We're on the floor an people're goin by all the time. Now an then some burd goes

OOOOOOOOOOOOOOOOOOOOOH through the plate glass an makes her boyfriend stare at the ornament they're goin to get when they're married. Me an him's sniggerin like fuck. I'm sure cunts can see us or the broke back door but they walk by an stop an look in, walk by stop an look in.

It's warm in the shop. Lookin up from the floor the strange shapes an colours of ornaments makes ye feel like a wane – terrified in some insane miniature waxworks. The ornaments're starin down. Street urchins wink. Jesus's lookin – I'm sure he's lookin. Standin at his table pointin his palms at us. I'm thinkin rays of holy light're any minute goin to

ZOOOOOOOOOOOOOOOOOOOOOOOOOM across an zap us. The Apostles don't seem bothered.

Fuck me! That cunt Daz stands up an walks over to the windie, lifts *The Last Supper* an shoves it under the door. Ten people walk by in that time but by a miracle none look in.

Daz! Daz! I'm goin in ma best shout–whisper voice, *get down on the fuckin floor before some cunt sees us.*

Ah Fuck it! he goes. *Who'se goin to see us? An if they do they'll think we work here.*

Half past ten at night? Aw fuck it!!!

I stands up too an gets *Street Urchins* an slide that under the door. Up an down we starts sneakin, through the alleys, to Hill Street. Carmen's got a briefcase I thinks'll be cool for keepin bits of paper an stuff in. By the time we've done five trips every cunt in Blackpool knows about it. Well, every cunt in Blackpool that's really from Coatbridge knows about it.

The last visit I does twenty-odd cunts're in the alley an they've all got statues. Hunner quid each. An the daft cunts're bouncin them off the walls like Buckie bottles. They're a pile of porcelain. Daz an Froggy're playin up-the-wall wi statues. It's where ye see who can chuck somethin an get closest to the wall. Only ye're supposed to play it wi coins not fragile statues.

I gets in the shop. It's covered in broke ornaments. There's fuck all left except the big *Horse and Carriage* pressed up against the windie. No way I'm riskin bein centimetres away from Joe Public. Daz comes chargin in – crunches across the room an shoves it under his arm. There's this *Bowl of Cherries* beside the busted till. I shoves it in ma pocket an me an Daz stroll back up the flat not knowin the thing under his arm is one of only two in Britain.

Anyway we sells the stuff. Slinky's Da buys the lot for ten grand. Ten grand for fucksakes!! But that's between us all. I've to pick the money up down The Windmill. Monday.

But that's not enough for Pieman. After they find the shop screwed an the Polis get it secured, the Pieman goes an screws it again. Tells no cunt. Takes all these Chinese ornaments about three feet high up Hill Street. They were in the basement of the shop. About thirty. Jackie phones the CID.

Monday. I'm comin back from an interview in Coral Island. I pick up the money at The Windmill. It's in hunner pound notes. I finds this empty can of Super an punctures the bottom on a spiky fence. I stuffs the money in an sticks the can in ma pocket. It feel less conspicuous. The sun's out an a breeze's comin in from the sea. Everythin's goin to be fine now. Just fine.

I lean over the rail an blow smoke out over the sea. I'm feelin clean inside. I'd mibbi be able to work for a livin an drink at the weekends just. Take Carmen out for a meal. Get a mortgage. A house. Dream dream dream. I walk up Hill Street breathin big gales of air. Feelin good.

When I gets to the top landin there's these two guys. I thinks they're Pieman's pals. I nods an tries to get by but they get in the road.

Do you live here? goes baldy.

Aye?

Do you know who lives in there? he goes openin Pieman's room door a bit.

Eh . . . some guy . . . Pieman or somethin . . . Scottish . . .

Know him well do you?

Say hello an stuff. How? Is somethin happened to him?

They stare. Carmen shouts ma name. I walks by them an she's sittin on the couch smokin. She's been greetin. The ashtry's full of douts.

What is it?

They cunts there!!!

The two cunts're right behind me.

Well, Mick?

Well what?

You know what?

Oh do I?

She's told us the whole story.

I know she's told them nothin. Not Carmen. They twiddle wi our stuff. There's this nine-inch blade hangin from the cupboard in case her family crashes in. This CID cunt's got it. You can tell shivers're runnin up an down his back. He's lookin at me from the side tryin to make out he's not scared.

This yours?

Aye.

Expectin visitors?

Any minute. All the time.

He feels the blade I've been sharpenin every day an looks at the other CID. He's in an out drawers. He lifts a pair of Carmen's knickers an he's rubbin the silky material between his thumb an finger.

These yours? he says holdin them up so the light shines through them. One by one he lifts her knickers an bras.

Fuckin Pervert! she goes.

What age are you? he says.

Sixteen.

There's only one pervert here. An he looks at me.

Not much stuff in here, goes the other one. *Leave Scotland in a hurry?*

Nothin.

I said, leave Scotland in a bit of a hurry? He lifts Carmen's chin an draws his hand slowly off it. She turns them on. The underwear's still bundled on the chest of drawers an every now an then one of them stares at it. That's when I notice the fuckin *Bowl of Cherries* on top of the fire. They must've walked by it a hunner times. It's gettin bigger all the time.

Bowl of Cherries on the fireplace.

Bowl of Cherries on the fireplace.

Bowl of Cherries on the fireplace.

Bowl of Cherries on the fireplace.

Bowl of Cherries on the fireplace.

Bowl of Cherries on the fireplace.
Bowl of Cherries on the fireplace.

C'mere, says baldy. We all get up an walk out in the landin. He opens Pieman's door an fuck me! It's like Aladdin's cave. The light's shinin off the heads of all these Chinese soldiers.

Nice ornaments he's got?

Aye.

What do you know about them?

Nothin. I've only been in his room once. For a light.

We're in the room denyin everythin an the one wi hair's in the scullery bangin the fridge an cooker doors. Next thing Jimmy McCann an Pieman come up the stairs. We're ushered back in our room. Jimmy comes firin in shoutin abuse about fascists an wavin his skinny arms all over the place. He pulls a can of Super out his pocket, crashes it an slumps on the couch. The CID've got Pieman in his room an ye can hear serious voices.

A car draws up an Pieman's stuffed in. Next three hours every cunt that comes for their money's lifted. I sees some out the windie. Jimmy's greetin now:

A Cos he's ran out of drink.
B Cos he's got nothin to do wi it anyway.
C He can't handle an hour without drink never mind jail.

I sits the can stuffed wi money beside the one Jimmy drank. In comes Baldy wi the briefcase.

Well well well! Look what I found behind the cooker, Mick.

So?

From the Capo de Monte shop no less.

Any cunt can get in there. Pieman could've planked it.

You two are down the station.

He starts radioin. I swipes the *Bowl of Cherries* an stuffs it in Jimmy McCann's pocket.

Ditch it! I whispers.

So we're huckled. Carmen's roarin. I tells her tell them nothin. She knows that anyway. When we get there I sees the names on the board. They're all lifted. Me an Carmen's separated right away. I hear her screamin up corridors.

Mick I love you Mick Mick Mick. It echoes mixin wi the disinfectant an clickin heels.

BAAAAAANGGGGGGGG

I'm in a cell pacin. I shouts out the openin.

Who's in?

Who's that?

Mick.

It's Daz.

Daz, where's Pieman?

Three down.

Can he hear ye.

If I shout.

Tell him the case behind the cooker's his.

What?

Tell him they found the briefcase behind the cooker in ma flat. Ask him to say he put it there.

How?

Polis've got fuck all else – that's how.

I hears Daz passin the message but at that Pieman's took for questionin.

It's an hour before I hears keys. This Polis opens ma

door. I meets Carmen outside. Must've worked. Fair play to the Pieman.

On the way back to Hill Street we decide we're movin out South Shore. Gettin away from trouble. Cut down on the drink an get a wee job each. We kiss an cuddle all the way up the road an we're cold as hell.

We walks up the stairs an Baldy an Hairy're amazed.

What the fuck are you doing here? says Baldy.

Been let out.

That right?

He gets right on the radio kickin up fuck. When he's finished he shoves us in the room. Right away I notice the *Bowl of Cherries* on the fireplace.

Notice anythin different?

Aye. Jimmy McCann's not here.

Ha ha. Anythin else?

An he's walkin over to the fireplace. He picks up the *Bowl of Cherries* an reads the bottom. *Capo De Monte . . . can you tell me why this was on the fire when we came in an then we find it stuffed down the sofa?*

So that was that. Lifted twice in one day. Back down the cells. On the way out I look round for the Super cans. Not there. Not in the bin. I hope McCann's got them.

Back in the cells. Up the court. Three weeks remand. Carmen's out after three days. Too young. It's not bad. Scotland ye get fuck all but in Blackpool ye get everythin except drink an burds. Swiss rolls sweeties, fags, books, comics. Two showers a day. Four wanks. Three meals. Hour in the exercise yard. An a visit every night at seven from Carmen.

Second week I notice Slinky's Da gettin marched about. McCann's still got the money even if the stupid cunt stuffed the cherry bowl down the couch. Every cunt makes statements except me, Daz, Pieman an Danny. Danny's another guy from The Brig. Every day the CID come an ask if I want to make a statement. Every day I nod. We play cards at Danny's cell mornin an afternoon.

I mind one of the cells all black an shut up. Some Paki set hiself on fire. Take shame to extremes some cunts. Anyway. This day I'm bored as fuck. I've had the picture an the dabs took the third time for some reason. The CID come an ask the usual. He's walkin away when I answer, *Aye*. He spins.

You what?

Aye. I want to make a statement.

I go to make a statement duckin at every cell. I not makin a statement cos I want to grass. I makin it cos I'm so fuckin bored. I tells them the lot. Who why where when, except I don't tell were the money is. *Slinky's Da never paid us*, I says. They question me a long time on that cos he's obviously said he's ten grand down.

After the statement they asked me if I wanted any TICs.

(A TIC: Taken into Consideration – allows ye to admit to crimes but not be sentenced for them. Ye're only sentenced on the one ye're up for. Some people take TICs to add to their street cred.)

Fuck off! I says.

There's an armed robbery up North Shore – bloke fits your description.

Get to fuck, I goes in a friendly way.

C'mon, Mick – think how that'll look on your form? Armed robbery. Lot of respect there.

You take it then.

Anyway they know I want fuck all TICs but they want me to look at this guy. I ducks at every cell.

SLLLLLLLLLLLLLLOTTTTTTTTTTTTTT

Look in there.

I has a quick look. It's Slinky's Da. He can only see ma eyes but I think he recognises them. I stands at the side of the cell door wi ma back to the wall an he comes to the peephole.

Who's there? he goes. *Who's that? How long am I gettin kept in here?*

Then loud as fuck one of the CID goes.

Well, Mick – recognise him?

Never seen him in ma life.

I says an shuffles down the rows of cells. Ye can smell the petrol where the Paki torched hiself.

Back in Danny's cell I'm feelin guilty as fuck. We're playin away an I can't keep it in. I mean I could hold ma own in a scrap wi them that's not what's botherin me. It's loyalty. I turns to Daz an says so Pieman an Danny'll hear,

I made a statement the day.

Big silent pause.

The look at each other.

They look at me.

Daz laughs. The others snigger.

I made one last week, goes Daz.

Me too, says Pieman.

An me, laughs Danny.

I bursts out laughin. It's a mad laugh. The kinda laugh ye might do if the person ye love most on the planet dies an ye crack up on the spot.

We get bail after three weeks. Back in two months for sentencin. We're on a curfew. Got to be in for eight o'clock every night an sign on at the Polis Station every day at one. Me an Carmen move out South Shore. She gets this flat in Reads Ave. The day we get bail we go there.

I mind walkin through the court. Every cunt's fell out wi every cunt else. Me an Carmen hold hands so tight our bones're nearly breakin. When we walk away from the courtroom I'm sure of a new beginnin.

Wrong End of the Rainbow

Reads Avenue's run by this old guy. He's doted but OK.
Keeps hiself to hiself. The whole place's been painted wi
sky-blue gloss. Nothin includin the paint job's under thirty
years old. I gets the job in Coral Island. Carmen gets one in
Snappy Bite.

It's a quiet time. We don't even fight much. We're nearly
like a normal couple. I go to work at eight in the mornin.
Meet her at one an walk up the Polis Station to sign on. Back
at two. Work till eight. Go home. She's got the carry out.
Some nights these cunts're in a car outside. CID.

The waitin's worst. Waitin to see what's goin to happen.
The lawyers're tryin to keep it in the Magistrate's but The
Polis want the Crown. Maximum's two years in the
Magistrate's. Sky's the limit in the Crown.

Ma job in Coral Island's walkin the floor wi a big bunch of
keys an fixin any machines that break. I've done it in
Glasgow. Twice a day ye're on The Yella Brick Road. The
Yella Brick Road's done up like the road to Oz. All these
kiddie rides an waxworks of the cunts in the film. I didn't
think hearin the words of the film a million times'd've
bothered me. But it reminds me of ma wanes. Ma fuckin
heart's breakin every time I sees a Da puttin his son or

daughter on a kiddie ride. I want to grab the wane maself an cuddle them. I can't give maself the luxury of feelin sorry for maself. I left them. This's a big empty fuckin sorrow. Eventually, every word of that film goes through ma heart like shards of glass. If I hear another fuckin

SOMEWHERE OVER THE RAINBOW

I'll murder somebody. I've got the wrong end of the rainbow.

There not much happenin in Reads Ave. I'm scared to make a move in case I get lifted. I'm feelin right low at work cos of The Yella Brick Road. Even the lone long hours on ma feet's a bummer. Ye can't carry money on the floor. So if yer found wi twenty pence even ye're sacked. No questions. Seen it twice.

So I gets Carmen to come in wi this specially prepared plastic bag. Waterproof. Lead weight in it. She leaves it outside the men's bog. I hangs it wi a bit of wire in a cistern behind the bog's wooden panels. They check behind the panel cos I glued a hair on it five times an it was broke every day. So I wander in an out all day droppin coins in the bag. Carmen comes in wi ma lunch box. I take it in the toilet an fill it wi as much twenties an fifties as I can. Hardly any pound coins cos they shoot straight in the cash box. We're gettin two hunner a week.

There's a million ways to get money. I make fifty pences wrappin tape round tens till they're the same size as flat to point on a fifty. I've got a coin mech in the flat to try them. So I know they work before I hit the arcades. Free money – thanks very much. Another thing's to Superglue a pound coin to a long thin bit of nylon. That goes down a treat but it's more easy noticed than bumpin dodgy fifties in. I've always got Superglue on me.

Every day for weeks on end's the same. Work – Polis – Work – Home. I think every cunt's watchin me. Every time a car stops outside I thinks it's the CID.

I think you're goin off yer fuckin head! she goes.

What d'you know about it? You're not on a curfew.

D'ye think they're goin to waste time watchin to see if you're away out for a pint? I don't answer – I just stare through the yella net curtains.

Borin time. The flat's got this gas cooker. Museum piece. Looks like Flash Gordon's spaceship. Got it's own smell – can't say if it's good or bad. It's work eat drink an shag. I'm fed up. Even wi shaggin. But sometimes it's a turn on hearin the burd through the wall screamin. She goes like fuck squealin,

Ooh ooh it makes me so *horny* it makes me so *fuckin horny*.

We used to wonder what makes her so fuckin horny. It makes us horny listenin. We belt into each other every time we hear it. So our sex life depends on if the tart next door's got a lumber.

I'd to pass her on the stairs. Butter wouldn't melt.

Hello.

Good weather,

. . . or somethin she'd go an wiggle that wee arse up or down the stairs. If ma eyes were pins she'd squeal all the way up or down.

We're gatherin money like nothin on earth. It's in carrier bags all over the room. Every now an then she goes to a different bank an changes it for notes. At one count it's four grand. We get curries an pizzas every night an drink constant but we can't dwindle it. A couple of times we sneak out durin curfew. We leave the light on. I wear a hat. We leave at different times an meet in Rumours. It's not the same boozin when ye've no option but to behave yerself.

What if some fucker gives ye the look or gets fresh wi yer burd? Ye can't just jump up an stick the head on him. Not under curfew ye can't.

This night we're out an this cunt keeps lookin at me across the other end of the pub.

That cunt keeps lookin at me.

Who?

Him wi the baldy head an glasses.

So he is.

I know him.

That's what I'm thinkin.

Anyway, we gets on at pool. Carmen's all in white. White ski pants an this lacy top's shovin her tits up. Her black hair's stretched back tuggin her white skin an red lips. She bends over the pool table an I can see her knickers through the ski pants. I turns an so can every other cunt. That bothers me. I've got this jealous streak. The baldy bastard's lookin at her arse. She pots a ball, stands up, spins round – he's lookin at her crotch. I mean – c'mon. He's not even tryin to hide it – right at her fanny. She gives him this smile I've never seen before. He smiles back. I want to kick his cunt in but I can't cos of the curfew. I gives him the look an he spits on the carpet. Cunt.

I gets her off pool an back to the seat. Baldy goes to the bog.

He liked yer fanny, I says in her ear.
What?
I said, he liked yer fanny.
Who?
You know fine well who.
What're you on about?
You ya fuckin slut flashin yer pussy at that baldy bastard.
Fuck off.
Ye smiled at him.
Is there a law against smilin now?
No. But there's a law about flashin yer fanny like a slut.

She stands, lifts her glass an pours it over ma head. This guy next to us is pretendin it's not happenin. They're wary of a Scottish accent in Blackpool.

What the fuck're ye doin ya stupid bitch?
I'm fed up wi you an yer disgustin patter.

I jumps up an for the life of me I want to smash the joint an Baldy. My hand's on the tumbler an she's darin me wi her eyes, head cocked to one side. The guy that's been kiddin nothin's goin on says,

Watch it, see that bloke over there wi no hair – he's the old Bill. CID.

ZOOOOOOOOOOOOOOOM

DONNYBROOK We're out the place punchin lumps out each other all the way home. But that's about as excitin as Reads Avenue gets.

Well except for when our Angie came down out the blue wi her five mad wanes.

I've escaped out the flat maself this Monday. Rubber out ma head. I'm strollin along the prom not givin two fucks about the Polis an swiggin ma third Buckie bottle. I'm singin, *Some fuckin where over the fuckin rain fuckin bow . . .*

I wakes at four in the mornin on the beach. The tide's

ticklin ma legs. Ma hand's bleedin. I can remember fuck all. I gets back to Reads Avenue. She lets me in but it's the point the arse treatment in bed. Know – from above we're touchin arses lookin like a big X. Ma head hits the pillow an,

BRRRRRRRRRRRRRRRRRRRRRRRRIIIIIING

It's Tuesday. Ma mouth's like a badgers arse. Know how when ye're fucked wi drink everythin's a blur? Next thing I'm walkin the floor in Coral Island. I've sent out an there's six Supers in the bog behind the panel. Drinkin on the job's OK so long as ye do yer work an keep it secret. Fuck! They've no option – every cunt in Blackpool's alkies.

Badger, this Black guy from Birmingham, tells me there's no Yella Brick Road the day. Thank Fuck! Some cunt pulled Dorothy's head off an Superglued it to the Tin Man's dick. Not a pretty sight for children our Dot blowin the Tin Man. They ripped the guts out the Straw Man an fucked them all over the place. An the Lion? Ripped his arm off an stuck it up his arse. The kiddie rides've been booted about the place. Must've been a team. In through the plate glass.

Fuck me, Badger – Probably the Munchkins Liberation Organisation.

The Wicked Witch Appreciation Society.

Done us a favour. They're havin to send away for a new Dorothy – ripped the lips off her gettin her off the Tin Man's dick.

Must've been lovin it.

Yeah – Tin Man's smilin.

There's oil drippin down his inside leg.

Badger walks away laughin wi a Birmingham accent. An hour later I'm feelin better cos I've sank three Supers. I own the fuckin place now in fact. The security guy – Bob – I'm friendly wi him. He's Scottish. From the Borders. He's easy to talk to. Been in Blackpool that long he knows not to ask

questions. We talk about Border collies an hills. He's an
ex-Polis but he's all right.

Quiet the day, Mick?

Aye – borin but.

Take the good wi the bad in this job.

Not too good on the feet.

Try on the beat!

An he walks away whistlin this song that I always think I
know but can't remember. He spins.

Some carry on wi the Yella Brick Road!

Aye – well out of order, Bob.

What kind of sicko does that?

You get the lot in this town.

Don't I know it. Don't I know it.

He tuts a couple of times an walks away noddin wi his
hands behind his back.

I've finished the last can an havin a fly smoke keepin the
fag in the ashtray. This wee guy goes by an I think, *Hey I
know him* when there's another an then a wee lassie wi red
hair, then another two wee guys. I've not been in contact wi
nobody up the road.

Here's ma wee nephews an niece. I spins an there's Angie
sittin smilin in the café bit. I looks right at her. I don't smile.
I don't know what to do. I'm a spare prick. She's lookin right
at me. I thinks – *fuck she's goin to give me a right bollockin*. She
smiles.

I thought that was you!

Fuck me.

I was up yer flat

Is Carmen . . .?

Aye she told me ye were at work

Where's John?

Carry out.

It's weird seein Angie there. Every cunt that goes to The

Brig comes back wi these stories. Ma family's disowned me.
So an so's goin to stick a blade in me soon as he sees me.
Another cunt's goin to blow me away – got a shotgun just
for the sake of it. If I know what's good for me I'll never set
foot in The Brig again. Half of me's glad to see her an the
other half's feart. Feart that she's up to somethin. Mibbi
there's a team up the flat. Carmen's Da an that down to take
her home an Angie's the decoy. Next thing Big John walks in.

HELLLLLLLLLLLLLLLLLLLLLLLLLLLLLLLLLO

Big Fulla! he goes an slaps ma back. *Long time no see how's the
shaggin?*

John! says Angie.

John's got this holdall clinkin wi bottles an clankin wi
cans. He holds it up.

Take the morra off – party time. I realises everythin's
hunky-dory. That's when I spot the wanes' anorak hoods.

Right I've got a plan! I goes to John.

They all go out an come back in half an hour actin like
they don't know me from Adam. John places the wanes
strategically at different machines. Every now an then one of
them goes,

Mister – hoi *Mister* this puggy owes me money.

They give it a swift kick for reality's sake. Big John's
taught them well. I don't know how many times I do it.
Must be thirty in two hours. I open a machine. Pump out
five or ten quid in tens an twenties. (All the other coins go
down tubes into the cash box.) Drop the coins in the wane's
hoods. Make the machine pay the two or three quid jackpot
an the wane walks away smilin.

Outside Angie empties a procession of silver filled hoods
into a wee leather holdall bought for the purpose. Two
hours. Two hunner quid.

We'll away up the flat an get tore in. See ye when ye get home. Goes John.

John get me a curry for eight the night, eh?

Right, says Angie. An off they pop. The wanes swagger like the five dwarves behind them.

I spend the rest of the day fixin the Yella Brick Road wi Badger. A new Dorothy's comin next day.

I goes on a bender wi Big John. Three days off work sick. Ends up the usual. Every cunt falls out an John an Angie go up the road not talkin. Carmen batters lumps out me when I'm lyin drunk. At least I've made contact wi home. Things don't seem so bad now. I decide not to listen to cunts from now on. An this thought appears – that somehow, not now, but soon, we'll go back to The Brig. Back home.

Headlines and Hairdressers

Things settle down a good bit. I've had Psychiatric an Social Inquiry reports an I'm waitin for sentencin. Coral Island's got us loaded. It's drink an Chinkees every night. I've started to go out – the CID don't know I've moved from Reads Avenue. I've dyed ma hair.

We're in this flat above Mario's in Lytham Road. Mario thinks Carmen's Italian wi her brown eyes an long curly locks. Twenty-five a week. Two levels. Ye go in the lobby an up stairs to get to the bog an bedroom. In the first room there's a chair, couch, breakfast bar, cooker, fridge, cupboards. I like it right away. There's this back windie overlookin a brick wall. Bog's massive. Big white bath like the Flake advert. Bedroom's amazin. When ye think of Marlyn's – fucksake – this's a palace. Mirrored wardrobes wall to wall. Double bed.

Fucky fucky, I says to Carmen when I sees it. The bedroom windie overlooks higher up the wall in the back alley. Soon as Mario leaves we do it on the bed, in the bog, on the floor in the livin room, an standin up in the cupboard.

They keep the case out the Crown. That's somethin. I'm sure I'm gettin two years. No cunts talkin. They're all blamin each other for grassin. We've kept ourselfs to ourselfs.

Carmen's had her charges dropped.

Two days before court day ma arse is makin buttons. I'm stoned every day an drunk every night. Even the Yella Brick Road's paradise compared to gettin dubbed up in England. I'm prayin an prayin – in case there is a God. If he lets me off wi a fine or community hours I'll stop drinkin. Get ma act thegether.

Blackpool Magistrates. They're all in groups not talkin. These separate briefs're takin last minute details. Slinky an her Maw an Da're well away from every group. Now an then they're lookin over. They're drawin me an Carmen looks. Carmen sneers in ma ear.

See if that cow looks at me once more I'll to stick a knife in her.

Fuck sake – just get this day over an we'll see what's what.

She's fuckin drawin me daggers.

Carmen draws Slinky a look.

Want yer eyes back! shouts Slinky.

Sorry – are you talkin to me? Carmen points at herself wi her knee turned out.

Yeah you grassin little slag.

Anybody grassed it was you, bleachy hair. Away an get yer roots done.

Slinky's black affronted. Carmen shouts to Slinky's Da,

Ask her – I was there she forgets that – ask yer hoor of a daughter who stuck ye in . . . Every cunt's silent an watchin. Next thing she's doin this stupid impersonation of Slinky,

Yeth it's my Dad has the stuff – it's all in a garage in Manchester I've got the addless in me puss.

Slinky's strainin to attack Carmen. She's twice the size but Carmen'd tear her to bits. Slinky's Maw an Da hold her back. She spits but the bold Carmen carries on.

You know what else yer precious slut of a daughter done? The whole Court's lookin an listenin. The Briefs're quite enjoyin it.

Yer daughter stuck ye in for knocked-off videos an tellies.
Slinky's Da looks at the Maw an they turn to Slinky. She
shakes her head wi her mouth wide. Daz don't know where
to stand cos he's close to me an Carmen but Slinky's his
burd. He's standin halfway takin ages wi this roll up. He's
shakin. All the tobacco's waterfallin out the joints. Carmen
goes for it again.

*Ask yerself: who knew you had a knocked-off telly an video in
the house, EH?*

Silent pause.

That cow – that's who!!

Slinky marches into Court Three. It's time.

This's the big day. I've told Coral Island I'm up the road
for a funeral. We file in the courtroom an we're called up one
at a time. It's like a school register from the old days. They
don't put us in the dock cos there's too many of us. They line
us along the front of the bench. Alphabetical order. The
public's laughin an jokin.

Slinky's Da gets passed to the Crown to the deep breaths
of the public. An us. The rest of us get the speel about how
we're from this socially deprived area. High unemployment.
High crime rate. No amenities. Usual stuff to make the
Magistrate feel sorry. We've all got bowed heads tryin to
look sorry. The Briefs're sayin it was a bungled Laurel an
Hardy type job. Makin us look like eejits. That's OK. I like
that. Better chance of stayin out the jail.

None of us get jail. 270 hours community work each.
Fuckin relief. The Pieman. I thinks he's goin down for sure –
an Daz: record's the length of yer arm. When it's Pieman's
turn all his Brief can say is he always turns up for court
appearances an never skips bail.

See he's from this posh joint near Stirling – Doune – old
historic village. The only burglar there. An a right ugly wee
cunt. Every time a pint of milk goes missin in Doune he gets

lifted. He moves here an carries on the same. His main story's about how he stole this hi-fi in Central an wheeled on it's castors through Blackpool to his flat. A fuckin ALBA. The Lada of hi-fi's. Ye can even re-arrange the letters. LABA. The worst. Probably found it in a bin. Since comin here he's spent more time in jail that out.

Daz gets an exceptional last chance.

We come out an everyone unwinds away. They're sick of havin their life's connected. They don't want to see each other again. I couldn't give two fucks if they got crushed wi a tram crossin the prom – far as I'm concerned they're a bunch of losers an alkies. Me an Carmen go to this pub in North Shore an get pished.

We get back late afternoon. The hairdresser's still open. Mario waves. I never liked any cunt that had power over me. He owns the flat an he smiles an I smile back. But that means nothin. Inside I don't like him.

People can see right through me. They know I'm no good. I half expect Mario to pop up through the floorboards someday an say, *You, ya Scotch cunt, you lefta your wife an children. You should be a shota basterdo.*

Nightmares about that all the time. I not scared of him physically. He knows ma thoughts. I hate people knowin ma thoughts so I don't look in their eyes. Worst thing's walkin past his windie to go in the flat. The door's next to the hairdressers door. I walk away round the block so as not to pass it. I sneak along the wall an open the door quiet.

I'm lookin in the fridge. I'm holdin the door wi one hand an swayin about. Every time I bend down the flat's spinnin.

Anythin for eatin? I says.

Look an see.

I'm lookin but I can see fuck all. What did ye get?

How's it always me that's to get get get?

Cos I'm workin an you're not.

*So cos you walk about that pussy puggy place ye expect me to
run after yer arse all day?*

No but at least make sure there's fuckin grub in the fridge.

Don't swear at me.

*I'm not swearin at you ya daft cunt I'm swearin cos I always
swear.*

You never swore in court the day.

Aw fuck off.

I slams the door of the fridge shut.

Don't slam the door.

I'll slam any fuckin door I want.

I can't stand you d'ye know that? Can't fuckin stand ye.

Well fuck off then ye know where the door is.

I might just do that.

Do it then. Ya fuckin loony.

I picks up this cup an flings it off the wall. It explodes. I
can hear them stoppin cuttin hair down in Mario's. There's
the silence of open scissors. I can tell Carmen's thinkin, *I
wonder if Mario heard that?*

She gets on great wi him. The schoolgirl act. Smiles an hair
flickin an, *Yes, Mr Mario. No, Mr Mario. Three bags fuckin full,
Mr Mario.*

I picks up a plate. I grins at her. She screws up her face an
half shuts her eyes as if that'll stop Mario hearin it.

BOOOOOOOOOOOOOOOOOOOOOOOOOSH

Some kinda Pyrex stuff flakes in a million slivers, sharp as
fuck. This bit sticks in her cheek. Ye'd think I'd run over an
comfort her but do I fuck. I laugh. I shouts,

That's you now – wasted ya dog. Scarred for life.

She's jumpin about

Oh! Oh! Oh!

. . . she's goin. Her hands're flappin up an down like she's
tryin to fly. I decides to terrify her more. Fuck knows where

all the badness comes from. I opens the drawer an pulls out the blade that hung on the cupboard in Hill Street. She runs out the room. I sweeps plates an cups off the board an boots them about.

He'll hear that all right the wee Italian poof! I shouts as she dashes up the stairs.

I starts up the stairs slow an creepy. Like a horror film. *Psycho.* All the time part of me's *sayin stop this, ya stupid cunt,* an this other part – this part that's takin over – it's drivin ma blood. If ye believed in God an the Devil ye'd think I'm possessed when I'm on the drink.

I gets to the room. I leans against the door standard an sticks the knife in an out relaxed.

An what the fuck d'ye think ye're doin?

What does it look like?

She's packin gear in this brown suitcase. I flings the bedside light through the windie. It hits the brick wall. Some cunt screams. Carmen's screamin an stuffin more an more clothes in the bag. The bottom door opens. I don't need to look. Mario.

He's runnin up the stairs but starts walkin when he sees the knife. I expect him to be team handed but it's just him an he's a foot smaller than me. Carmen flumps on the bed greetin an stuffin the odd pair of knickers in the case.

What ees thees?

Fuck off! I goes. First time I ever speak to the guy in the middle of wreckin his flat an I tells him to fuck off. He might be Mafia for all I know.

Are you OK. Carmen?

SOB SOB mmm mmm.

He touches her hair. That's when he sees the windie's broke.

What ees wrong wi you man?

73

Everythin – the whole fuckin universe that's what! He looks puzzled.

Throw him out, Mario, says Carmen. Mario stares at me.

What are you dooing to my propertee?

Fuck knows why – probably him havin his hand on her hair – but I reaches over an lifts the other bedside lamp an crashes that through the glass mirror on the wardrobe.

That's what I'm doin. I'm wreckin the fuckin joint

WRE-CKIN THE FUCK-IN JOINT. Eh? Eh? is *that what ye want, Tally bastard? Eh? Eh?*

I starts bootin the other mirrors. They won't break so I turn the bed up on it's edge. She dodges by me an Mario an stands out in the lobby. Ye'd think Mario'd have a go or at least say somethin. He doesn't even seem angry. He stands there till I stop wreckin the joint. I wrench a door off an fire it out the windie. It posts itself neatly between the ragged blades of glass. I look straight in his eyes as it crashes to the ground. Nothin. I slide down in the corner holdin the knife upwards. He walks away. Carmen goes wi him.

Ye'd think he'd get the Polis. No. Doesn't chuck me out the flat. Doesn't bill me for the damage. Says nothin about it. Still spoke as if nothin happened.

I goes to Coral Island next mornin wi a cunt of a hangover.

All the way along the prom the wind's blowin in ma face. I'm takin deep breaths an gettin cold sweats an hot flushes. I smoke a fag an it's stinkin. *Fuck off fag,* I says an fling it under a car. I get to work an there's somethin wrong. Know how sometimes ye walk in a place an the atmosphere's different? Well it's one of them days. Badger an them're normal. *Good mornin,* an all this stuff. But I sense somethin wrong. I gets ma gear an starts walkin the floor. No Yella Brick Road for me till afternoon.

Just Stonkers. They use a nylon strip an stuff it in the coin mech an ring up ninety-nine credits. They hide the number on the credit indicator wi a personal stereo or tobacco tin. I usually let them fleece the joint. Coral Island makes a million a day in the season. But Bob the security guard's dossin about an keeps lookin over. I think he's checkin to see if I'm goin to lob the Stonkers out cos they're on ma patch so I goes,

Ye'll have to leave, lads – come back another time when the big guy's not here.

Sound mate! they go.

I know most of them. If I meet them in town they buy me drink. One from Newcastle posts the odd tenner through ma door. Out they go an Bob walks over. I'm vibratin cos I've not had a chance to get more drink.

Eh, Mick, got a minute?

Have I got a minute? The place's fuckin dead. I looks round about.

Aye, no problem, Bob.

Bring your keys.

I thinks he wants me to fix some machine nobody else can fix. I'm the most experienced here. But that's not what he wants. He takes me up to his office. Fuck sake! It's full of wee tellys an there's a telescope lyin on the polished table. Tidy as fuck. He stands at the other end of the desk an leans on it wi both hands. The spotlight's shinin on his head. It's like metal an it's givin me brain damage. He starts speakin an I notice the *Blackpool Gazette* on his desk.

How's things?

Good, Bob – OK. I notice two words peekin in the paper.

De Monte

I knew then – an he knew. But he never knew I knew he knew.

Enjoyin the job?

Aye – right hangover this mornin but, Bob.

He liked a drink. He laughs. Not his normal laugh. It's cut short like he remembers his Maw just died or somethin.

How's things outside, Mick?

Fine.

Still goin wi that wee lassie.

Aye – fell out last night . . .

Anythin else ye'd like to tell me about?

I decided to stop fuckin about so I points at the paper an goes, *Well, you've read it, Bob.*

He does his stupid laugh an picks up the paper.

Aye – I'm afraid we're going to have to let ye go. Nothin personal, Mick, but you know these places.

Aye right.

I goes to walk away, thinkin mibbi I'm sacked at the end of the week but he calls me back.

Eh, Mick? he goes.

Aye?

Keys an yer overalls. Ye'll have to go now.

Now?

But I knew the score. In case I robbed every machine in the place – but I've been doin that anyway not knowin his office's full of wee tellys. He shakes ma hand before I go. Like he's not really bothered about ma court case, like he likes me despite him being an ex-Polis an a security man an me being a crook. I don't expect him to shake ma hand. I'm nearly cryin. Well – I am cryin. I don't know if he sees the tears but he goes,

Good luck son. Take care of yerself.

As I get to the bottom I don't turn. I say *Aye* in a thin shaky voice an walk out. I walk out The Yella Brick Road an I thinks the new Dorothy's laughin at me all the way out.

He must know I was stealin out the machines. I mean all them tellys – he must've seen me at least once. There's even a camera in the bog. He let me steal that's it. It's normal to steal. It's not normal to get caught. It's not normal to get in the paper for burglary. They've got to sack ye. The whole town'd know a crook's workin in Coral Island. The whole town knows the whole town's crooks but they don't like ye to advertise. That's why I'm unemployed.

I buy a paper. Headline news. Daz's goin to love it. His ambition's to make the front page of the *Daily Record*. Front page of the *Blackpool Gazette* – good start. What the fuck does it matter anyhow? Jimmy McCann's got a few grand stuffed in a tin buried in the Windmill. Only me an him know about it. He's allowed to drink some of it. I decide to take it easy for a while.

The tide's out an the sand's flat an hard. I start thinkin how fit I was before I ran away wi Carmen. Runnin ten miles a day. Weird thing first thing I do when we hit Blackpool's buy a tin of roll ups an get pissed. Like I've been waitin to explode for a long time an this's the result.

I look at the sand. I'm goin to give up fags an drink an get down here every mornin. Must be a good four mile from South Pier to North Pier an back. Keep ye fit. No drink – good grub – mibbi go to College that's it – get ma act thegether. I lights up a fag. *See you fag,* I goes, *you're the last fag I'm ever goin to smoke. I swear on ma wane's lifes. I'll never smoke again.*

I sits in the sand an stares out to sea. I feel wee. I feel outside maself. Wave after wave echoes up the beach. Here an there people're dotted about. Throwin balls. Frisbee players. Couples wrapped round each other tryin to get the wind to catch their coats an hair so they look like cunts in films. An me. Me runnin ma troubles through ma head. I decides life's like this for everybody. Always sad. Always pain. The thing to do's stem the pain much as ye can. I do it wi drink an drugs but from now on I'm runnin. Any time I feel like a fag or a drink I'll run like fuck till I can't run no more. Fit as fuck I'll be.

When I get back Carmen throws herself, legs an all, round me an kisses me like a lost puppy dog.

I was down at your work.

Was I there?

Ye're sacked, Badger says.

Seen ma name in the paper.

I know. Headlines. Front page news. Our address an everythin. We're famous!

Fuck sake, it makes us look like idiots – a bunch of bunglers.

C'mon we'll get drunk.

I've stopped.

Since when?

Five minutes ago.

I'm away to get ready.

She's halfway up the stairs an shouts, *Mario says not to worry about the mess he's gettin it fixed.*

Ma hangover's disappearin. I decides to have one last fling before I really stop. I'll buy a track suit at the weekend, then I'll start. An I might as well finish these roll-ups.

Down the Noggin. Celtic's playin an they win. The owner's a big Polish guy an he's a Celtic supporter so it's a closed door job. At eleven the next day we're still there pished an talkin shite.

Simon Templar

I don't miss a days drinkin till I end up in hospital six weeks later. See the money Jimmy kept? Drank the lot. An the money we had all over the house. Every penny. Ye don't actually drink all the money. Ye buy for the whole pub. Big shot. Pizzas an kebabs an curries all the time. Taxis everywhere. Fuck washin yer clothes – sittin in the launderette wastin drinkin time. No way. Buy new stuff. Knickers an socks? Chuck them when they're boggin.

I'm only kinda sober when I do ma community work on a Saturday – cuttin gardens for aul wrinklies.

Ma skin's yella after four weeks. I thinks it's jaundice or somethin. I drink on.

Breakfast: we sit down the front washin the burgers an onion an chutney down wi cans of Super an a toke.

Twelve: the pubs open for pool, pints an vodka.

Six: a curry or a Chinkees then more pool.

Midnight: kebabs or fish suppers. Nightclub.

Three in the morning: boakin on a pavement or killin each other up an down the street. Day in day out's like that except Saturdays. After five weeks I start not eatin. I still go to the burgers in the mornin an the curry at six an the kebab at midnight, but I'm only nibblin an flingin the rest at seagulls.

This mornin I wakes up. Carmen's been goin on about ma funny colour for ages but I didn't give a fuck. I'm pickled. But this mornin I gets up to go to the burgers. Carmen's already away. It takes me half an hour to walk to the burgers. Ma head's spinnin. Every step on the concrete slabs's a hammer over the head. I thinks it's a bad hangover. Two burgers – the wummin's got them ready. We're a ritual now. I looks along Waterloo to them sittin near the Windmill. Even lookin's sore. I nips in an gets a half bottle of voddy an two cans. Usually I get six Supers – four for me an two for whoever's beggin. But I thinks a couple of slugs of voddy'll clear ma head. I gets to the front speared an sliced by rods an sheets of sunlight.

Oh I am fuckin dyin!

Somebody passes a joint.

Carmen's on the beach wi Daz playin headers wi this wet teddy bear. Jimmy McCann takes the joint out ma mouth.

Voddy? he says.

Aye I'm dyin.

Ye're a funny colour man – look rough as fuck.

Every cunt's gettin tore into the drink. I fling the burgers to seagulls. Even movin ma head's sore. I cracks the vodka an drinks as much as I can. I grue halfway down it but don't boak. I keeps it down. It rushes round ma veins an I feel OK for a minute. But by the end of the voddy I stand up an start wanderin home. I feel like a bad flu.

Carmen comes in about three in the mornin pished. She tries suckin me hard but I can hardly move. I'm not sleepin. I'm lyin wi this thump thump thump goin in ma head an bein sick now an then. There's nothin left in me. It's the sticky water stuff for a couple of hours. I've got the basin

in the bed. Then it's the green bile. Tastes mingin. Then its
the yella bile. Tastes ten times worse than the green. Then
stuff I never had before. Know when ye're retchin an retchin
an yer stomach's hard as marble? This brown sludgy stuff
starts comin up.

I'm like that four days. I take aspirin, paracetamol, night
nurse, day nurse, every time of the day ye can think of nurse
an Carmen – give her her due – after two days she decides to
stay in. She sticks wet cloths all over me. I'm seein things
comin out the walls. Big fuckin monsters openin an shuttin
their jaws at me. I don't scream. They don't frighten me. I'm
too sick to be scared. Five nights I don't sleep. I decide to go
up the Victoria for painkillers. I've no doctor in Blackpool.

Casualty. We wait.

An wait.

An wait.

Carmen's got dancin gear on dyin to go out but two hours
go by an nobody. Nothin. All I say's is I've got a sore throat
an need painkillers. I keep hallucinatin. People walkin by all
look like somebody up the road.

Did ye see that? Did ye fuckin see that? I says to Carmen.

What?

Him goin by there?

Where?

Wi the white overall.

She spins round. *Him down there?*

Aye.

What about him?

He works in the chippy down Mitchell Street.

She looks at me. Her face's glowin like melted plastic. Her
eyes're two dark planets an they're goin round an round.
She's askin if I'm all right.

Your eyes're rollin, she says.

But it's her's that's rollin. She's a planet. She's a solar

81

system. A spinnin fuckin galaxy an I'm bein sucked into her spiral or thrust away from it. It's a fuckin tunnel. If I go in it's a pin-point of heavy darkness. If I get thrust out it's the biggest widest empty space in the universe. I'm scared. I'm scared. I don't mind sayin it. I'm fuckin scared. I think of Ma Maw.

Excuse me? Excuse me? Carmen's goin to these people passin. She's doin the lost girl but people keep walkin by.

Ma Maw, her Maw, her Da, ma teacher from Primary. They all smile this treacherous smile. People that's been dead for years're walkin by an grinnin. Grinnin like they know somethin I don't. Carmen's at reception. She's mutterin. Sounds like Hail Marys. The wummin sticks her head out the windie. But it's not a head it's a spacehopper wi these wee rubber horns stickin out the top. She joins in the Hail Marys wi Carmen. It's not a hospital. I thought we were in the hospital. It's a train station. Carmen's buyin tickets to get back home. She'd better get me off these tracks soon. There's a train comin. I'm slidin down the red plastic chair. This wummin wi a cut hand's holdin me. I'm hangin off the Statue of Liberty an she's got ma sleeve an it's rippin all the time.

BANG!!!!!!!!!

I'm on the floor. I've been shot. It's the North Pole. It's fuckin freezin. Carmen screams across a massive expanse of ice an she's tryin to run across it but her feet're slippin. An the ice's crackin into big lumps an the water's scooshin through.

Next thing I'm sittin up in a cubicle.

I hear Carmen's voice somewhere. But I don't know if it's in ma head or real. I want her. I want her arms round me. I want her mouth in ma neck. I want her warm breath rushin down ma chest.

I usually like nurses but I can't lift ma head. Nice ankles.

Sore throat?

She's pissed off dealin wi a sore throat. She's got this thermometer in ma mouth an she's mumblin. I'm usin all ma energy to stay conscious. After four years she takes it out, squeaks, panics an bolts.

A hundred and four – a hundred and four deari deari me a hundred and four.

I looks at this clock. Five minutes it's took. But what about the years?

She's away. The clock's a trick. Like the used to do wi The Champions when they caught them. There's this empty space glowin where her white uniform used to be. I feels panic. *She ran out. Why did she do that?* I'm sayin in ma head.

I don't get to panic much. Witchcraft. Cos next thing I'm on this trolley gettin wheeled down a long corridor. Carmen's goin,

On My God he's dyin he's dyin.

Plantin kisses all over ma face. I'm bein attacked by gumsy Piranha fish. I'm drownin. This nurse's trying to rip Carmen's fingers off the trolley. But it's not Carmen. It's a chimpanzee. This Paki doctor's mutterin gibberish an stickin a Fairy Liquid lid in ma left arm. He whips out a turban an says he's called Sinbad. He slices the heads off this seven necked dragon an we're whizzin along the tarmac. BZZZZZ. We have blast off. This bag's swingin in the air. Flop flop it's goin. It's a see through liver. Transplant. Transplane. Liverpool.

Whizzzzzzzzzzzzzzzzzzzzzzzzzzzzzzzzzzzzzzzzzzzzzzzzzzzz zzzzzzzzzzzzzzzzzzzzzzzzzzzzzzzzzzzzzzzzzzzzzzzzzzzzzzzz along a corridor. Carmen's screams're fallin behind like a

weddin dress. We're gettin married. It's not Sinbad. It's a
priest. The nurse gets Carmen's fingers off an gets between
her an me – smilin. She's the *Any Objection to this Weddin*.
She's kissin me. Carmen can't see it. She's forcin her tongue
down ma throat. It's a snake. The Paki's back an he's got a
chanter. He charms the tongue snake out ma mouth. But the
fucker bites me on the other arm. When I looks down it's
another Squeezy lid. But it's not Fairy Liquid. It's another
cheaper brand that only does half a million dishes.

Hospital I think that's what it is. Two drips puttin fuck
knows what in ma blood. She's roarin an greetin.

He's goin to die. God's repayin us for what we done, she's goin.
All this alleluia music's playin an angels everywhere singin:

I

   p

     a

       s

         s

           o

             u

               t.

I come to in this room on ma own – bollock. The windie's
open. It's night. I can see the lights of rows an rows of
windies surrounded in deep silent black. This big fan's
whirrin an blowin cold air on me. I goes to switch it off but
someone's tied lead weights on ma arms. I gets ma arm in
the air an lets it fall so ma hand's near the switches.

I fall asleep. I wake again an the fan's still whirrin but the
rows of lights're out except for here an there in an order.
Must be corridors. I'm proud of maself guessin corridors. I'm
quite happy ma brain's workin. It's the only clear thought
I've had for years. The only thought wi no emotions
attached. No lies in it. It's just there. It's not good, not bad. I
like it. This time I switch the fan off an fall asleep.

I wake to birds whistlin in clouds of perfume. The fan's back on an perfume fills the room. The sky's gettin red. I suck the perfume an touch ma dick. It's big an soft. Sometimes yer dick's wee an soft but when yer sick an ye've not used it for a while it gets big an soft. The nurse must've switched the fan on. Must've seen me in the scud. Wonder if she looked right at ma dick? Specifically at ma cock? Must see a million. I'm not bothered lyin bollock either. The drips're still in ma arms. I try readin the bags but it's the name of the company that makes them. I fall asleep again an wake in light. It's just wakenin up – switchin off the fan – goin to sleep an wakenin up wi the fan switched on.

After four days punctuated wi visits from Carmen ginger an swedgers're pilin up. I feel better. I've had plenty fluids but so far no pish.

I feel like a pish.

The nurse gives me this Simon Templar terry towlin housecoat. There's me shovin this drip on wheels to the bog. The man wi the standard lamp I called maself. It's like comin havin this pish. Nothin's been along that tube for over a week. It's yella – nearly brown.

I looks in the mirror. Fuck me! I never looked in the mirror much since we came to Blackpool. I'm like the fuckin wolf-man. Against the whiter than white walls I can see the yella of ma skin. Ma cheekbones're stickin out an there's hollows in ma cheeks. I look just out Hartwood. I'd run a mile if I seen maself in the street.

I start drinkin an eatin like fuck. Next day I'm orderin hospital dinners. None of the nurses talked to me except to say here's yer medicine an all that. I gets a shower an shave an comb the hair. They start chattin me up. Not that I'm handsome. But this's the nearly dead coffin dodgin ward an I'm more sexy than a corpse-bound geriatric.

Turns out its the drink. Ma temperature was a hunner an four for days. Brain-fry.

Week later I'm havin a rerr time. Carmen's visitin every two days. She smells of drink an she's always got Daz wi her. I starts gettin jealous. Her an him. He's barkin but I can't budge it out ma head. This wee nurse brings me a poetry book. She reads them to me. Treated me like a King. I'm feelin great. The drip's off an so am I – that night out the windie. Away wi the Simon Templar an the poetry book too.

I got to the flat out of breath an shakin. It's been three weeks. I half expect Carmen to be sittin knittin – fuck knows why? But I half expect her to be in bed shaggin Daz. In I goes quiet. Up the stairs. No cunt in sight. Up to the bedroom to put the Simon Templar by an there she is on top of the bed. Pished out her head. I looks at her an wonder how if she loves me she could be out an about boozin wi me lyin in hospital. She's got this long black velvet dress on but it's worked it's way up. I can see the whole white length of her thighs an her black satin knickers. I starts workin the knickers off her. She jolts a couple of times but I slide them off easy. I inspects them. That's where the aul jealousy takes ye. I sees stuff that looks like spunk. I slide ma hand up her thigh. She starts moanin but I'm not turned on. The inside of her thigh's all wet. I want a close look at her fanny. I want to see.

BZZZZZZZZZZZZZZZZZZZZZZZZZZZZZZZZZZZZZZZZZZ
Fuck me! I jump. So does she.
What are you – who's what?
She's rubbin her eyes an I answers the buzzer.
Who is it?
Who's that? comes this voice.
It's Mick who's that?
Oh oh ye out hospital?
Aye?

Carmen's gettin herself thegether now.

It's me . . . Daz – I got a Chinkees for Carmen . . . is she in?

I opens the door. When I looks round the knickers're gone. Daz comes up the bottom stairs an in the livin room. He's got a Chinkees an a carry out. Carmen decides she needs a bath. We all sit an get drunk till the mornin light filters in on the weird atmosphere.

Fuck a Duck

Its not long after the hospital escapade that I'm back to ma old ways. Sometimes we run out of money. Do the Giros an Housin Benefit in. The end of this bender were sittin skint. Sometimes there's nothin to eat a day before the Giro. But this time it's two days we've had no food for.

The mornin before the Giro we're Hank Marvin. She's goin on an on. An I'm all this.

What the fuck d'ye expect me to do?

No fags. We're chokin. I gets up an has a dark yella pish vergin on the edge of brown. It stinks of everythin I ate an drank last few days.

Mug of water. Can't be bothered combin ma hair so I shove on the black tammy. I'm starin out the windie an she appears in the doorway. I feel her stare stickin in the back of ma neck.

So? she goes.

So what?

What're we goin to do?

Ha! What ye really mean's what am I goin to do?

She blows up the fringe. Ma eyes run down her jumper an rest on the dark shadow between her white thighs.

There's silence except her bare feet movin over the sticky

linoleum. She opens a cupboard.

No tea bags.

I say nothin.

She's bangin doors an pullin out empty boxes an throwin them over her shoulders.

No fuckin nothin.

Ah ha! she goes, an I turn round. She's got this pre-historic loaf.

Mibbi we can toast this? She says openin it.

ARRRRRGGGGGGGGGGGGGGHHHHHHHH

She drops it like it bit her. It's got a blue mould fur coat. I grin careful she doesn't see me. She slumps heavy in a chair.

Well?

Well what?

What're we goin to do?

Me ye mean?

Well what the fuck're YOU, she says in a funny voice, *goin to do?*

I walk out the room like a man wi a purpose not knowin what the fuck to do. I have to do somethin cos:

1. She'll nip ma head in all fuckin day.
2. I'm Hank too.

I comes down dressed. Soon as I sees the hairy loaf on the floor this idea comets in ma head.

Get yerself ready.

How?

Just get ready an ye'll find out.

She jumps up an I catch a glimpse of her pubes. I watch her goin up the stairs an the two boiled eggs she's got for an arse dancin cheek to cheek.

Bring that wee duffel bag down, I shouts.

She grunts.

I'm emptyin the bin in the sink. I pick out all the tattie peelins an put them to the side – shove all the other stuff back in the bag an put the peelins in a sinkfull of water.

Mountain Goat's got no juice so we're walkin. She won't carry the duffel bag cos the hairy loaf's in there. Soon as we walk on the street I smells nicotine. I spots half a fag on the pavement. There's people but I'm gaspin. When ye're gaspin ye can smell fags for miles. I twitch like a cartoon dog. I swoops. Carmen, without turnin her head, sees me an does five quick steps forward an to the side so she's not wi me. I'm surprised. It's not as embarrassin as I thought. No cunt hardly looks so I picks up a few more.

I light up an suck in a length of smoke. An instant paradise of dizziness rushes through ma veins.

AHHHHHHHHHHHHHHHHHHH! I goes an she turns.

She blows the fringe an waits, hand on hip. I give her this big dout. She looks round, spits on the tip an cleans it on her jumper leanin in for a light. A smile rings across her face. We feel better. We're goin to Stanley Park.

She's gettin enthusiastic about this fag business. She's shovin me out the road an divin for good ones. She holds one up ma nose goin *na na na na na* an pops it in the crisp pokes we're usin. We've got green Rizlas so we sprinkle the tobacco in the bags. I've kept this fag that's nearly full an she's tryin to find one bigger. People passin must think we're mad. There's me holdin her back by the hair an her fingertips an inch from a good fag. Same time I'm tryin to lean down an get it maself. She suddenly bumps me right into people an dives like Grobbalar. Laugh so it is. A fuckin laugh.

We get to the park wi enough tobacco to choke a horse. I

feel better wi the Giro comin next day an tattie peelins
cleanin in the sink. Ducks're swimmin on the lake in Stanley
Park.

There's people sniffin flowers an helpin wanes on an off
swings an monkey puzzles an through tunnels. I blank ma
wanes out ma head best I can. But every time I sees a Da wi
wanes an big smiles an laughter an runnin at each other it
smashes ma ice. I can feel Carmen thinkin ma thoughts an
our air's gettin darker. She hates me thinkin about ma
wanes.

Round the other end, I says.

Eh?

Round the other end – hardly any cunt there.

We find this clump of trees an get the loaf out. I'm breakin
the hairy loaf an sprinklin it in the water. The ducks've got
their radar switched on. They're at the other end of the lake
an ZIP they turn an their wee feet're goin like the clappers
under the surface. In seconds they're all round us quackin
like fuck.

Aw they're like wee babies, says Carmen. *Look at their shiny
wee eyes.*

Quack quack, says the ducks.

Dinner time! I'm sayin in ma best Boris Karloff voice.
They're that innocent ducks. They don't know what's
happenin.

It's posh around Stanley Park. Nothin like South Shore.
This wummin's walkin her poodle. Stupid tartan coat.
There's this wee lassie wi her. About five. She stops to watch
us feedin the ducks.

Look at the nice man feeding the ducks, Cynthia, Isn't that nice.

Yeth.

Aren't the little ducks pretty?

Yeth. Me want Duc.

I smile at the wummin. Her dog. Her wane. What else can I do. The ducks're gettin closer I'm throwin bread closer so some of it's on the grass at our knees. The bag's lyin open. The ducks're gettin closer but so's the wummin.

Lovely day, she goes.

Oh Aye nice an sunny, goes Carmen in her nicey nicey voice.

Oh are you Scottish?

Aye.

Fuck this, I thinks. *I know someone called George from Scotland'll* – be the next thing . . .

This little girl's father is Scottish.

Is your Daddy Scottish? says Carmen.

Ye-eth. Says the girl foldin her arms behind her.

Some ducks're next to the bag.

From Dumfries – do you know it?

Heard of it. We're from Glasgow.

Oh. Looking for work?

Day off.

A duck's at the black openin of the bag.

Where do you work?

I think, *Fuck me! Carmen's talked herself into a hole now.* But no.

I'm a stripper down South Shore.

Ahemm, the wummin says. *Are you really?*

An starts walkin away shovin the girl's back an sayin, *Come along now,* that's the instant I grabs this duck an stuffs it flappin in the bag. It's quackin like fuck. Ducks take off at all angles quackin like there's a nuclear war. The wummin turns to see a duffel bag wi wings. There's these green-black mallard wings stickin out the top flappin. It looks like the bag's tryin to fly.

Well really! she stamps an storms towards us.

Leave that poor creature alone you animal. The wane bursts out cryin.

Me want a duc. Me want a duc.

I shoves the wings in an pulls the strings.

Carmen's walkin away. I lifts the bag, dodge the wummin an catch up. Carmen's doin her straight legged walk. She does that when she's tryin to get away inconspicuous. Lookin direct forward.

Come back here this instant, the wummin's shoutin.

What she expect? *Oh OK, missus, seein as how you put it like that,* an give maself up. This's our dinner.

I give her the fingers. As I do that this big seagull swoops out nowhere, lifts the loaf an flaps big an slow in the air. The wummin jumps wi fright an by the time she gets herself thegether we're too far away. She tries shoutin across the lake at tourists but her voice's dragged down by gravity to the surface of ducks an ripplin water.

We don't pick douts on the way home. We go a weird route in case she phones the Polis.

Back in the flat I put the bag down. It's quiet. Fed up strugglin. I puts the tattie peelins in a pot an gets them on the gas. I thinks she'll give me the *I'm not eatin them* routine but she looks in the pot an goes MMMMMMMMMMMM.

There's this big soup pot under the sink. We've never used it.

Get that big soup pot under the sink out.

Her eyes light up. Rattle rattle an there it is, sittin like a tomb.

Check it for shite – McCann's been in here.

She laughs. The bag jerks like it gets the joke. There's still the question of killin. She reads ma thoughts.

Are ye goin to wring it's neck?

Eh?

How're ye goin to kill it?

Chop it's head off.

Her mouth grins to rows of mad teeth. I take out this big cleaver an lay out the wooden choppin board on the worktop.

Turn that telly on loud cos this fucker'll scream the house down.

She puts the telly on. The Old Spice advert's on wi the Omen music. I feel evil – powerful. I gets the fucker out. I've got it by the feet. It's flappin it's wings thegether an risin on the end of ma arm to the ceilin. I'm holdin it that tight I'm sure I feel it's feet breakin. It scunners me.

DA DA DA DA

the music's goin. I lies the duck on the board. I've got it's wings shut holdin it by the shoulders. I lifts the cleaver. I looks expectin her to be cringin in a corner wi her hands on her face waitin for the thunk of death. She's not. She's starin right at the duck's neck. Not at me. Not at the cleaver. Right where the metal'll make contact wi feathers an flesh. I've got a carrier bag against the wall to catch the scoosh of blood when the head comes off. The fucker won't stay still. Keeps liftin it's head an lookin at me. It's beggin me not to kill it.

Hit it!

DA DA DA DA

I can't get a swing it keeps movin it's head.

DA DA DA DA

Fuckin chop the bastard.

DA DA DA

DAAAA DA DA

It's too wriggly.

Take it's fuckin head off.

DA DA DA DA.

I can't kill it. I lets it go. It sits up. It's thinking, *Duck heaven?* When it realises it's in Lytham Road near a big pot it flaps up an bounces off the ceilin. Ye'd never think a duck's so noisy. Quack quack it's goin an lucky the Shake an Vac

advert's drownin it out. It sees the windie an woosh woosh woosh three massive flaps an it THUMPS right on it.

It falls like four pound of mince on the floor an starts runnin round quackin.

Do the shake an vac QUACK QUACK an put the freshness back. QUACK QUACK Do the shake an vac QUACK QUACK an put the freshness back. QUACK QUACK.

Do the shake an vac QUACK QUACK an put the freshness back. QUACK QUACK Do the shake an vac

95

QUACK QUACK an put the freshness back.
QUACK QUACK.

Do the shake an vac QUACK QUACK an put the
freshness back. QUACK QUACK Do the shake an vac
QUACK QUACK an put the freshness back.
QUACK QUACK.
QUAAAAAAAAAAAAAAAAAACK!!!!!!!!!

Carmen's got it. I expect her to give me it. Before I get out
from behind the telly she's got it over the sink. She whacks it
three times wi the soup ladle, shoves it on the board, lifts the
cleaver an THUD!

There's a mini-quack. A queek really. Blood's oozin all over
the board. She turns an smiles. Her white teeth seem to
reflect the blood all over her white hands. She's standin wi
the cleaver an black hair everywhere an blood on her hands
an the body of the duck jerkin like a feathered orgasm on the
board. For a minute I feels she's goin to come at me.

Dinner   is served   master.

We laugh. I turn the telly down an pluck the duck, gut it
an fuck it in a big pot of boilin water. Carmen's washin.

The duck an tattie peelins're boilin away nice when in she
comes. Black bra – sussies knickers stockins – the whole bit.
She's got this look in her eye an I know what it means. Over
she goes. Shuts the curtains an kneels down. Undoes ma
button, down wi ma zip an starts suckin.

I'm on the floor an she's givin me this ride like I've never
had. Every time I try leanin up like the duck done she
shoves me back down. Every time I try to hold her tits she
leans away. Total control an she's lovin it.

It's a bit tough the duck. But wi rollups an us bein pure
Hank an the tattie peelins it's a banquet.

Necklines

We're all at the Noggin. Some of the team're goin to the Red
Lion an some're goin to Raffles. Raffles's this disco under the
ground on Waterloo Road. You go down underlit stairs wi
blue glittery walls. There's all sorts in there. Poofs. Tarts.
Cows. Trannies. Mad cunts. Me an Carmen walk round
holdin hands to Raffles.

It's a fiver in Blackpool discos. If ye're a local it's a couple
of quid to the bouncers.

Local.

Four quid, mate.

They're lookin at Carmen's arse.

We get in standin near the dancefloor. She's shoutin in ma
ear all about how the music's great. Every now an then, just
to show any predators she's mine I give her a good winch.
She's rubbin the cunt off ma thigh. The blond Trannie's
smilin but I don't know if it's me or at her. The Poofs're
checkin ma gyratin hips an holidaymakers're squeezin their
eyes round corners to see her knickers through her ski-pants.

SOLID

I grabs her hand.

SOLID AS A ROCK

We're on the floor an givin it close-up sexy dancin. She

flicks the tongue out an licks ma lips. The energy level in the place goes up. Every cunt's dancin. Carmen starts gyratin wi these holidaymakers. They're about eighteen. I starts feelin alone. I'm on the dancefloor an to anyone lookin I'm lovin it. I've got the rhythm automatic but ma mind's back home.

Carmen's back's swayin side to side an I'm catchin ma son an throwin him up. He's pausin in the air an fallin to the safety of ma arms. They say there's nowhere more lonely than a city. But they're wrong. There's nowhere more lonely than yer own head. It separates ye from the world an all the flashin lights an wafts of perfume can't pull ye back. I need more drink.

SOLID AS A ROCK

That's when I noticed I've never had that. Love solid as a rock I mean. There we are on the dancefloor an she's turned away singin 'Solid as a Rock' to these young bucks. She's got an arm above her head wrigglin like a belly dancer an thrustin her hips at every beat of the rhythm. I'm dancin like I don't give a fuck – like this's how it always is for me – like I'm so fuckin irresistible she'll turn round any minute an shag me on the dancefloor.

But that's not how it is. I'm a spare prick. I'm glad I don't loose the rhythm. The Tranny knows. He sees ma pain. He winks. But it's not a *I want to shag you* wink, it's a knowin wink. There's another thing risin inside me. A black thing. Somethin dangerous. Somethin that wants to scream an wreck the joint. Somethin that wants to die, but in fire. To die in fire rather than the ice of suicide. An the thought of her writhin on a bed wi four young bucks turns me on. The same thing turnin me on's makin me jealous. The same thing makin me jealous's coaxin a mad fatalistic streak to the surface like the beginnins of a giant uncontrollable oil slick.

The music stops.

Over she comes.

I'm bobbin up an down like I don't care about the right good lookin cunt givin her a peck on the cheek.

Solid, she sings.

I grabs her hand an shoves it in ma balls.

Solid as ma cock.

See you, she goes. An laughs. She bends her head forward an sips her drink. Her hair falls an shuts like curtains but I know she's peekin through the chink givin the sparklin eye to the guy than pecked her cheek.

You don't mind me dancin wi other guys do ye?

Me? No way. Hm.

Daz says he'd have none of it.

I'm too old for that stuff – so long as ye're comin home wi me at the end of the night I don't care if ye shag them on the dancefloor.

She gives this big smile that melts me an sticks a vodka-sodden tongue in ma ear.

Anyway that's not the story. This's the story. At the end of the song I'm dancin feelin like a spare prick an Daz comes in. He's not got Slinky. He's got Sally. I thinks, *Oh ho here we go Daz's goin to put a tail on her the night.*

Carmen withdraws the tongue an eyes the young bucks again. Daz walks over.

This's exactly what happens. See how ye always swear blind that if yer mate got stabbed ye'd do this an that? Daz walks over. Takes a sip from his pint. Sally's still walkin over. Daz starts talkin. I notice this guy comin from the right. Daz's eyes swivel. The guy cuts his throat. Daz stares at me. The guy walks away. The cut unzips into this big insane mouth runnin from under his ear to his Adam's apple. Sally's glass's on its way to the deck. Carmen screams. The stuff hangin out Daz's neck's shiny. Looks like fibreglass. Sally's glass explodes on the floor. The blood starts pishin out his neck. Carmen starts shoutin,

Get that bastard. Him there!

She's throwin ashtrays an glasses. The guy's duckin. He's not runnin. He's grinnin an walkin deliberately towards the stairs. Carmen's goin to town an cunts're divin off the dancefloor.

Daz starts shakin. The music stops. The DJ shouts for bouncers. Daz's vibratin now an his eyes look like a stuck pig. Sally's roarin an greetin. Cunts've suddenly got necks like swans. Burds everywhere start screamin. The Young Bucks slink into the shadows. Blood's actually pum-pin out his neck. SQUIRT SQUIRT I whips off the T-shirt an shoves it against his neck. The cunt walks by the bouncers runnin down the stairs. First thing they see's some guy vibratin an another guy, stripped to the waist, covered in blood down the arm an chest. They're lookin at me like I done it.

Get to fuck out ma road, I shouts shovin Daz through the crowd.

Out ma fuckin road!

I'm screamin. I've got him on Waterloo in seconds. Carmen's holdin screamin Sally.

I looks frantic left

looks frantic right

Not a car in the street. Waterloo Road an not a fuckin car in sight. First time ever. Daz's lost blood. He's on his knees. Carmen's runnin in an out broke phoneboxes. Sally's in the middle of the road roarin. Then a miracle. A Polis car comes round the corner. They nearly mow Sally down, so they stop. We stuff Daz in the car explainin quick an

zoooooooooooooooooooooooooooooooooooooooooooooooooooooooom off they go.

I'm goin to kill that bastard if I ever see him again, says Carmen an blows her fringe.

I've got the arm round Sally. She's shakin. Then I realise so am I.

I'll remember that bastard. Know how? goes Carmen lightin up a fag.

How?

He's got this big black birthmark right on his head.

What?

A black mark right there – right fuckin there, she goes pointin hard to the middle of her head.

No No, goes Sally bubblin. *It's not a birthmark.*

Eh?

On his head. That's not a birthmark.

How? D'ye know the guy?

No.

Well?

It was Daz.

By this time we're all on the kerb smokin.

What d'ye mean?

When we came in that guy's on the stairs. He says somethin to Daz. Liverpool accent. Daz says somethin about Scouse cunt an he says somethin about Slinky. Daz puts the fag out on his head. That's the black mark.

So that's what happened. The guy shagged Slinky. He worked beside her on the Pleasure Beach. The guy says every cunt on the Pleasure Beach shagged her. So he's an ashtray now an Daz's in the Victoria wi his head hangin off.

Twenty-eight stitches. Lucky to be alive. A minute later . . . if The Polis weren't goin by . . . If I never got him out quick – I liked that bit . . . One lucky man, an all that shite.

Murder

This night Sally's covered in face dust an perfume. I'm right across from her an she's got this wee skirt on. Black tights or stockins, can't see right. She knows I want to shove her over an give her it so she's hot an bothered. I'm givin it *nice day* an *how's yer Maw* an all this shite but really what I want to say is,

Get on that floor an start moanin ya tart.

So she's got her knees stuck thegether like magnets an her shinin tights (or stockins) are like train tracks parallel right up the black cavity between her legs. She catches me lookin at the wee vee an bats the eyelids like two butterflies landin on her face. The dust off her make-up puffs up an she coughs an smiles all shy like. She tilts her head forwards an to the side an some hair falls over her face. Fuck me. That makes me worse – a wee girl wi a wummin's body. *Get to fuck hard-on.* I'm sayin in ma head tryin to think of rent money.

Somethin's tellin me I can make the move. I can smell it. Are ye tryin to tell me when they're wet an the tip of yer cock's glistenin it doesn't fill the air wi hormones? Fuck off! When ye're horny, ye're horny an every cunt knows. It's the social membrane that stops complete strangers shaggin each other to death.

102

Anyway. Carmen's movin about up the stairs. She'd blade me if she could read ma thoughts. Next thing I hears the wardrobe door slide. She's lookin for what to wear.

Away to get washed, Sally, I goes, spins quick tryin to hide ma semi. She glances quick at ma crotch an smiles.

I gets up the stairs.

WOW!!!

There's Carmen, this long flowin sky-blue skirt an top. All her black curls fallin wet from the bath. Shinin. I'm rock solid. She smiles through her hair. She's got a leg on the bed fixin this white stockin. I grabs her hip bones an starts rubbin off her. I think cos Sally's down the stairs she'll tell me to fuck off but she presses back moanin. She's still got the leg on the bed an leans forwards to the side an grips the headboard. I rolls the skirt up an I bend her over wi the flat of ma hand on her back. Her moans get lost in her hair. Five minutes an we've came.

We go back into the livin room thegether an Sally doesn't crack a light about the squeaky bed an Carmen moanin like fuck.

Down the Noggin – pool, jukebox an beggars. In fact the first thing I heard in Blackpool was,

Gees a quid Jimmy.

All the way from Scotland to get begged by some Scots guy.

Daz's in the Noggin wi his burd. He's got this scar round the left of his neck.

Mind that? says Carmen liftin a black eyebrow.

Fuck aye, says I.

Thought he was dead.

We've left the Noggin an hold hands all the way to Raffles. We get in an we're standin at the dancefloor. She's eyein talent thinkin I can't see. Next thing she goes,

There's that bastard there. Don't look!

I looks an it's him.

I told ye not to look!

He's stood at the bar nice as ye like. Drinkin on his own. *Always be wary of a guy that drinks on his own,* ma Granda used to say.

That's him all right.

Well? she goes.

Well what?

What're ye goin to do?

What the fuck d'ye mean?

Kill the bastard.

Shh . . .

Shh fuck all. Look at the snake drinkin like he thinks he's somethin. Kill him.

I don't want no blade in me. But at the same time she's goadin me. Slightin ma manhood. An this blackness in me – the thing that's makin me not give a fuck any more about anythin – it's sayin, *get over there an crush the weasel.*

Well?

She's got the folded arms, one toe turned up an she's blowin the fringe back. I decides to prove ma manhood.

Right. Shut yer fuckin mouth an I'll tell ye what we'll do.

She leans in an we conspire.

So we're dancin an she's got this smile on her face all night. I'm hopin he'll slip away early. But there's not much chance of that cos the bold Carmen's got a bead on him out the side of her eye all the time. Fuck it.

As if that's not enough. We gets this table in the corner an I'm firin the drink in for berserkness. Who comes over but the very cunt. He sits at our table.

I looks at Carmen.

She looks at me.

How ye doin? he goes in his Scouse accent.

OK.

Come in here a lot? I asks him.

Haven't been for a while now.

He looks at Carmen lookin for a response. She's not sayin nothin.

Local?

Yeah.

Workin here?

Pleasure Beach. Yer Judy don't say much do she?

Wait till she starts. Carmen smiles.

A smile. Yer alive then?

He prods her an she laughs. But there's a glint in her eye only I understand. Anyhow it soon becomes clear John – that's his name can't remember us from the night he slashed Daz. I've got a gram in ma pocket so I asks him if he's into goin down the Windmill for a smoke after Raffles. He glances at Carmen an says yeah. He thinks he's in wi a shout if I conk out. She's givin him footsie under the table.

We're in the Windmill an I've skinned up three joints. I've put all the dope in so they're strong. He's first on this one. The noise of the sea's right up. The tide's in. Me an Carmen's sittin each side of this guy. In the dark I can see the glow of his hand on her leg. His fingers're foldin round her thigh an she moves close so he can feel the warmth of her arse against his.

Meh-low, he goes an blows a long line of smoke up the concentric darkness of the Windmill. Darkness gets thicker as the point of the Windmill crushes it into a smaller space. I'm thinkin that's the way ma life's goin, into that small space of immense darkness. It's the night I let it happen. I decide I deserved fuck all good in life. I decide that whatever happens I deserve. Ma thinkin changes.

I'm seein better in the dark now an his fingers're flickin light over her pussy now an then. Just like the dancefloor it's makin me jealous an turnin me on. Me an her're takin wee tokes on the joint an sippin the Supers. We're passin the joint to the daft cunt in the middle. Carmen-him-me-him-Carmen-him-me. He's probably thinkin we're a pair of eejits – *life of Riley here* – but he's gettin drunker an more stoned by the minute.

Don't know what time but all there is's the rush an fall of the sea an the silence pushin down from a Blackpool that's drunk itself to a stupor. Not a sound. Not even a voice screamin down the labyrinthine alleyways to the front.

Want to go a walk? Nighttime paddle?

She peers at me.

I'm stayin here – too welded. I goes.

He jumps up, staggers a bit to the side.

I'll go for a walk. No problem. Paddlin's ma middle name, goes The Scouse.

They clamber out the hole. He's not givin a fuck now. He's got his hand right on her arse as he's shovin her out the hole. Out they go an I hear them pad off towards South Pier. I hears groanin up in the Windmill.

Who's that? goes this rough voice. Jimmy McCann's home.

It's me Jimmy. Froggy. Me an ma burd.

I reach up an hand him a can but he mumbles somethin an falls asleep on his ledge again. I spring out the hole right away.

When they come into focus he's got her bent over holdin onto one of the upright columns under South Pier. Her ski pants an knickers're a pile at the bottom of the line of her white legs an he's bangin her from the back. She's shovin side to side in a rhythmic motion an the rage's buildin an subsidin in me wi the push an withdrawal of the waves. I walk away down the water's edge an start comin at them along the line of columns. She's moanin an he's givin it,

D'ye love it tart – ma big cock?

Yes yes, she's goin.

She loves danger. I'm two columns away when she comes. Her moans're muffled by him slappin her arse.

Stay there tart, don't move, he goes.

An starts bangin it into her. His breath's risin an his moans get higher. By this time I'm a couple of feet behind him. I waits till he's shudderin in orgasm an fuck him one on the side of the head. He screams. I punch him about the head rapid. He's on his knees. His wet hard on's shinin in the moonlight.

Carmen's pullin her knickers up an I'm layin the boot in good. Flurries of sand blow up wi every kick. She starts puttin the boot in too. But we underestimated this cunt. He corkscrews up through the tornado of blows an limps sideways a couple of steps. I catches him a hook full force on the beak as he tries to pull his trousers up. Just as I aim to crash a couple of boots in his ribs he's standin wi mad eyes. His dick's flopped between his thighs an he's wavin this blade about. His eyes're swellin. I jumps at him an he swings the blade.

I jumps at him an he swings the blade.

I jumps at him an he swings the blade.

I jumps at him an he swings the blade.

Your Judy's a good ride, he says, sneerin.

He doesn't give a fuck. Dangerous. But I'm gettin more dangerous by the day. The thing that's growin in me launches me at him. He misses wi the knife an we're strugglin in the sand. I've got his two arm's cos I don't know what one the knife's in. The cunt's sinkin the teeth in. Carmen's found driftwood an I can hear the slap as she hits skin an the clunk as she hits bone but the cunt's still not givin up. I'm tryin to think of a way out an he flops on me. I thinks he's fainted. Ran out of energy or somethin. I push him off an there's Carmen wi the blade shinin in the moon. There's blood runnin down over the guy's arse an he's jerkin an moanin like he's havin another orgasm.

Gimme the knife!

I take the knife an sticks it in an out the sand till there's no blood. She's stock still watchin him jerk. I walk into the sea, up to ma waist an throw the blade as far as fuck. It splooshes in the water like Excalibur. The sea around ma body's cold. So cold.

I get back an he's stopped movin. She's sittin smokin a joint. Snifflin. We say nothin for a while an smoke. The tide's creepin up. We'll have to do somethin soon. The sky's lightenin. I keep feelin his neck hopin for a pulse. I don't feel nothin. I always thought if I got involved in a murder I'd feel a massive sense of guilt. But I feel nothin. Just relief the fight's over. It'll probably come themorra.

But what if somebody seen us in Raffles wi the guy? I start to panic. I'm twenty-four. She's sixteen. I'd get life an she'd get a couple of years. Premeditated murder for fucksake! That's what it looks like. We only meant to give him a hidin for Froggy. It's lookin bad. I feels his neck again – nothin. I say a couple of prayers. I feels the pulse – nothin.

What the fuck're we goin to do now?

I asks her expectin her to burst out greetin. But cool as ye like she nods up South Pier an says,

Take him out to the edge pier an chuck him in the sea.

I laugh. It comes home to me that this is a dead man. An this is a murder. An this is a body. Ye get rid of a body.

Ye get rid of a body.

Ye get rid of a body.

Ye get rid of a body.

So we struggle. I get his back against ma back so we're knockin heads an start draggin him up these stairs. They go up to a trap door under the Pier. The two of us bundle him out onto the deckin. I drag him over the wooden boards to the far edge of South Pier. Carmen picks up his shoes an stuff that's fallin out his pockets. We get him to the edge an let him fall wi an almighty thump on the deck. His dick's dead wee now. Weird. Here's a guy that a couple of hours ago was shaggin ma burd an now he's dead. Doesn't exist. I hope there's no such a thing as ghosts.

Right. Over the edge, I says.

We get under an arm each an shove him up to his waist on the railins. Then we get hold of his feet an tip him over.

TIIIIIIIIIIIIIMBEHEHEHEHEHER! she goes.

There's two feet of boards between the rail an the edge.

What does this guy do? Clunk His head hits the boards an he's crumpled there like he just got blew in off the sea. She reaches through the railins an gives him a push. Over he goes.

Silence.

Splash as he hits the sea. A terrible relief.

Next day we're in Coatbridge. Stuffed the Mountain Goat full an buzzed up the road sayin nothin about what happened.

Floorboards

The first thing that hits ye about Sikeside's the wanes an dogs an burnt-out cars. Rough as fuck. Ye can get a house no problem. Rows an rows of four-high flats wi verandahs an the odd cottage type here an there to make it look good.

Boarded up windies. Wooden boards an the new metal ones that're dead hard to get off. Most of the flats're empty. There's the odd burnt-out buildin here an there. If ye're not born there or mad as fuck ye can't stay there. Ye'll get yer house screwed when ye go out to the van for a Curly Wurly an ten Club King Size.

At one end of the main street through it the sign says *Sikeside Street*. At the other end it says *Sykeside Street*. How d'ye expect **them** to get the place in order if **they** cant even spell it?

Sikeside? says the burd up the Housin. She knows I'm desperate. They get to know who wants a house the now an who's got the stamina to wait ten years for a good area. It's crazy: half a mile from Sikeside – the worst council scheme in the world is Cliftonville, the best council scheme in the world. I'm desperate an she senses it. Half of me wants it an half of me's sayin, *Don't be so fuckin daft*.

But I says I'll take one if there's anythin goin. Next day I gets a letter at ma Maw's offerin Cumbrae Cres.

ZOOOOOOOOOOOOOOOOOOOOOOOOOOOOOOOOOOOM

I shoots up an gets the key. I walks over to Sikeside. 3B. Turns the key. There's cunts peekin in the close an whisperin all about here's a new guy. Wonderin what I'm all about.

Two bedrooms one left one right. Lights're not workin. Fuck – not a light fittin in place. I can smell damp burnt wood. There's hissin water comin from down the lobby. I hold up ma lighter an move to the bog. Can't see nothin nearly. The windies're boarded up wi metal. Lucky I looks down when I gets to the scullery – no floorboards. None in the livin room either. The metal shutter on the scullery's been bent back an there's enough light to see without the lighter. Under the joist's full of water an this fine spray from a hammered over pipe's hissin as it moves through the air. It's cold. I balances the joists an walks in the livin room. Foundations full of water. The copper pipes an wires're stripped bare. There's raggled lines round the walls where they've been tore out. I makes ma way to where the sink used to be an turn off the water.

The room to the right seems the best bet. If somebody's goin to break in they're comin in the back room or scullery. Give me time to get ready. I goes up ASDA's an gets a set of keys made. I goes up the Housin an it's the same burd.

I'll take it, I goes.

She's expectin refusal. She coughs a couple of times an looks round like she's lookin for handers. She's got big blue eyes. She's not givin me a second look. She blurts out, *It's undergoing repairs at the moment according to this . . .*

This was an aul yella bit of paper. What she should be sayin is, *Every empty in Sikeside's been screwed and wrecked by the young team. Stripped for scrap. We don't bother doing them up till some dick takes one. Usually they look an say, ye can get*

yersel to fuck wi that midden!!! **But you've fucked the system**
right up saying you want it.

She's threw off balance so I goes, *I can wait.*

Be a few weeks.

No problem.

Pretty bad down there. The houses.

Looked all right to me.

She looks right at me.

So you want it?

Aye.

She pauses an scratches the top of her head wi one finger
an off she goes. Comes back wi these documents full of
stupid lookin questions. She's pissed off I want the house cos
it's Interview Room now. Emerge two hours later through a
fuckin mangle. Every question's designed to trip ye up. I
fully consider every sentence cos of the questions she's askin
an the ones she's goin to ask. Mind's racin like fuck. Same as
the Social game. Mental Cruelty Chess. This dame's no
match. Beginner. I fuck her up every turn. I pull the classic.
Make her think I'd never played before an before ye know it
she's all flustered an lookin about for handers again. I gets
right up to

ADOPTED AS HOLOGRAPH

Fuck knows what it means but when ye get there, ye've
won a house. I gives her the **fuck you** smile an saunters out.

It won't be ready for some time, Mr Riley.

I swings open the door without lookin round.

We'll inform you!

What she really means is,

*Cunt. I'll make sure your house goes to the fuckin bottom of the
repairs list. Smart arse.*

I swivel an grin an close the door. She's talkin to other
cunts about me.

She done her job right. It's March before they start repairs, ye know like put a floor down. It's a laugh so it is. Oh! by the way, by this time Carmen's pregnant.

She's done that to trap ye ya stupid cunt, our Angie goes.

Never bothered me. Kinda liked it. An I thought I'd be trappin her. How wrong can ye get? Anyway she's moved in her Maw's till Cumbrae's fixed up. Ma family's talkin to me but I can't visit or stay or anythin so I move in the day I sign

the ADOPTED AS HOLOGRAPH wi the keys I got made in ASDA's.

I get some lights workin. I gets a kettle, mattress, sheets, a towel an one of them slow cooker gadgets off Angie an off I pops in a hackney.

Cumbrae Cres, mate, I goes, *Sikeside.*

See his face when he drops me off. Thinks he's in Beirut.

I find this floorbrush in a cupboard an brush the room out.

FLOP the mattress on the floor. I've got a wee thirty bob tranny too. I plug in the kettle an go to the shops.

It's dark. My breath's glowin in the orange street lights an people're peekin out curtains.

You new?
Aye.
Got a wife?

Naw.

Aww!

But I'm gettin one.

When?

Soon.

Got wanes?

Aye tw – three.

Our age?

Aye.

Are they good fighters?

They don't fight.

Everybody fights.

Except ma wanes.

Aye right.

You a good fighter? Ye look like a good fighter? Bet you can fight?

I don't fight.

Aye ye do – every cunt fights.

That's terrible swearin at your age.

So it fuckin is!

By this time were at the corner of Cumbrae an Sikeside Street.

Shops're over there.

This wee guy says noddin as he lights up a joint. He's about eleven.

How d'ye know I'm goin to the shops?

The other wee guys an lassies tune in.

They always go to the shops, don't they?

He turns to his pals an like primary wanes they all say at the same time,

Aye, Dinky.

Who? I goes.

New cunts.

What d'ye mean?

They come in an put the lights on an go to the shops for scran.
I'm gettin a better picture of this place now.
Does a lot of people move in?
We've crossed the road now an they all laugh. Dinky grabs his red hair an shakes his head side to side like I'm really daft, like I can't understand.

Aye!!!!! in one night – out next day.
How's that, Dinky?
He scuffs his feet stoppin dead.
How d'you know ma name?
I know yer Da.
Do ye fuck.
Aye I do.
What's his name then.
Mr Dinky.
Shut it ya wanker.
Dinky's not too chuffed. I need as many pals as possible round here so I starts bein nice again.
What do they move out for then?
Same reason you will.
An what's that?
We'll tan all yer windies the night.
I'm about to say *that'll be fuckin hard they're made out wood an metal,* when all the other wee cunts start laughin an dancin round singin,

> *Got no windies got no floors*
> *Can't see through yer wooden boards*
> *Got big holes instead of doors*
> *You are fuck-in Mi-ingin.*

Dinky joins in an I slide in the shop. I can hear them singin this other song outside the shop.

Oh they're tough
Mighty tough in Greenenn.
Oh the wummin they are tougher than the men.
Cos they wash their clothes on Sunday
An pawn them on the Monday.
Oh they're tough, mighty tough,
in Greenenn.

There's a pause an then they burst into,

You are ma woodbine
Ma forty Woodbine.
You make me happy when skies are grey.
You steal ma Giro an fuckin lie low
Oh don't take ma sunshine away.

I hears their feet clickin away.
Silence.
Frosties milk bread marge cheese coffee sugar tea bags an
onion an spuds. I goes home an has a feast. Goin round the
road wee Dinky comes up on his own.

What's yer name, big man?
Mick. What's yours, wee man?
You know what it is!
Oh aye Dunky?
No Dinky.
That's right.
I know it's right it's ma name ya tube.
What's the story then, Dinky?
What d'ye mean?
How come ye're smokin dope at your age?

He shrugs an kicks a stone. He walks beside me to
Cumbrae. I know he's goin to say somethin cos he's lookin
away real quiet.

Know how ye said ye know ma Da?

Aye?

Were ye really kiddin?

Aye. I was only kiddin, wee man – I might know him. What's his name?

Don't know.

What d'ye mean ye don't know?

I don't know.

I catches maself on.

Oh well, wee man, Da's aren't all they're cracked up to be.

Mine was a right bastard ma Maw says. Right rotten bastard.

Better without him then eh?

It's just the scrape of our feet in the darkness. Wee Dinky turns an nods at Sikeside itself.

They screw yer house.

Who?

Junkies.

When ye go to the van they kick yer door in. Take yer telly an video.

Think they'll kick ma door in?

He tilts his head up at me, sticks his hands on his hips an draws out:

Naaaaaaaaaaaaaaaaaaaaaaaaaaaaaaaaaaaaaw.

How?

Fuck all in there worth stealin.

How the fuck d'you know that?

I was in.

When?

There the now.

Through the scullery shutter. Took nothing. Fuck *near got drownt. Ye've no floorboards. A swimmin pool it is in there.*

What the . . .

Don't worry, Mick. I'll no go in again. Ye'll not get yer house screwed – every cunt knows ye've nothin.

The wee cunt zooms off. Lucky I've got the Rambo knife. The light in the room's shinin through the metal shutters like straight rows of tiny stars. I'm surrounded by flats. There's music from all angles. Shoutin. The odd screamin wummin an shoutin man.

There's no close door. Stinks of pish. I stops in ma tracks. There at the door's this wee bedside table. I opens the door an takes it in. Scraped out on the top wi a bit of glass, splinters of it still embedded in the wood, is:

WELKUM TO SIYKSIDE DINKY YA BAS IRA

Plumber wi the Burgh

Sometimes ye hear rats scratchin below. I get in a good routine. I wake about ten an smoke a fag waitin for the kettle to boil. I have Sugar Puffs or Frosties – they're great. I got this toaster out a skip up Cairnhill. They throw good gear out up there so their neighbours'll think they're well off.

Mrs McGinty throws out a half-decent three-piece suite so Mrs McGonigle chucks a couple of beds an a wardrobe. McGinty hears about the bed escapade at the knittin bee, storms down the road an rips out the kitchen just fitted a year ago an skips it. McGonigle responds wi her kitchen an the cooker an fridge. On an on they go till they've got to buy stuff out Comet to throw out. OK for the likes of me scavengin up through the woods from Sikeside.

See when I find the toaster it's a great day. It might mean diddly to you – a fuckin toaster – a toaster that never even worked for fucksake. But I'm a spark. Remember the fruit machines?

Anyhow, this mornin I comes out the house.

Yo big man! shouts Dinky an draws on his fag.

It's half ten an he's waitin for his Maw to go out so he can sneak in to dog school. I gives him the nod wink combination.

Half way round Cumbrae there's this gap. Zip – I'm on the red ash path that used to be the canal. Up through the woods.

A good bit. Could be anywhere. If ye pick the right angle ye can't see the sewer away down the hill or the shut down Imperial Steelwork up the top. There's only trees an the smell of mushy ground. There's sometimes young birds cloppin about on horses on the criss-cross paths. Up the top's Cairnhill House. Like a house out Frankenstien or Dracula. Don't Watch Alone. Remember that?

I couldn't stay away from it. It attracted ye. Not like one of them daft burds that goes in cos it's the very thing she shouldn't do,

Oh I know, there's a house full of vampires an werewolves. I'll go in there an get murdered.

I'm never out it. Square beams of light fired through the big dark rooms. When I reach the main hall half of me wants to explore the other half wants to run like fuck. I think of ghosts, or one particular Ghost wanderin the beach at Blackpool.

This day I'm past the big house walkin through posh streets. It's amazin how completely different kinds of people can live so close. It's all shiny cars an the aroma of different wife's cookin an the scents of different wife's passin wi go-chairs. They're great some of them. Like out a catalogue. They're lookin. They know I'm Sikeside. It's all over me. In ma walk. Ma gear: Army trousers, donkey jacket an this black woollen tammy.

Four wummin're talkin an noddin over. I'm hot an bothered. They think I'm up to no good. Paranoia's rippin right out me. I see why they're bothered. Doors lyin open. Levis on the washin line. Bikes on their own. I could blag the lot if I wanted. I know I'm gettin watched from dark windies an through hedges an washin lines. Quick look at this blur of red an white. This wummin's kinky gear's on the line – even the knickers're posh. Some cunt's probably phoned the Polis already,

Eh excuse me there's a chap walking about our estate and he seems rather – well rough if you know what I mean. He's acting very suspicious and I suspect he's planning a job. I've written a description!

Up ahead's this skip, on the road out the scheme. Yo ho, I love a good skip. I walks by slow peekin over the edge. It's lookin all plasterboard an old timbers when somethin glints. I scan the street. Empty. They probably breathed a sigh of relief when I turned the corner wi their wanes appearin like Munchkins out their hidin places.

I harden the belly muscles an balance into the skip. A wire. Tug tug an on the end's a silver toaster. Morphy Richards. I dusts it down walkin away. It's rainin a bit so I catches the drops on it to wash off the plasterboard dust. I goes this path to miss the houses.

I gets to the wee burn. There's a pool. I dips the corner of ma donkey jacket in an shines up the Morphy Richards. Fuck me! Thickness Settin. It can do outsiders. I always wanted one of them. Ye can set it light brown to totally burnt. What the fuck do they keep puttin the totally burnt settin on toasters for? Who the fuck wants their toast totally burnt? An another thing, how do they get that non-stick Teflon stuff to stick to the fryin pans? But it's a brammer of a toaster. Wane wi a new toy. Can't wait to get in about it.

I gets in an plugs it in. I switch the plug on wi a stick cos the toaster's wet still. Nothin. Changes the fuse wi the slow cooker. Nothin. I gets the side off wi a knife. The element's broke in the middle. I twists the two ends thegether an hey presto it's glowin spittin an hissin.

Yesssssssssssssssss-sssssss-ssssssss. It's sayin.

The Paki never seen any cunt that excited askin for a plain loaf. The toaster opens a whole new world for me. Toast on beans – the beans done in the slow cooker. Toast on Kraft Cheese slices – put the cheese between two slices of pan bread an toast the bread meltin the cheese at the same time. Fuckin luxury. An Kraft Cheese slices're easy to steal. Just si liip them in the aul donkey jacket pocket as ye're bendin over for the milk. Presto hey!

Another thing I learnt, fuck knows where, is how to bake a tattie wi no cooker. Ah ha! Got ye there. That's how it got me. Somebody goes, *I can make a baked spud without a cooker.*

Microwave, I goes

Nup. No cooker. Two forks – that's it.

Fuck off! I goes. *Two forks an what? A bonfire?*

Bet?

Tenner.

So there goes a tenner.

Get a plug. If ye're tryin this in yer house cut the plug off the hairdryer an leave three feet of wire. Split the wire an ye'll see a blue an a brown. Sometimes they're the same colour – that's OK. Bare the ends of the two wires till ye've got a couple of inches of copper (sometimes it's aluminium). Wrap the bare bits round a fork handle each. Metal forks only. Wooden handles're no use. Stick the forks in both ends of the tattie. Plug in. For fuck sake don't plug it in before ye start or ye won't be needin a tattie – ye'll be a fuckin tattie. Anyway, the spud acts as a resister. Electricity runs through it an cooks it in about ten minutes. If ye're under sixteen get an adult to supervise the whole procedure. Use a big spud. For two reasons:

1. It won't frazzle so easy.
2. It'll fill ye up.

Another thing, after ye boil a kettle sit an egg in it for five minutes exactly an ye'll have a perfect soft boiled egg. Saves the mess when ye boil eggs in the kettle an they rummle about an leak an ye can't use the water for tea. These things're handy to know cos ye never know when a run of bad luck might hit ye.

I'm in a good routine. Carmen comes round every second day an we shag till we can't breathe. I don't mention the rats. After six weeks I start wonderin what the fuck the Burgh's up to. I goes up the Housin an the same burd tells me they'd been workin on it for weeks. Unbeknown to her I'm livin there an not a soul's been near the joint. Lyin cunt. What can I say? If she knew I'd get lobbed out.

Seven weeks. Half eight in the mornin the door makes this noise. I sit up an don't breathe. I hears keys. Fuck me I'm thinkin Polis an Housin an all sorts. This whistle comes driftin in. La-la-la this guy's singin. There's another voice.

Right, Charlie, put it all in the lobby. There's this clatter as all this timber's flung in. Footsteps back an fro to the van an they're fillin the place up wi stuff. The Burgh've finally got round to doin the house up. I get shifted snappy an stick the kettle on. The van draws away. Sawin starts an the guy's singin away. I'm laughin. What if he decides to have a wank or somethin? Imagine he's chuggin away an I pop out at the tickly bit. Get the fright of his fuckin life. I lights a fag an coughs. He hears nothin. I coughs louder.

Ahem! Ahem! I'm goin.

I shout it out an his sawin stops. The door opens. He comes in an jumps back at the same time. I know what ye're thinkin,

How the fuck can ye come into a room an jump back at the same time?

Well this fella done it.

123

Christ son're you dossin here?

He's scared an concerned at the same time. This boy's good at doin two different things.

Aye, well, I mean it's ma house. I got a key made . . .

How long ye been here?

Six weeks.

He looks at his sheet of paper.

We've got it empty.

Got a key made.

He's hardly listenin. He's checkin his chit.

Aye there it is, an empty. He moves closer.

Aye I got a key made, I'd nowhere to stay.

He looks. He understands.

Ah right, he says real slow.

Nowhere else. I'm waitin on it gettin done up so ma burd can move in.

He looks at the floor an tightens his lips, thinkin. *Right, son, I'll get to work. Don't worry, we'll have this place spick an span no time.*

I never believed him but two weeks later it's like a new house. Floorboards in every room new sinks an wardrobes the lot. I'm called up the Housin.

All this time I'm havin nightmares. The Scouse's face keeps loomin in through this fog. But he looks different. He's six feet tall wi all these bits hangin off him like black seaweed. It's wet an shinin in this red an yella light that's burnin beneath him. Like Hell. That's what it is. Hell. His eyes're this luminous yella an starin. The wee workman's always nearby saw saw sawin away. Scouse is comin at me wi a big lump of wood an there's this knife just out of reach. I'm tryin to get the knife but I'm in invisible treacle. Scouse lifts the club an I flash ma eyes open to escape – but – an this's the weird thing – I still see the knife on the floor. I feel him behind me. I reach for the blade but I can't grab it. Ma hand goes through an hits the floor. I cover ma head for the blow an wake up breathin like a pervert. Sweatin like a pig.

Here's the keys, Mr Riley, she's goin explainin how the work took so long an all this. Cow. I want the shutters off the windies. Can't wait for the light to flood in. Carmen says she's not livin in no house wi boards on the windies so I struts down wi a smile to take them off.

Giro Jackpot

I rip the boards off an sweep the place clean. Every week
I've been buyin buckets an stuff for the house. It's kinda
good cleanin an arrangin stuff. The kitchen's got new Burgh
cupboards an shinin Formica worktops. The wells work an
there's a multipoint on the wall. A multipoint's this gas thing
that gives ye instant hot water an heats the radiators.

I goes on the verandah an breathes in ma new world.
Rows an rows of four-high flats. Half're boarded up – metal
on the bottom, wood from the first floor up. Best thing's the
light. Like the house's flooded wi football lights. I'm that
used to the dingy daytime an pitch-dark nights ma eyes've
not adjusted. It's like somebody turned up the voltage on
me. Like I've flitted from a cave into a greenhouse.

Carmen still won't come. She's not stayin somewhere wi
no cooker.

But look, I says, sweepin over the neatly arranged kettle,
slow cooker an toaster lined along the shinin worktop.

How can ye expect me like this, she goes pattin her belly, *to
live in here?* That's her new war cry – pattin the belly
whenever she wants the world to go away. Stumped. Can't
pat ma belly an say somethin smart. So it's a shag an home
to her Maw's. Usual.

126

I starts thinkin she's not wantin me any more. I gets the jealous head on. Some nights I sneak by her Maw's watchin for boyfriends. Nothin. Wasted night but it makes me feel better.

Light bulbs in every room now. Burgh delivers wardrobes for the bedroom. Big white things. Nice in a gigantic kind of way. I gets this great carpet out a skip. Fitted carpet, wardrobe, mattress. I start hangin up ma clothes. I've not got much but it's good to hang them up. I wash the Ys an socks in the sink wi multipoint instant hot water. Luxury.

This day I'm back from a scavengin mission. I've found ten fat chrome tubes two feet long – they screw thegether – obviously some shop display. I chucks them in the back room. Be handy for somethin. I'm depressed. Right down. I'm makin roll-ups for the rest of the day an lookin at the food. I'm sittin on this bar stool out the Big House. Ma smoke's dark against the painted walls. Burgh white – everythin. If ye were pished an went to the bog ye'd have to feel about its that white. The Burgh usually splash ye wi Magnolia but Charlie boy puts the word out an I gets white. Pure white an good gloss.

Anyway, I'm blowin the smoke an thinkin maself into depression. Nothin worse than bein alone wi yer own head sometimes. Bad company. I'm tellin maself Carmen's not comin back. It's her an her wane from now on. I starts thinkin how to get her back an she's not even left.

I feels

     the black

         anti-tornado

             of depression

                  suckin

                      me under

when the letter box clicks an a letter falls to the floor. It's funny the things ye can miss in life. There's me twenty-five an it's the first I know THEY deliver letters in the afternoon. I've got a lot to learn. It's a Giro. Ma Giro's not due so I thinks it's an extra for somethin – five quid or three – ye get that quite a lot for fuck knows why.

I rips it open – wait for it – I'm lookin – Can't believe ma fuckin eyes – One thousand two hunner an eighty-six pounds an sixty-seven pence.

Yeeeeeeeeeeeeeeeeeeeeeeeeeeeeeeeeeee-HA

I'm bouncin about the joint. I calms down. I applied for all sorts of stuff off The Social. Somebody that knows somebody's auntie's uncle's cousin's wee sister's boyfriend's maw told Booda about a list of all the stuff ye can claim when ye get a house. Ye've got to claim each item individual or ye don't get it. They cunts tell ye nothin. But Booda got a list. I mind thinkin he's comin the cunt but there ye go.

Ye claim the usual stuff – suite, cooker, carpets, that made sense – beds (Blindcraft deliver them). But it's thousands of wee things that make up the difference. Corkscrew. Plugs. Plug covers for safety. Bulbs. Fuses. Fusewire. Cutlery. Dinner set. Cleanin stuff. Cloths. Pots. Fryin pan. Pot scourers. Carpet tacks . . .

On an on this list goes. I was a whole night writin it out.

I spins an starts leggin it up Airdrie market.

There's five carpet dealers. They all know the score. I've not measured the rooms but they know all about Sikeside an the size of the rooms. They know I want all the rooms done wi the best cheap carpets I can get. An they all ask how much the other cunt's fittin them for an offer a better deal. This fat bastard wi an Edinburgh accent sways me wi curtains for the whole house for fifty quid extra – nets an real curtains. He'll be down in a week.

By the time he comes I've got a kitchen table an four chairs off a jake for ten quid. Wood chairs the whole bit. I've got a brand-new automatic cos I gave the guy deliverin for The Social a hunner quid an the twin tub he brought. It's plumbed in cos Charlie up the Burgh got it done for a fiver. A three ring brand spankin cooker. I wired it. Fat Bastard never counted for lino. Fly as fuck so there's another fifty quid. I've ripped out the carpets I got in skips. An hour after I slung them some guy's trailin them in the close across the road. I've got a double an single bed off Blindcraft. I'd to give the guy thirty quid or I was gettin three singles.

Blindcraft's in Edinburgh. All these blind people make beds an sell them for next to nothin. Cheapest beds ye can get. Silent Night they're not – that's why The Social use them. Fat Bastard fits the carpets an this wee thing fits the curtains. She's one of them burds wi an ugly face but a body that turns ye right on. She's stretchin an I see the white hollow of her back. Probably seventeen. He's soon got the lino down an I'm cookin out the book that's free wi the cooker. Fruit loaf.

Soon as the guy's away, I gets the beds in position an has a good look at the rooms. I look wi the lights on. I look wi the lights off. I look wi the curtains shut. I look wi the curtains open. I look wi the curtains shut an the light's off. I look wi the curtains shut an the lights on. I'm lovin it. The heatin's on an its nice an warm. I goes up the woods wi a bottle of Buck an two Supers feelin happy.

Next day the suite comes. Hunner quid. Brand spankin. Blagged – take whatever they get. I got a telly an video out Stepek.

I put all the lampshades up. Pictures out Poundstretcher's – ornaments an stuff. A palace. I'm tellin Carmen she can't come up cos I'm paperin an I want her to see it finished. I'm phonin twice a day. I phone at eight cos the phones in the Paki's an it shuts. I get a bottle an go home.

Anyway. I lets the place settle a couple of days an this

Friday I'm meetin Carmen up the Galleria. A meal for a quid in there. Burger an chips.

Ma Maw says it's not a good place to bring up a wane.

We won't be there all our lifes.

She says she'll keep the wane if I want to . . .

Fuck off no way . . . it's ma wane . . . ain't it?

Ye fine well know it is.

I'm shovin chips in ma mouth wi one hand an pattin her belly wi the other. MMMM. Perfume. Night Mist – best of stuff. Next minute I'm horny as fuck.

Fancy comin down to see the wallpaperin?

Och! through the week eh?

How what's up wi the day?

I want to relax.

I looks up at the Humphrey Bogart mirror an give him this shrug. He twists his face an says, *Ball's in your court, boy.*

I grabs her by the hand.

C'mon to fuck, Carmen – I've got a surprise.

Eh?

I've got this surprise.

What surprise?

Somethin yer never goin to forget.

I know what you want.

Aye. I want that too but there is a surprise.

Her eyes light up.

Is there?

Aye.

Promise?

Cross ma heart.

Swear?

I swear.

Swear on yer wane's lifes!

I swear on ma wane's lifes.

What?

That there's a good surprise down there for ye.

Say it all thegether.

Och – right – I swear on ma wanes life's that there's a good surprise down there for ye.

Down where? Down where?

Cumbrae.

She's goin to stand an then she flops back in the seat.

No ye're just after one thing.

Cross ma heart hope to die. I'm after that, I gives her fanny a squeeze under the table, *but there's a surprise too.*

Swear on it. Swear?

Aye?

Swear on the wane's life.

I done that.

No not them, the new wane.

I'd never though of the lump as a wane. It's a wane sittin next to us in the Galleria an it's Da's stuffin hiself wi beer an burgers.

Right! I swear on the new wanes life there's a surprise.

That does the trick. ZIP we're in a fast cab down Sikeside. I gives her the key an she's at the door wonderin if it's a practical joke. She's dressed in bright yella baggy gear an her hair's all over her shoulders an her eyes're buzzin in the darkness of the close.

Shag her, big man! wee Dinky shouts, goin by on a skateboard.

She's got the key turned an her hand on the handle.

Go in. It's not a fright.

She looks nervous like the cells in Blackpool.

Go in!

She opens the door a wee bit. The smell of clean an new comes waftin out. She's sniffin – wonderin. She looks scared again. I gets on ma knees.

Look if there's anythin wrong – if it's a trick – may all the people I love in the whole world this neighbour goes by *drop dead this minute.*

She goes in an switches the light on.

I stands in the close. Waitin in silence. I can hear her feet shufflin about the new carpets.

She comes out ten minutes later. Throws the arms round me an lifts one heel like in the films. In we go an shag. An we shag that night on every floor in the house cos she moves in.

Bombs

So we're settled in an things're goin OK. She visits her
Maw's a lot an I walk about the woods an along the canal an
think. I think a lot an deep but I've not got words to say
what I think. Even if I did no cunt'd understand what the
fuck I'm on about. So I keep the thoughts in ma head
spinnin like a washin machine. I'm readin books. I don't
know how. This voice says,

Read a lot of fuckin books! So I start stealin them out the
library. It's the meanin of the universe I want to know. After
ma Eric von Daniken stage I'm readin five books a week. I
don't let on about the books – do ma street cred in. The more
I reads the more I wants to know. I've got to know somethin
but I don't know what. I keep readin an readin like it's a
fuckin bad trip. It's a drug. If I'm not readin I'm thinkin. If
I'm not thinkin I'm lookin an if I'm not thinkin readin or
lookin I'm out ma head on drink an drugs.

I go up The Street sometimes but I'm still on the edge. I'm
still on the lookout for her Da an her cousins. Sikeside's ma
territory. I feel safe here. No cunt else feels safe in Sikeside.

All the time in Blackpool I kidded on I never gave a fuck
about nothin. But I was scared.

That doesn't matter now cos I'm really off the rails.

Crackers. People used to think I was a headcase. I fooled them. I was only actin. This's the time I really became a headcase. What we done in Blackpool never pushed me over the edge. It only pushed me over so I could look down in the abyss but it never shoved me off.

I remember exactly how it started. I decides to walk Carmen to the Whifflet this day. She's goin to the Bingo wi her Maw. The Whifflet's ma limit. I feel safe up to the Whifflet. On Calder Street I slaps her belly, *How's the bun cookin, fatty?*

She looks all worried.

D'ye think I'll get fat?

No.

Ye sure?

How can ye get fat when ye're already fat?

Oh ha ha limp dick.

Can't be that limp. It was me that stuck the bun in there.

Sure it's yours?

Sure it's yours?

I slaps the bulge again. She's quiet for a hunner yards. I feel her electricity buildin. Cars swerve to avoid her field. She's for explodin. Still lookin dead ahead she goes,

What about the wanes?

Eh?

Yer wanes?

What about them?

Ye said ye were goin to start seein them when we moved back.

Aye so I did. I'll need to do somethin about it.

I know she's pokin about to open me up. To let go wi a blast of abuse. More quiet. But I'm an oyster. I'm stayin shut. Cars're swervin even more.

Have ye done anythin yet?

No. Not yet.

What ye goin to do?

I sees her tactics. She's got a picture of me an Caroline standin chewin the cud. Me leanin on the doorway wi an elbow. Only Carmen's not thinkin it's Caroline's doorway. Carmen's thinkin it's ma doorway. In fact it's even worse than that. Carmen's thinkin it's OUR doorway. Me an Caroline.

I'll phone, I says, hopin that'll stop her.

Phone? she goes.

I kids on I'm interested in passin cars. But she's not givin up.

Ye'll phone? Oh I can just see it now. Hello, Caaaaroline, it's Mickey here. Oh hello, Mick. Why don't ye come FUCKIN up an have a wee cup of tea an a shag!

The word FUCKIN's Carmen's. Her anger leaks out there an she bungs the word in. But I'm ready for her.

No. I'll phone our Angie an get her to arrange it.

She goes quiet an we're nearly at the Whifflet. She's still tryin to get me at that doorway leanin on an elbow. But I've got her. She's fucked. She's that angry she's changin the Whifflet lights just lookin at them. Her long black hair's bouncin up an down off her back. She spins an spits. The spit explodes like a star on the slabs. She doesn't notice it but every other cunt in the vicinity does. They all turn round an she's shoutin.

An how're ye goin to get them Eh? Eh? thumpin her finger in her chest hard an loud.

What d'ye mean? I goes.

Ye'll have to go an get them. Won't ye? Won't ye?

Not unless I want to leave them standin waitin.

She mumbles, *Hmm. That's what they deserve.*

What did you say?

You heard.

I never heard fuck all. What did ye say?

You an yer fuckin wanes. Wanes wanes wanes – go an fuckin get them.

Fuck off.

Go an get yer scrawny wee wanes an yer fat wife.

You're sick as fuck know that – sick!

You're the one that's sick, she screams an turns to the movin audience, *See him he's a bastard a right rotten bastard.* She's screamin at the top of her voice. I manage this stupid fuckin grin but it goes no way to persuading these cunts she's mental. I've no chance. She looks that pretty an hard done by. By this time she's changin the lights like fuck. The green man an the red man're on at the same time but no cunt takes notice they're all lookin at me an her.

I'll send ma Da up for ma stuff – cunt, she goes.

Before I know it she's through the volume of traffic an on the other side of the road. Her hair's bouncin off her back an swingin from side to side.

I'm left alone in the Whifflet. I turns to face the crowd an their heads flick away like fish in a stream. Only this stream's polluted to fuck. Even the pavement's're bleak. No cunt can look me in the eye. They're suddenly interested in things in Pender's an the Paki's. A hangin pig an cheap Buckfast.

I don't fancy the hangin pig so I comes out the Paki's wi a bottle of Buckie an three Supers. I wander angry down the Whifflet. I goes up this big close. Soon as I'm there I remembers it's a close were me an Daz dogged school.

It starts rainin. I tries to feel sorry for maself but I can't cos I feel like a bastard. You probably expect big flashin lights an thunder an stuff at the moment I go over the edge. It's fuck all really just a moment like any other. Some aul wummin's buyin four slice of ham out the butchers.

I'm standin there an the anger's dyin wi every slug. The rain's good on ma face. I've got ma Army jacket on an a good thick jumper under it. I pulls the collar up an coories into a wall. I'm still tryin to feel sorry for maself but I keeps thinkin of ma wife an wanes an that stuff in Blackpool. So instead of crumblin an greetin an snotterin this's what happens. Because there's a mental gate stoppin me feelin sorry for maself I go the other way. In ma head I try this big gate an it's locked. So I turns round an there's this right sleazy red light district down the road. I walks into that an opens ma eyes.

All this arrogance an aggression rises up in me like a deep monster. My inside's go black an so does the sky. I'm that evil at this point that the young team come up the close – take one look an fuck off. I feel like Dracula an look into the rain wi ma mouth wide open. I laugh like the Don't Watch Alone films. The wind howls an this wolf glares down over the rooftops. It's got big yella eyes. I laugh again an it's gone. The rain's runnin in ma mouth an down ma face. But that's not what it is. It's blood fallin out the sky. An I laugh an I laugh an I laugh.

But to any cunt watchin I'm just this drunk guy laughin. They don't know what's goin on inside ma head. I spark a joint an start thinkin. I want revenge. Thing is, I don't know who I want revenge on but I've got to have it.

I must be two hours later. I've found this hideaway under the stairs. I notice a stream of guys in one's an two's sometimes three's, but never more than four, comin an goin from the door above me. I'd not normally take much notice only they're super confident. An another thing, they're built like tanks.

By this time I've no drink left so up I goes. It's a bodybuildin club. When I walk in they all glance at me. I've got no build compared to them so they don't see me as a threat. Back to hooshon an shooshin an shovin weights up an down an shoutin *Beef it* an *Keep tight* an *C'mon, Benny, it's yours – it's yours*, an bein macho as fuck.

This guy wi blond hair who's been beefin it an pumpin up his pecs stands up an whips off the shirt. It's for me. He's probably showed off to these morons a million times. He's squeezin his tits thegether an puffin up the shoulders. I catch him glancin out the side of his eye in the mirror. Every bit of wall space's mirrored so they can see their selfs.

Loo-kin good Vic.

Ripped.

Beef.

Solid Vic.

Vic does a couple of half-turns. His fists're clenched at his belly button an his arms're curvin to his balloonin shoulders. He's pressin his muscles so hard he looks like he's doin a shite. Next thing he drops the keks an he's got these wee shiny satiny knickers on. Sky blue. Like wummin's panties.

I thinks, *Oh oh somethin a bit strange here is there not?*

He starts stickin one leg forward an flexin an then the other leg. I'm walkin about but no matter where I go I see him an his fan club admirin his muscles. I must admit he's fuckin massive an there an then I decide I want to be that size. I want to be like that cos I've got violence to unleash. I've got to get rid of ma fear. What better way to do it than have no fear at all? I decide I want to be a bodybuilder.

Thinkin about joinin? says Vic.

He's sweatin an he's well covered up now wi tracksuits an stuff.

Aye. I've done it before.

Where was that.

McShane's.

Oh. I thought I recognised ye.

Did he fuck. He's just sayin that. But, I'll give him this, for all his fearsome looks an massive build he seems like a nice guy. I starts to feel at ease. Every cunt's stopped listenin. Back to shovin weights about shoutin the odds.

Ye can't drink an train.

I know I've . . .

Come in the same time themorra an we'll show ye round.

Much is it, Vic?

Oh that's right. I'm Vic, an he shoves his big hand out for me to shake.

Mick, I goes, an shakes his hand. He doesn't try to crush ma hand like I expected.

I walk back to Sikeside decidin to get as big as Vic in a year. I've got forty quid in the house so I decides to go to What Every Wummin Wants next mornin an get kitted out wi track suits an T-shirts an stuff. I looks at the fag I'm smokin an decides mibbi I'll stop smokin too.

I nod's at wee Dinky. He's drinkin a bottle an smokin a joint. He waves me over by flingin his head back like it's a big secret.

What is it wee man? I've no dough.

I'm not on the beg.

He hands me the bottle, takes a long hard draw at the joint an hands me that.

There's two cunts at your door.

Ma door?

Aye. Been there a couple of hours.

Polis?

Fuck off! Polis? No way. It's this big Slagbag an a guy.

What do they look like, Dinky?

I hands him the wine but he waves the joint.

The Burd's got blond hair an a skirt up to here. See her fuckin knickers – good wankin material . . .

I've got the eyes screwed up wonderin.
An the guy looks mental as fuck. Looks like a boxer.
Dinky's flattenin his nose wi his finger.
Black hair.
Are ye sure it's ma door?
Aye. I went round the back an listened up the close. They were talkin about you an Carmen.
Must be for me right enough.
I think the Burd's from London.
How?
She talks funny an she's a big fuckin Tart. Dinky's got his fist clenched where his dick'd be if he had one an he's wankin away sayin *big fuckin Tart* over an over. I walks away an he follows.
Fuck off Donkey.
Fuckin Dinky.
Fuck off Dinkly then.
He boots ma arse.
Dinky.
Right right Dunky.
He ignores me as we get to Cumbrae. He starts singin this song:

> *She's a rag bag*
> *shag bag*
> *automatic hoor*
> *she's got a fanny like a big barn door*
> *you can hop skip jump*
> *shove a barrel up her cunt*
> *that's your wi-ife the hoor.*

I ignore the wee cunt an he sings it again. He walks away down the street backwards singin. I look in the close an who's sittin freezin on the stairs but Daz an Slinky.

Dinky'svoice disappears in the distance.

She's a rag bag
shag bag
automatic hoor
she's got a fanny like a big barn door
you can hop skip jump
shove a barrel up her cunt
that's your wi-ife the hoor.
Na na na na na na na na na na na na na na na na na na na na na na na na na na na.

Daz An Slinky Blether

I can't believe it. It's like I'm back in Blackpool.

DAZ! I goes, like I've been sayin Hail Mary's for him to turn up.

MICK! he goes, like he's been doin the same.

Me fookin arse's freezin hurry oop an open the door.

Slinky's lost weight. Her face's clapped in an there's a yella bruise over her right eye.

They're lookin in all the cupboards an stuff an I stick the kettle on.

Nice place, an *ye've done it up good,* an *this's a big room,* an all this they're goin from different rooms. It's not big. The flats in Blackpool're just pokey.

Tea's out an we all sit down. Slinky can't look at me cos of the black eye but Daz's talkin ninety to the dozen. He's speedin. Ye just know he's done her in an then he's offered her a holiday in Coatbridge. *Get away from it all hen. Things'll be different,* an all that shite. Probably meant it. Probably greetin an cuddlin right in an really really meanin every word. Ye get that aul drink in ye an out come the claws an the horns.

Where's Carmen?

Down at her Maw's. She might not come home the night.

Phone her.

Sikeside. Ye kiddin? There's no phones.

Is there a wine shop? Goes Daz.

Aye. It's just over . . .

Slinky, want anythin?

Yeah snouts an some Supers

I'll take ye over, I says. I want to make sure he doesn't notice the phone in the Paki's.

Out on the street Slinky's lookin out at all the boarded-up houses. Daz waves an blows her a kiss. She kisses the glass at him.

Gave her a right tankin last week.

I don't say nothin.

See her eye?

I thought it was bruised.

Bruised for fuck sake? Shut tight. Had to keep her in for a week!

That's the way to treat them, Daz. Eh?

He's not sure what I'm meanin an goes, *Aye aye that's it keep the fuckers in their place,* an throws lefts an rights snortin air out his nose.

See told ye he's a boxer! shouts wee Dinky out the darkness from behind the glow of a fag.

Who's that?

Wee Dinky.

Oh.

I like wee Dinky. We've got somethin in common but I can't figure out what it is. I buys him a Super. Sometimes I get him fags. Sometimes I get him lager.

Yo! shouts Dinky.

Here, I says, an, without stoppin, pull the can out an pass it like a relay baton. He's off in darkness an Kshhhhhhhh he's gluggin away waitin like a spider on the next fly bastard comin past.

What d'ye do that for?
What?

Our voices're echoin in the close. Big Frank, the neighbour, comes out, grunts an slams his door.

Makes sure no cunt screws ma house.

That wee cunt? How could he stop them.

Don't know? I'll ask him the next time.

Big Frank's fuckin daft. He's listenin at his door but the lobby light's on an there's his big meaty head in the glass. What a fuckin Sammy. I points liftin the eyebrows. Daz laughs.

Got the guns? I goes.

Eh?

I points again cos Daz's a bit slow.

The fuckin guns – how can we do a turn without shooters?

Oh AYE the SHOOTERS right, he nods.

Pick them up the morra. Usual place.

Rounds.

Eh?

How many rounds?

What?

Bullets – did ye get bullets?

Twenty each.

Big Frank's head's as still as fuck. He's whisper-shoutin his wife *Chantelle! Chantelle.*

Pop.

We're in ma lobby laughin at the big cunt.

Frank's one of them guys that walks about like he's got a rugby ball under each armpit. He's got a cowboy swagger too an a wee moustache. He tells the best lies ye ever heard. Looks hard as fuck but Dinky says he's a shitebag.

Slinky's lyin in the chair half sleepin. No wonder she's freezin she's got hold up theirself stockins on. Brown. A flash

of white thigh. We crash a couple of cans an open the Buckie.
'Ma Home Town' is on an we sit there listenin.

We're in the Brig an Slinky's in Barnsley.

I don't like it. It's a good song but it reminds me of things.
I want to blank the past out. Some cunts can do that no
problem. I always need drink an drugs. In ma head there's
these accusations. I try to switch them off but I can't.

The snib goes. The door opens wi Daz an Slinky's eyes.
Carmen's comin down the lobby wi *I'm in a right fuckin bad
mood* footsteps. Clump clump. She swings in the
scullery an stands wi her legs apart in the big Artexed arch.

Her face goes angertosurprisetoallsmiles.

Slinky stays flopped in the chair. *Hi, Baby,* she coos.

Fuck sake, Slinky, what happened to yer eye? goes Carmen.
Him!

Daz lifts the shoulders, shows his palms an makes his eyes
dead wide.

There's this silence.

The tape clicks off.

Who do I look like? he goes?

What?

*Who the fuck do I look like? I mean who the fuck am I the
spittin image of eh?*

Oliver Reid, Daz, I goes, *spittin image of Oliver Ried, ma man.*
But I says it like I'm bored out ma skull wi the whole thing.
He's wantin laughter. He wants rid of the silence so he pats
Carmen's belly, *Oh well ye're lookin swell,* an turns to me for a
reaction.

Oh well ye're lookin swell! he goes again an gives me the
wide eyes an open mouth.

I turn up the edge of ma mouth. Carmen sits beside Daz
an there's me in one chair an Slinky in the other.

More silence.

Get some party music on, goes Carmen. She's crashed a Super. Daz lights up a joint an places it in her mouth. His fingers're against her lips. He holds them there too long but I don't say nothin. Three or four puffs an she sticks on

NOW THAT'S WHAT I CALL SHITE NUMBER FUCK-KNOWS-WHAT

'When the Goin Gets Tough' comes on wi this thump thump thump.

I'm singin *Go an get stuffed,* instead but no cunt likes ma patter thenight. Carmen's spinnin an her hair's goin everywhere. Her long flowin dress's liftin up an up an Daz's slidin down an down the couch.

So. It's hours later an we're pished. Welded. We've even sent Dinky for another cargo.

So what brings yous up?

The coonts were all accusing me of grassing.

For what?

The ornaments an my Dad's videos.

Mmm mm, should've heard them, says Daz all sympathetic.

She's nearly greetin an Carmen moves over an puts the arm round her. The 'Phantom of the Opera''s on: pure pish.

Fuck sake, Slinky, ye'll never find out who grassed down there. Daz an me have a fly smile.

She sob sob sobs an Carmen's pattin her back.

C'mon **PAT PAT** *hen it's all in the past.* **PAT PAT PAT** *No cunt* **PAT** *cares about that now.* **PAT PAT PAT** *Forget it.* **PAT** *It could be worse.* **PAT PAT** *It could've been murder.* **PAT PAT PAT**

Carmen gives me this sleekit smile. I avoid eye contact.

Murder!! shouts Daz. *FUCK that's right.* I jump out

ma pants an Carmen swings round quick.

Ohh Fook me I forgot that, mutters Slinky Sobbin.

Me an Carmen look.

What's THAT?? I goes.

The fuckin murder – ye don't know about it. Youse were away before it happened. We got lifted – every cunt got lifted!

The electricity's buildin. Slinky an Daz think it's cos they're about to tell a good story.

Mind some Scouse cunt cut ma throat?

In Raffles? goes Carmen as if she half-remembers.

Aye, fuck what am I on about youse were there that night, goes Daz throwin his hands out at us.

We got you to the Victoria, I says.

Well the Scouse got found washed up at Central Pier.

No way, I goes.

Knifed.

Central Pier? goes Carmen.

Daz looks at her like she's daft.

Aye Cen-tral Pier. Anyway, this wee guy's passin on a donkey an it leans in the water an starts lickin what looks like a burst air-bed.

Yeuch! says Carmen.

Turns out it's the Scouse's face an the skin's that soft it's comin off. Know how Donkey's tongues're dead rough?

Me an Carmen's noddin like fuck. As if we've rubbed many a donkey's tongue.

Awwwwwwwww stop it, Daz, goes Slinky coverin her ears. She lifts her knee an I want to run ma tongue up her thigh.

Been in the water three days, all blew up. The wee boy on the Donkey shat hiself.

Me an Carmen look at each other.

Fuck sake. How come you got lifted?

Daz's tryin to give the impression he done it. That he's a

147

murderer. He's smilin like a secret.

They lifted all the cunt's that had to do wi the Capo De
Monte.

Why?

How the fuck do I know, the Polis are mad!

Aye?

They found out the Scouse cut ma throat an I had stuck a fag
in the guy's head.

But what did you get lifted for? says Carmen. I can see
worry.

Slinky buts right in angry. *Fook me – that's when they all
started calling me a grasser, that right, Daz, darlin.*

*Fuckin re-run of Capo De Monte. Every cunt in the same cells
an everythin. Except youse.*

My heart's fuckin throbbin. I look over an I can see
Carmen's chest goin in an out wi every beat like a ball
blowin up an burstin-blowin up an burstin faster an faster.
This lump in her throat's goin up an down-up

an

down.

How come we heard fuck all about it?

It was after youse went away.

It was what?

Youse were up the road before it happened.

Slinky buts in again, *I told the fuzz that, but it don't make me
a grass.*

They found yer Giros at Mario's. I heard her sayin what
Scotch cunt would leave a Giro?

So just after we left it happened? I goes.

Aye a couple of nights. Carmen gives this sigh.

That's wild.

See after **they** *got us in the cells, know what* **they** *done?*
This's true ain't it, Slinky?

She nods.

Some new thing **they** *do wi skin. They guy had skin under his*
nails . . .

I looks at Carmen. She looks at me.

They take a bit of yer skin . . .

What? Cut a bit of yer skin? shivers Carmen.

They *take a wee swab in yer mouth an scrape dead skin off yer*
hands – that right, Slinky?

Slinky nods.

They *look that up under a microscope an* **they** *can tell*
exactly who done it. That's how we got out. That right, Slinky?

Slinky nods.

The electricity goes right up. It only takes one cop to find
out when we left Blackpool. Fuckin life. Don't fancy that one
bit. No sir. Not me. Not this cunt here. She stabbed him
anyway, I thinks. An then I thinks, It's ma skin that's under
his nails.

Tell them about McCann, goes Slinky.

Oh Jimmy McCann, that's right.

That cunt stuffed the **Bowl of Cherries** *down the couch.*
Hope they lock him up for ever.

Kept him in for ages. The guy was in the Windmill the night he
got done in. Battered an stabbed.

Me an Carmen get electric shocks. I put this other
Springsteen LP on. *Nebraska.* This song's a right laugh
considerin. Only I'm not laughin an Carmen's not laughin.

Jimmy tells the Polis there was this party. He never took part.

No cunt knew he was sleepin on the ledge. Says there was about thirty there.

Me an her start breathin easier.

Couldn't make sense out McCann. Drunk as a monkey an in DTs comin off it. Fuckin useless really.

Got chucked off Central Pier. It's hard gettin some cunt over them railins, says Daz tryin to hint he done it.

He thinks we're not takin the bait.

Anyway, that's how we're thinkin about movin to Coatbridge too much trouble down there.

I starts to get all cocky for some reason.

Right yar I know why yese're movin here.

What?

Youse done the Scouse in, eh Carmen?

That's right yese done the guy in an're movin here in case the Polis decide to start liftin cunts again.

Ha ha, goes Slinky but Daz smirks like we've caught him out.

Miiiiiiiiiiiiiiiiiiiiiiiiiiiiiiiiiick, you know I'm not the kinda guy to do a murder. Ha ha.

I know ye all right, Daz.

He laughs. Fuckin prick.

Slinky's had enough of Polis an goes,

Ye'd better watch what ye're sayin, Daz . . .

But Daz loves it even more now.

Slinky's startin to a get this Glasgow accent. Daz must be rubbin off on her.

AAHHHHHHHHHHHHHHRGGGGGGGG!

Goes Slinky. There's this face at the windie.

Who the fook is that? she goes.

Carmen an Daz get a fright.

It's just wee Dinky, I says, an they all settle down.

Dinky drops out of sight. Daz starts up again.

They charged me but *they* let me go. *They* think I done it *wi some other cunt. All* they *need's Jimmy to say I was in the Windmill wi some cunt else an the Scouse.*

Yea but the NDA fingerprint thing – that was what they let him go on. They never had his NDA in the skin sample, says Slinky.

Suppose so?

I thought I'd be worried sick. Carmen looks worried sick. This's the new Mick. I've changed. Remember behind the bodybuildin club? The new aggressive mad-as-fuck Mick. I don't give a fuck. I'm startin bodybuildin in the mornin. I feel dead strong already.

But it's four days before I start.

Flyin Nudes

Slinky an Daz decided to stay the weekend (probably a week before they left Blackpool).

Oh I know? Why don't we stay here a couple of days? goes Slinky.

Aye, is that all right? says Daz.

Me an Carmen's noddin goin *mm mm mm mm* but I really mean, *Get yerself to fuck back to the clingin hole ye crawled out.* Daz claps, rubs his hands, an crashes another can.

So that night we all hit the sack in good moods. Daz's on the couch wi Floyd on low an Slinky goes in the back room on this sunbed I stole out a delivery van. Bollock. One of them ye lie on. Cost a few bob probably. I fall asleep floatin on fast movin clouds that only a certain mixture of drink an dope produces.

That's why I think it's strange the way everyone's actin next mornin.

I scuffs along the lobby holdin up ma jeans. Walks in the livin room an there's Carmen, Daz an Slinky. Silent. No music. I thinks they've had a fight an whistles Floyd again. 'Another Brick in the Wall'.

Ham an eggs?

No answer.

152

Ham eggs tattie scones fried bread tomatoes beans black puddin mushrooms waffles toast an tea?

Still no answer.

OK OK, who's goin out for the Sugar Puffs?

Nothin. There's somethin wrong.

Been doin battle?

Hmm!!! comes out through the Artex arch. I can tell it's Carmen's *Hmm* an I can tell it means:

Ye've got a fuckin cheek ya bastard askin us if we want Ham eggs tattie scones fried bread tomatoes beans black puddin mushrooms waffles toast an tea? PAUSE *Sugar Puffs? Sugar Puffs for fuck sake?*

She knows how to hate me an can cut the words down to the bare minimum so it's only me knows what they mean. So I know I've done somethin.

What is it then? I goes.

Slinky spins an stares out the windie wi her hands wrapped round her knees. Daz sparks up a fag an in the yella light I sees he's got a black eye.

You're a right rotten bastard, says Carmen.

What? I goes tryin not to grin.

You know.

I laughs.

You fuckin know all right.

Leave it, says Daz.

Slinky's starin out the windie.

What the fuck is it? I says droppin limp ham in the fryin pan. Pink. Dead pig really.

Danishshshshshshshszzzzzzzzzzzzzzzzzzzzzzzzz

is what I'm sayin in ma head.

Oh ho he's doin the, an she puts on this stupid voice, *I can't remember nothin about last night routine.*

Youse're all mad.

*Danishshshshshshshs*zzzzzzzzzzzzzzzzzzzzzzzzz

but this time I says it out loud lookin for a laugh. No cunt flinches. I know I've done somethin. I'm always doin that – gettin up to all sorts on drink an not rememberin next day.

You came in here in the middle . . .

Leave it out, Carmen! says Daz, like some cunt in that wee pub in *American Werewolf in London*. The Slaughtered Lamb, it's called.

He's fookin crazy! says Slinky, screwin her finger in her temple without turnin round. Carmen's not for lettin it go.

*Danishshshshshshshs*zzzzzzzzzzzzzzzzzzzzzzzzz

I says again knowin none of them's goin to laugh.

Ye came in in the middle of the night screamin about him an me . . .

Eh?

Accusin Me an Daz of havin an affair . . .

Yeah – I heard ya, Slinky's turned round now. The only eyes that's not drillin in me're Daz's.

She was on the sunbed.

I remembered that. I'm cookin the breakfast an sniggerin. But it's only me that's laughin. Carmen's still tryin to edge her story into the mornin. I lets her.

You stay away from ma fuckin wife ye're goin, says Carmen, *d'ye hear me?*

Daz turns an his face's covered in bruises. He smiles an one of his teeth is missin.

This big knife ye had at his throat.

I checks – thank fuck – head's still on. I'm sniggerin. The pink pig in the fryin pan's curlin up wi embarrassment.

What the fuck're ye laughin at? It's no laughin matter. You're fuckin mental.

*Danishshshshshshshs*zzzzzzzzzzzzzzzzzzzzzzzzz

goes another slice of ham into the hot fat.

I came runnin in an ye flung the knife at me, she shows me this bruise on her thigh. Must've hit her wi the handle.

An ye dragged him by the hair up the lobby punchin an kickin an flung him in the close.

Daz buts in, *Fuck it. Leave it out. He was drunk.*

He's smirkin away an he's got a dose of the shakes. Slinky's pullin her knees into her big tits.

Fuck sake – mibbi I should go an see a shrink cos I remember fuck all about it.

That's your war cry ya bastard.

An that's yours.

What.

I puts on a voice, *Ya-baaaaaaaaaaaaastard.*

Think ye're fuckin smart? Slinky nudges Carmen wi her leg.

*An her **point** she comes runnin in without a stitch cos of the commotion an you're kickin fuck out of Daz . . .*

Daz bows his head in shame.

. . . an what do ye do eh? Eh? What do ye do?

Somersaults?

Fling her in the close an every cunt watchin. You were bollock too.

I keep on layin the table an makin the breakfast.

Turns out I flung Carmen out too. They all went in Big Frank's an got clothes an tea.

After a while I went out an up the woods a walk. They all sneaked back in. Carmen's tellin me what happened next.

. . . an we're all sleepin quiet in here an . . .

KERRRRRRASH

. . . there's this earthquake. I runs in the lobby an the front door's on the floor an you're standin on it. Ye never said nothin – stripped an went to bed.

The front door's sittin in the right place but around the

hinges an locks there's white splintered wood. The smell of ham's makin me hungry.

I sit them all down an say I'm sorry an blame it on the drink. Usual. They're happy an do impersonations of me. Carmen decides no drink the day an Daz an Slinky agree. I've got no say in it.

That night we're watchin some film.

Ding dong dong ding dong ding ding dong.

There's the van, says Carmen but she knows we're skint.

Daz jumps up an out he goes.

He comes back wi a pile of sweeties, Strike Cola, Irn Bru an sits down. I automatically thinks he'll chuck a Mars bar or a Marathon but no, the two cunts scoff the lot. Me an Carmen look at each other wi *who do they cunts think they are?* looks. We do it even after they've finished the stuff.

Night night, an off we all pop to bed.

Next mornin I've got the Ham eggs tattie scones fried bread tomatoes beans black puddin mushrooms waffles toast an tea. We're all in a better mood for eatin cos we never drank last night.

But we're at the table an I looks at the two cunts woolfin in. There's egg runnin down Slinky's chin. Daz's munchin an rollin this slice of ham between his back teeth. Slinky slurps her tea an chow shlap chow Daz's goin an

FUCK IT!!!!!!!

I chucks the whole table up in the air. Plates an hot cups of tea an sugar an teapots're slidin an rollin across the floor. There's this sudden aroma of Ham eggs tattie scones fried bread tomatoes beans black puddin mushrooms waffles toast an tea flyin up ma nose at the wrong angle. Then

SILENCE

an Daz's got this rasher hangin out his mouth like a dog that's been caught in the fridge. He's not movin. He's got his knife an fork where the table used to be an he's definitely not movin. Nope. Slinky jumps up unzippin her white jeans cos her fanny's roasted wi hot tea. Carmen's mad wi me an mad wi them. She can't attack no cunt. She's bewildered. There's this other silent pause an it's only Daz's ham swingin like a creakin door in *A Few Dollars More*.

Get fuckin out!!!!

I shouts

an ma voice frightens me cos it sounds like the Amityville horror when the Devil tells the Priest to

GET OUT

GET OUT

an the place's covered wi flies an the Priest – Rod Stieger I think it is – bolts the coarse boakin his guts up on the way.

Before I know it the house's empty an Carmen's in the street pointin an shoutin. I walks in the close through where the door used to be. The street's empty now so I starts fiddlin wi the door. Creak – an there's Big Frank.

Need a hand? he says, an whips out a tool box.

I do that all the time, he says.

Slinky an Daz go back to Blackpool never goin to talk to us again an all that shite.

Months go by anyway an I'm settled right in. I've taken to

sleepin up the big house when I'm welded an fell out wi her. She's swellin up bigger an spendin most of the time at her Maws. I'm readin this book when there's this chap at the door. I looks out. No car. I opens the door. Fuck me. Daz. On his own.

What does Adopted As Holograph mean? he goes.

He's movin in five doors up. Slinky's slung him for a much older guy.

DNA Phd

Daz goes to Coatbridge Tech.

Still boxin ma man? Cunts say.

No. I'm at collidge now. He'd go puttin a 'D' in.

Anyway. At the Tec he finds out DNA means deoxyribonucleic acid. That's the worst thing that ever happened. He starts askin people if they know what it means. That wee cunt can get DNA into conversations about yer Granny's carpet. He's a Phd in that.

He's never done doin it wi me. If any cunt knows the meanin of DNA it's me. For two reasons:

1. I've got a personal interest in it – you know why.
2. He keeps tellin me every chance he gets.

But he keeps tellin me an every other cunt for two reasons:

1. To look clever.
2. So I think he's interested cos he done murder.

Anyhow – he moves in a one bedroom flat. I wire his meter. He's got the heatin on full blast. The place's dry as the inside of a packet of cheese an onion. Golden Wonder. Gives ye a splittin head. There's this smell an it's sour. It's Daz. It's as if Daz's a pint of milk an he's off. He's curdled. He's bitter an stinkin. Fuckin mingin.

Next thing – big surprise. He goes back to the boxin. Stops drinkin an smokin. Not drugs but he tells every cunt he has. Loves speed especially. I couldn't give two fucks for speed – all it does's keeps me wakened all night. Every cunt wants to get high or get low – speed or dope – but I like to go sideways. Acid mushies an booze. An another thing, Daz starts all these airs an graces. He starts to care about clothes.

Do I look OK?

Aye

Ye're not lookin.

Ye look OK.

Sure?

Aye for fucksake – ye look great.

What d'ye think people think when they look at me?

Eh?

What d'ye think they think?

What the fuck're you on about?

Nothin.

We'd walk a wee bit.

Are ye sure I look OK?

Good for some cunt the spittin image of ET.

He grinds to a halt.

What d'ye mean?

Ye've got a big wide face an bin-lid eyes.

Fizzin he is, fizzin. He wants a go at me but there's this fear in his eyes stoppin him. Even Carmen's makin comments about him.

This day he goes by an waves in the windie. He's got

ILLUSTRATED HUMAN

AND SOCIAL BIOLOGY BY B. S. BECKETT

stickin out where every cunt can see it. He's got this long *I'm a student now* coat an a stupid lookin scarf on. He's swelterin but at least he's got the book angle right – the sun's glintin off it. I swear there's this haze of sour trailin behind him. He's stopped hangin about wi me much. It's me an Booda most of the time anyway. Booda? I'll tell ye all about him after.

Anyway. Daz goes by smilin an wavin an checkin the inside of this book an noddin like some cunt on *Mastermind* who just remembered the answer when Magnus Magnus Magnus reads out the *you passed on just thirty, Mr Extraterrestrial.*

Carmen squints the eye round the curtain.

See him! she goes.

What?

Look at him – look at him.

That's what he wants.

Thinks he's somethin. COLLIDGE.

She's squeezin her nails in her palms an bitin her bottom lip.

Collidge doesn't make ye better than every other cunt just like that . . .

She

SNAPS

her fingers.

All of a sudden he's Mr Fuckin Brainbox.

She whips the curtain shut.

He's thick as fuck that's what.

I laughs cos I've really went off him too.

Know what he always asks me?

Give me a ride, Carmen?

Hmm. She does this stupid voice: *Carmen, d'ye fink I'm an all right guy.*

What d'ye mean? I go.

D'ye think people like me? he goes, an I say, *Who gives a fuck what people think.* But I know what he's workin up to. *On an on he goes askin all these questions.*

Tell him ye hate his extraterrestrial guts. See how he likes that.

He ends up askin if he's good lookin.

Aye! Right yar.

Honest to fuck.

Do you fink I'm a good lookin guy, Carmen? If ye seen me comin up the road would ye fink I'm a good lookin guy – if ye never knew me? I mean what the fuck d'ye say to that?

Say what I say – ye're the dead spit for ET, Daz. Dead spit.

Oh! That's another thing – heard his latest . . .

Fuck that. What else does he ask?

She sucks her thumb a bit.

If he's better lookin that you?

An I hope ye give him the right answer?

Don't want to hurt his feelins.

What d'ye say?

She sucks her thumb some more.

Some burds'll like you, some burds'll like Mick.

I'm happy enough wi that answer but she's suckin her thumb harder tryin to stop her words spillin out. I keep quiet so she'll need to talk.

But all in, he goes, who's the best lookin?

I lifts ma eyebrows at her.

Put an advert in the paper. Who's the best lookin?

1. Daz.
2. Mick.

He's after you that wee cunt.
Carmen smiles an spins away.
No way, she says, really meanin to say:

1. *I know he's been tryin to get into ma wee black silky knickers for years.*
2. *Worse; I know he's been into ma knickers for years behind your back.*

An his latest what is it?
What?
Guess what his latest is? ye said a minute ago.
Aye – that's right – if anybody says, hi, Daz, he goes, Don't call me Daz! an squares up to them.
No cunt knows his right name so they go, *What'll I call ye, Daz?*
I said don't fuckin call me Daz! He goes an grabs them.
Fuckin prick – he was happy enough wi Daz all the years I've knew him. Some cunt'll do him in.
He's bouncin now.
Him? Couldn't beat Casey's Drum.
Well he's a bouncer.
You stickin up for him now.
I'm just sayin he's a bouncer.
I'll bounce his head off the walls if he tries his pish wi you again. Cunt.
So that's it. Silence for ages.
It's hours later an she waves at Daz joggin wi an ultra-dear track suit an brand spankin pump them right up trainers. She's wavin that hard her hairs swingin from side to side.
I'm started not to trust the wee cunt for two reasons:

1. All the things he's sayin to Carmen behind ma back.
2. The way the snobby wee cunt's actin.

163

Here's an example. We get a carry out. He asks me to carry it an tells every cunt he's off drink. Buys a big bumper bottle of

LUCOZADE

an swigs it all the way down Calder street whizzin out his head on speed.

Or what about this. The week before his Granny dies. We're in her house an he's talkin an she's answerin. It's yer usual Granny an Grandson shite. But somethin's not right. Know how ye can tell these things. Nothin in the words. It's a feelin. They don't like each other. In fact they're talkin like a couple that's broke up an met at a funeral. Forced to be nice. I should've knew. He's got sisters but they never visit him an he never visits them. They visit each other all right. He's the odd man out.

I'm uneasy in people's houses. I always feel they can see right through me. Read ma thoughts an stuff but she makes me feel all right. Coffee, Wagon Wheels, Carmel Logs an Carmel Wavers. I'm munchin away an he's eatin nothin cos he's on speed. He's tellin her about him bein changed. Off the drink. Back at the boxin. At collidge studyin biology an does she know what DNA means? She's noddin away sayin it's good to see him on the right tracks now. She's noddin at me an smilin. He smiles. I'm noddin back an smilin. He smiles more an his chest's comin out an out. Like it's a balloon an her approval's a footpump.

I'm tryin to persuade this man to go. He's clever too ye know. Eh Mick?

An he slaps me on the back.

First I fuckin knew about it ya wee patronosin bastard, I say. Only kiddin. That's what I want to say. What I really say is,

MMMMM, an smile this crazy cartoon smile at the Granny.

She flings me the same smile an he fucks off up the stairs for another snort. I'm embarrassed by the whole side-show. After the silence I turns an say,

Good weather we're havin.

She widens the eyes an looks like a mad starin witch an goes,

Don't trust that wee bastard. He'll stab ye in the back first chance he gets.

I go to say, *Eh!!!??*

an the door opens an in spins Don't-Call-Me-Daz, all smiles an white powder. He kisses his Granny like a luvvy an we leave. She struggles to the door. When he's round the corner of the buildin she goes,

Remember. Mark my words, son. Ye're a nice laddie. I can tell. He's evil. Evil.

Anyway. She dies an we go to the funeral. Relatives're talkin to him like his Granny. The words're thin but a thick pot of treacle emotions's slushed round about them. I can see blackness surroundin the words as they float over the gravestones like sparrows that want to be bats.

Same night we're up the woods wi a bottle of voddy an a gram. We fall asleep in the rain. I'm tryin the supportive pal bit but I can tell he's soakin in the attention not givin a fuck about his dead Granny.

This's the very bit I shagged Donna Murphy. Lumbered her from Stars an brought her up the woods. Dark hair. Tight white top on an half-cut jeans. Good fanny bulge. Brown eyes. We sits on the very log me an him's leanin against an right away she's got the tongue in ma mouth.

Well. Under the trees the night of Daz's Granny's funeral I tells him all about it. He's lovin every detail.

Later we're listenin to the rain rattlin soft on the leaves. He goes,

What would ye do if ye found somebody wi Carmen?

Kill them.

We fall asleep in the rain.

After that I see him less an less. He pops in now an then an tells me all about these babes he's shaggin. But every time I see him wi one they're plug ugly. I think he's dealin – he's never out Boffa's an Plastic Belly's. Armani suits, right good shed an this wee XR2 thump thump thumpin pump up yer trainers music out the sunroof rain sleet or snow. Fuckin prick.

Carmen hates him more when he mentions burds. She's jealous that me an him're talkin about burds. I cringe every time he comes near me. The odd time he's in ma house when I come in from the weights. I don't like it.

I'm trainin Monday Tuesday Thursday an Friday at Vic's. I'm trainin wi Vic an Benny – the two strongest cunts in there. I'm gettin strong. Two things happen within days. They're not really related but in ma head they are cos they happened thegether. Nearly.

1. Don't call me Daz's ex-wife moves in wi him. Bolt from the blue.
2. I start on bombs.

Daz's wife movin in makes me think all his fitness an new suits're about gettin her back so I feel a bit sorry for him.

The steroids'll make me massive an strong as fuck.

I start injectin every day. First day testosterone – 10ml. Next day Decca Durabolin – 10ml. It's not so easy at first. Ye split yer arse cheek into four sections by drawin an imaginary cross on it an inject into the muscle in the upper outer quarter. I fill the syringe an chase ma arse round the house for half an hour. Eventually I do it the way Benny says.

Slap yer arse sore an ye'll feel fuck all.

SLAP SLAP SLAP

I goes an slides the needle in. No problem. The sorest bit's injectin the stuff. I've got a freckle on each cheek exactly where the needle goes in. I know steroids'll have a massive physical effect what I don't know's what they'll do to ma head. An I'm mad enough already.

The Horrible

All of a sudden he's back wi his wife, Daz. Walks hand in hand ignorin us except the odd nod now an then. He's up an down the street slabberin her wi kisses. Holdin hands like some blind cunt's goin to steal her off him.

An he's got this big Boxer dog. Guess what it's called? Rocky Two. Not Rock or Rocky but Rocky-fuckin-Two.

C'mere Rocky Two, he shouts. He takes it runnin to save him carryin a knife. He's scared. Young team's on every corner shoutin the odds. The funny thing is, even though he got the dog full size in Easterhouse, it looks like him. They say dogs come to look like their owners, so some cunt in Easterhouse looks like ET. It's a laugh watchin them runnin down the street. Bowly. Exact same except Rocky Two's got four bowly legs an Don't Call Me's got two. It's got a big fat folded fuckin face just like him. You could hide fag packets in the folds in it's face. Two ET's comin right at ye down Cumbrae. Frightenin stuff. *Muppets out for jog*, wee Dinky says.

Booda calls it, *Don't-Call-Me-Rocky-Two*.

Up an down the street joggin. Up an down wi the best Armani suits on. This day right out the blue The Horrible comes stormin in. Ye can tell her arms been straight out an

168

pointin right along the lobby. Her finger tip's throbbin for Carmen.

That slutbag's shaggin ma man!

Never even chapped the door. Carmen's lookin right at her.

The Horrible folds her arms.

Tell him – tell Mick all about it, You an an Brown Teeth.

I looks at The Horrible.

You are fuckin mental, says Carmen stickin the chin out.

The Horrible's not movin she's tappin the toe in mid-air an foldin her arms tighter. She sucks on her teeth a couple of times an goes,

Are ye goin to tell him? Cos I will.

You are fuckin crazy! Carmen points three times exactly. The Horrible bulges her eyes an lowers her head so she's lookin out through her bushy eyebrows,

Don't call me crazy, she goes like it's a final warnin.

Crazy.

Don't call me that!

Crazy. Crazy. Crazy.

Don't call me that.

But she's blew it. Carmen's wantin a fight an Helen's detected that. She's crushed, apologetic even,

Just don't call me crazy, Carmen. Don't call me crazy.

Never show Carmen yer weaknesses. Never.

Away back to yer aul hoor of a Maw's. Look at the state of ye, ya strag.

The Horrible puts her hands over her ears sayin,

Shut up shut up shut up shut up shut up shut up shut up shut up shut up shut up shut up shut up shut up shut up shut up shut up shut up shut up.

But Carmen's right in there.

No fuckin wonder yer man left ye – fat cow.

The Horrible starts hummin an pressin her palms on an off her ears.

Cow. An ye stink. Yer fuckin mingin.

HMMMMMMMMMMMMMMMMMMMMM
COW
HMMMMMMMMMMMMMMMMMMMMM

Yer man's shaggin every hoor in town.

The Horrible screams an bolts.

Silence.

All this shoutin's comin from up the street. Next thing two big cases goes by wi The Horrible in the middle. An **whooooooooooooooooooooooooooooooooooooooooooosh** Don't Call Me's runnin behind beggin her not to go.

An there's Don't Call Me Rocky Two woof woofin away an shovin it's nose in Daz's crotch an he's shovin it away so it shoves its nose in passin crotches. Aul Mrs McVicars is the first. *Ooh!* she goes, an limps on past.

Fuck off go an get yer wee slag, screams The Horrible an nods in at us.

He's behind her, in front, that side, this side, makin sentences wi his hands but she marches on between the cases like a mad tank. Some Verandahs're shoutin the odds an cheerin her on.

Please oh please, he's goin.

Fuck off, Brown Teeth, she goes.

I fall about but Carmen's foldin her arms an blowin her fringe.

What did you say. What did ye fuckin say? shouts Don't through his brown teeth.

You heard.

Say it. Say it again.

She knows if they were on their own he'd be poundin the

punches in. But there's people watchin from all angles now so she shouts,

Fuck off, Brown Teeth!!!!

He can't take it. She marches on an I move round the room to see them leavin the street. But he doesn't leave the street. Just as she gets to the corner he hits her this almighty boot up the arse. She squeals an funny walks away tryin to keep her dignity wrigglin wi a sore arse an two big cases. I guess she's cryin.

Don't's marchin back throwin punches in thin air an all the Verandahs're shoutin the odds.

Ya wee cunt. Pick on somebody yer own size.

No get a hard on any more, son?

Midget.

He can't take it.

Get yer fuckin man down here ya fat cow, he screams.

He's flingin lumps of dirt at Verandahs. Wilder he gets the more they laugh.

An the more they laugh the wilder he gets.

Great! He storms off like Elmer Fudd. Five minutes later
he comes out wi the joggin gear on like nothin's happened.
But plenty's happened an all the time Carmen's standin
starin at nothin except wanes wi the elbows out their
jumpers an fat wummin on Verandahs.

Wummin're mental.

The Horrible's back a couple of days later an they're
holdin hands goin down the street wi floor cloth face shovin
it's fat nose in passin crotches of old ladies who walk
backwards in semi-circles to get away.

C'mon, Rocky Two, shouts Don't, as if the old wummin's
sniffin the dog's crotch.

Rumplefuckinstiltzkin

Skint.

Drank the Giros.

She's fucked off down her Maw's.

The house's warm enough seein as how I've wired the meter an electric radiators're everywhere. Three in every room – four in the bog. Got them out Weirs when it shut down. I'm heatin the whole street.

Shut that door d'ye think I want to heat the whole street, is what ma Maw used to shout just before she slapped me.

I'm warm but I'm starvin. Down to the last onion an a bottle of salad cream. Diet. I'm dippin slices of the onion in the cream an thinkin up a plan. I'm smokin ashtray douts an drinkin tea from a five-day tea-bag.

I gets a plan.

Fuck you onion! I says an pops off to find grub.

I chaps Booda's windie. He jumps up an gives me the *two minutes* look. She's goin radio cos he's promised to take her to B & Q. Ye can hear bangin pots an swearin echoin out the close when he opens the door.

An I'll not be here when ye get back, CUNT, she shouts an SLAM goes the door.

Here comes Booda swaggerin down Sikeside street cuppin

his hands in front of his face lightin up a J.

Fancy a doss up the canal for spuds?

Fuckin spuds? he goes givin it the question-mark look.

Aye, I'm cleaned out. Not a sausage. Lee Marvin.

He shrugs the shoulders, *I'm Geme.*

He hands me the joint, rubs his hands, an we march off. I feel her eyes poppin out like Walnut Whips drillin in our backs but we don't turn. I hands him an ASDA bag an he shoves it up his jook.

Later on we're comin back along the aul tarmac road. I'm thinkin roast tatties an five-day tea. We've got a bag of spuds each an he's skinned up. He found a bit in his wee jeans pocket. Survivor of a Persil number one soap sud boil wash. When ye've nothin next to nothin's a feast. We lights up. I closes the eyes an blows the smoke out over the field like a crop duster, well that's what I'm thinkin . . .

when . . .

dust dust dust dust dust dust dust dust dust dust dust dust dust dust dust dust dust dust dust dust dust

whoooooooooooooooooooooooooooooooooooosh

dust dust dust dust dust dust dust dust dust dust dust dust dust dust dust dust dust dust dust dust dust

up comes this pick-up wi a big red face. Ye don't have to ask. Farmer. Spins it round like the films. Ma mouths blowin the last of the smoke out. Ma eyes're amazed. He gets the dust cloud right but the noises're rock chunks an slippin tyres instead of screechin rubber.

The door flies open before the thing's stopped right an he's stampin his boot off the movin gravel. It stops. He heaves hiself upright.

Up he comes – chin on chest – eyes swiveled up at us – elbows out – arms swingin – steam comin out his ears – right out the fuckin *Beano*.

Get the tatties ower ya perr a ignirnt pigs yees. I sat at ma breakfast there an watched yees – the height a cheek howkin ma produce oot thon park.

Rantin. Pointin at thon park like a demented referee. Barkin mad. Can't get a word in edgeways. Booda's flabbergasted. He's puffin away at the joint, half laughin half not laughin.

Ah ken yer faces so a dae. Ah ken yer faces an I'll find oot yer names so a will. I'll find oot yer names an it's the Polis for ye – oh aye – the Polis. I've seen yees round here a hunner times an I kent yees were a perr of good for nothin shysters.

He's right next to us. I can smell his saliva an the reek of cow dung. He snatches Booda's bag out his hand.

A split second stillness, that's what I notice.

It's that freaky quiet when Booda does two things:

1. Kicks their cunts in.
2. Starts laughin.

He bursts out laughin, thank fuck, an Ken Yer Faces goes fuckin ballistic.

Ya cheeky ignirnt pig yee steals ma produce an ye've got the lip tae laugh right in ma face. Right in ma bloody face . . . Whit kinda world we livin in fur Goad's sake? But I ken yer faces an mark ma words I'll find oot your names – oh aye – don't think ah won't. Then he says to the hedges, *Right in ma face he's laughin . . . wid you credit it?*

He's stampin in circles. Rumplefuckinstiltskin. I've snuck sideways. Booda's creased. Doubled. He's got a hand on the ground stoppin him fallin on his face. Ken Yer Faces comes marchin at me but this's ma dinner. This's roast tatties an five-day tea. No fuckin way. He crunches by on the path an goes to snatch the bag like one of them mail trains that catches the bag whizzin through the station only he's no

Flyin Scot an I'm no wooden post. I snatch the bag back violent an give him the snarl. It's a real snarl I'm not just kiddin to frighten the bastard. Ye can see he's scared. I look crazy as fuck sometimes. Booda's dragged hiself off the ground; he's comin over. Ken Yer Faces's runnin in circles lookin desperate for help. The hedges're still ignorin him.

Ya pig ya big ignirnt pig them's ma produce mine!!! *Ma produce . . . Mine ya* big *ignirnt* pig ye *. . .*

On an on he's goin an me an Booda's passin the joint rapid an fallin all over the place. We're at the holdin each other laughin through the nose stage.

An we'd've laughed all day if Ken Yer Faces never whipped out the knife. A big fold over job – eight inches anyway – like a pocket scythe. GULP! I goes.

Booda pulls a straight face but I'm in fits still an pointin at the knife wi this crooked finger.

Booda pulls out his blade.

I pulls out mine.

Compared to Ken Yer Faces's folded Claymore they're toothpicks, but Ken Yer Faces doesn't even see them. He's runnin down the hill screamin like an Indian attack. So we hop the hedge an follow bent over. We're almost parallel an all the time he's screamin back up to where he thinks we are:

Ye'll no be gettin away ya pair a thievin louts. Ye might hae the produce but ye'll get caught. Ye'll hae tae come back for yer caur.

I looks at Booda.

He looks at me.

What fuckin car?

We thinks at each other. There's this sky-blue Escort parked squinty halfway down the hill. Ken Yer Faces's right on it tryin to force the pocket sword through the tyres

PSHHHHHHHHHHHHHHHHHHHHHTTTT

That'll sort yees oot, he shouts up, an moves to the next tyre.

PSHHHHHHHHHHHHHHHHHHHHTTTT

We crouch down vibratin as aul Ken Yer Faces sets about the other two tyres.

PSHHHHHHHHHHHHHHHHHHHHTTTT

Aye . . . the Polis'll be here when yees come to get yer motir caur. Hee hee hee . . .

PSHHHHHHHHHHHHHHHHHHHHTTTT

He's laughin like Dick Dasterdly's dog.

When the exhaust's kissin the tarmac he storms back up the hill shoutin about how that'll teach us, an how the Polis'll be there when we come to get the car back, an if he ever sees us again on his land he'll be well within his rights to blow our arses off wi his shotgun that he just wishes he brung an in fact he thinks he's got in the pick-up, an off he goes runnin.

So do we just in case.

I've still got the spuds an we're wanderin through the trees below Cairnhill House smirkin away an laughin at aul Ken Yer Faces. Booda stops dead lookin up this tree. I can't see nothin.

What is it.

Nothin shh.

I looks again. Nothin.

What're ye lookin at? I goes.

Up the tree.

What at?

Nothin. I'm lookin for . . . what're you lookin at?

I'm not lookin – I'm thinkin.

Fuck. There's me thinkin ye've seen an Extraterrestrial or somethin.

No.

He hands me the joint.

I've got a few bob comin the day.

What for?

A claim. Mind I broke ma wrist.

Aye fuck, that was years ago.

I know but I've to collect some of the dough the day at
Flannigan's. I just remembered this's the fourth – am I right?

Aye.

That's it then.

Our two grins float through the woods like slow-flyin
doves. We're lookin forward to a bender.

That night it's me Booda an Shaz drinkin an smokin an
listenin to Floyd. She's rippin open all these B & Q carrier
bags an openin bolts of wallpaper like they're the Dead Sea
scrolls.

BZZZZZZZZZZZZZZZZZZZZZZZZZZZZZ

The buzzer goes an we jump.

I'll get it, Boooooods, goes Shaz.

She seems away ages cos we're stoned. There's this
gigantic gap between me an Booda an I'm foldin into the
cushions. I can hear murmurs out in the lobby. I look at
Booda an he's not bothered so I assume time's stood still
again – it does that a lot for me but usually when I'm on
mushies or acid or comin out a bender. It never usually
happens on the gange.

FLASH!!!

An there's Carmen an Shaz in the livin room. Carmen's
got on all this new white gear on her Maw must've bought
her. She bedazzles us.

Bedazzle bedazzle bedazzle, goes Booda.

Look who it is, Boodssssssssss, says Shaz an Carmen's smilin
away.

Booda jumps up an pats her belly.

Swell hotel for you soon hen.

Her smile fills the room. I'm too stoned to move. I'm waitin on her reaction. She sits down an kisses me hard on the cheek, wipin her lips round slow to ma mouth.

Wooooarrrrrr, says Booda, *Get the knickers off her.*

Boooooods!

Love yooooooooooo, she whispers in ma ear an suddenly the world's glowin an warm an I'm smilin. Definitely smilin. I can move. I feels her belly an looks right in her dark eyes.

Wohhhhaa they're in lurve, says Booda.

Aww, see you, that's nice, says Shaz.

I laughs. This moment wi ma friends an Carmen an ma wane in her belly, all bad things're fallin away an I feel real. I feels like we're a couple round at friends for drinks – an aye fuck it, a wee smoke – who doesn't smoke the gange now? I feel glad to be human. It really do. I stands up for the bog but ma legs get the signal too late so I topple into Booda. But he's quick. The wummin've screamed an he's up out his chair steadyin me. I give him a full arms round yer back hug an he kisses me on the cheek.

Hey, that's ma man, shouts Carmen.

Aye an that's ma man, says Shaz.

Pair of poofs.

I'm beginnin to wonder about yous two.

The crack's good an soft an warm. I'm goin the long walk to the bog but it feels good as I leave the room cos I know there's somethin to come back to.

Hey there's Don't Call Me Daz walkin down the street! goes Booda.

I looks out as I leaves the room. The second I claps eyes on him the softness disappears.

The walk to the bog's long. Right along one lobby an down this other lobby. It's me an this cold solitary light. Sixty-watt bulb. Almost yella. Dampness's creepin up the walls. All that lies between me an the glow of comfort in the distant livin room's darkness an a journey so long I think I'll never get back.

But I do.

On the way back I hear Carmen's voice driftin up the lobby. She's singin. I stand listenin in the lobby.

> In a neat little town they call Belfast
> Apprentice to trade I was found.
> And many an hours sweet happiness
> Have I spent in that neat little town.
>
> A sad misfortune came over me
> Which caused me to stray from the land,
> Far away from my friends and relations
> Betrayed by the black velvet band.

An Booda an Shaz join in.

> **Her eyes they sho-one like diamonds**
> **I thought her the queen of the land.**
> **And her hair it hung o-ver her shou-ou-lder**
> **Tied up wi a black velvet band.**
>
> I took a stro-oll down Broadway
> Meaning not long for to stay.
> When who should I meet but this pretty young maid
> Come a traipsing along the highway.
>
> She wa-as both fair and handsome,
> Her neck it was just like a swans
> And her hair it hung o-ver her shou-ou-lder
> Tied up wi a black velvet band.

Her eyes they sho-one like diamonds
I thought her the queen of the land.
And her hair it hung o-ver her shou-ou-lder
Tied up wi a black velvet band.

Christ I never knew Carmen was such a good singer.

I took stroll wi this pretty fair maid
And a Gentleman passing us by.
Well I knew she meant he doing of him
By the look in her roguish black eye.

A gold watch she took from his pocket
And placed it right into my hand,
And the very first thing that I said was
Bad Sess to the black velvet band.

They're – singin – almost shoutin – at the top of their
voices.

He eyes they sho-one like diamonds
I thought her the queen of the land.
And her hair it hung o-ver her shou-ou-lder
Tied up wi a black velvet band.

Before the judge and the jury,
Next morning I had to appear.
The judge he says to me, young man,
Your case it is proven clear.

We'll give you seven years penal servitude
To be spent far away from the land,
Far away from your friends and relations,

> Betrayed by the black velvet band.

I get to the livin-room door amazed that she knows all the words.

Her eyes they sho-one like diamonds
I thought her the queen of the land.
And her hair it hung o-ver her shou-ou-lder
Tied up wi a black velvet band.

So come all you jolly young fellows
A warning take by me,
When you are out on the town me lads,
Beware of the pretty Colleens.

I open the door an the party hits me right in the face.

They'll feed you wi strong drink me lads
Till you are unable to stand,
And the very first thing ye'll know is,
Ye've landed in Van Deemin's Land.

Her eyes they sho-one like diamonds
I thought her the queen of the land.
And her hair it hung o-ver her shou-ou-lder
Tied up wi a black velvet band.

I'm on the couch holdin her hand. Every now an then she gives ma hand a squeeze. I can smell her clean an perfumed body an even though her belly's away out to here I want to shag the pants off her. So does Booda. He makes it no secret an that's OK. I know he'll never do it. There's some people've morals an there's some people've none. But usually the people who look like they've got them, they're liars an cheats. The ones that look like right bastards, they could surprise ye wi the morals they've got.

Two o'clock he hands me a gram. I load some lager in an ASDA bag an me an her head down the road. It's one of them nights when the walk goes on an on. All I want's in bed stoned an dream dream dream the night away.

After three million light years through the empty streets of Sikeside we get home. Zip we're in bed an she lets me shag her from the back. She's not carin about herself I'm just pushin it in an out slow. It's beautiful. I've got a hold of her swollen tits. I comes – an orgasm's slow an warm when ye're stoned. Ye feel every drop of spunk scooshin up an out an explodin. I moans an rolls on ma back. I mind it well. I fall asleep wi all these wee birds an cartoon characters spinnin round ma head an tweet tweetin an singin this little song, fuck knows where from. It sounds like it's comin out the pillow.

zzzzzzzzZZZzzzZzzzzzzZZMICK!zzzZZ

zzzzzzzzzzzzzzzz MICK! zzZZZZZzZZZZzz

MICK! zzZzzzzzzZZzzz MICK!

zzZZZZZZZzz MICK! zzzZzZzzZ MICK!

zzzz MICK! zzzzzzZZZzzzzzzzZzzzzzz

MICK! zzzzZzzzzzzzzzzzzz MICK!

183

zzzzzzzzz MICK!

zzzzzzzzzzzzzzz MICK!

ZZZZZZzzzzzzzzzzzzzzzz

MICK! zzzzzz

MICK!?!?!?!?!?!?!

zz Zzzzz

MICK!?!?!?!?!?!?!
?!?!?!!!!!

Eh!
I think I'm away.
Where?
Away, the wane.
What now?
Aye! she goes an cringes wi pain.
Oh fuck it's dead sore. It's killin me.
Aw shit! Could it not wait till the mornin I'm totally stoned out
ma head!

Ohhhhhhhhhhhhhhhhhhhhhhhhhh!

So up we get. I nips into Big Frank's an phones a taxi an

down to Bellshill. An ye know all she can go on about? If the doctors an nurses'll know we had sex last night. I mean it's a bit obvious we had sex wi her bein swol up like a balloon but she doesn't want them to know an while the taxi's hootin the horn outside she's in the bog cleanin herself wi the face cloth. Face cloth – that's a laugh. They should be called everythin but yer face cloths.

It's a boy. Patrick we call him. When it's all over I go over to the bing across the motorway.

Look out the windie in ten minutes an I'll wave from the top of that hill, I goes.

I'm feelin like I've got to do somethin momentous but the only thing I can come up wi's climbin the bing an wavin. What a prick.

I'm breathless gettin up it. I stands lookin at her windie but she doesn't come.

I wait an still no Carmen. It's gettin dark. That's what I remember most about that day. Not the birth or the screamin wane or holdin the wane or Carmen all sweaty an greasy in the bed. What I remember's me alone on the top of this slag hill an the sky gettin dark. The lights glow in the hospital windies an below Lanarkshire spreads out in straights an spirals. The rain starts an the moon rolls over the tops of the trees.

When I get back to the empty house in Sikeside I don't even have a drink. I sit there. I don't think. I just sit an fall asleep in the chair.

Mad about the Milk

When ye've got a wane ye get milk tokens an family allowance an single parent benefit. Carmen's down as livin at her Maw's so she moves in there after she gets out the hospital. I'm allowed in now we've got a wane. They're that nice to me too. She stays in her Maw's a month an then comes back to Sikeside.

I've got two pints of milk a day comin on the milk tokens an I've done the room up goodstyle for the wane. But to tell ye the truth the wane's more in her Maw's than Sikeside.

Sometimes the milk's only one pint an sometimes it's none. I says to the milkman but he swears blind he delivers it. He gets the milkboy by the hair an he swears blind he's delivered it.

Sure ye've not got yer own customers up a close or somethin, he goes.

He nods his head like he never knew what havin yer own customers means . . .

Someone asks ye to start deliverin milk an ye don't tell the driver. Ye steal extra pints from the van or cunts doors an deliver them, collectin the milk money at the end of the week. When ye've collected about ten customers ye can make a fortune. This milkboy looks thick as fuck so I believe him.

I ask Dinky an he looks wi his mouth to one side an his eyebrows halfway up the street. I know what he means. He means Sikeside's too tough for poofy milk stealin. But some cunt's stealin it an I'm goin to find out who.

I'm fifteen stone now an doin weights every day an jaggin up wi steroids. Steroids make ye mad. It's like, know how ye get the fightin head on when ye're drunk? Well on steroids ye've got the very same fightin head on without drink. So I've got to smoke as much dope as possible to keep calm.

Sometimes it's no use. Sometimes The Rage gets hold an there's no stoppin me. I burst into temper all of a sudden wi enormous strength.

This mornin I'm pacin about. The milk's went missin again. Twenty grams of protein in a pint of milk. I'm cursin in the scullery an she scuffs in wi these big stupid lookin Mickey Mouse fluffy slippers. It's like the mouses're starin at me an laughin. I'm glarin at them but they won't stop starin.

What's up wi you? goes Carmen.

Nothin.

What're ye thumpin about in here for then?

Nothin.

The slippers keep starin an I want to choke the life out them. They shuffle her over to the sink an make her put the kettle on. I'm at the table I overturned for Daz an Slinky.

The light's comin in the scullery windie an I can see the shape her thighs make as they meet her fanny – it's like wine glass. A tall wine glass. I stand up feelin horny. But not the horny ye want to share. I want to shag her hard. Treat he like she's not there. Rough. I want to shag the fluffy slippers right off her.

She pulls out the grill an flops some pieces on. Even the pieces're annoyin me. I like bread to be thick. This bread's thin pan slices. Ye could do origami wi them. They're in the grill curlin up. There's never any softness in them when ye've toasted them – it's toast all the way through. Toast toast an more fuckin toast. I want to smash that fuckin grill.

I'm leanin on the scullery door now an I've got ma hand on the top of it. She's got this fag hangin out her lip an her hair's fallin round it. I can hear it singein an smell the burnt hair.

Need to go down an get the wane the day.

I grunt at that.

Any milk?

Ye fuckin asked that already. Some cunt's stole it again.

Just cancel it an get it at the Paki's. He gives ye fags an drink for tokens anyhow.

That's not the fuckin point is it? Some cunt's stealin ma milk. Our milk.

Aye . . . but they know I live here.

Probably wanes.

Wee Dinky says it's not wanes.

Wee Dinky? I think you're shaggin wee Dinky.

An she crunches into a bit of the toasted right through toast.

I keep thinkin of some cunt stealin ma milk an laughin at me. Laughin an tellin cunts in Sikeside I'm a dick. Been stealin ma milk for weeks an I've done fuck all about it.

Years ago I'd hardly walk through Sikeside for fear I'd get done in an here am I now wantin to take on the whole scheme. She rattles the grill an turns more cardboard bread. Her fag hisses out in last night's tea cups. The kettle boils an she says through her hair,

Ye'll never find out who it is.

Will I not? I'm tryin to say but by the time I come to *not* this white rage's lightenin bolts in ma head an I'm standin wi the door in ma hand. I've wrenched it right off.

You are fuckin crazy, she says.

Don't call me crazy.

You're fuckin away wi it so ye are.

Don't call me fuckin crazy, I'm sayin through ma teeth.

I've got ma lips stretched across ma teeth an ma eyes're wide an throwin blue at her. They're sayin,

Say no more cos he's just about to take a flaky.

She nods an puts her head down

What did you say?

Nothin.

What the fuck did you say there ya cow.

Nothin, she says, through her hair, an she's slowly butterin toast wi margarine wi her shoulders hunched up waitin for the attack. An that's what she gets. I fly across the linoleum an grabs her hair.

Ahhh!! she goes, an drops the knife on the fluffies. She's tryin not to look in ma laser-beam eyes so I twists her head round. I feel some rippin out. I don't want to do it. I don't care if ye believe me. This wee voice in ma head's goin, *Stop it stop it don't be daft let her go* but this bigger voice keeps sayin, *Ye said somethin what the fuck was it?* Her hair's tearin an she's screamin. She flings a hand out an opens the drawer fumblin. She gets a big spoon but she thinks it's a knife an tries to stick it in ma leg.

Eeee. Eeee. Eeee. She's goin an the spoon's bouncin off ma leg.

Ya daft cunt! I says, an flings her on the floor. She's curled up greetin. I flings the hardboard toast all over the joint. I want to rub one of the slices right in her face an hair but I've calmed down a bit. So she's sobbin on the lino an I march out an slam the door.

Out in the street there's Verandah after Verandah talkin. They've heard the noise. They're lookin at me. Every time I zap on Verandah wi ma eyes the cunts look away or drop the heads. They won't look me in the eye. I can only zap one at a time. ZAP I go but soon as I take the beams off them an Zap another one they're right back on me again. It's like tryin to get rid of midges. Their eyes're burnin through me like weldin rods an their whispers surround me like whirlwinds.

He's he's her her door door slut slut baby baby sitter sitter wanes wanes mad mad

I get to the woods. I need the trees. The whole street's laughin when I get to the ash path red wi rage. I decide to get this milk stealer.

When I get home she's not in. I go up the weights an train like a demon. No cunt talks to me. They know when to not talk. I get back to Sikeside still mad about the milk. No cunt's goin to make me look like a dick. No cunt.

Carmen's back an the wane's in our bed snorin. I go in the room an kiss him. He feels that safe an smells that clean it's like he's from another world. An I feel sad. I want to be in that world. I want that comfort. But I'm too far gone now an know it. Who's ever goin to love me? Ma world's in hate. Patrick's world's love an care. His powdered skin an long eyelashes speak a language I can only hear through ma nose now. He gurgles an moves like only wanes can. I smile a real smile first time in years an I wish it was all real. I wish we were really a couple an we had met at some disco an fell in love an winched an went on holiday. That I had a job. Or we both had jobs an had a wee house of our own somewhere an no fights. I wish the world Patrick smells of was the one we lived in.

But that's not our world. It's black an it's hard. Outside's crushed glass an boarded-up windies an junkies an mad stabbers. But they won't beat me. No cunt's goin to stab me. No cunt'll make me look like a dick. I lost ma passport to the real world in Blackpool, on the South Pier wi that heavy splash into the cold sea. So did she, but she weathers it better. It's drivin me fuckin insane. I kiss the wane an curl his hand round ma finger. He's like a wee chipmunk. They're that innocent wanes – they don't know what's happenin. I hear the kettle goin on an she shout-whispers

D'ye want coffee.

I know this mornin'll never be mentioned till the next big argument. I shuffles in an there's a good film on. She sits beside me an puts her head on ma chest. We breath in unison for a while an she says, like she's readin ma thoughts,

He's beautiful eh?

Aye he is that he's . . .

Lyin there – that innocent.

Aye it's a pity . . .

Shhh, she goes an I know she's readin ma thoughts. We go to bed each side of the wane. We don't shag. I spend half the night wi ma nose in the nape of Patrick's neck smellin maself into the other world. Me an Carmen hold hands over his cuddly body. We hold hands like we're drownin an he's the only object floatin in the sea. Like we're tryin to save each other. Like we've got a reason to live now. I fall into nightmares about bein torn away from ma Maw by a black claw. I'm sweatin buckets.

Next mornin I'm up at six. Carmen an Patrick turn lightly on the bedsprings. They look lovely wi her black hair fallin on the wane an him tuggin it unconscious. She's half awake

an half kisses him an I'm sure he half smiled. An that's a
world I'll not be in either. I keep thinkin of the Paul Simon
song, 'Mother and Child Reunion'. In that reunion there's
somethin I want. But I don't know how to get it.

Anyway this's the day I sorted out the milk stealer. The
milk comes at half six. Clink clink an out the close shoots the
same boy the milkman interrogated for me.

Once he's gone I sticks the ear on the door an makes sure
no cunt's shufflin about the close. No cunt. I opens the door
an ties white thread round the bottles. I slips it under the
door an lie back. I've got ma steelies on an ma army jacket
an a hammer. I ties the thread round ma fingers an dozes off.

TUG
SNAP

an I'm at the door handle in time to see a shadow move
out the close. I gets to the close mouth an sees a big lanky
cunt jump on this different milk van halfway up the street.

You're a dead man, I shouts, an Instead of ignorin me he
gives me the fingers an shouts,

Ya fuckin wanker c'mon.

It's that bastard Trunk's sidekick. Trunk delivers milk to all
his junkies so this's probably how he gets it.

Cunt's always shout c'mon when they're travellin away
at speed. I walks out onto the main Sikeside road. Cumbrae
joins the road at two points only, an it's the last street in the
scheme so I figure they have to come back by the end of ma
street.

I'm in the middle of the road. I've got a black tammy on,
an Army jacket an big steel toed boots. I'm fifteen stone. I
look wild. I'm the wild man of fuckin Borneo. I've got ma

Estwing hammer at ma side in full view of the swervin cars on their way to work. Five minutes've passed an the big lanky cunt wi a mop for a hairdo's probably forgot about me. He's probably decided not to steal ma milk any more. Probably thinks that's all I want. But he's got another think comin. I want revenge. I want somethin in return.

The van turns onto Sikeside Street. It starts accelratin. I can see bodies stuffed in the cabin. The driver sees me an moves to the left. So do I. He moves to the right. So do I. He toots the horn. I stand still an stare. He's thirty feet away an dips the clutch an revs the engine. I don't flinch. He brakes. He stops an ma face's right on his wipers. He winds his windie down a couple of inches.

Before he talks I've unloaded two crates of milk.

What the fuck're you doin?

I look at him. Cars're slowin up cos they sense somethin's wrong but they can't see what.

That cunt's been stealin ma milk for weeks.

The driver turns swift to lanky. He's all palms an shrugs.

I'm takin this milk . . .

The driver looks. He doesn't know what to say cos I'm tappin the windie gently wi the hammer.

He revs up an jerks away leavin me in the middle of the road wi two crates of milk like suitcases. He stops fifty feet away an gets out.

That's the last milk ye'll be stealin off ma van!!!

For a milkman he's not got much bottle. If he done that to me I'd've knocked him down at least. So I humps the two crates home an drink milk all day. Carmen makes rice puddins an coffee wi milk an semolina an custard.

I don't get ma milk stole again an I'm the talk of the town for holdin up a milk van wi a hammer. Good. Fuck them all.

Debt-Collecting

We owe forty quid still for this Provvy cheque from Big Maggie. She rattles the door Saturday mornins but we don't answer it. After a couple of months she takes to shoutin through the letterbox. I whisper to Carmen, *There's nobody here but us chickens*.

Then she starts on Plan B. Lookin in windies. There's this big archway between the scullery an the livin room, the only place she can't see ye's in the bog. This Saturday mornin she goes.

THUMP
THUMP
THUMP

an her man's in the car – engine's purrin. He's resigned to the fact that we're not payin so he sits smokin wi that look long term naggin brings. Probably hates her as much as me. Maggie lifts the letter box an shoves her eyes through. She sticks her fat nose in to see if she can smell toast an tea. The flap falls an I hear her walkin out the front. I nip in the lobby lookin for a hidin place. Carmen beats me to the bog. But there's quick steps an the lid lifts again. Fly as fuck. Tryin to catch me out. I zips in the scullery an slide over crouched to the sink. I hear her at the back room windie thumpin, shoutin,

I know ye're in there.

Nobody here but us chickens, I whisper.

She rattles the bog windie. I can hear Carmen holdin her breath.

I crouch under the sink. The scullery windie's right above the sink. She rattles it. I can't believe it. Feet away an I'm findin it hard to stop laughin. She's hammerin that hard I think it's cavin in. There's steam on the windie an stuff lyin about that makes her suspicious. The fuckin kettle clicks off.

I know ye're there ye haven't paid me for months. She's nearly greetin.

Her voice's tremblin angry. She thumps one last time an her footsteps crunch over broke glass in the dryin green. I waits for the engine. A door slams an a car drives away. I gives it to the end of the street an stands up.

FUCK ME!!!!!

She's still there. Fat as fuck. Pink as a pig. Snortin in the windie wi this smile that bitter wummin do – a grin an a growl rolled into one. The colour flushes out me. I stare in her bloodshot eyes an the steam's buildin up on both sides of the glass. What do I do? Drop – that's what. I drop back behind the sink an curl up. She's thumpin away tryin to break the glass.

Ya Bastard get out here an pay me. Get out here an face me like a man.

I hear Carmen really curlin up now an holdin her breath. Maggie knocks for a good quarter hour. Then there's these other footsteps. An a voice.

C'mon hen! What the fuck's keepin ye.

He's in there that bastard.

But he's not goin to answer is he?

But he's in there, I seen him.

Did he see you?

See me? See me? He was that away from me – right behind that windie there.

He seen ye?

Seen me? Aye he fuckin seen me?

She's shoutin for ma benefit an chappin again.

Aye he fuckin seen me all right . He bobbed up an bobbed back down again like a shite in a sewer.

Answer the door ya shitebag, goes her man.

Then he starts chappin the windie.

Get yerself out here now an get this bill paid.

He's shoutin. Fuck! All the Verandahs must be watchin. No way I'm gettin off the floor, even if half of me wants to kick his cunt in. They chap an shout abuse for ten minutes an then off they pop givin the front door a good bootin goin by. They don't come back to Sikeside. But we're not there much longer anyhow.

Carmen's got her name down for a house since she got pregnant. Single parents're treated like fuckin royalty in Coatbridge Housin so she gets offered this cracker of a flat in Kirkshaws. Two bedrooms double glazing, the works. We're goin to get it done up right before we move in.

★

We're not goin to get it done up before we move in now. These debt-collectors catch up wi me. The first time they come to the door I goes,

Who? Mick Riley? No he doesn't live here but if ye find out where he is tell me, I'm goin to kill the bastard. Left ma sister here wi a wane.

Away they go. Next time they come they slip a note through sayin,

Nice one Mick. Hope your sister's OK.
Us

One lucky break when a debt-collector turns up.

Chap chap chap goes the door. I'm in a cunt of a mood. It's Jamie Mac.

Fuck me, Mick! he says.

How's it goin, Jamie?

He's got the suit on an the tie.

Come in.

We sit down an he's got this bill for two grand for a car.

I'm payin fuck all, Jamie.

Och I know that.

He's skinnin a joint an it looks right out of place against his suit an shirt an tie. We tokes away an laughs about the old days.

An hour later he's got to go.

Put ye down as a deceased. We laugh. Smokin wi a dead guy. He even offers me a job on account of ma new found muscles.

Could do well in Easterhouse an Barlanark wi a build like that.

Tenner a door. Just stand behind me an stare. Say nothin.

Jamie, I wouldn't do that job for all the fuckin money in the world.

He laughs. Thinks I'm not serious an hands me his card. Jamie Mac. Debt-Collector an Private Investigator. Fuck I thinks he's goin to stop at the door an say,

Oh! Just one more question before I go,

But he doesn't. That's *Colombo*. That's America. That's the movies. This's Jamie Mac. This's Sikeside. This's the real thing.

So he puts me down as deceased an that saves me for a couple of weeks until another note pops through the letter box. But this time I don't move or turn the music off. They look in the windie an I close ma eyes an loss maself in the music. Carmen stands up an dances in a skimpy skirt. Lifts the skirt an flashes the knickers. A note comes through the door.

Mick — sorry to hear about your death but we will be arriving on such and such a date wi a warrant etc.

Us

This's the real thing too. The final warnin. Final fuckin frontier – million light years after the red final reminder that isn't a final reminder at all. I need four grand or get ma door broke down an all ma stuff pounded an sold for ten bob to snide neighbours. Fuck that.

I've got a week to get the stuff out. They don't know about

Carmen's house in Kirkshaws. We move all the stuff.

Oh, there's this nosy neighbour watchin us move in right at her windie. She's in the flat below us – we're one up. Doesn't even have the decency to peek behind curtains. I know first time I see her pile of rocks for a face that she's trouble. An she is. Big fuckin trouble.

After we move the stuff I go back wi Booda to Sikeside. Daz turns up an helps Carmen to move stuff about the new house. He's a fuckin pussy anyhow. I think he's feart to come wi us cos he knows what we're goin to do. Ma Giro's switched to No Fixed Abode. Ye go up an pick it up wi Gypsies an hobbos on a Thursday afternoon. If ye ever do that take yer gas mask cos some of the cunts're hummin.

Me an Booda get back to Cumbrae an the first thing's the multi-point. In the car wi that. Next we smash up all the furniture that's left. All the walls inside, apart from the one where the heaters an meters are, are breezeblock so we kick them down. The place's a pile of rubble like when the council gave me it. The mad room at the back where I keep all the clocks an mad stuff out closed-down Steelworks's great. We smash that in a frenzy. When we're finished we pan all the windies in. The Sheriff officers're comin on Monday. I paint on the wall.

When me an Booda get back to Kirkshaws, Carmen an Daz've got the place done right comfy but they're nowhere to be seen. Turns out they're up the Galleria celebratin flittin. Carmen doesn't get in till yon time. I'm lyin in the new house stoned. Her Maw's got the wane. She flumps on the bed steamin. I stick ma hand down her knickers to see if she's wet. No wetter than ye'd expect so I suppose she really has been out drinkin.

Daz gets a hard time when he gets home. The Horrible doesn't let him in.

Flyin Panties

Next day Booda's got a gram an I've got money. I walks over Sikeside an the Captain's (Booda) got three joints skinned. Expectin me.

Comin out to play, Captain?

Shaz's at her Maw's so Booda can stay out an play all day. Carmen's up Airdrie market wi her Maw to order curtains an carpets for when she gets her movin-in Giro from The Social. Another Giro Jackpot. We're ready for a good day.

But who do we bump into on the way down Sikeside street but Don't. Lookin rough as fuck. He's all speckled in this white stuff.

What time did Carmen get in at last night, Mick? asks Booda, an I know exactly what he means by that.

She was out wi that wee cunt at the Galleria but she came in about twelve.

Awright, Daz?

Don't call me Daz, Booda.

Sorry.

Booda takes a deep breath an says it all over again in his cowboy drawl.

Awright, James ma man.

Aye. Slept in Weirs last night.

Weirs – not got a bed?

Me an Booda laugh. He doesn't like it one bit.

She wouldn't let me in.

Punch her, goes Booda.

She starts all that shite about . . .

He pauses. I know it's Carmen. Booda knows it's Carmen. An Daz knows we know it's Carmen so he says . . .

All that shite about other wummin.

Booda uses his *takin the pish out them* voice. But it's only me an Booda that knows his *takin the pish out them* voice. He makes the words longer an there's somethin else in his voice. The thing ye'd have in yer voice when ye're talkin to someone ye kicked fuck out last week.

But Daz . . .

Do . . .

James, ye're always tellin the lads how good ye are wi wummin. No wonder she's jealous bein married to a stud like yerself.

Booda's pattin him on the back.

She threw a pot of pancake dough round me, goes Don't as if she stabbed him.

The yella goo's dried to flaky pastry. Booda's pickin it off.

Yer a walkin cake, Jamesy.

James!

James. Want to come for a wee smoke?

At that he sparks up a joint.

Have to go round the road first.

So me an Booda go wi him. We're behind him sniggerin at his swagger. He's goin on an on about names she called him. Brown Teeth, Smelly Dwarf, Limp Dick, Horse Breath an on an on. Me an Booda's laughin at every stupid fuckin name an Don't Call Me Daz's not pleased at all.

We turns up Cumbrae. Wee Dinky an a team's outside Daz's close. An they're not standin like they usually do. They're waitin. It's like they're waitin on a scramble. But there's no weddin. They're waitin on us. Or more to the point, they're waitin on Don't.

Daz swipes a boot at them at the close door. They all jump back like a shoal of sticklebacks.

ET ET
got to sit on the poe to pee
face is folded like an aul hankee . . .

Some of the younger wanes're singin. They sing that quite a lot.

Hey, James, what's that they're singin? goes Booda.

Some stupid wane's song.

What's they words but? goes Booda.

Fuck knows. They're all wee toerags round here.

An he shouts for the benefit of the Verandahs.

They're clatty aul Maws don't even wash theirselfs how d'ye expect them to wash their wanes?

The wanes're still singin.

ET ET
got to sit on the poe to pee
face is folded like an aul hankee . . .

Booda buts in again.

What's that about ET?

Daz stops an glares then spins quick an marches in the close. Booda knows the words anyhow me an him learnt them the song.

The wanes're laughin an throwin wee stones at Don't's arse. Dinky an his mates're at the corner smokin an gigglin, squirmin in an out each other like snakes. That's when I notice the Verandahs're quieter than usual. Usually they're chatterin away like crows not botherin about the world below apart from the odd nod an the odd

See him. NOD *Well see his Maw.* NOD *Well see her sister.*
NOD *Well she's a right slut.* NOD *See the Barnyard.*
NOD *See the Thursday night disco.* NOD . . .

That's the way they go. Like every time they say *See* an
the other Verandah vultures nod, a picture's transmitted in
their heads. Who knows. Mibbi it is?

Anyway. The picture here's Daz goin in the close an the
attention's squintin on him. The street knows somethin we
don't. Booda grins an we step in the pishy close.

His flats the top. Three up. First thing's the door's lyin
wide to the wall. Don't sprints in an me an Booda walk in
his lobby. He's comin in an out rooms slammin doors.

The cow, the fuckin cow, he's goin. Then, *Rocky Two!? Rocky
Two!?*

No answer. No bark. Only that terrible empty ye get in
houses in schemes like Sikeside. She's fucked off an left him.
We know that. Took all the furniture. We know that too. Fuck
Daz knows it but he's got to go round an round every room
to make sure again an again.

The only carpet left's the lobby carpet. She's left the cooker
an a couple of brown bedroom units. An there's this black an
white portable on the floorboards in the middle of the livin
room. The cow's plugged it in an knocked it off station so it's
hissin an flickerin like an electric snake. Daz's standin at the
scullery windie, fists clenched. The place smells of
floorboards an spilled perfume. The heatin's on full blast.

Daz! I says, an that's enough. He flies in the livin room an
picks the telly up above his head. He jumps off the floor an
flings it wi violence at the Verandah windie shoutin,

Don't call me fuckin Daz!

On ye go, James, shouts Booda, bootin a hole in the

Gyproc wall. We're all set for a total house wreck. We've
been practicin. But the telly's still plugged in.

TUG

It stops halfway to the windie an crashes explodin on the
floor. There's a second's silence as the glass tinkles over all
the wee electronic bits an bolts of lightenin spark out like
telly blood.

Outside ye can hear them all lookin up. They've seen the
removal van an The Horrible marchin about wi folded arms.
Burd wi a purpose – nothin worse. There's a smell of bad
electricity now an I don't know if it's off the dead telly or
Daz. As the last bits of telly implode he explodes. Ballistic.
Radio fuckin Rental. If there's one thing he hates more than
his wife leavin an takin all the furniture it's lookin like a
right dick. An he looks like a right dick.

He starts shoutin on the dog,
Rocky Two Rocky Two-oo. She even took the dog.

Oh Don't Call Me Rocky's took away, says Booda in a wanes
voice so Don't can't hear.

I nudges him but he whispers laughin in ma ear,
So the dog took the dog woof woof.

Daz's screamin in our smirkin faces an then he goes to
town. He starts bootin the walls in.

She Boot

even Boot

took Boot

the Boot

dog Boot

Chalk dust's flyin up an all over him mixin wi pancake
mix. He sets about the place. But there's nothin exitin about
his house wreck. We help him but he's only half hearted an
he doesn't really want help. We want to crash the walls

down an I've got ma eye on the multi point. Daz's choosin the bits to boot an punch. He needs lessons on takin a fit. We give him a few minutes an Booda shoves him onto this big bean cushion. It's the only bit of furniture in the room. The stinkin cushion where Rocky two used to lie lickin his balls.

Daz Daz, we're goin, *calm down it's your house. Ye're wreckin the joint man.*

He's not wreckin the joint really. We tell him that to make him feel good. I feel like sayin, *Daz Daz, sit down an I'll show ye how to wreck the fuckin joint!* He breathes in an out fast an gives it mad starin eyes. He's even pish at mad starin eyes but we don't tell him.

D'ye want a cup a tea?

He grunts. An stares like he's in another world.

Booda slaps him a couple on the face. The slaps're harder than they need to be so I've got to turn ma grin away when Daz snaps out his coma holdin his face.

Eh? Eh? he goes, dodgin Booda's next slap.

Tea. D'ye want tea?

Aye . . . aye . . . he goes. Booda sticks a new joint in Daz's mouth an he puffs away. Centre of our attention – that's what he loves. He's enjoyin it really.

I opens a few cupboards. They're all bare. I do the Old Mother Hubbard routine openin door after door.

Where's the tea bags? I goes an he gets up an stomps in, opens an slams a few cupboards. Nothin there.

The Cow the Slut, an all this he starts goin an wreckin the house a bit more determined now. He's got two war cries now.

1. *She even took the dog.*
2. *She even took the teabags.*

Two good punchlines lookin for jokes. Me an Booda's in the lobby while he trashes the two brown fake teak bedroom units. Booda's miles away an I'm tryin to think up two good jokes.

WHIZZZZZZZ
ZZZZZZZZZZZ
ZZZZZZZZZZZ
ZZZZZZZZZZZ
ZZZZZZZZZZZ
ZZZZZ
KELUNK
KELUNK
KELUNK

This door wi a plastic brass handle whizzes past an bounces down the lobby. Booda nudges me an sticks a hand at his mouth.

For fuck sake ye're wreckin the place, James, he goes, an holds me by the shoulder laughin through his teeth.

Next thing these other three doors come bouncin out the room. Two big one wee. A wee pair of red knickers comes by. A cream suspender belt. A bunch of tights an stockins all tangled. There's a trace of perfume in the lobby now. A wee tartan skirt. A pair of shiny black knickers trimmed wi lace. A bra. Big tits. The Horrible.

Booda pockles some knickers an tights. This pair of lace stockins comes by attached to a white satin suspender belt. I roll them in a ball an suck air through them. A sex filter. I stuffs them on Booda's nose an he sucks. I can smell perfume an the sweet-sour scent of her fanny. I never thought about shaggin his wife but now I've seen her tackle I want her bent over somethin. Twin tub mibbi. Or the bonnet of a car.

Panties're still comin out an we're stuffin the best knickers in our pockets. Good wankin material. We're gettin rid of ones we collected earlier if somethin better comes along.

It's the knickers that Mick an Booda reject that makes Daz's wife's knickers the best, goes Booda.

Good advert, Booda. Fish – smelly salmon.

That's right sexy gear, James, goes Booda in his rippin the pish voice.

That makes Daz worse but he's exhausted an a pile of bras flumps on the floor an so does he.

No Poundstretcher underwear there.

Nothin worse than yer wife leavin ye an you thinkin about her sexually. It does yer head right in. An that's what Booda's up to.

The wreckin's finished an Daz starts laughin. We give him pats on the back an all that. I know it's not right to ask for the multi-point cos he's not done the damage ye do when ye're leavin a place for good. He's only done the damage ye do to impress yer mates. He's impressed us fuck all.

C'mon, James, I know somewhere we can wreck.
Eh?
D'ye want to smash somethin up?
I want to smash the fuckin world up. See her . . .
Forget about her. D'ye want to really wreck someplace?
Aye?
Right follow the Captain.

If Don't never impressed us he impressed the street. He made plenty noise so they think he's really wrecked the joint. They clap an cheer an he raises clasped hands above his head an thrustin them in the air over an over like he's won a title.

We go to Weirs. It's this big work that's shut down. That's where I got the radiators, mind? There's these guards in it so its hard to get near. Booda was there a couple of days ago an no guards

We'll sneak in from the burn an make sure the guards're really away, says Booda.

I've got visions of us sneakin about dodgin the guards an liftin anythin that's not nailed down. Been in a few times since they shut it down. That's our main hobby, stealin out works that're shut down. We're not short of a shut down work or two Thatcher made sure of that. Good on the aul cow.

We get to Weirs prepared to sneak in. Fuck me! It's black wi Sikesiders. All over it. On the roof, in the ground, in the buildin. They've dug a trench across inside the main gate so the Polis can't get cars in.

Some of them's never worked in their lifes an some worked in Weirs. They're doin shifts diggin up copper cable underground, strippin lead off the roof, smashin cast drainer lids an barrowin them to the scrappy. The place's nearly bare. Piranhas.

We run the corridors smashin white globe lights wi iron bars. It's a good game. Ye've got to smash it runnin so the glass'll shower behind ye. But Daz wants to go home. We've got no tools for scrap so we walk him back. Lookin back at Weirs it's like a plague of locusts devourin the buildin.

First thing I notice walkin up Cumbrae's a trail of knickers an stockins. I know right away it's wee Dinky. That's what they done when ye wrecked yer house. We're nearly at the close when Don't notices they're his wife's knickers. He bolts up the close. So do we.

The place's booted to fuck. Boot holes all over the walls an doors. Knickers an stuff in the bath an the water's left on an overflowin. On the wall it says:

Daz goes crackers. He curls in a ball an rocks side to side cryin. I feel sorry for him – even though I hate the wee cunt. Booda tugs ma jacket an we leave. His sobs trail down the close after us an echoin. It's like one of them films where someone's locked in a secret room an ye hear cryin at night but ye can never find the door.

I leave Booda at his close an walk down Kirkshaws.

To Be or not to Be

We're up the Galleria me an Carmen an Daz. He's tryin to get over The Horrible so Carmen suggests takin the wee cunt out. He's never done talkin biologyspeak an rantin about these two Comp O-levels he's got.

To be or not to be? That's Hamlet. *Shakespeare,* he goes every time he gets the fuckin chance.

Do you like Shakespeare?

Some stupid burd'll say an he's off all about how Shakespeare's a genius an all the plays he's wrote (specially if the burd knows fuck all about Shakespeare).

Oh aye, James, not that old shite again, Carmen goes an leans over to the bird an says,

We've heard this pish a million times. C'mon, James, EastEnders! Eh? What about that then?

That's what I'm tryin to say!

An he'd come out wi the punch line;

Hamlet *an that was just the EastEnders of its time.*

But Carmen's as pished off wi him chattin up burds as me. She stands swishin about her drink singin the EastEnders tune.

Doo do do do do do doooo do do do do do do do do do do do dooo.

Don't grins out the side of his mouth an leans in closer to
the burd but Carmen shoves her head between them, it's like
a coconut shy out there.

*Doo do do do do do doooo do do do do do do
do do do do do dooo.*

She's blastin their ears an laughin. But its not a laugh. It's
to taunt him. She's sayin, *I know what the fuck yer game is,
James. Don't kid me.*

I've worked his game out too. He sits in at night
memorisin lines an quotes them to burds. It's impressive the
first couple of times but after three or four ye know the exact
same stuff's comin out an ye cringe.

He's fed up wi Carmen rippin the pish so he goes to buy a
round. He buys a lot of drink; specially if there's a new burd
in the company. He takes tenners in the bank an changes
them into twenties. If he's got enough he gets a hunner
pound note an whips it out. Had the same hunner pound
note for six months once. He'd just wraps whatever money
he's got inside it.

Another thing, he always buys a fresh orange wi two
voddys in it an lets the town know he's on the orange juice. I
feel like shoutin,

*D'ye want yer usual two voddys slipped in
here while ye're off snortin whizz in the bog,
Don't Call Me Daz, or I'll punch yer cunt in?*

But I don't.

We're in the Galleria. He's goin on about *Hamlet* but no
cunt even knows who Hamlet is except if it's mibbi a cigar.
They're specially thick this night when it comes to
Shakespeare so he's in the huff. This tart sits at the table wi
her fat ugly pal. The tarts filled the holes in her skin wi make
up. Big red lips an tight black strides. Ye'd shag her – that's
about it. Good body. She's lookin at Daz the same as she's

lookin at every guy in the pool room. Carmen's up at pool an she's won four games so Tart thinks I'm on ma own too. There's this zip on her black top. She looks in ma eyes an

WIDTH FOUR INCHES OF CLEAVEAGE

I'm not into tits so she flaps them at Don't. He loves tits. He is a fuckin tit in fact. He's mesmerised. It's as if her tits're that snake out *Jungle Book* only they're not singin,

They're singin, *Suck me now an my sister beside me wobble wobble.*

Daz goes to the bog an nudges for me to follow. In the bog there's a guy slumped in a pizza of sick. Slabberin an gruntin. He couldn't commit suicide if ye gave him a grenade wi the pin out. He must know Daz cos wi this super human effort he says,

Daaaaaaaaaaaz . . .

An **BLAM!!** Daz KO's the guy wi a hook.

You're a fuckin liberty taker, I goes.

He laughs. Blood's tricklin down the guy's mouth an his face's swellin up. I hate that. He's always takin liberties. What can ye do? I can't lift the guy up, sober him up, an tell him:

Sorry for the missin teeth but ma mate's a fuckin liberty taker. I'm a nice guy but.

Daz's pishin away like nothin's happened. He's got a wee dick, an he's right close to the pisher tryin to hide it wi two hands. Mine is nothin to write home about but it's an elephant's trunk compared to Daz's. I always wonder what the burds think when he whips that out.

I starts tellin him this joke. He doesn't want to listen to cos he's not sure if the jokes on him. We're walkin out the bog an I hears the thud of one last boot at the pile of sick.

There's this guy right?

He nods.

An he's got this wee toty dick . . . I wiggles ma pinkie an he looks to see if I mean him. I do but he can't tell if I do so I wiggles the pinkie again.

Deedly deedly dee . . . I goes.

As we pass Carmen bent over the pool table an he slaps her arse. She looks over her shoulder without straightenin up an laughs. I feel like bootin him round the place. But I don't boot Don't. There's still the joke about his dick.

Deedly deedly dee . . . I go again, but louder, an he detects anger an listens to the joke.

So this guy – he lumbers this Tart – that tart over there in fact . . .

She fancies me . . .

Aye . . . well . . . good luck to ye then. Anyway he lumbers this tart an she takes him back to her place. She whips the gear off an

*she's lyin wi all the tackle on . . . sussies . . . open crotch
knickers . . . he whips out the pinkie dick – pinkie dick . . .*

I repeat it an laugh right at him. I say *pinkie dick* like
I'm callin him names. He doesn't know what to do. Thick as
fuck when it comes to catchin hiself on. That's how he gets
angry an punches cunts for nothin. He can't tell if they're
laughin at him or not.

*. . . right he's standin wi the pinkie dick out an she bursts
out laughin . . . pointin . . .*

Who ye goin to satisfy wi that thing? she goes fallin back on
the bed.

Know what he says?

What? He's fuckin ragin now.

*He say's me! That's who an fucks the pinkie dick in. Wiggle
wiggle. Chuckin a sausage up a fuckin close.*

He likes it if it's him in the joke an he comes out tops. He
sits close to Tart an I says,

*But he has to send her a postcard next day to let her know she's
been fucked.*

He lifts his fresh orange an secret vodka an starts talkin to
Tart who's rollin a joint on the table.

Bad for ye that.

What dope? she goes as if it's a life-givin elixir.

Does ye right in.

Who the fuck says?

It's a scientific fact.

Carmen's lookin. I don't know if she's watchin me, Daz or
the Tart but she's got the mad stare an she's whackin the
balls harder. I can hear then thrum across the table an collide
in anger.

That right? Scientific fact is it? goes Tart.

Aye . . . messes wi yer DNA.

Yer what?

DNA. Know what that stands for.

Fuck me – a world record for gettin deoxyribonucleic acid into the conversation. I claps an he ignores me.

Deoxyribonucleic acid, he says an leans back foldin his arms.

Poxy whit acid?

Acid? says Fat Ugly Burd. *Where?*

She's out her tree the now on acid.

Fat Ugly Burd's fascinated by the exit sign above her head.

I'm a boxer, goes Daz.

I thought so.

Yes. Fuckin Yes. He hates that. When they say they think he's a boxer. That means they noticed his bashed in face.

How? How d'ye know that?

Yer nose, it's flattened right in yer face.

Ma shoulders're goin up an down. He wants to punch lumps out her. Fuck. She's tearin him to bits an she's not even tryin. Ma kind of Burd. I wish I could work her voice. Say somethin about his wee dick or his folded ET face.

He's had enough. Up he gets an stands too close to Carmen. I can't hear what they're sayin but she keeps lookin over an pullin her eyebrows down. But fuck it. I leans over to this Tart an fills her in on what to say when Daz comes back from the bar.

He sits an dunts a pint of Guinness for me an makes a show if his half pint of orange.

You on the ginger the night? goes the Tart.

Fat Ugly Burd laughs. *Granny know your out?* she says.

My Granny's dead, he goes, all sombre, expectin the burds to burst out greetin sayin how sorry they are. But they spray the place wi Super lager an fall about laughin. He's fuckin boilin mad.

The Tart's quick.

Know who you look like? she goes.

He sits up ready to forgive them, an ready for a Steve McQueen or a Patrick Swayze or a Richard Geere.

EEE fuckin TEE, she snorts an the joint's hangin from her limp hand. She's wrapped round her pal an they're pointin at Daz goin,

EEE TEE, phone home.

He's starin in the distance an dribblin his secret voddy. His Adam's apple's goin up an down. He's got a big Adam's apple I'll give him that. He's tryin to ignore them.

Hey where's yer fuckin spaceship?

He takes another gulp. The whole pool hall's lookin. The Burd's're like two laughin-faced hyenas now. Climbin all over each other wi laughter. I'm creasin maself. But Daz's still lookin at the wall. Tart's doin her best gruff extraterrestrial voice.

Phone . . . phone ho-ome, EE TEE, Pho-one ho-ome.

She leans right up to him.

EE TEE, phone home yer Granny's dead.

His eyes turn black. I'm expectin him to go in the bog an weld the drunk guy again cos no way he's hittin burds in front of the whole pub. He stands slow. Fat Ugly Burd cottons on an shouts,

Aye EE TEE, yer Granny's dead – ye've to phone home right away. She got ran over wi a Zanussi.

The whole pub's sniggerin. Wee guys're turnin away in case he takes the head off them.

BOOSH

He smashes his glass on the floor an storms out. Carmen tries to get him to stay. She holds his jacket an he whips it away. Usual. The bouncers wait till he's halfway out an walk behind him.

What a night. Fuckin magic. I'm lovin it that much I leans over an gives Tart a kiss.

ZINNNNNNN
NNNNNNNN
NNNNNNNN
NNNNNNNN
NNGGGG

Big fuckin mistake. There's Carmen behind me bangin the blows in.

D'ye want her? D'ye want her? Take the fuckin Cow. Tart. The two burds laugh all the more. I struggle away but Carmen's Limpet Mine Naggin.

Yap yap yap yap yap . . .

She won't stop. In an out the guy's bog an she follows me. In an out the wummin's bog an she follows me callin me all the perverts. All over the pub an she won't leave me alone. Glued at the fuckin shoulder.

Yap yap yap yap . . .

Ye let him go an he's out wi us for a night out . . .

Some fuckin pal you are, he's away home.

It's goin right through me. How to get away?

Bright idea.

I lift ma pint. Drink it, an launch the glass in the Humphrey Bogart mirror. Poor Humphrey explodes in a million bits all over the pool players. The bouncers run at me an I knock the first one clean out wi a straight right. But the other one gets his arms round ma an wi the help of a few cunts they shove me out the door. I kick a few chairs over an smash the front door on the way out – but that's it.

I'm outside waitin on the Polis. They don't come. Somethin worse comes. Her. Carmen.

She's goin an won't stop.

I've got ma hands over ma ears an I'm shoutin.

Stop it. Stop it. Please stop it.

I go to grab her hair but she ducks an drags her nails down ma chest an face at the same time. Nails're like knives. Blood's runnin out me. Still got the scars. She runs like fuck but only as far as the Job Centre an stands givin me abuse wi her head tilted to one side an her hand on her hip. The Polis don't come an she follows me all the way to Kirkshaws keepin behind me an nag nag naggin.

I go to bed an she sleeps on the couch.

Fuck me! I wake up the next mornin a mile in the Douglas Estate wi a bin bag over ma legs an this other bin bag, wi a hole poked for ma face, over the top of ma body. I'm doin this a lot now, goin to sleep in one place an wakin up in another. Rememberin fuck all. I just put it down to sleep walkin.

Bin Bags an Bushes

Somethin prods me. First thing's the hardness of the ground an all these jaggy bits. Next the smell: unmistakably damp ground. The rustle of the bin bags's thunderin through ma hangover. I'm in a black plastic womb reluctant to be born into the day.

I pokes the head out. When ye wake up in yer house yer sight bounces out an stops on walls a ceilins. But here it bounces out an keeps on goin. Grass bushes trunks branches twigs blue air white air clouds – out into space. Or sideways across rollin fields undulatin like yer stomach. The whole fuckin world's sick. Sick.

Ma mouths like a barber's floor an there's green sick an Buckfast on the back of ma tongue. I sit up an I don't know if it's the bags or me that's creakin. I'm twenty feet in from the path an down towards Viewpark there's a man an a dog. They keep lookin back. The dog's tuggin on it's leash. The leaves're blowin an rattlin in the breeze but the world's hard. Hard an fuckin heartless. An me. A solitary figure in shinin black in the green an yella landscape.

The guy sees me lookin an drags the dog an picks up pace. Mibbi he prodded me to make sure I'm alive as he passed. Mibbi his dog sniffed me out.

Hello hello, woofity fuckin woof. What's all this then owner?
Some cunt in a bin bag.

Owner lets doggy woggy sniff ma crotch till I move an then he fucks off. He's lookin at me again, unless there's this special bush he's in love wi. I puts ma hand up to ma cheek cos it's itchin like fuck. It feels like a relief map of the Himalayas an then I remember her nails rampagin down ma face. The long grooves of cuts've froze over wi their own wee ice age of blood. The snaky crusts crack to the touch an itchin on ma face tells me blood's tricklin. I try smilin an it's like I'm wearin a restrictive rubber lattice. More cracks, more blood. I try frownin an it's much the same only I don't look as happy I suppose. I looks down ma jumper an see the same arrangement on ma pecs.

There's crushed fags an loose matches in ma pocket. I'm like the SAS when I do this stuff. Methodical right down to twenty quid down the sock. That's for the pub. Thing is, I never remember it. All I ever remember's fallin asleep on the couch, or the floor, or in the bed. I never ever remember preparin for sleepin rough in woods. I light up. I don't even like it. It's makin me gag an I boak a wee pile of green sick on the grass. Ye'd expect the grass to shrivel up like bean sprouts in a wok, but it doesn't. I finish the fag anyway an last night comes back in film clips.

There's drizzle comin down on me. I don't move. It's coolin ma head. I'm hot an dry. Every drop's hissin like I'm a fryin pan under a leaky roof. I'm smokin wi the drizzle droppin down on ma hair. I feel I'm the only cunt in the world. No – that's a lie – I wish I was the only cunt in the world cos then they'd be no one to face. I never want to break breath to another human bein as long as I live.

See when things're goin bad. When yer down? That's when ye shouldn't think. It's bad for yer health, thinkin.

WARNING BY HM GOVERNMENT.

THINKING CAN SERIOUSLY DAMAGE YOUR HEALTH.

IN FACT IT CAN BE DOWNRIGHT FUCKIN FATAL.

EVERY HUMAN BEING CARRIES A GOVERNMENT HEALTH WARNING.

I starts thinkin. An right when the rain runs off ma nose first time, I wish I never left ma wife. Ma shoulders start goin up an down. From a distance I could be laughin. I wish the past three years was a bad dream. I could be wakenin up to wanes runnin about right now. She'd be makin coffee for ma hangover an headin up her Maw's wi the wanes. I'd mibbi watch black an white films wi a couple of bottles of Irn Bru. Mibbi get a Chinkees after. Chicken cashew nuts. No, Kom Po chicken – that's great for a hangover. Andrews' Liver Salts mibbi.

But there's no goin back. There's me, the bin bags, the drizzle an the big empty Douglas Estate. Wi food an drink an fags I'd sit here forever. Tired. That's what I am. Fuckin knackered wi life. I could settle for death if this's what it was like – under this tree for eternity. I could handle that. But see if there is a God, I'm fucked. An see if there's no God? I'm fucked. Too many things've happened. I try disappearin in loneliness but I can't. How can I experience self-pity? There's nothin to like in me. I'm seein the wanes every fortnight. I can't bring them in the house. It's a battle leadin up to it an a battle after they go back. Carmen's gettin worse an I'm gettin weaker.

Don't know what it is about these woods.

In Blackpool it was big walks along the beach. Lookin for somethin. I used to think it was a good shell or a good bit of wood, or better a pile of treasure from some Spanish galleon wrecked in the Irish sea.

In Sikeside I thought I found it wi mushies an acid an

walks up the canal an the big house. There *was* an answer
but fucked if I could see it.

In Kirkshaws it's walkin for hours down the Estate, or
sittin lookin in the burn, or at trees wavin in the wind. Mibbi
up the trees wi Booda – holdin on tight – gettin blew about
by some wind or gale. Lettin it happen. Nearly there! No
answer. Still lookin.

When I wake up down the Estate I go for long walks an
see it in things. Daffodils, they've got it. Pine cones. Mibbi
the odd Robin. Even leaves fallin out trees. Blackies singin
after a shower of rain an movin circles in puddles.
Somewhere through the woods it's shinin like a crashed star.
But every time I get to the other side it's further on – or
further back.

This milky mist's leavin the fields. The M8's buzzin faster
an faster as the mornin gets a grip. I pick some daffodils. Ma
guts flop up to ma head when I bend over. I change to a
crouch an walk about on ma hunkers. She'll like these. The
stems break like rhubarb stalks an the heads've got trumpets
ye could drink tea out. They're so good they look artificial.
Twelve. Good number. Like a dozen red roses. Ye see it in
films: he brings a dozen red roses an next clip the roses're on
the silk sheets. An ye know they'll be in there grindin away
soon. A dozen red roses an she'll let ye shag her. Thirty quid!
Ye can get a hoor down Anderson for twenty. Ten for a blow
job. But this isn't sex. This's *let me back in the house*. Her
house. I've wrecked mine. She's already said it. She said
she'd never say it. She fuckin promised.

Promise? I goes.

I'll never say it.

But ye're sayin that now what about when we fall out?

*We'll not fight down there an make a cunt of ourselfs in front of
the new neighbours.*

Right. No fightin.

No fightin. Fresh start.
Fresh start.
An ye won't say it.

It's OUR house.

An over she comes an kisses me soft on the cheek, then soft on the lips, then wet an hard on the lips. Presses her bone on me an tongues me. YAHOO bedtime.

But she still says it. First time we're arguin.

I want you out ma house.

I don't say nothin.

I don't want you here. It's over.
Fuck off.
Out.
You said ye'd never . . .
Don't give it that pish. It's ma house an I want you out here.
Ye'll need to get the Polis to get me out.
I'm tellin ye I'll get them if you don't . . .

I wondered how long it was goin to take. She takes a flaky right between the word *don't* an *move*.

MOOVE!!!!!!!!!!!! I'll phone them right now ya baaaaastaaaaaaard.

So that was that. You could hear the whole close listenin. She's stampin about. The wane starts roarin an she's goin . . .

See – see what ye've done now ya rotten bastard.

Away an fuck a duck.

I says an walks. Fuck her. Fuck every cunt. Fuck me an all.

But that was another day. This's the daffodil day. I reach the motorway. I look good on the edge of the M8. Somethin out the Hillbillies. Unshaved. Bloodshot eyes. Hair like fibre-optics. Scarred down the right side of ma face. Crusted blood. Cars're slowin an lookin. Not cos of the blood but.

I've got this big bunch of daffodils fluorescent yella against the grey exhaust-stained sides of the motorway.

I chaps the door an she opens it, glances at the daffodils, an walks away. I can tell just looking at her that she's been with somebody last night.

Hurricanes and Hatred

We were a hurricane, whirlin passion. Now I'm death warmed up. The mornin sun's sore on ma eyes an her make up's slurped all over her face: *Rocky Horror Picture Show*.

Want tea?

Bitter. Her head's tilted. I want to shag her white skin, to defile, to come all over her neck an shoulders. To show her she's mine.

No I don't want fuckin tea, I says.

Sharp breath. Folded arms.

Make it for maself then, she goes, an storms across the room. I want to shag her an I want to kick the shit out her.

You do that.

Don't worry I will.

SLAM

She knows I want to know who the fuck she was wi last night. Even the doors just painted look yella – tarnished. The white doesn't like bein white.

I tries to kiss her. She bites me the cunt. Right through ma skin. Bleedin. Now SHE'S rattlin pots an pans like I came in late – like I'm fuckin about. It's ma grass that's gettin cut here.

Wrap more barbed wire round ma heart – don't bother about me.
I shouts

What?

Fuck all – that's what.

BOOSH BOOSH BOOSH

Cups explode on the scullery floor. Who the fuck does she think she is? Who the fuck does she think she's dealin wi? Ma veins're poppin out an I'm takin deep breaths.

Did ye smash another cup dear . . . tut tut, you're always breakin things, I goes in ma best posh voice.

She says fuck all. She's even stops movin but Aul Cunt down the stairs hasn't. She's all over the house tryin to find the room where the argument is. I try an rile her again.

If it's not hearts ye're breakin it's crockery dear.

Silence. She's still not movin. All I can hear's Aul Cunt shufflin from room to room starin at the ceilin for dents.

Then.

BOOSH BOOSH BOOSH

Three beauties. I feels Aul Cunt jumpin an shrapnel's rattlin like ice all over the scullery. Carmen's in there in a flurry of mad snow. Fuckin Snow White.

I hear her comin so I tap the fingers lookin at the telly. She waltzes in sippin her tea like a seal.

Mmmm. This's great tea.

Cool as ye like. As if some fuckin poltergeist wrecked the kitchen. Fuckin maddie. Ma veins're out more now but I'm not lettin on. I'm lookin at the telly. Open uni fuckin versity.

Legs crossed. I see her inner thigh. Last night's perfume's floatin in the room. Sometimes I watch her contortions as she watches the telly. Pullin her lip, screwin her eyes up. A pause on a half-smile before it flowers to the real thing. An sadness.

She can do sadness too. Fuck me! The worse she treats me the more I'm fallin in love wi here. What a fuckin dick.

D'ye like nuclear physics? I says.

Eh?

I said d'ye like this – nuclear physics.

More than I like you but less than Neighbours.

Cunny funt.

I get maself a coffee. I'm pleased I haven't cracked up. I think about a walk in the woods. A walk in the woods. Calm. We could talk. In the woods.

Carmen . . . ?

Espiside park an she slams the door. She turns back wi this stupid lookin smile an swaggers off. Short skirt. Schoolgirl legs. I'm jealous. Some cunt's been rubbin up an down them legs. Seen her from the back in Stars an thought,

Oh aye – a schoolie out to get herself fucked the night. An I'm just the man for that job.

So he slides up, *hello there doll, fancy a wee dance?*

Fuckin wanker. An she's sayin *aye* an dartin her eyes about for cunts that might know me.

Lust. I wish I never had it. I wish sex didn't exist. It's doin ma head in. I'm dyin cos she's been wi some other cunt. But in a couple of weeks I'll be chasin some other schoolgirl legs in some dancin somewhere. What I want – an this's the truth – what I really want's her to be faithful an me to fuck everythin in sight. That's what every man wants. But that's not goin to happen. Is it?

Love? What the fuck's love? She swears blind she loves me. Fuck! The way she looks at me. I imagine she's a gypsy.

Raglin fuckin road. Know the song?

> *On Raglin road*
> *Of an autumn day*
> *I saw her first an knew*
> *That her dark hair*
> *Would weave a snare*
> *That I might one day rue.*
> *I saw the danger an yet I walked*
> *Along the enchanted way.*
> *And I said let grief,*
> *Be a fallin leaf,*
> *At the dawnin of the day.*

The grass's wet an she's leavin milky tracks. She turns an there's this look. She's hurtin. I feel sorry for her. I don't want to but I feel fuckin sorry. Guilt an remorse – that's what she's feelin.

This wee bird's rustlin it's wings an floatin near her. I shakes rain off ma feet an it makes wee arches. It's quiet as fuck.

Carmen.

What?

I smile but she turns away. She can't want to look in ma eyes. People that just meet look in each others eyes all the time. But soon the badness gathers like cataracts an they don't look. They keep the other eyes in their mind somewhere. Every time ye look at the eyes ye keep in ye're mind ye see the gap between them an yer lover's an ye cry. Ye cry inside. The depths ye cry're gouged by the difference between the eyes that WERE an the eyes that are.

Fuck I'm greetin now. Out in the open. She sees me an turns away. I look up twistin branches. Mibbi It's up there.

Up where twigs reach at the sky.

She's rollin this bud between her forefinger an thumb. The syrupy moisture's tricklin down her fingers. *Sweet tears* I says into maself. She's cryin out her fingers.

I stare at the canal. Terrified of it when I was a wane. Called it the Nicky-naull. Had nightmares.

Fallin in brown water an the banks gettin further away. Ma Da an Maw an all these other people reachin, but I'm sinkin. I'm smotherin. Water gurglin up ma nose. Can't breath. I wake an I've pished the bed. If ye pish the bed ye'll know this. Sometimes ye pish on yer own face. Ye pish the bed lyin on your back wi a hard on in yer sleep. The pish goes all over yer face.

No cunt needs the canal. I can't remember it gettin used. Except swans. Swans on it. Their bellies're always covered in rust. But that's where they live. Swan slum.

There's this web of drizzle on Carmen's hair. She looks like a wee girl goin to her communion.

I love you, she goes right out the blue.

Oh aye ye showed that last night.

Can we not forget about last night?

How the fuck can I forget it?

She comes over an grabs ma arm.

It'll never ever happen again. Promise.

She kisses ma cheek an sinks her head on ma chest.

I'm lookin at her neck thinkin of some other cunt's lips there. She looks round the place an goes.

I'm goin to make sure I'm here every day from now on it's . . . it's . . .

She jumps like a fuckin primary wane. Fuck I shat maself.

Look a little robin . . .

A robin? A fuckin robin? Ye nearly give me a heart attack.

It lands shakin waterdrops from a twig. Cheeky wee cunt

stares at her then me. We're smilin first time in ages. Really smilin.

Hey Robin, stop lookin at ma burd an get yerself to fuck, I goes.

Tweet tweet, she goes, an it looks at her as if she's mental.

It blinks an fucks off. She keeps wonderin when I'm goin to crack. But I don't crack. I say,

See if we stand quiet all the animals'll gather round like we're not here.

She licks this drop of water from her lip an as her tongue slides back the jealousy tears through me again. It's a real pain in yer veins. It's not just an emotion the aul jealousy.

I feel dead, she goes.

Wish ye were.

No honest – I feel dead . . . It's a calm dead. That's what rest in peace means . . . it must be this.

What the fuck're you on about?

She's got her hand out palm upwards an I know she's goin to try an explain.

I mean . . . we could've died right . . . an we're . . . wanderin . . . if ye know what I mean. We could be wanderin about not knowin we're dead . . . know . . . not knowin we're wanderin about but . . . but not worried about it cos . . . know what I mean?

Clear as fuckin pigshit.

See you.

No I'm only kiddin I know what ye mean.

Do ye?

Aye.

I touch her shoulder an her arm snakes round me. We're welded thegether by bad things. In the cold rain she kisses me an her lips're sticky wi the stuff off the bud. I drags her out the rain.

We're under this tree holdin each other tight. Not sayin nothin. All the words ever invented hold spikes in them for us now. There's not a lot we can say without barbed pain

tearin at us. So we talk wi hands an kisses an breath on
necks. We talk like animals talk. There's silence an chirpin
birds an hissin rain an she goes,

Marry me.

She squeezes ma hand an water's runnin down our skin. I
squeeze her hand back an kiss her.

When? I goes an she laughs.

An I laugh.

An there's this wee robin peelin an unpeelin it's eyes at us.

Big Love Star Talk

It's like I've never been in love before. Thinkin about us gettin married I starts fallin in big love. Been divorced a year now. Gettin married might stop all the shenanigans. I'm doin things like wakin up in the middle of the night an watchin her sleepin. Sleepin beauty – that's what she's like. Or Snow White. Her hair's fallin over the covers like shadows an her face's white. The moon sometimes lights her skin an she looks gentle – aye – gentle. Breathin so light I think she's dead. I nudge her an she groans. Not a sex groan – more like a wane. A frightened wane. Frightened an trapped. Trapped an stopped strugglin.

I shove ma nose in her neck an lock ma knees in the back of her legs like Lego. I love the air draggin itself along her skin before gettin sucked up ma nose. I shove ma arms down by her belly an rest ma hands between her thighs. Not sex. Somethin else. But not sex.

This night I wakes up an ma right arm's numb wi pins an needles so I works it out from under her easy. She gives the wee moan again an a rush goes through me like an electric shock without pain. I realises I love her too much. It scares me an I go an stand at the windie. Big stars're up there an one on it's todd's skinklin away. It's me that star. It's up in the night an there's nothin talkin. It's burnin an there's no cunt lookin. So I send maself out there. Right out through deep space. It sounds mad but that's what I do. Not ma body. Me. I'm beside this star an we're talkin. Star language. Carmen's thrashin about in some nightmare. It's lonely in space but it's a good lonely. It's not the big empty lonely ye feel on this planet, it's a new lonely. It's got clearness an coldness an bigness. Ye can breathe cool an deep an yer pain's burned up by the white light.

What the fuck am I on about? See me! See ma head, it wanders all over the shop sometimes. Most people make their head think for them. Open a shop or a business or somethin. But me? Ma head? It thinks for it's fuckin self an off it goes wherever it wants. An it makes me do things. It thinks an there's me doin it. No in between. There's no:

Oh hold on there old bean mind. I'm not chuckin this petrol bomb in that pub no no not me . . .

Ma thoughts're ma actions sometimes. I'm arguin wi a guy in the pub an next thing I'm punchin lumps out him. Fuck ye. We're on the deck rollin about an cunt's're puttin the boot In left right an centre. See if I could just go . . .

Don't throw that punch.

or

Don't stick the head on him.

or

Don't fling that glass through the gantry,

I'd be all right. But I can't. Even worse, on the drink I don't know what I'm doin half the time. On the drink ma head makes me go wild as fuck.

But where am I? I'm tellin ye how much I love her. The reason I'm on the subject of ma head is that now I know one of two things're goin to destroy me:

1. Carmen: cos I can't control ma love no more.

2.   Ma head cos I can't hardly make it do anythin I want
     any more.

I goes back to bed an locks into her again. It's matter of time now. I crush in about her. An I cry. I cry a lot cos I wake up who knows how much longer an her hair's all stickin to ma face. Ma tears've dried to glue an outside the skinklin star's disappeared an deep purple clouds wi black linins rule the sky.

Is that Your Car, Sir?

But I might've knew it'd take more than thinkin about gettin married to change things. I'm in ma own wee dream world for a while. But when life starts happenin all about me ma dreams crash. All the wee people an situations I invented fall away wi their mouths wide an no screams comin out. No screams at all.

Reality. This neighbour. A right sleazy bastard. I hate him but he hates me more. He phones The Polis an The Housin all the time. I can't move for him peepin out the curtain an whisperin. He's a wee fat bastard that looks like he sprays his body wi chip fat every mornin. His hair's black an welded to his head. His wife's the exact same only wi tits an a fanny. Christ ye should get jail for lettin them breed.

But they breed all right. Oh aye. Skweek skweek skweek their bed goes every night. She howls like a laughin faced hyena an he grunts an flops on her belly like a walrus. Make ye puke. An Carmen'll not go near me cos it makes her sick an all. So ye can imagine it. He's gettin his hole every night an all I can do's wrestle wi it like it's a crocodile. Know what I mean? Choke the bishop . . . German tank. Wank.

I'm prayin for an excuse to kick his cunt in. Any excuse.

I'm not a violent guy but sometimes ye've got to teach them a lesson. Well he needs teachin.

Get the picture? So listen to this.

Carmen goes to the van this night: *Two bottles Irn Bru, two Marathons, forty Club King Size, a Double Nougat, a Curly Wurly an whatever ye want for yerself* . . . I shouts out the windie. She nods all the way to the van without lookin up. Her arms're folded an she's got this white woollen dress on. It's glowin in the yella streetlights. Stickin to her skin. Can see every groove. I decide I'm goin to shag her so I shoves a porno in to warm her up.

I flops on the couch an sparks up a joint. I'm still at the bodybuildin an I'm jaggin maself up wi Deca Durabolin an Testosterone. Solid. Fifteen stone now so I am. I relax at night wi a couple of joints a few cans an a bottle of Buckie.

So there's me lyin on the couch. Restin from a chest shoulders an arms night at the gym. Stoned. A long time passes cos the porno's nearly finished an no Carmen. I rolls off the couch an looks out the windie. Nothin. Only the young team wi baseball bats an stuff gettin it thegether to mangle the Mad Squad. *But where the fuck is she?* says I. Ma brain's doin overtime. The young team waves up an I wave back. *YO!* I shouts, *Mick ma man!* they shout back.

All this the I'm noticin this Pump Up Yer Trainers music.

doof doof doof DOOF WHOO WHOO

doof doof doof DOOF WHOO WHOO

doof doof doof DOOF WHOO WHOO

I realise there's a party in Greasy Bastards. I know what yer thinking, but that's where she is. Fuck me!!! She goes to the van an halfway back up the close she disappears. I goes fuckin mental.

Aul Nosy Bastard down the stairs phones,

Oh by the way, she goes, *Carmen's in the party next door.*

Carmen's in the fuckin what? I goes. *What the fuck's goin on?*

Carmen's never spoke to the Greasies in her life. Nosy Aul Bastard down the stair's not content wi that. No way. She starts sayin stuff like:

I'll tell ye this, there's no way I'm goin to a party wi the like of her again . . . Hussy . . . I'm tellin ye she's a scrubber.

I'm callin Aul Bastard all the hoors under the sun an shoutin, *Don't you talk about ma burd like that!* But on an on she goes all about how she left cos Carmen's in the room wi this bird's man . . .

BLACKOUT RAGE

. . . AN THERE'S THE PHONE SWINGIN ON ITS WIRE . . .

I'm bangin at the fuckin door. Ye could fry eggs on me. I'm hot as fuck. Electric. High fuckin voltage. There's scurryin an tooin an froin then Greasy Bastard opens the door. He's sweatin an right there I think he's been shaggin ma wife. But Carmen comes sideways out a room an so does this guy. A right flashy good-lookin bastard. The kind ye keep well away from yer burd.

Well. I'm goin mental an Carmen worms out an stands behind me. I can smell sweat an perfume. One string of hair's stickin to her neck. Flashy Bastard lifts this big fancy vase an swings it right at me. I fuck the head right on it as its comin at me an it splinters in a million bits. The blood's runnin out ma head an he's shitin hiself. He can't move. Froze. I crash the head on him an cos he's already against a wall he's out like a light I put the boot in a couple a times so he gets the message. Turns out he's a commando type in the army. *Special Forces? Some fuckin Army!* says I.

Greasy Bastard whips out this big blunt bread knife an lunges. I've still got the scar. I grabs the blade an laughs like Jack Nicholson in *The Shinin*. He shites hiself. I grab his hair wi ma left hand an swings him round into the close. I mind the first punch. It's a cross between a hook an a straight right. I get fifteen stone behind it an whack. But he ducks a bit. I'm tryin to break his nose but I scud the forehead. It bursts like a kipper an down he goes. I take the boot off his ribs an leave him wrigglin on the close floor.

Carmen goes to bed wi her clothes on so I can't see the love bites an ripped knickers.

The Polis don't come.

I goes to the Paki's next mornin for a couple of Supers. I comes in the close Greasy Bastard's on his hands an knees wipin blood off the floor.

Good Mornin, I goes, an he's said it back before he realises.

He's got stitches across his head. Puts his head down an scrubs frantic like he can't get this bit off. I goes in the house an bursts out laughin. Probably never got The Polis cos he tried to rip me wi that knife an then there's Action Man wi the big fancy vase an all that. He'll not want the Army to know some ordinary guy welded him. I mean, how'ye supposed to save the fuckin country wi that talent? Special fuckin Operations? He'll be needin special operations if he goes near ma burd again.

Next week Greasy Bastard sends a hunner people to ma door.

The Priest comes an asks if we want to get married.

The Housin comes an tells us to stop annoyin the neighbours.

The Polis come this night when I'm watchin *Flight of the Condor*. They tell me to stop the wild party an ask to see Carmen. I'm supposed to be doin her in. Wonder who the fuck that was? She's sleepin.

The Social comes. I'm in the lobby cupboard. Carmen's on a Monday Book an I'm still gettin ma giro no fixed abode. They look in the wardrobes. Carmen says the clothes're mine but I'm in London in jail or somethin.

A Jehovah's Witni comes.

Fuck off we're Catholics, says Carmen.

Off goes the Witni all humble an up come the Mormons.

Slam. Off ye pop Mormons. Good night.

An then we're out this night an the Polis break in. Greasy Bastard tells them we left the washin machine on an flooded the close. We might've left it on. If we fuckin had one. I goes bananas wi The Polis, *Fuck youse*, an all this I'm goin jumpin about like a madman. They don't even apologise. They're goin to lift **me** in fact. Carmen's holdin ma arms behind ma back an they're tryin to get me to hit them. The neighbours're all out to see what the fuck's goin on. The only one that's not out's Greasy Welded Hair Bastard an that's how I knows it's him. As If I need proof.

I decide to get the bastard once an for all.

Next week he putters in the street wi a beat-up Metro. Make ye sick they're all out there Mammy Grease, Daddy Grease, assorted Granny an Granda Greasies an some wee Greasies. They're inspectin this car like they know about motors. Christ, I don't know fuck all about motors but from behind the curtain I can see it's a fuckin rust bucket. An he's smilin up as if to say;

Well, Hard Man, what d'ye think of ma new car then? Us Greasies're really comin up in the world now eh!

I want to punch lumps out him but he's still wearin the bandage.

The next mornin do I not see the openin I've been lookin for? There's this horn beep beepin so I looks out the windie along wi a million other fuckers. It's not for me. It's drivin lessons. I waits in case it's the seventeen-year old blondie. An who comes bobbin out the close like he's goin to collect the European cup? Right: Greasy Bastard. Off he pops for drivin lesson number one. Right there Nosy Bastard phones up an goes,

That not terrible him drivin about wi no licence no insurance nor nothin.

I'm still not talkin to Carmen so I hands her the phone without sayin nothin. Nosy Aul Bastard fills her in.

Later on when Grease's back an skweek skweekin away there like drivin must turn him on. Or she's turned on cos he's a real man now wi a car. She starts her laughin faced hyena an I pick up the phone an phone The Polis. He flops on her belly gruntin an I'm thinkin it might be the same bed Carmen got her special operation on.

Hello, Coatbridge Police, can I help you? goes this posh voice.

I tells them there's this maniac in the street who's got a car. *It might be stolen,* I goes. I tells them he's screechin in the street like Mad Max an he'll kill a wane soon. The rust bucket wouldn't do twenty but I lays it on thick. An him just gave his wife one. Sittin sharin sweat soaked roll-ups an restin their bellies on their thighs.

The Polis come in the street an they're lookin round the cars. *Yes!* I says, *fuckin yes!!* I can't wait to see his face.

Fuck you an yer smelly wee Metro, I shouts. *Come on see this.* I tells Carmen an fills her in on what the score is.

She loves it an takes the scullery windie. I takes the livin room. The Polis look up an look in their wee books. Up they come. Windies're twitchin everywhere. Me an Carmen run to the door an press the ears on it. Probably that's what Greasy Bastard's doin too.

BANG
BANG
BANG

goes ma door. Me an Carmen jump up. We looks at each other.

BANG
BANG
BANG

goes the door again. Carmen crawls in the toilet an swings the door shut. I opens the door an there's two big Polis – the ones I was goin to do in the week before.

Mr Riley?

Aye?

Is that your car out there?

No, the wee Metro? IT BELONGS TO MA NEIGHBOURS!!! I shouts.

No . . . not the Austin Metro, Mr Riley, the Renault Four.

Fuck sake. Shut ma fuckin mouth. Do they not go an do me for no tax on the Renault Four an Greasy Bastard gets off scot-free? I'll stick to dishin out doins in the future.

Virtual Unreality

For some reason Don't Call Me's down at ma house when I arrive back from pickin the mushies this Sunday. It's me an Booda an we've got about five hunner. He's in the livin room wi Carmen.

Oh aye! What's goin on here then? goes Booda.

Carmen says ye'd be back soon, says Don't smilin lopsided.

So we are an look at this.

Rustle rustle.

Booda opens an ASDA bag an shoves it up to his face.

What's that?

Mushrooms, they're mad, says Carmen.

Fancy a wee shot, Jamesie?

He looks at Carmen but she looks away.

C'mon James – a day out wi the boys down The Estate.

So, anyway, we persuade him an boil up the mushies. Two cups each an we're zooooooooooooooooooooooooooooooomin down the Douglas Estate.

Crossin the M8's all right on the way down but I'd like to see ye crossin it two hour's later when yer right out yer chunkie. Ye can't tell the cars from the spaces.

The mushies're different from acid. It takes up to two hours to come up on acid an the trip's twelve or twenty-four

245

hours. The mushies take half an hour to get ye an they only last about six hours. A bad trip's easier to handle when ye know it'll be over soon.

By the time we're in the middle of the Estate we're trippin like fuck. The trees're movin all over the shop an the clouds're racin like a fast film.

We go through Vietnam – all these rhododendron trees. Behind them there's a steep slope down to a stream three feet wide. Another steep slope rises out the other end. We starts sneakin through the trees. We're comrades. Brothers in arms. All in a line watchin out for each other. I keep gettin these rushes from ma toes up an

DOING!!!!

Rattlin the inside of ma skull an

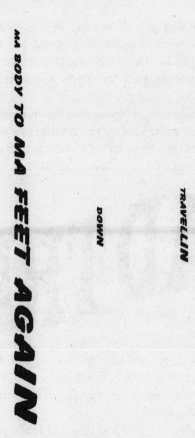

Like gigantic orgasms without a hard on. Ma body's a big dick an it's comin an comin an comin.

Out through Vietnam there's a dog an pony graveyard. Belonged to rich cunts that owned the land. Makes me laugh. I keep imaginin this funeral, an a hearse, an all these mourners an a big pony wi it's legs stickin out holes in the top of the coffin.

It bores us quick cos me an Booda's tripped there a million times.

If yer trippin they say always trip wi somebody ye trust. Somebody ye can stand bollock in front of. Me an Booda're like that. But this day Don't Call me Daz's makin me uneasy. An I know he's feelin bad. An I know Booda knows he's feelin bad.

Sometimes he's a right bastard Booda an seein as how we're in the dog graveyard he starts tellin this story about a dog. Fly as fuck. Winks at me so I know he's tryin to put Don't in a

He starts the story an starts movin deep into Vietnam.

Booda's no good at stories so I'll tell you it like you're Don't Call Me Daz. Imagine ye're on acid or mushies. Virtual Unreality. Freaky stuff.

Booda's neighbour's got this dog that looks like a Labrador but acts like a lump of wood. Thick as shit this dog. Irish Labrador, Booda calls it. We don't give a fuck about Irish jokes. Every other cunt's into the Provo's an the RA an Brits Out an all that shite. Fuck, some cunts we were at school wi're livin in Falls Road. But me an Booda couldn't give two fuck about it.

So there's this dog. Don't know it's right name but Booda calls it Sideboard.

Sideboard, c'mere, he shouts an Sideboard skulks off wi it's ears pressin on it's head.

Here's why:

Booda's neighbour starts her dabs. A bit young for them – eleven or somethin. Every time it's her bad week Sideboard gets in the washin basket an gets her knickers. There's trails of blood stained knickers up an down the street. They try everythin. Booda shows it knickers an kicks fuck out it a few times. But the mutt's obsessed. Usually underwear lyin about gives ye a thrill, but not knickers wi blood on them – fuck sake. Especially when it's rainin an they're sodden wi muck. Aw fuck!

His neighbour's scunnered wi the dog, wants it done in. Booda takes it down Vietnam an ties it to a tree. He takes out a hammer an lays in about its head. Of course Sideboard's not for puttin it's head down an screwin up it's eyes waitin for the blows so it's dodgin about goodstyle. Booda's missin five times for every good crack an the piercin whimper's ringin through the rhododendrons. Eventually it's lyin still an he sticks his ear on it's nostrils to see if it's breathin. Snortless. Dead as a fuckin doornail. He thinks.

Next day, he goes back down wi a can of petrol to burn it. It's gone. Fuckin offski. The rope's chewed through an blood's jellied on the grass an paw prints pad away to the darkest part of the forest.

Booda shouts an whistles.

Nothin.

Here, Sideboard, dinner.

Sideboard's in the trees goin, *Aye! So an I fuckin will!!!!*

So that's that. Escaped dog. Three days later it comes wanderin up the street wi a dented head matted wi blood. It avoids Booda like the plague specially when he goes near the hammer cupboard.

Don't is horrified at this story an starts lookin at us funny. Para. That's good cos I know, an Booda knows, the story's not finished. Booda starts tellin the rest of it into two moons in Don't's face.

A month later it's the neighbour's dabs again. Sideboard's got knickers planked all over the scheme. But the hammerin's made it even more crazy. It's bitin any cunt that goes near its buried panties. So there's cunts all over the Brig wi knash marks an they don't know what for. They're walkin by long grass an Sideboard jumps out an sinks the teeth in their leg. As they hop about Sideboard sneaks off an lies in wait at another pair of blood-stained panties.

So Booda's neighbour orders him to,

Take that fuckin thing away an do it in.

He arrives at ma door wi a bit of steel-fixin wire. Sideboard doesn't look too pleased at all. Not one bit. It's givin it flat ears an touchin its belly wi its tail expectin the whizz of a hammer.

This fucker's got to go, Mick.

The neighbour shouts down,

An I don't want to see it staggerin up this lane next week. Fuck sake, it'll start thinkin it's a cat.

Off we pop to do poor Sideboard in. We go down Vietnam. Booda gets a copin stone off the Roman bridge an wraps one end of the wire round it. Sideboard's very interested in the proceedin. She's been here before so she's also keepin a sharp lookout for hammers.

He shoves the stone to the edge of the bridge. There's no parapet. He lifts the dog. He's cradlin it like a wane. It shrinks into itself like all it's bones got shorter. I smell fear. Right before he chucks it in the river I think he's not goin to do it. But it's Booda. Next thing's the scrape of the boulder as he shoves it over the edge wi his foot an then the silence of the boulder fallin an him lettin go of the dog. Then

SPLOOSH

Birds an stuff explodin out everywhere.

WHIMPER

SPLOOSH

It's deep an still. Circular waves fragment on trees an rocks at the edge. Some waves make it back to the stream an get washed away like they never existed. The water's black. There's no bubbles. I mean ye'd expect bubbles as Sideboard gives out it's last. But nothin. Fuck all. Just the burn's stink an birds landin an water pushin past.

The water's that settled seconds after it ye can see trees an leaves reflected. I'm starin in to take ma mind off the dog. I imagine it . . . Arrivin sudden under cold black. Engulfed. Would it hold its breath? Do dogs do that? Do they **know** about drownin. Fuck! Do they know about dyin? Booda sparks up a spliff. It's all quiet.

Ever seen that film *Carrie*?

Ever seen that quiet bit at the end when her hand shoots out the grave? Every cunt in the pictures screams an shites theirselfs? Well that's what happens here. The bold Sideboard

up like a Trident fuckin missile. It's pullin it's lips over it's teeth an it's eyes're mad an wide. Booda flings the joint down thinkin it's a fag. He soon picks it up when he realises it's a joint.

Fuuuuuuckin baaaaaaaastaaaaaard! he says wi long vowels.

Superdog, I goes, *fuckin Superdog.*

I'm thinkin Booda'll say, *Well, deserves to live after survivin two tries.* But he says fuck all. He stares at the dog. So do I. He hands me the joint all absent minded cos he's noticed somethin.

It's paddlin like fuck but the wire's still attached to the stone. The stone's an anchor so it's round an round we go. Booda starts hurlin huge rocks at Sideboard tryin to KO it. By this time I don't want it to die. A real underdog – under the bridge, under the water an under the threat of death. But I can't say that to Booda. He's in his Hit Man mode.

Booda, there's cunts in them trees watchin.

He stops.

Where?

Up there I seen them an then they bolted to Viewpark. They'll be phonin the Polis. Let's get to fuck.

He believes me an chucks a whizzer that only hits Sideboard on the back wi a wet slap an thud an we're off.

By this time Don't's terrified an starin at Booda. I don't need to look at Booda. I know he's givin Don't the mad eyes an evil grin. Don't struggles for somethin to say to break the evil blackness that's sweepin through his body. There's a tremble in his voice. He's talkin the way ye'd talk to the bigger team searchin ye for money years ago. D's mind's doin overtime on Booda.

Have ye really been done wi attempt, Booda?

He goes all apologetic like.

Aye, Booda says an opens up this knife.

D jumps back a yard.

An now it's your turn — ye'll never leave these trees alive.

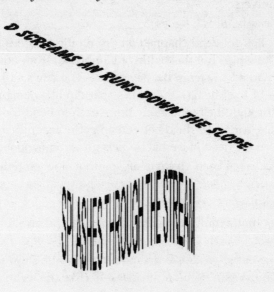

By the way, James, me an Carmen's gettin married, I shouts

Fuck me he falls to the ground an starts beatin the wet muck wi his fists an feet like two year aul.

No yer not no yer not! he shouts an bounces up an runs off again slippin all the way up the hill to darkest Cambodia.

Last we see him he's crashin through trees an screamin:

*AHHHHHHHHHHHHHHHHHHHHHHHHHHHHHHHHHHHHH
HHHHHHHHHHHHHHHHHHHHHHHHHHHHHHHHHHHHHHH.*

An we're laughin:

*Haaaaaaaaaaaaaaaaaaaaaaaaaaaaaaaaaaaaaaaaaaaaaaaaaaaaaaaaaaaa
aaaaaaaaaaaaaaaaaaaaaaaaaaaaaaaaaaaaaaaaaaaaaaaaaaaaaaaaaaaaaa
aaaaaaaaaaaaaaaaaaaaaaaaaaaaa.*

An then quiet. Like heaven. The uneasy goes away cos D's gone an it's me an Booda now. Our day. Our trip. Our Estate. Our universe.

I'm chokin, Booda, I goes.

The lips get dead chapped an dry on the Mushies. Fuck me – he whips out this bottle of Lambrusco from nowhere. They had a Christenin the day before. The day's still bright an cos of the Mushies the wine's sparklin like mercury. We look through the bottle a few times each to bend the world. Booda's grinnin at the other end an gettin magnified. The sky's on his head like a hat. It feels great. Smooooooooooth.

Ergonomic I keep on sayin an spinin it slow an tight in ma hand. *Er-go-no-mic er-go-no-mic er-go-no-mic er-go-no-mic . . .*

What the fuck's erganomik?

I don't answer. I keep goin . . .

. . . er-go-no-mic er-go-no-mic er-go-no-mic er-go-no-mic er-go-no-mic er-go-no-mic, an spinnin the bottle slow an pressin ma skin tight on the glass. It's like the feelin of the

glass an the wine inside an the word ergonomic's the Truth
of the Universe.

*This's a regal wine of cosmic proportion, Captain, I goes, a
shining nectar that needs no partaking of in the low terrain of mud
and cow slush we now traverse. This liquid needs a special place to
be consumed and **you!** Captain are charged with the finding of that
aforementioned place . . .*

He laughs like a plastic doll, his skin all bendin. I'm full of
that kinda pish on the Mushies. He laughs like we're two
wee boys an, for a split second, inside, I go infrared wi
happiness.

Words come pourin out like ma tongue's a page out a
book an the wind's shakin the words off. I see them screw
their way across an twist their way in his ears. They're
words of colours an transparencies. Big loud words've got
legs an arms like fat ladies an wee words look half starved to
death an scrawny like Ethiopians. Words like *blood* an stuff
ye can taste – they drag their selfs off ma tongue. Once the
words corkscrew in one ear, an drill through his brain an
cackle out his other ear he starts lookin serious for
somewhere to guzzle the plonk an spark up spliffs.

★

Hello!
   We've found it.
   It's up this tree.
   It's perfect.
   Yer feet

are on this big branch that's twenty feet up but it's like a
magnet. I could let go an slant back an not fall. Superglue
shoes. Rooted.

No way we're fallin off this thing. There's this other branch right at

elbow size

an its like a bar in the sky. At first it's a laugh an we do some *bar up a tree* jokes an laugh up through the last yella leaves of autumn into blue sky an cold white clouds. I looks round – the colours rape into me. It's like the ecstatic cramp of orgasm in ma head an I goes:

. . . shall I look back at you – autumn – in the gloamin of life an remember ye rollin yer golden starkness through ma scrapbook of a mind . . . shall I . . .

. . . but Booda places a joint in ma mouth. Gently, like yer Maw givin ye an unexpected lollipop when ye were a wane.

Lollipop, I starts to say. Then, *Loolipop looooolipop loo ooooo ooooo ooolipop*

The spliff's in ma lips an he lights it like it's somethin automatic he's done a million times. A surge runs through me an I cry a bit. He doesn't see me. I look the other way into the copper leaves of a maple tree.

All these things filmstrip ma head. Not black an white – brown like Victorian films an sometimes burstin wi Spielberg colour. I'm cryin like waterfalls inside cos the films're all about things we never got: good dinners, the love that never came our way when we were boys. The beatins, the screamin an shoutin, the absent cuddles, voices in the distance, the Da's fists. Then it all comes out me in one long but quick film strip in 3-D an plays for Booda on a grey cloud. He watches it an right down his ear I see the turbulence of his waterfalls all blue an foamin white an this black black water where these deep deep things are an I look away cos Booda's got things in him too dark to see – he's proved that.

It's as if all the love we were deprived of's in the tip of the joint he placed between ma lips. I feel his shoulder pressin close to mine an this tremendous voices in the distance warmth thrummin from him into me. We're twenty feet above the ground an a million feet above the ground.

Big black bars of silence fill the gaps between the trees.
Voices in the distance. Voices in the distance. Voices in the distance. Voices in the distance. Voices in the distance.

D'ye think we'll still be up trees when we're eighty? he goes.

A   long   pause

I turns sorrowfully an says,
No,

an turns away. The world'll drive us apart. He reads all these thoughts goin round ma head like a Hotpoint number four soapsud wash.

Everythin's gettin drove apart. We cling to the next thing that comes along. Voices in the distance. Then we're drove apart. It's you against every cunt, the whole world, no cunt wants to know. It's you against the whole sky, the universe, the whole fuckin shebang! Then it's The Big Empty. A wind made up from all the things ye hate about yerself an the world blows right through ye an all the coal fires an pieces on sausage won't warm ye. Then ye cling to somethin or somebody. Then ye're drove apart. Then The Big Empty. Then ye cling. Then we're drove apart by The Big Empty. The Big Empty's what Hell's like. There's no one there to cling to. Ye wander about inside yer own empty heart searchin for the things ye missed out on in life. But ye'll never find them cos ye don't know what they look like.

Voices in the distance.

Here – have another smoke of heaven, goes Booda.

We laugh an *kshhhhhh* he cracks the cork. It goes down ma throat ticklin like Christmas tinsel. It's light's comin out ma nose like two search beams an I'm torchin the ground below.

*MMMMMMMMMMMMMMMMMMMMMMMMMMMMM
MMMMMMMMMMMMMMMMMMMMMMMMMMMMMM
MMMMMMMMMMMMMMMMMMMMMMMMMMMMMM,*
I'm goin makin ma best searchbeam noise.

Ma eyes shine like billiard balls. They throb out onto some yella an red in the trees.

Next minute I sees all these wee fellas in the trees. It's all these elves an fairies an stuff holdin hands an dancin round an singin a song I can understand – but the words mean nothin. I nudges Booda.

What? he goes.

Elves an fairies! says I.

So it is! he says after I point them out. *So it is!!!*

So we watch them come over the grassy knoll beneath the trees an dance towards the river. Five. It's them dazzlin red an blue Pounstretcher colours an they're happy an they're dancin, an they're skippin. I never seen that much happy in the one wee bit in all ma life. They can't see up the tree an that's great. We see them at their play an they don't know we're here.

But that's not what they are. They're a man an his wife an wanes. They're dancin in the grass an springin up off the curvin daisies an every now an then the sun sends down a tube of light to wash them. The Maw an Da're smilin an sometimes they hold hands wi each other an sometimes they hold hand wi the wanes. An when they think the wanes aren't lookin they have a fly kiss. An they've got a dog. An guess who it looks like? Right. Sideboard. Me an Booda don't need to say nothin we look down an we know they've not got The Big Empty. We feel like two demons now lookin out of hell down into heaven.

They don't know where hell is. The wine an dope an mushies an a strange hunger burns fires in ma heart.

There's a

FLASH

an I'm transported to this place. There's rows an rows an lines an lines of people on their bellies an they've got a shoulder propped up wi a stick. Their heads're tied up by their hair so they're all lookin right at me an there's pain of all sorts contortin their faces an under their hearts a wee fire burns an burns inflictin eternal unbearable pain.

FLASH

an I'm back lookin down out the tree gaspin an white.

They're walkin lightly, sometimes skippin. The wanes're singin. One looks up the tree.

Mammy there's two men up that tree. Look, look two men, she goes.

They angle their heads – Da mumbles an the distance between them's zero an they fold in the one bundle till they're a pile of just-washed washin movin up the hill. The smiles hide, the laughter dies, an the colours fade.

This raindrop's got ma face reflected in it. It hits a leaf an the leaf breaks an falls leavin aluminium tracers in the cold autumn air. The raindrop explodes sendin ma face out an out in minuscule mercury moons but fallin,

fallin.

Booda hands me the wine. The family scurry off an we sigh grey clouds over the comin winter. In the distance ye can hear the happy bark of a dog.

Your Flexible Friend

I'm seein less an less of Don't now. In fact we're seein that little of him we've started callin him – That Wee Corner at the Top Left-Hand Side of the Letter D.

Truth be told, I couldn't give two fucks if I never see him again. His stupid-lookin ET face annoys me. Never smiles. Always looks like the world's done him wrong: twisted, bitter like a bulldog lickin the pish off a jaggy nettle.

But there's somethin I'm a bit worried about. Carmen's been spotted wi him a few times up The Street. In Lighbody's an the Galleria. Says she always bumps into him unexpected. I think the wee cunts followin her about. Don't think she'd go wi somebody as ugly as that. But ye never know wi wummin Booda says. I keep shovin it all out ma head. I don't want to know for two reasons:

1. No cunt wants to know that some cunt's shaggin their burd.
2. I've got this picture in ma head – we're happy married an walkin through these trees. I'm holdin the wane's hand an he's skippin an the sun's shimmerin on the ground like it's water. Carmen's up ahead an she's got on this thin flowery dress. The sun's shinin through it an ye can see her white underwear. She turns slow an

smiles. The leaves above rustle in a cool rush of breeze an the golden light dapples her.

So what I do's I keep the picture in ma head. When it starts breakin up I think of other things. I go runnin till I drop. I push weights. Or I drink an smoke till I'm welded completely.

So. We're gettin married an I've got to earn the money to pay for it. Booda was banged up wi this guy from Possil in the Bar L. Worked on the scrap thegether. Bizz he's called. Right wide cunt. Slide a blade in ye no problem – an smilin all the while.

Anyway. Booda an me go on the M8 headin for Possil.

Possil's like Sikeside so we feel at ease in it. Bizz gives it all the funny handshakes an the *Yo ma man!!!* stuff an takes us up this close. In the livin room all these junkies're flaked out on the deck. Booda's done smack –

Don't go near it, Mick, ye'll love it too much, he always says when I ask him what it's like.

On this room there's this big fuckin metal door wi locks like Fort Knox. Bizz starts undoin them. We're doin the *not sayin a word* bit – that always makes ye look a lot harder. The rooms piled wi all sorts. Boxes of car radios, telly's, videos, a fuckin rubber doll (don't ask – we never), Armani jeans an this wee safe. Must weigh half a ton. He opens the safe an hands us three Access cards.

A week, he says an guides us out the door. The place stinks of rancid sour milk an hash an smack burnin. The carpet's littered wi wee balls of tin foil like the sky fell out the ceilin. If ye look long enough ye start to see constellations. Orion's belt – that's one I remember from the primary.

Booda an him do this stupid lookin Bar L handshake at the car an a couple of *mind the time's* for ma sake – to show how hard Bizz is an we're off.

What it is's we've got three blagged Access cards an he wants a grand in a week for them. Usually he want's the grand up front but when ye've shared every fart an fiddle in a cell wi a guy for four years he can let ye off for a week.

If ye spend more than fifty quid in a shop they check the cards out for stole an cut them up in front of yer face.

I need five grand for the weddin.

We go round every town in Scotland wi Mountain Goat. Buy all sorts of stuff under fifty quid. First we get new gear, haircuts an curries. Restaurant meals twice a day. Sittin in. An booze. Imagine the hoors took them? American Express? That'll do nicely sir – an they slide the card along their fanny slits. Booda won't drink when he's workin but I've got this case of lager on the floor all the time we're drivin.

Can!

KSHHHHHHH

He pulls the pin an hands me one. Joints sittin in the ashtray. The tape's *Negotiations and Love Songs* by Paul Simon. We'd sing it wi the wee car full to the gunnels rockin from side to side buzzin down the motorway.

I always think of Booda at that bit about the house of detention. I don't tell him, but I feel sorry for him. Sometimes when I think of him in the Home when he was a wane an then in the Mary's an then Borstal an then Detention an then YOs an then the Cons I feel like greetin. Sometimes I do greet. That's what I do. Greet.

Seven in the mornin we're up an shoppin till nine at night. We take orders. Everythin's half price. Fifty quid watch – twenty-five. Fill yer petrol tank – half price.

It's amazin what the most popular thing is. Guess? Emulsion fuckin paint. White matt an silk. They can't get enough of that. The car's weighed down wi it twice a day. A grand for Bizz out the paint alone.

Half-decent personal stereos about twenty odds. CDs of

any cunt ye like – four for twenty quid. Tracksuits. Wee
Frenchie wants as much sexy underwear as we can get –
eight's an tens. We rub her knickers an stuff down our balls
before we give her them. Me an Booda's perverted the same
way. It's good that – havin a pal that's perverted the same
way as ye. No need for embarrassment.

We pay Bizz two days early. I keep ma money in Booda's
cos Carmen'd do it in.

Three weeks later the cards're burnin the fuckin hands off
us. We've got nine grand in Booda's punch bag. We decide to
do a run on garages for fags expectin caught any minute.

What ye do wi garages is ye go in for petrol an when yer
payin ye start this conversation about a party at the weekend
an how ye'll need plenty fags for it. Then ye buy fags up to
what's left out fifty quid. Remember – don't go over the fifty.

Ye travel the garages all day doin that. Ah ha! If yer sharp
ye'll've guessed it's not so simple. Ye can't go on fillin a car
up wi petrol. An ye can't just put half a gallon an go:

*Oh Mr guy that works in the garage that's a half a gallon of
petrol an six zillion fags please. Oh an a curly wurly.*

Well ye can – if ye want to spend the next year strippin
copper cable in the Bar L.

So if yer doin cards this's what ye do. Fill the car right up
at the first garage an get some fags an a petrol can. Get some
Pepsi too cos it's thirsty work. Park a hunner yards before
the next garage an walk in wi the can. Moanin. Argue a bit
wi yer pal about it bein his fault. No hittin.

Ma car's ran out of petrol just up the road there.

Ye buy a gallon an get the rest in fags an more Pepsi an
sweeties to keep ye goin. Then pour the petrol on the ground
on the way back to the car an do the same thing all night all
over the place. Easy.

We've done thirty garages an we were fucked. We're that
bored we start lightin the trail of petrol soon as were out of

Des Dillon

sight of the garage. Lot goes up like fuck

WHOOOOSHHHH

Anyway. We give up when the car's crowded wi fags.
Booda give me five an a half grand. Extra for a weddin
present. We half the fags an flog the cards to the young team
down Mitchell Street. Course they get lifted after a week.
Walkin in Princess Square boggin an pished an buyin
watches. Five yobbos out their heads. Thick as fuck.

So that's that. I give Carmen five grand an keep five
hunner. The next month's her runnin about doin this an that.

Wake me up on the mornin of the weddin, I says.

Ding-Dong the Bell Tolls

It's summer. Ding-dong the bells are goin to ring. Marriage? Access? That'll do nicely sir.

I'm in Memory Lane wi Booda an hour before the weddin. I'm trussed up like an animal to the slaughter. The bow tie's diggin in ma neck. Carmen's at her Maw's. Bad luck to see her or somethin. We've been smokin but I'm still nervous. I'm shakin an he's laughin an firin voddys in ma head.

Next thing I'm in the registry. They're fixin the roof. These scaffolders're lookin in the windie an some cunt's hammerin on the roof. Married in a buildin site. Next thing the registrar sticks a tatty TDK tape in the wee machine on the table. A tape recorder ye got for Christmas when ye were ten. Here comes the bride starts playin. It's all

whooo ooh ooh

an there's Carmen all in white. It's all through a fog – like soft focus an if there's a time I loved her more I can't remember. She smiles an her eyes glitter. The scaffolders're nudgin each other an poppin their eyes. Even the hammer stops. She rustles up beside me.

The registrar says all her stuff an we go:

I do.

I do.

I will, an all that a million times an then I may kiss the bride an the thirty people cheer an clap an the music comes back on an it's *Annie's Song*. The scaffolders turn away in pain an the hammer beats away at the roof.

Reception's in the chapel hall.

Ding ding. Time for the speeches.

Welcome to ma weddin it's so much better than ma last one. But the present's aren't as good.

That's what I want to say but I don't. I say the usual stuff an every cunt gets drunk an batter each other round the place an nip each other's wife's an tell people they used to hate their guts but now they're spot on. Irish rebel songs. A couple of fur coats march out in disgust.

In mounta joy jaaail Wan singer wan Bitta order here for fucksake. BANG BANG BANG GOES THE PINT TUMBLER Order. shng. *Mixshed cumpny* Wan singer wan shong. ***one monaday mornin*** Wan singer wan shng. Wan singer wan *Mixshed cumpny* shong. Wan *Mixshed cumpny* singer wan shng. Wan singer wan shong. ***high uuuuupon the galla treeeeeee*** Wan singer Bitta order here for fucksake. BANG BANG BANG GOES THE PINT TUMBLER Order. wan shng. Wan singer wan *Mixshed cumpny* shong. Wan singer ***Kevun Baaaaaary gave his yung life*** wan Bitta order here for fucksake. BANG BANG BANG GOES THE PINT TUMBLER Order. shng. *Mixshed cumpny* Wan singer Bitta order here for fucksake. *for the cause of liberteeeeeee* BANG BANG BANG GOES THE PINT TUMBLER Order. wan shong. *Mixshed cumpny* Wan singer wan shng. Wan singer wan shong. Wan singer wan shng. Wan Bitta order here for fucksake. BANG BANG BANG GOES THE PINT TUMBLER Order. singer wan shong. *just a laaaaaad of eighteen suuuu merzzzzzzz* Wan singer wan shng. Wan *Mixshed cumpny* singer wan shong. *Mixshed cumpny* Wan singer wan shng. Wan Bitta order here for fucksake. BANG BANG BANG GOES THE PINT TUMBLER Order. singer wan shong.

Usual.

Later on Daz's talkin in Carmen's ear an they're lookin over. He smiles at me. Cunt. The Blackpool mob're here. Froggy, Edinburghslut, an Jimmy Pot Shite McCann.

I'm outside smokin an Jimmy staggers out.

Awright Jimmy.

Zat . . . zat you, Mick?

He's right out his tree. I hands him the joint.

I think a lot about how the head works. Psychology. That's what it is. I try figurin people out. This's a good night for practice. It's just me an Jimmy McCann an the dark. There's a breeze that smells like the sea. But it's Coatbridge. Jimmy smokes the joint talkin gibberish. Well – It sounds gibberish to any other cunt . . .

Who . . . who . . . who's you? He goes an points a crooked finger at thin dark air.

The thin dark air whirls an says nothin.

Eh? Eh? I said who's you?

Jimmy turns an asks me who it is. I shrug an he tilts his head to the side peerin at this figure he sees. The music's bouncin the walls in an out. I feel isolated out under the quiet stars wi Jimmy.

Jimmy throws a punch.

Scouse cunt! he says.

Ma ears prick up.

Ma fuckin windmill. MINE! Out cunt.

Mick . . . Mick . . . kick . . . his Scouse cunt in . . . fucker's hand's on Carmen's leg last half-hour.

He remembers the Scouse. Fuck me. Me an Carmen's there an it's dark an there's music an lights an a breeze. The mince that's Jimmy's head thinks we're all back in the Windmill. Remember fuck all in the mornin. But he knows. Somewhere in that booze infested brain he can piece thegether what happened.

He collapses in a heap tryin to punch the Scouse. I walks back in the hall wishin Jimmy Pot Shite'd choke in his own vomit. Don't's dancin this smoochie number wi ma wife an I want to kill him. It feels like a mess. I down three of four quick voddys get the DJ to fuck on the Pogues – *Irish Rover* – an I pogo round the place tryin to bounce out maself into another life.

I collapse wi some cunt singin *Fields of Athenrye* an wake up in a taxi wi Carmen. Kirkshaws. I get her to put the weddin dress back on an shag her. All them frills rubbin an ticklin yer skin. Yee Ha. St. Andrew's next mornin for the honeymoon. Ma mate Sam's got a caravan up there.

Higher

After the honeymoon, I'm seein less an less of Don't. But when I do he goes on an on about two comp O's he's got for Higher English. By this time I'm sick an fed up wi it so I decides I'll go an do the Higher.

I'll help ye if yer stuck, the wee cunt says. Who needs help off some cunt that's failed twice? That's what a comp O is. Ye get that if ye fail but can read an write. Thinks I'm thick as fuck so I'm dyin to beat him. I don't give two fucks for deoxyribonucleic acid. I'm readin books a lot now but there's things I don't understand. Ever tried readin that *Zen an the Art of Motorbike Maintenance*? Don't.

I quite like College. Or Colli**d**ge as Don't says. Don't's sniffin an tellin me who he's shagged but the burds draw him looks behind his back. The only burd that speaks to him's got a face like a plate of porridge flung in a bin. I want to pass the Higher an fuck it to him goodstyle.

Anyway we starts this poetry stuff. Quite like it. Specially the about 'Fernie Hills' by Dylan Thomas. Turns out I'm quite good at it. Sharpened by years of crack in the boozers wi Jim Gal probably. He's got the best patter in the Brig.

Don't's pullin me aside every five minutes an givin me advice about Shakespeare an shit. But see when we do *Othello* – he knows fuck all. Thick as pig shit. I'd be as well sayin,

Hey stupid cunt. Tell me a lot of shite about this play then.

An he'll answer,

If there's no deoxyribonucleic acid in it I know fuck all about it . . .

Well get yerself to fuck then, ET.

But that's not what I do. I listen to him repeatin the teacher's words like he's a fucked up tape machine.

But I must be stupider cos I'm fuckin listenin. I even hate the way his nostrils flare in an out when he breathes. I hate his Adam's fuckin apple goin up an down. I hate him swaggered about chewin an thinkin every cunt's lookin at him. If they are it's cos they've never seen a extra fuckin terrestrial wi it's nose flattened in before.

But when he looks at me sometimes I see a secret in his eyes – mibbi he's still tryin to kid on he done the Scouse in. Prick.

Christ! A couple of years ago if ye told me I'd be readin Shakespeare books I'd've stuck the head on ye. Anyway. I think ma life's a fuck up – always goin wrong. But see after readin Shakespeare books. Christ *Macbeth* an *Othello* an that *Hamlet* that Daz's always goin on about? See after readin them I feel good cos ma life's no worse than theirs. Everybody's life's a mess if Shakespeare's anythin to go by. Murder, jealousy, rape, incest, nippin about – the whole bit.

I'm right into Higher English. Dont's phonin me every night nearly,

Just to see if ye need any help wi yer English.

No. None, an the phone goes silent an then . . .

To be or not to be. that's Hamlet. *That's the main bit in* Hamlet.

It's Othello *we're doin.*

Oh – what's that about again? Em em, an I can hear him clickin his fingers an turnin the pages of *Shakespeare for Dummies.*

It's complicated . . .

Why don't I come round an we'll go through it together?

It's all right . . .

I've got experience in it . . .

Othello?

No – but Hamlet's *just the same thing . . .*

I'm goin to ma bed . . .

*Meet me in the Colli**d**ge library the morra an I'll take ye through it.*

The library?

Eh?

The library – take me through the library?

Oh. Ha ha.

Rocky three's on the telly . . . I goes.

BZZZZZZZZZZZZZZZZ.

Big pause. While he figures it's not on.

Ring ring. Pause. Ring ring. Pause. Ring ring. Pause. Ring ring. Pause. Ring ring. Pause. Ring ring. Pause. Ring ring. Pause. Ring ring. Pause. Ring ring. Pause. *Ring ring. Pause. Ring ring.* Pause. *Ring ring.*

Even on the phone he gets on ma tits.

I like *Othello.* I mean who'd've thought it? Me likin Shakespeare. I don't tell no cunt I like Shakespeare. It's a good story. This guy *Othello* – he's a darkie. Big strong cunt. Hung like a donkey. Army commander or somethin like that. Anyhow. He's married to this burd Desdemona. Pure loves him. Thinks about him all the time. But there's this wee cunt called Iago an he gets the big darkie jealous so as he thinks his wife's shaggin this other guy Cassio. Cassio's a soldier but he's not got the gumption big Othello's got – he's more yer posh cunt. Anyway. Othello gets the jealousy bad an smothers his wife wi this pillow. After it he finds out Iago's a lyin wee bastard an – I think he kills hiself or somethin – I'd need to look at the book to find out.

But here's the thing – Every time I read

IAGO

on the page it spins like they sometimes do wi titles on films an changes to

DAZ

when it hits ma eyes. Even the film's got Daz in it. Says Bob Hoskins on the titles but I keeps seein Daz doin dirty deeds all round this big fuckin castle.

I keeps thinkin about him an Carmen. Sometimes I think they're at it an sometimes I don't. I'd rather be a fuckin frog an live in a shitehole than have any other cunt touch even a wee bit of Carmen.

It's daft wearin yer heart on yer sleeve so the burds can see it – that's been ma problem all along. When I'm not near her I think some other cunt's givin her one. An when I am near her – like I said before – when I'm lyin in bed lookin at her sleepin I could die. I could die there an then an I'd be the happiest man alive cos I love her that much I can't think of anythin else I want. But I'm always on the look-out for jealousy. The Green-Eyed Monster ma granny called it,

It'll eat into yer marriage son an laugh ye in the face when it's finished.

I think heaven'll fall in on me if she's at it wi that wee cunt. If I catch them I'll take nine years killin him slow. Takin

his skin off in bits an burnin the nerve ends wi
two-for-ninety-nine-pence lighters out What Every Wummin
Wants. Cunt. She looks that innocent – like she'd never do
me wrong: Fuck. I wish she'd never been born.

See when I'm crouched over her an the breath's comin in
an out her nostrils, an the slight twitchin of her top lip, an
I'm wonderin what she's dreamin – is she dreamin about
me? Am I in her head? See when I'm lookin at her an mibbi
the moon's shinin on her face. Well I feel like takin
weedkiller an knifin her an dyin wi ma lips pressin on her's.
When they find us we'll be stone. A statue. A fuckin
sculpture. A man made sculpture made out of man an
wummin. Fuck sake see ma head – I've got some mental
thoughts. We'll be the opposite of Adam an Eve. We'll create
somethin dead. No Garden of Eden. Two dead bodies locked
in rigor mortis an a pool of jellied blood on the sheets.

Yeuch!

Fuck that. See ma head. This night I'm goin to see *Othello*
in the Theatre Royal – me an Booda an Carmen. At the last
minute she decides she's not goin. Huff. Instead of the usual
coaxin an stuff I drives off an leaves her. Me an Booda toke a
couple of joints an a bottle of Buckie each. The play's fuckin
magic.

When we get back Carmen's in hospital. I notice the
windie's smashed. The young team tells me she's up the
Casualty. Ripped her arm open punchin a hole in the windie.
Fuckin maniac. So up I goes an gets her. I drops Booda off.

When I get there she's sittin in this orange plastic chair. I
come in the side door. The place smells of blood booze an
disinfectant. I feel that sorry for her. How lost she is. Lost as
me. She's still got her good clothes on like she's on her way
out. Drunk cunts're arguin about how they couldn't stop
their mate gettin chibbed an there's some gypsies smokin in
the corner. She doesn't see me so I stands an watches her.

She keeps lookin at the main entrance for me. George Michael wouldn't make a dent on her if he walked in. This time it's only me she needs. Trouble – an she needs me. Happiness an party time – I'm ditched. Her skin's whiter than usual an the blood's all over this white satin dress she got special. Her hair's hangin into the blood stain. Make a pretty good picture I thinks. Black, white, red. Her head tilted to the one side an tears track down her face. The picture of war. She shivers every time I look. Definitely shivers.

Soon as she sees me she's over kissin an bitin ma neck an throwin the good arm round me an greetin. I'm pattin her on the back.

S'all right, s'all right hen there. C'mon.

I'm sorry, I'm sorry, she cries. The gypsies look up an give me a knowin glance but the drunk cunts laugh into theirself an start arguin again. I hooks ma finger under her chin an tilts her head. I search down through her brown eyes. Deep an deep. Past all the shite that's happened, past time an past places. We shrink to **US** in a mist of disinfectant. I look deep an deep. Deep an deep. An there it is. The only time I ever glimpse it. The light that's her. The light I'm in love wi. The light that glows a bit when I'm propped on one elbow in bed an starin. An next to the light. I see me. The light loves me. The light loves the almost extinguished flame that's ma light. But there's no hope of recovery from this casualty cos the light's covered an veiled by screens an walls of pain an crime an lust an violence an death. An this sea's ruckled over the blackness. An the world surrounds us. Not as a couple but individually. The world surrounds us individually an more an more people an things come minute by minute an pushin us apart. Pushin.

One day the light'll be small. An white. A pinhead buzzin.

The light'll be a million miles across space. The water'll be too deep. The oceans'll be wide. I won't be able to swim. An darkness'll cover the face of ma earth.

Fuck me. Ma head runs away sometimes. Runs away.

Chips an Curry Sauce

We're comin out Stars this night an she's givin it *couldn't take yer fuckin eyes off her!* an all the usual stuff an marchin off wi nearly folded arms smokin. I goes in the Chinkees an gets two chips an curry sauce an two cans of coke. She takes hers without a word.

We turns down towards Cuperhead an I sits on these stairs. Tearin in. She's standin sayin nothin an slabberin into hers.

When ye're drunk all these things come in yer head that normally don't get anywhere near it. I cant get Daz out ma head. I keep wonderin if it's coincidence that she keeps meetin him up the street. There's stars above her head but she doesn't notice them. She's on another planet.

What ye thinkin about?

Nothin. She keeps ignorin me. Makes it worse by turnin one degree away. Exactly.

I can read your mind.

Hmm.

Think I can't?

Who gives a fuck what you think.

Me . . . an some other people.

Aye the TARTS ye can't take yer eyes off.

At least I'm not spotted wi them in every cafe in the Brig.

What's that supposed to mean?

Whatever ye want it to mean.

There's this charged-up silence an even the stars take a leap further into deep space. They're havin fuck all to do wi this. She's eatin the chips an curry sauce faster an faster an gurglin every mouthful down wi fizzy gulps of cash-an-carry coke. Critical mass. Supernova. The buzz of her electricity's makin ma hair stand up. I know she's about to go so I puncture the force field wi,

You an that wee cunt Daz — ye're never done goin about thegether up the street.

Who says? One of yer tarts?

Every cunt's always sayin it.

Is that how ye've never mentioned it.

I never fuckin mentioned it cos I never believed it.

Hmm.

Don't hear ye denyin it.

Hmm.

I said I don't hear ye denyin it.

Well I've met him a couple of times. It's not as if we live in New York is it?

I hate that wee fucker.

The sun shone out his arse in Sikeside.

Did it fuck.

It was Daz this, Daz that an Daz the fuckin next thing. Don't try an kid the kid that kidded them all.

She's started the pointin games. Know — thumpin her finger in her chest wi bits of the words. I just goes,

Oh aye you think ye're the kid that kidded them all but this kid — this fuckin kid — ain't that easy kidded by the fuckin kid that thinks she kidded them all but kidded no cunt cos the whole town knows yer a fuckin slut.

Boom.
New universe. I sees
this **flash.** But it's not a white flash or a blue flash. It's a dull flash. An right as I registers she's booted ma curry sauce in ma face I feel the curry startin to nip ma eyes.

YA FUCKIN SLUT I'll kill ye when I get ma hands on ye.

I starts throwin wild hooks an punches. I can hear her click clickin away in quick sharp steps.

My eyes're burnin. I fling the coke in her direction. Missed.

Go an get yer fuckin tarts now. Click click.

Oh! Oh my God ye've blinded me. Ye've blinded me ya stupid fuckin cow.

I'm layin it on thick. Right out World War 1 films. Mustard bombs.

She's goin, *I hope ye walk in front of a bus.*

I'm staggerin on an off the kerb shoutin,

I can't see I can't see. Oh God help me I can't see. I'm blinded.

She's not affected. Anyway. The nippin's stoppin an I can see a couple of seconds before the nippin starts again. I'm staggerin almost in front of cars hopin she'll come to ma rescue but does she fuck.

Die ya bastard, she's shoutin. *You ruined ma life. D'ye know that?*

Ruined ma fuckin life.

Anyway I'm probably borin ye wi all this – we go on like that for half an hour. What stops me is I gets to the bottom of the street an there's all these little redbrick houses where there used to be slag hills.

Fuck me look at them, I slabbers. She's mesmerised too. It's like a miracle. They must've chucked them up in weeks. I'm singin inside ma head an clearin lumps of curry sauce from ma eyes wi the button of ma shirt when she comes over, flings the arms round me an goes,

I'm sorry darlin, I'm sorry. Look I won't go near Daz again. I don't like him either.

I want him out – our – life. I goes pointin three times exactly to the tarmac.

We've got the arms round each other. An mibbi cos I'm drunk or mibbi cos Daz's more in ma head than I think, I starts cryin. It's just tears at first an I thinks I can hide them an they'll be good for washin away the last of the curry sauce. But the lip starts tremblin an this wee noise comes out. The shoulders start to go an it's obvious. Carmen starts pattin me on the back like a wane.

There there – it's goin to be OK It's goin to be OK.

Cos she's showin me affection I let go. Never knew I had it in me. I'm cryin like Frankenstien. Big loud howls an she's holdin tighter an tighter.

Shhh. Don't worry. We'll not let any cunt come between us again darlin. From now on it's you an me an the wane. C'mon.

We start walkin.

Nice houses, I says an at the same time we goes,

Let's get one.

So that's that. Not a job between us but our hearts're set

on these houses wi wee windies wi hunners of squares on them an the red bricks.

Three weeks later I've arranged a dodgy mortgage an we've put a deposit down.

It's all goin to be different. No carry on. No makin a right arse of ourselfs. We'll cut the drinkin down an I'll get a job on the buildin sites. We'll do it no bother. Carmen'll get a job in a pub or somethin. Everythin's goin to be hunky dory. Everythin's goin to be just fine.

Iron

So we gets one of them nice houses wi wee fancy windies. It's goin to be great. No makin an arse of ourselfs here. This's Poshville Tennessee. This's the good life. The easy lane. I've got this job on the side an we've bought a brand new motor on tic. A Skoda. Free toolkit. Good cars.

Some daft cunts say where ye live doesn't effect what kind of person ye are. Bull. There's us – Carpets down. Rag-rolled walls. Black ash furniture – the whole bit. Snobs we are. So we're in Glasgow this day an she stops at this windie across from Central station nearly.

Ohh let's look at the watches, she goes, an I notice the start of a posh accent in her voice. She drags me over an we're standin there. I'm watchin passin burds reflected in the windie. She's pointin at this watch.

You'd look good wi that.

It's price's kinda focused on the outer rim of ma vision. Looks like £1250 an I'm laughin.

They do tick in there c'mon in an see if we can get a watch, she says.

The mention of tic brings her voice back where it belongs. Ma focus gets better. Rolex. That's what it says. Fuckin Rolex. Big ugly things ye wouldn't give a spacemen to go to the moon wi. But she loves it. Big an chunky. She wants me to be the cunt in a fancy suit flashin the watch in the sun an lookin through her skirt cos the light's shinin hard.

Heloo daarling would you like to go out tonight to a quiet little restaurant just the two of us? I'm sure Auntie Mabel will look after our nice little children.

Ohh yas dear (KISS) let's do that shall we. (KISS ONE HEEL UP IN THE AIR.)

Good, Cynthia, an then on the way home I can bend you over a hedge an fuck the arse off you.

So I starts laughin at what I'm thinkin.

What ye laughin at? goes Carmen.

I can't tell her I'm thinkin about Cynthia bent over a hedge an George rammin it up her arse so I tells her about the Rolex's they sell down the Barras.

They sell they stupid fuckin things down the Barras for thirty quid.

No way.

Fuckin right. Thirty quid. No different.

Then the real price of this fucker catches ma eye. It's not £1125 at all. It's fuckin £11,250.00. No it's not a misprint. Eleven fuckin thousand two hunner an fifty quid. Fuck sake. If I paid that for a watch I'd want to travel through time wi it.

I'm laughin again.

Stop laughin yer gettin me a red neck.

You ha couldn't ha get hu a ha red ha neck ha in ha a brothel ha.

Aye an you couldn't get yer hole in a brothel.

She folds the arms an bumps her way along Gordon street. I'm followin wi a half smirk. It's a half smirk that only cunts wi burds like Carmen can understand. It's somethin like when ye start laughin in chapel. Ye know ye've got to stop or ye're in big trouble. But ye can't. An there's adrenaline in yer blood. That's the fear. That combination twists the smile into that certain curvature that only cunt's in ma situation can understand.

A couple of times out in the open guys've passed me when I've had this smirk an recognised it. They nod an I shake ma head meanin,

I know I know, an funny thing is that's not what I mean. What I mean by the nod is, *I know you know how I feel cos ye've been here before an we're brothers in arms on this one.* Thank fuck for the dictionary of nods. One time this guy goes,

Aye ye'll be buyin her a curry the night.

He knew what he was talkin about.

I catches up wi her. By this time she's in Buchanan Street deliberately bumpin into posh burds comin out Princess Square. They must do lip transplants in there cos all these burds've got lips like folded over lifebelts. Next time yer in Glasgow go in Princess Square an see them tryin to outlip each other on the movie stairs. Fuckin fishfaces. The bold Carmen's knockin them for six. That's ma burd. I catches her.

Hey! Fancy a curry the night?

She gives me this wee kiss. That guy really knows his stuff.

We end up down the Barras. A Rolex each. Fifty quid. Solid gold plate that flakes off on the way home. After the curry we christen the house. The only thing we're wearin's the watches. Things're hunky dory. Right hunky dory. For a wee while.

I'm readin a lot of books wi me doin the Higher English. We're hardly in the house three weeks an here's what happens. She's naggin away;

Books books books ye're always readin books what about ME have you no time for ME – yer Wife?

She's got the book pressed against ma face wi her face an she's shovin a pointin finger in her chest an shoutin. I puts down the book an gives her the usual reply. Fuck knows why cos I know what can happen wi this reply. A wee feel at her mop-box'd be better;

Get yersel to fuck ya maddie!!

Don't call me mad.

Ya fuckin mental case.

Don't call me mad.

She's diggin her nails in ma arms at this bit. Up I gets an flings her on her arse. She glares up through cracks in her hair an draws air through her teeth. I starts movin away from her an I'm halfway up the stairs when,

WHIIIIIIIIIIIIIIIIIIIIIZ-ZZZZZSMASHSHSHSH

another cup bites the dust. I'm at the top of the stairs goin *tut tut dear did ye drop one of our new china tea cups* when she's leapt halfway up them an the talons're out.

BOOKS books BOOKS books BOOKS books BOOKS books BOOKS books BOOKS books BOOKS books BOOKS books BOOKS books BOOKS books BOOKS books BOOKS books BOOKS books BOOKS books BOOKS books BOOKS books BOOKS books BOOKS books

She's slabberin an shovin her head forward on her neck.

Fuck you I'm out of here, I goes, but she follows me back down the stairs goin;

BOOKS books BOOKS books BOOKS books BOOKS books BOOKS books BOOKS books BOOKS books BOOKS books BOOKS books BOOKS books BOOKS books BOOKS books BOOKS books BOOKS books BOOKS books BOOKS books BOOKS books BOOKS books

The new neighbours're millin about tryin out garden hoses an paintin their fences whiter than every other cunts. Last

thing I want's Carmen doin her limpet naggin routine
followin me down the street an me tryin to read *Great
Expectations*. She changes her tune an if I thought about goin
out before this put me right off.

Quick check for blades an I nip past her an bolt up the
stairs. In the front room, through the blinds I sees some
neighbours crouched down lookin for weeds but really
they're lookin up here to see what the fuck's goin on.

HOOOOOOOOOOOOOOOOOOOOOOOOOOOOOOOOORMASTER
she screams an if any weren't lookin before they're lookin
now. What the fuck can I do? She's comin at me across the
top lobby an her mouths goin like fuck. Like one of them
clockwork mouths ye get in Blackpool. I know I'm in for
the history of every little thing ye've ever
done wrong to me ya bastard wi all these bits
added on an all these things I never done stuck in the
middle of sentences an no chance to interrupt so that they
become truths for the cow to use the next time. I punch a
couple of holes in the wall but that doesn't work anymore.
They look quite good through the rag-rollin.

*That's right go go wreck this house ya bastard. Wreck it like ye
wreck everythin else. Wreck it like ye wrecked ma fuckin life.*

She opens the windie an starts shoutin down to the
neighbours.

*That's right – look – look c'mon see Mr Nice Guy in action;
HOOOOOOOOOOORMASTER he's a
HOOOOOOOOOOORMASTER. Don't let him near yer wifes.
C'mon in an see him smashin up his nice new house – c'mon.*

I can imagine them linin up to watch me in action.

I don't think they're comin in slutface, I goes, *mibbi ye should
offer them cookies buns an rock cakes. Oh that's right ye're a
couple of cups short dear.*

She starts chuckin the books at me. I nips out the room an

holds the handle tryin to think up a plan. She's pullin like fuck at the other end.

Open loft – that's handy. I chucks the book up an ma feet're disappearin in darkness before she comes chargin out the room seein as how she fell on her arse the second I let go of the door. She's searchin everywhere but I starts laughin.

I keep this wee torch just over the lip of the loft so I slides away into the darkness an starts readin the book. I can't really read it for sniggerin. Then:

THUMP this book lands somewhere in the shadows. She's got wind of what I'm up to.

THUMP THUMP two at a time.

THUMP

THUMP THUMP

THUMP

THUMP

She's tryin to figure out exactly where I am. Like that battleships game.

THUMP one lands nowhere near me.

AWWWWWWWWWW!!!!!!! Ya fuckin bastard!!!

I shouts. An

all these books land exactly in the wrong bit.

Silence.

I can hear her listenin for blood. I lets out this weak moan,

Carmen . . . Carmen . . . Carmen . . . I'm . . .

She's listenin like fuck so I funnel ma hands an shout.

I'M STIL

L READIN THE BOOK

YA FUCKIN IDIOT

HA HA HA HA HA HA HA HA

O VER

HE RE

YA STU PID CU UNT.

THUMP *AWW!!* THUMP *AWW!!* THUMP *AWW!!* THUMP *AWW!!*

The bitch thunders me wi a rapid four on the dome an shoulders. She sprints in the room for more piles of books.

Then – another great idea! There's this big cardboard box up the loft that the washin machine came in. I sticks it over ma head an switches the torch on an starts readin:

My father's family name being Pirrip, and my Christian name being Philip, my infant tongue could make of both names nothing longer or more explicit than Pip. So I called myself Pip, and came to be called Pip.

She starts chuckin books again. I'm sniggerin in the dull echo they make as they hit the cardboard an slide through the blackness onto the fibreglass insulation.

I give Pirrip THUUUUMPIPIPI as my father's

family THUUUUMPIPIPI **name on the**
THUUUUMPIPIPI **authority of**
THUUUUMPIPIPI **his tombstone and my sister**
– Mrs Joe THUUUUMPIPIPI **Gargery,**
THUUUUMPIPIPI **who married the blacksmith.**

She gives up. There's this big long silence an I'm settlin
into the first chapter at long last:

As I never saw my father or my mother . . .

FUCKIN
WHAM!!!!!!!!!!!!!!
!!!!!!!!!!!!!!!!!!!!!!!!!!
●●●●●●●●●●●●●●●●●●●●●●●●
!!!!!!!!!!!!!!!!!!!!!!!!!
●●●●●●●●●●●●●●●●●●●●●●●●

This thing hits me on the head. Comes burstin through
the cardboard. I'm not expectin it. The iron. The cow's
climbed up an saw the box an went an got the iron an fucked
me right on the dome. The blood's already tricklin down ma
forehead an I'm scramblin to shove the box off. But I'm that
fuckin angry I rip right through the box an I've dropped out
the loft like a *Star Trek* materialiser before she's even half way
down the stairs. She looks back an lets out this shriek cos I've
got The Iron in ma hand an I'm chargin at her. When I gets
out in the street the gardeners're out in force to see the
carberet. She's tearin down the street wi

 an

slantin back up at me an the neighbours. An there's me,
blood runnin down ma head, screamin out all the different
ways I'm goin to kill her. Runnin after her clickin heels wi
the electric flex an the plug danglin an bumpin behind me.
We disappear round the laughin corner. I can't catch her an I
don't go back till it's dark. The front door's still wide to the
wall an the house's freezin.

Parenthood

Funny. Round about this time I sees that film *Parenthood* wi Steve Martin in it. Next thing I'm wantin it. Husband, wife, wanes, nice nights watchin the telly – the whole bit. I'm fallin more an more in love wi the idea of bein a Da an a husband. I starts takin the wane walks up The Lochs an every time I'm at the shops I'm buyin her a bunch of carnations. I mind the wummin in the shop says,

I wish I was that lucky wummin.

I feel good when she says it. I feel like Steve Martin. I want wanes in ma garden at Patrick's party. I want them to say how funny his Da is. I want a horse an Carmen standin proud as fuck. But fuck me the grass's needin cut an no wanes ever come near our house. Not a one. Patrick spends his life in his Granny's. But I want to change all that. I want to make it all different. I want a fuckin life.

I want us to've just met. Not Blackpool – Sikeside – Kirkshaws – the South Pier. That fuckin Scouse – he could've ran away like any other sensible cunt. But no. He's got to stand an fight an pull out a blade. He's got to fuck it all up.

I wish it was all gone. But this isn't the Yella Brick Road is it? This's Coatbridge an this's real. Too fuckin real. An hard. It's fuckin hard.

An there's still reports of her an Daz meetin. I'm startin to lose it. Crumble. At one time I could've crushed her. Fuck! I crushed her regular so I did. But now she's in control. She's in control an she knows it. I'm fucked. Unless I reel her back in. She needs to see this family stuff's good. I've never got *Parenthood* off the video.

Aw not that heap of shite again, she goes, an ma head drops.

What the fuck's up wi you?

Nothin. Nothin.

So *Parenthood*'s not for her. I keep tellin maself it's all goin to be OK but right inside me, where the flame's goin out, I know I'm fucked. A bit of me gives in. Ma soul's got a slow puncture. At night, alone in bed, I hear it hissin like a snake.

Soon it's all back to square one. All the same things're happenin that happened in Kirkshaws, Sikeside an Blackpool. I'm always tryin to blame it on somethin else.

I blame it on the drink. I stop drinkin. I blame it on not drinkin. I start drinkin. I blame it on drugs. No drugs. I blame it on reality. Back to the drugs. I blame it on too much money. I spend it on drink an drugs. No money. Every other cunt's fault. No cunt's fault but ma own. God. No God. Luck. No luck. I blame it on the guy up the road cos he's got big fancy motors an I've got this laughin stock of a Skoda.

I don't blame Carmen.

Enemies

Get close to yer enemies. I decide to get all pally wi Daz again so I can drop into his house unexpected.

How do I do it? Easy. I approach him when he's makin a couple of burds sick up the college an ask him for help wi ma English. He's givin them the zygote an chromosomes pish this time. I leans over into his bad breath an gives it,

Hey James, any chance of helpin me wi ma English sometime?

The wee cunt waves me away wi a right royal wave an a *no problem.*

D'ye know what DNA means . . .

An just as the burds – thick as fuck picked special – are about to say *no-o* I shouts,

The British Dyslexic Association.

None of them laugh an he looks as puzzled. But he smiles like he gets it.

Get it? Get it? He asks the two short planks.

Duuhh? they go.

Och I'll tell ye's after . . . To be or not to be – know who said that?
Who?

An I leave him to it. Wee cunt.

I meet him regular. Rumours die away an, ye know what it's like, I soon forgets what I'm up to in the first place.

The Vulcan

It's the night of ma uncle Peter's wake. Daz's up Airdrie
bouncin. One night – twenty quid. After the Hail Marys're
over an we've walked Peter to St. Augustine's I decides to go
up an see how Daz's doin.

First thing's the atmosphere. Cut it wi a knife. They're all
drinkin in the side of their mouths an lookin out the sides of
narrow eyes at me an her walkin in. She's got the good togs
on an I'm dressed: black suit, black tie. Daz's at the door wi
these two giant cunts six feet big an the same round about.

The Duncansons.

Mad as fuck.

I gets two voddys an a Guinness an she's talkin to Daz at
the door. Already the bouncers've horsed a few pissheads
out an Daz's done the business. We gets talkin – how's the
wake an how's the bouncin an all that. He's quite happy an
he introduces the two fat cunts. They shake ma hand like
they're trying to break it an give me the grin. I stares them
out an ye can see the only reason they're not on me like
dogs's that I'm wi Daz an he's a boxer.

The wake an the greetin an our powerlessness over dyin
an all that stuff's goin through ma head an the adrenalin's
squirtin in ma veins every heartbeat.

I've been drinkin steady all day but in the Vulcan I've had three Guinness an three voddys. Ma eyes're lightin up psycho an ma chest's out fierce an unbeatable. I know, even if no other cunt does, I'm goin RIGHT ahead.

I looks slow round the pub. Terminator style. All the tables're took up wi Orangemen an their burds crouched towards each other rollin joints an snortin speed. Some catch ma glance an look away. Other's draw me a look. I'm not interested in startin just yet so I give them a quick **fuck you** look an move on round the pub again. Away at the other end there's this guy an he rivets onto me. I look over another couple of tables an then back at him. He's still starin. I think I know him. Fuck me. Jesus Christ it's him. It's the Scouse. He's on his own. No cunt's talkin to him an he's starin right in me. This fearsome shiver rockets down ma spine. I looks for Carmen's attention but she's rattlin away about somethin in Daz's ear. I turns an he's gone. There's just this purple empty space an the sound of the sea in ma ears. Ma head's fucked. Must be the drink. Got to be.

It's this big fat Orangeman in the space now an he's givin me the stare. A flashback from the mushies. That's it. That's what it is.

Anyway. We're at this door an the bouncers're wary. They're in ma mad electricity an it's makin goose pimples on their skin. The hairs on their necks're like toilet brushes. Carmen's beside Daz an he's got the arm round her. Ma mouths straight across ma face an shut except for blowin smoke out. I can read the bouncers' minds. They want me out.

Daz, you can knock off at eleven – there's fuck all happenin the night, says one, an the other one nods. A double act.

They're brothers – can probably read each others minds. Carmen's all over Daz an they're gettin more scared of ma mad stares by the minute. He's got the arm round her an I'm sayin nothin. The bouncers're not psychic but they know if they flung the arm round her I'll rip their fuckin heads off. The rest of the pub, all dressed up in Orange Lodge gear're givin it *the Aul Orange Flute* an all this stuff. Fair play to them says I.

I'm at the liable to do anythin stage now an it's quarter to eleven. The two fatties're countin down an ye can feel them easin off like ships as the wee hand swings up to eleven. Even if ma head's sayin, *drive Daz back to The Brig an get a cargo*, somethin else right in the quick of me's goin wild. Ma hearts starts pumpin like I've done a line of speed but I'm into fuck all drugs this night. It's booze – fuckin airplane fuel.

Right, Daz . . .

. . . an he hands Daz twenty quid. Carmen's slippin her jacket on an the bouncers open the door. The cold night forces its way in an above the rooftops the stars're burnin like dogs eyes.

She goes to walk out an she's pushed back by these two even bigger even fatter cunts an they stand in front of the Duncansons. I'm givin Daz the *what the fuck's this all about?* look when this wee skinny dyin-off runt comes in dressed up wi big stupid lookin lapels like a seventies film reject. His hair's dyed to fuck an his tie's loud. He's unfoldin a wad of notes an the edges of his sharp features shine in the disco lights. He's got his jacket hangin off his shoulders. Ye can just tell that he fancies hiself as some super cool Brooklyn drug-dealin pimp.

One of the heavies's pressin back into me like I'm nobody – like I'm nothin. The rage's whirlin up ma body an ma eyesight's wavin about. I'm holdin the brass rail wi one hand an I'm puttin the pint glass down easy wi the other.

The Duncansons're shitin theirselfs. Hatchet face's wavin

slow at cunts like he's God. He's been at the door at least a minute an he's still countin this dough. Fuckin thousands. He stares me in the eye but sees somethin he doesn't like an swings round an sees Daz, the new bouncer.

Hello, says the skinny bastard, *an who might you be?*

Awright ma man, name's Daz.

An Daz shoves the hand out to shake but the prick withdraws an laughs. I want to crush him. I looks into the heads of his two bodyguards an instead of faces there's just these two big black fuckin holes an all this laughin comin out. Daz's starin.

Fuckin kill him, Daz, I'm sayin in to maself, *kill the cunt.*

I'm waitin on him layin a few lefts an rights in. The Duncansons're laughin wi this cunt now. Carmen lifts two good cider bottles, one in each hand, an lowers them down into the folds of her long black dress.

Is this yer first night here wee man?

. . . goes the skinny bastard wearin his takin the cunt out somebody grin.

Crush him, Daz, I'm sayin into ma teeth.

The two bodyguards think I'm tryin to talk an they nod at each other an then at me like I'm a dick. Only seconds left. Carmen's not took her eyes off me the last twenty seconds. Daz answers.

Aye – first night ma man.

I can't believe it. I'm waitin on Daz bustin this guys head an he answers him back. The Bodyguards're dustin Daz's jacket down an fixin his hair all rough makin him look like a right prick. It never occurred to me before but right there an then I'm thinkin that mibbi Daz's feart. His bottle's crashin. I'm searchin in his eyes an the skinny bastard says,

It might be yer first night wee fella but it's goin to be yer last.

Fuckin kill him, Daz!!! I goes.

Daz's mouth drops open like he can't believe what I'm sayin.

Kick fuck out the prick. I says, without partin ma teeth.

The bouncers an the two bodyguards're lookin at me wonderin who the fuck I think I am.

Do you know who I am? goes skinny.

I don't give two fucks who ye are – PRICK

Carmen moves the bottles from under her dress an blows me this kiss. The cunt's still talkin but ma temper's comin up like aul Nick out the black pits of hell an there's no stoppin now. Time's ran out an he's still tryin to tell me who he is. I only hears one word but: MONEYLENDER. He could call me a Feinian bastard, call ma Maw all the cunts under the sun but that one word, that's what does him this night.

Next minute I've got the cunt an he's above ma head. I'm strong as fuck wi the bodybuildin an I throws him on the dance floor. There's plenty confusion cos his notes're flutterin everywhere an all the Orangies're whippin it in their pockets. He hits the floor like a sack of spuds an the floor clears. No cunt knows what to do. They're froze. By the time they even move I've jumped up an drove the heel into the bastards ribs seven times. All the time I'm ravin about,

Moneylender . . . fuckin moneylender . . . Crack breakin ribs.

Moneylender . . . fuckin moneylender . . . Crack breakin ribs.

Moneylender . . . fuckin moneylender . . . Crack breakin ribs.

Moneylender . . . fuckin moneylender . . . Crack breakin ribs.

Moneylender . . . fuckin moneylender . . . Crack breakin ribs.

Moneylender . . . fuckin moneylender . . . Crack breakin ribs.

Moneylender . . . fuckin moneylender . . . Crack breakin ribs.

He's not movin an only eight seconds've went. I turns an the two Bodyguards're only startin to move.

C'MON YA FUCKIN PRICKS!!!!!

I'm on the middle of the dancefloor an ma ferocity's froze

all the cunts halfway out their chairs. Slow motion. The
Bodyguards're off the startin blocks an wobblin towards me.

CRASH CRASH

Two well placed Grolsch bottles an one's on his knees.
Carmen's diggin the bottles in the back of his head an he's
screamin like a wane. The other cunt's full tilt at me now an
I sinks down a foot, keeps the eye right on his fat beak an
comes up when he's nearly on me an drives a right in his
face. Feels the shock down ma arm an through ma body to
the wooden floor. Burds're screamin like fuck an we're only
twelve seconds in. I'm checkin all round me now – eyes wide
an mad an sayin,

C'MON C'MON C'MON C'MON C'MON C'MON C'MON C'MON

That's when I notice Daz's still not moved. I mean I expect
him to be bangin heads. Cunts're ready to go. Ye can see
them gettin their burds to hold them back. But it's the usual
– one wee cunt breaks loose an he's first at me across the
dance floor. Then there's hunners of the cunts five steps
behind him. I launches him an he's sprawled on top of the
moneylender.

Daz's still not moved but Carmen's launchin bottles an
chairs an tumblers in the crowd. Some duck for cover behind
tables an still no Daz. I gets ma back against the bar. It's toe
to fuckin toe on the white line. They're a pack of fuckin dogs
bootin an swipin an punchin. I'm gettin the odd blue flash
but nothin too bad. I've covered up well an the stupid cunts
can't get a right good swipe cos they're packed too tight. I
keeps crouchin down an springin up sendin out long straight
lefts an rights to a face picked before I sunk. Gifts – they
don't expect it. Down they go every time. The only thing's
the barmaid's behind me shoutin an greetin.

Ya evil bastard! she's sayin over an over an smashin every

fuckin spare glass in the bar over ma head. I can feel the
blood runnin down. I'm thinkin this's it. I'm thinkin I'm goin
to get it here. Cunts're shovin me along the bar sayin,

Get the bastard in the toilet an we'll rip him open.

DAAAAAAAAAAAAAAAAAAAAAZ!!!!!!!!!

It's like he wakes out a dream. *Thank fuck*, says I, as he
comes chargin across the dancefloor. The Bodyguard that
Carmen fucked wi the bottles's back on his feet an he picks
Daz up an throws him through the disco lights.

Fuck me! I says.

The fat bastard's smilin an lookin for applause an that
takes the pressure off me a bit. This wee cunt whose been
diggin me an gettin away stops concentratin an I side kick
him on the knee an break his leg. Stupid cunt – he's on the
ground squealin like a lassie. Fuckin wanker.

Daz gets back up an starts skippin towards the big cunt.
The big cunt's laughin an givin it *Watch this – watch me
annihilate this wee cunt*. He doesn't know Daz's a boxer. He
reaches out to throw him through the disco lights again.
Daz's right in there bam bam bam bam bam bam an the fat
cunt's on his knees an the only thing holdin him up's his
pride an Daz fucks a few low hooks in an down he goes.

Meanwhile back at the bar I'm gettin closer to the toilet an
cunts're rainin the blows in. Daz's crackin head from the
back an I'm crackin them from the front. But we're
outnumbered. Lucky thing is the barmaid's ran out of
tumblers so she's slappin ma head wi this soakin wet
dishcloth thing an shoutin,

Ya bastard ya bastard ya bastard,

an greetin wi anger.

The force of them draggin me into the bog's too much. I'm
strugglin to stop them. I meets this wee cunts eyes an I can
see he's evil. I can see he means to do serious damage. He's
not puttin the blows in. He's standin behind the maddies an

lookin right in me. He looks a bit like the Scouse but I can't be sure. His eyes're dark holes in his head an he's got a hand in his pocket. Just as I smell the piss from the bog he cracks into this grin.

That's when I decides to use the blade.

I'm still taken them on the head but the blue flashes've stopped cos I'm used to it now. I drops the head down so's the blows're hittin me on the roof. I keeps one hand up punchin wild so's to keep them at bay. At the same time I take the blade out the left hand pocket of ma suit jacket. It's a foldin lock blade. I opens the blade partly wi ma thumb an opens it to a click by pressin the point into ma thigh an leverin it. The blue flashes're back again cos they're gettin free punches. I see the evil cunt's eyes as he opens the bog door an the orange light floods the black gaps in the writhin bodies.

They're like a pile of eels wrigglin an strong. I'm gettin weak cos I've nearly punched maself out. I decide to stick the blade in some cunt. Any cunt. No way they're gettin me in that bog – they'll cut me to bits. I pulls the knife back so its heel's hard against the bar. Him wi the eyes comes closer. Is it the Scouse? He's got a blade. I sees it shinin in the weak toilet light. He turns to slide into the bog but he's close enough so I lunges forward wi all ma strength knowin that when I stick it to him the rest of the cunts'll shite theirselfs an bolt the course. Honest to fuck I'm swingin the blade through the thick air of an Airdrie pub – I'm a micro second away when ma head puts on the brakes. I flicks the knife away into the legs of the throng an then I see Polis hats bobbin through the pub. The mob fall away like wanes off a roundabout an I'm on ma own wi the barmaid slappin me wi this wet dishcloth an goin,

It was him . . . that bastard . . . that evil bastard . . . he started

it . . . slap slap slap she's goin an this Polis's lookin at her like she's mental.

I walk to the other end of the pub. Carmen crouches down to her hunkers an when she stands up straight there's two big Whitbread bottles on the floor. She slides the arm round me. Daz's standin wi the bouncers wipin blood off his face an the barmaid's pointin at me hysterical an goin,

That's him . . . him over there wi the suit on . . . that bastard . . .

She spits. This wee Polis comes up an I thinks, *oh ho here we go. Lifted.* Weekend in the cells – three months if some cunt's got it bad up the casualty. An this's the most amazin thing about the whole night. He walks up an he grabs ma shoulder.

I suppose you seen everythin? he goes.

His eyes dart to the black tie. I'm just about to do some explanation about how the money lender threatened me wi a gun an all that shite when the Polis walks away. Carmen looks at me. Daz gives it *What the fucks goin on here?* look an the barmaid's dragged off screamin by two Polis wummin.

It was that **bastard** *there wi the black* **tie** *on.* **He's** *the cunt that* **started** *it all . . . get that* **bastard** *he's* **evil** *. . .*

She's makin some words louder than others an saliva's runnin down her chin.

We spend the next two hours drinkin wi the bouncers an tellin each other how tough we are.

Carmen's listenin intently lookin at me wi a glint in her eye.

An that's that. Or so I think.

Next thing I hear's Daz's tellin the town how me an him done in the whole pub. I mean – ye always exaggerate a fight then let other cunts exaggerate it more. Ye point them in the right direction so as to wind the story up an up. No pub fights're spectacular but they always sound like fuckin cowboy films in the tellin. I always let other cunts do ma main exaggeration for me. But what makes me mad's the wee cunt's puttin hiself in the picture as a killer. Seven cunts he put in hospital. He's boastin an boastin can be dangerous.

I play the night down when any cunt asks me. It was only a fight. I defended maself best I could. I give the Moneylender's bouncers their due an the Orange cunts their due an all. In Coatbridge an Airdrie anythin ye say gets to every ear that's got an interest. Things get round right quick. Fuck me – cable TV? That's nothin new – they've always had that here. The reason I always give cunts their due's to stem any comeback.

This's what ye do:

When some cunt's praisin ye up about how much of a killer ye are ye play it down an say stuff like:

Them Moneylender's minders could go to town. Fucked me good on the head. Nearly had me out.

Or,

See them Orange bastards? They're not to be fucked wi – kill ye in a minute.

What happens's this stuff goes back an gets exaggerated so it arrives at the other end like.

Mick Riley's shitin hiself – says ye's done him right in.
Wouldn't want to meet guy's like youse again. In bed three weeks. Couldn't move.

So that's the Moneylender's bouncers feelin like they actually won the fight.

The Orangies might get,

Mick Riley's feart to leave the house in case the UVF're goin to do him in.

Bringin in the sectarian element's always a good move. Makes them feel like real terrorists.

Ye usually get a message back that everythin's squared up an so the two lies can co-exist. But Don't's not got a clue about the psychology of street violence. He goes about tellin every cunt how wi one hand tied behind his back – fuckin Lion Man on the Yella Brick Road – hospitalised the whole pub. Critical list for ten. Saved ma fuckin life. That's good for me. But it's bad for him. Five Orangies break in his house this night, pull out the fuses an wait in the dark.

Clop clop. Keys. Jangle Jangle. Squeek. Clop clop. Click. Nothin.

Click.

Nothin.

Click click click.

Nothin nothin nothin.

Squeak – livin room door. Swish of dark wind. Blue flash. Hospital for three months. One month in intensive care. I'm half glad half angry. Carmen? She was greetin.

Man in Garden Centre with Axe

Don't's in some state right enough. I mean, I think he deserves the doin but I can't help feelin sorry for him when I see him. He only looked a wee bit like ET before but now he's a dead ringer. For the first three weeks he's got a face like a melted basin an can only talk Extraterrestrial.

He gets better but his eyes're dull. He's lost it. Gets out an falls to bits. Drink an dope all the time. Stops washin. An – bad news for some cunt livin in Sikeside – he's lost his bottle completely. It's all right to loss yer bottle sometimes. Even better if no cunt sees ye runnin away. But to lose yer bottle completely means yer housebound.

AGGRO-PHOBIC. He's even stops the deoxyribonucleic acid stuff. Every time I go round he's starin at the walls. An this time he's not lookin for sympathy.

He starts writin to Slinky.

Slinky starts writin back.

To tell the truth seein him in that state frightens me. I give all the cunts their due an there's no rumours that they're goin to get me. But there's this fear knawin away inside. I decides I need tooled up.

I decide on that trusted an feared West of Scotland weapon: the hatchet.

How to get a hatchet?

B & Q it that's how ye do it.

I goes up to B & Q. They've got el cheapo hatchets that break if ye hit anythin hard. The two I choose from in the end up're a black Stanley an this blue-handled Estwing. I pick up the Estwing – no competition. Sleek an hard. Cold to the touch. That's the one.

It's a Tuesday afternoon. It's rainin. Not a cunt on the streets. B & Q's empty apart from the old age pensioners tryin to buy one nail the way they buy one slice of spam. Good on this aul cunt – he argues till the manager decides to give him a nail for nothin. In the chaos I stick the hatchet up ma jook an make off to the garden centre.

Done it a million times. Anythin not too heavy. Stick it up the jook, take it out the back to the garden centre an lob it over the fence. See where it lands. I count the amount of paylins on the fence from the wall to whatever I've nicked. Out I goes an launches it over the fence. Twenty-six paylins.

Exact same time as I'm chuckin the Estwing over the fence this announcement comes over the tannoy in the staffroom. (Wee Joe Smith works in there) The whole team's drinkin tea an playin a right borin game of pool. The speakers crackle:

MAN IN GARDEN CENTRE – WITH AXE.

Eh? They all say an stop still. The pool players elbows're jaggin out. The speakers says again:

MAN IN GARDEN CENTRE – WITH AXE.

No mistakin it this time. Out they file. The B & Q shoplifter catchin posse're tooled up wi all sorts of hammers, hatchets, shovels, spades an one's got a Black an Decker four speed drill wi hammer action. Fuck knows why.

Wee Joe Smith sees me from a distance. *Fuck me it's Mick Riley,* he says, an they all slow down tryin to fall behind. Shoe laces suddenly undo an there's somethin interestin in the paint section.

Of course I don't see none of this stuff. It's wee Joe that tells me later on.

First I know these red uniforms appear all over the garden centre like mad flowers. Invasion of the bodysnatchers. They're keepin away from me. But I know they're there to get me – what I don't know is if they seen me fling the hatchet over the fence. So I finds out. I walks at three of them quick as fuck – straight legs nearly. I jerks ma hand in ma jacket like I'm goin for the axe. They bolt.

ZOOOOOOOOOOOOOOOOOOOOOOOOOOOOOOOOOOOOOM
So they never seen me. I walks right through the place an they're all yards behind me like that Sicilian courtin episode in *The Godfather*. At the door but I can see them arguin about who's to go first. No cunt flinches but.

From Lock Street I see them windin round each other in their wee red uniforms. Shitebags.

I go back for the axe at night but some cunt's stole it.

Surprise Surprise

I've got this job labourin on the side. This Saturday, fucked wi the drink from Friday night, I'm lyin on the bed about one o clock wi ma workin gear on – boots the lot.

I hears the door. I know it's her. I try gettin off the bed but I'm fucked. I decide to take a naggin.

The room door flies open an she pokes her head in smilin. Her hair's hangin down her face. The smile reminds me of the smile she gave me when she'd chopped the duck's head off in Blackpool. But the drink can conjure up some strange interpretations.

C'mon!

Eh?

C'mon wi me.

What?

I've got a surprise?

She's still smilin an ma head's doin overtime wonderin what she's all about. I sits on the edge of the bed.

Do I need to get changed?

No. Hurry – c'mon.

Might be somebody's won the pools or somethin. She runs down the stairs an I follows an every step ma head's poundin.

The Skoda's in the street wi the passenger door flung open an the engine revvin like fuck. She's wavin like we're goin to miss a plane or somethin. The radio's playin this stupid fuckin song an it's goin round an round in ma head.

I reach over to touch her arm an she whips it away an clicks the radio off. Funny thing is she's still smilin. Or is she grinnin? I feel sick.

I jerks back as she accelerates away. Turnin out the street she goes,

Met Daz up the street the day.

What was the wee prick sayin.

Nothin much – went for a coffee.

Is his face still a special effect?

She ignores me an hits the kerb. I decides to wear the seat belt. Carmen's starin straight ahead an never looks at me all along Bank Street.

Mibbi we're goin to some pub for a surprise party for me or somethin. What the fuck for I don't know – there's nothin I've done an it's not ma birthday.

Ah Ha! Surprise party? I goes.

Wait an see.

Right by the graveyard. Turns left. Whifflet lights an I'm gettin strange thoughts. I think we sometimes underestimate the power of our minds. I've got the right answer right there at the lights but I don't even tell it to myself cos it might be a right answer but it's a bad answer. We're headin towards Sikeside.

She stops outside Donna Murphy's flat.

Who lives in there?

Eh?

Who the fuck lives in there.

She's pressin her finger on the windscreen. I'm sure its goin to break.

Where? What're you on about? But I don't have the energy to look puzzled.

You know fine well what I'm on about, an she pulls out this big blade.

Aw fuck!

She's clickin the blade off the windscreen now. I give up. I know she knows. Guys always say deny it all the way, admit nothin, even if ye're caught on the job. But under Carmen's spell the words're pulled out like a string of magic hankeys.

Ye know who, I goes.

She screams an jumps out wi this blade an the car keys. She goes to the door an starts bootin it,

Come out here ya wee hoooooooooooooooooooor.

The curtains move but Carmen's too busy layin into the door an shovin her eyeballs through the letterbox to see it. Whoever's in there's not comin out. No way. She's stabbin the knife over an over in the door. Verandahs an starin but they're not sayin nothin.

She nips round the side an a windie shatters. I get out the car. I walk towards her. Away. Towards. Fuck me I don't know what to do. Another one shatters. From here I can just see her steppin back an lookin on the grass for bricks. The door opens an Donna Murphy an her pal run like fuck up the nearest close. Carmen's in the house now rippin fuck out furniture, curtains an clothes wi her blade. Supposed to be some mess. Talk of the town.

I bolt through Cumbrae an up to the Big House.

In the dark an damp of the house I wish I never had to leave. I wish I had a wee cooker an a stash of food an some books. I'd sit it out for a month. Mibbi two. I could prowl in the nights an mornins for milk an rolls an screw the odd shop. Fuck I could live here forever. Cunts'd think I was dead.

It's the drip drip of this gutterin when the thought comes in plain as day. That wee bastard Daz's the only cunt that knew except for Booda.

Watch that wee bastard he'll knife ye in the back first chance he gets, says his Granny. An she's right. An he does.

Ye'd think I'd want to kill him or at least want him to die of somethin horrible. But I want him to live. I want him to roast in his own pish. To light his own furnace. To fuckin rot in his own bitterness an jealousy. Far as I'm concerned longer he lives the better. CunT.

Home Help from Hell

Two months after the Donna Murphy incident I'm back in the house. Carmen's only talkin when she needs to.

Got yer keys? Payin this bill? Yer Maw phoned . . . Stuff ye see on EastEnders.

I'm out wi Booda. He wants to go an see that wee corner at the top left hand side of a D. Even though the wee fucker stuck me in for Donna Murphy.

I decide to go. I want to see his face when he sees mine.

There's a feelin in his close. We just know there's somethin wrong. Last time we were in his house it was the knicker flingin incident. Still had a few select pairs.

Chap chap.

Nothin.

Chap chap.

Nothin. I looks at Booda wi ma eyebrows up.

Booda looks at me – eyebrows down.

Chap chap chap . . .

The door swings open.

The upright bit of the door standard's not there. Gone. Booted out an lyin on the floor. In we goes. First thing's the smell. It's stinkin. There's this rancid smell an a powerful guff of fish. Black bin bags're lined up along the floor. That's

311

Des Dillon

where most of the smell's comin from – like a bin lorry on a summer day. There's more flies than the Amytiville Horror. The place's pitch black – there's aul curtains over all the windies. Turns out it's cos they're broke most of them.

We hear rustlin from the other end of the house, an the heavy spring of a fold-down bed. But it's not a fold down bed. It's Don't wi a big slug gun cos when we gets to the livin room he's pointin it at us an glarin this torch in our faces.

Who's tha? he goes an starts coughin his lungs up.

It's us, James, the Captain an Mick.

The gun thumps down on the floorboards like it's too heavy anyway.

In them gas flats. There's this partition between the livin room an the scullery. It's all these glass panels about two feet square. But there's not one of them intact. They've not been smashed wi bottles, bricks or flyin plates. Some's gone completely but most've got holes from his slug gun.

A quick look about the place now our eyes're used to it. Fuck sake. It's clingin. The wallpaper's hangin off at the top. Right round. It looks like a cave. An there's stalactite things comin out the ceilin. A water tank burst. He's been shootin holes in the ceilin an the water an the cold an the years an years of dust an muck up the loft's formin these things.

Fucksake – nature takes hunners of years to make them an here's Don't in Sikeside makin them in a matter of months. The place's like a cave inhabited by a strange animal. He's perched up on one elbow.

Ye suit that wee beardie, goes Booda tuggin it.

Don't scratches it like it's the first he knows he's got one.

Watch!

He shouts an whips the gun up an shoots between us through the partition, an out the scullery windie – well it's a big hole in the wall really cos there's no glass. A couple of

312

pigeons flutter up like toilet roll on the wind an land again like nothin happened, like they travelled back in time an the flurry an slap was the transition . . .

FUCKIN BASTARDS!!!

He shouts,

FUCKIN BAAAAAAAAAAAASTARDS!!!

He's loadin the gun when I notice wee piles of dead pigeons here an there in the scullery.

Fuck sake, James, you better get a grip of yerself.

He looks. We're seein a lot better now. His face's corn beef where there's no hair an his eye's're yella where they should be white.

You look fucked, goes Booda.

He smiles an half of his lovely brown teeth're missin. He looks about eighty. His light's cut off. His gas's cut off. The multi-point's gone. The wee cunt's sold it. This burst pipe in the bog's hissin like a snake lyin in wait. That's when we see the needles. Three. I mean I'm usin needles all the time for steroids but ye whack them in yer arse-upper outer quarter. The needles an syringes I use're brand spankin but these things're fuckin hingin. There's wee scabs up an down his forearms. The fishy smell – I see what it is now: millions of sardine tins an squashed milk cartons appearin through the darkness in the other corner.

When were ye last out the door? goes Booda. He's really concerned. It takes me back a bit. But then I realise that I'm concerned for the wee cunt too. I can't believe it after all he's done to me.

Wha wha what is it . . . day . . . who?

Ye need to get yerself out, goes Booda walkin in the scullery an crunchin pigeon bones.

The only good thing I see's a wee pile of letters from Slinky beside him. There's a notepad an a pen an stamps.

How'd'ye post the letters?

He does it.

Who?

Trunks.

Trunks – fuckin trunks? Booda – he's dealin wi Trunks.

Plastic belly? shouts Booda potterin through the squalour. Don't looks at the floorboards.

Hey there's a fuckin nest in this sink! This pigeon flaps out the space in the wall. Booda comes back in lightin up two joints in his mouth. He draws an inhales deep before handin one to Don't. He sits on the edge of the mattress.

What the fuck're ye doin dealin wi a cunt like Trunks?

Don't don't say nothin.

He's the biggest cunt in town, Booda says crouchin down an liftin James's arm tuttin at every scab he sees.

Smack. What did I always tell ye? Stay away from smack. Cunts like us can't go near it. We like it too much. Instant oblivion.

You don't know it's it's . . . stutters Daz but Booda cuts him off.

I was never off it in Bar . . . look at the fuckin state of ye.

Booda hold Daz like he's a baby an keeps runnin his fingers through his hair. Daz's smokin the joint an cryin.

Trunks operates wi the worst junkies in town. Cunts that're too para to leave the house. Mobile's no good to him. He wants the sick an the helpless. The limp an the lame. The poor an the meek. The lost an the loster. The ones wi not enough spirit for suicide.

He's got Daz's Monday Book an he's bringin two bags every day. He's like a postman that misses the houses of the livin. The round of the nearly dead he does. Skinny fucker. Me an Booda's been lookin for an excuse to weigh him in. He's the best sloper in The Brig. We'd see him an look at each other wi that *let's get the cunt* look an soon as we change direction he's disappeared – like aul Nick hiself.

So every day he turns up wi the smack. The sardines an the milk comes from Trunks too. He gets the wanes to steal as much as they can an he delivers to his housebound junkies for a price. Home Help from Hell.

Even though we don't like Daz that much we want to help him. Even though I think he's been pokin ma wife I still want to help him. There's somethin in us that stops us hatin cunt's when they're helpless.

When they're helpless I want to help them. That's not a good thing for livin in the Brig. Tell no cunt ye've got feelins or ye're a dead man.

So we do ten things for Don't:

1. Phone Slinky an get her up here.
2. Get him booked into re-hab.
3. Weld Trunks – hospital case.
4. Pay his bills wi Trunks's stash.
5 Pay five young burds twenty each to clean his house.
6. Buy a bed for twenty off the Blindcraft van.
7. Get him some gear out What Every's for his wee holiday.
8. Tie him up an deliver him.
9. Steal his slug gun.
10. Emulsion his house.

Cos of the state he's in an us freakin him out on the mushies that time, Don't's terrified of Booda. So when we take him down to the place in Peebles Booda pulls out a big blade. It's a farce. No way ye'd carry a blade like this – a Gurka – one of them big curvy things. He gets it on Don't's neck an tells him if he doesn't get clean he's goin to cut his fuckin head off.

After the pigeons're shovelled up an the bins flung out the place smells not bad. Slinky's comin up a couple of day's before Don't gets out the re-hab. But we've got all these bags of smack. Fifty odds. An somethin else cos Trunks's in the Monklands: all these junkies of the night – cave-dwellers – start appearin on the streets lookin for him. It's Night of the Livin fuckin Dead in Sikeside only it's broad daylight an Sikeside's in Scotland not America an these people're actually alive.

We could sell them the smack an make a fortune. But no fuckin way. Booda changes his mind about anythin day by day. But see smack – somethin's happened in the jail. He never changes his stance on that. No sir.

WARNING IF YOU ARE A JUNKIE CLOSE YOUR EYES

We fling it in the canal. Smokin dope an sprinkled bag by bag on its oily surface. These pond skaters that live by walkin the tightrope of pressure on the surface of the water're burstin through it an topplin. If ye zoom in they look like them big Tripods on *War of the Worlds*. Tiltin into the water goin *OOOO LAAHHHH.*

Or *Hey Man Reggae set ma face ablaze* more like seein as how they're out their scientific eyes wi smack. I'm half-expectin fish to pop up an ask for the works. But they seem quite content beneath the surface slidin through the slow waters of the canal an havin the odd soft chew at a passin pondskater's leg that's poked down into their underworld.

I know not to ask Booda to try a bit. He'll give me the, *are ye fuckin mad or something? Have ye not learned nothin from me?* look.

It's not that Drugs are for Mugs. It's that there's different mugs for different Drugs. Don't's been one mug an now he's another kind. Mibbi yer muggery changes as ye get older or as yer life gets better/worse – who knows. No cunt – that's who. But there's plenty'll talk about it all for hours on the wireless. Funny thing is they're the people that know fuck all about it. Read a book an think it qualifies them to talk about drugs, drink an despair. But the only thing that qualifies ye to talk about drugs, drink an despair's drugs, drink an despair. But the only cunts that experience drugs, drink an despair're the least likely to get a career on TV Radio Papers *Dandy* fuckin *Beano Hotspur*. Poverty's a lot easier to handle when ye've got a few bob. So I can't talk about smack. I don't know it from the inside. All I know's Booda knows me inside out. An Booda says I'll like it so much I'll be dead in a year. I trust Booda. Why? I love him. He loves me. But ye don't go up to some cunt in the Brig an say,

Oh by the way Booda, I love you.

Oh do ye? Well here's a swift kick in the balls then,

GROUNDSHAKIN BALLBREAKIN THUD!!!!!

that's what ye'd get.

No.

Love isn't in words an wee stupid fuckin kisses in midair beside some cunts cheek in Princess Square.

Booda loves me. I loves Booda.

317

He cares what happens.

Don't take smack – ye'll love it that much ye'll die. Ye'll be the biggest junkie the world's ever seen. Stick to dope an acid.

He doesn't like me drinkin either but I love drink.

The drink'll be yer downfall . Yer too crazy on it, he'd go.

But not that wee cunt Daz. I don't love him. I just can't see a man down. An there's plenty of them in the Brig since they done the place in. Men're down. Men whose wifes hate them that much they shag their pals on the fly. An their wifes shag other pals an wanes run about wi blades at midnight. But ye can't raise a whole town from the dead so ye look after yerself an them that looks after you an fuck the rest of them. Fuck them all.

Windmills Always Come Round

Slinky an Daz get back thegether. Carmen meets Slinky up the street an she's goin on about Jimmy McCann. Nearly forgot about him. Jimmy's off the drink. He's at AA.

An ye know what he says? goes Slinky lookin right in Carmen's eyes.

What?

You an Mick were in the Windmill that night.

What night? goes Carmen fly as fuck.

Slinky lifts up her eyebrows, *The night the Scouse got murdered.*

Carmen screws her eyes back at Slinky an goes, *He's mad that Jimmy. Still shitin in pots?*

Big Slinky keeps goin at it, *Swears you were there.*

We were here for fuck sake!

I says that but he swears he remembers ye both. There.

Carmen shrugs it off wi a cup of tea in Lightbodys but when she comes home she's worried as fuck an it's all, *What'll we do now,* an all this.

An what's he goin to do about it? I goes.

I don't know do I?

No cunt'll believe him – his head's fucked up.

I'm never goin to get away from it am I?

Us ye mean.

Eh?

We're never goin to get away from it.

We're never goin to get away from it, she says wi her chin jutted out.

Nothin'll happen. Forget it.

But that's easy to say. How can ye forget it?

What'll we do.

She's picked up this knife an right there an then I know she wants to kill Jimmy. I mean it'd be good if he was dead but I never thought to kill him.

I looks at her. She gives it the dead duck grin holdin the blade up.

No way!

How not?

Fuck me the Scouse was an accident. What else could ye, we do? He was goin to plunge me!

But Carmen's on one train of though an she's not lettin it go.

Invite him up here for the weekend. You could pick him up at Buchanan street.

An what?

Bring him here at night.

You'd do that wouldn't ye?

She shrugs. *Better him than us!*

I shrugs.

Bring him here. Get him pished.

An how're we to know he's not told some cunt where he's goin?

But she's not listenin.

Bring him here. Get him stoned. Get him back on the drink.

He's off the drink. He's at AA for fuck sakes.

AA? A fuckin A? They're the worst. It's easy gettin them on the drink. They go back on it if they trip over a kerb. Fuckin alkys.

Right right right but what if he won't take a drink?

How the fuck do I know? Stick somethin in his joint.

Like what?

Heroin.

Who the fuck d'you know that takes smack?

Daz.

How d'ye know.

Every cunt knows. He's a junkie. Big Slinky told me.

So we invite Jimmy up an kill him in his bed. Is that it? That yer plan?

She nods an lights up a King Size. She walks to the windie an watches the trees wavin in the wind.

Every cunt'll suspect us.

I never knew the trees were so close to our house. She goes absent minded. Fuck. She's not even listenin.

Ye're not even listenin!

She turns wi the dead duck look an says, *he's got to go. If the Polis pull us we're gone.*

It was self fuckin defence.

Try tellin them that. I can just see ye up the Polis station, Oh by the way me an ma wife accidentally thundered this guy over the head wi a lump of wood. Beat him up, stuck a knife in him an threw him in the sea – but it was self defence really.

Then she's doin this other voice.

Oh that's all right, Mr Riley, and all the time we thought he got murdered. Thanks for letting us know. Humph, she goes an stares out the windie again.

There's no way I'm killin Jimmy McCann to cover up for that. He might go back on the drink an die.

What if he stays sober?

Fuck sake ye're just after sayin alkys go back on it dead easy.

Aye if ye give them their hole an tell their wife, or break their hearts.

I looks at her up through ma eyebrows.

No fuckin way – Jimmy McCann?

She spits a dry spit an stubs her fag out hard.

Look! Why don't we play it by ear? If Jimmy goes back on it he won't remember anythin anyway.

Know what I think?

What?

You couldn't do it.

It's not that.

Oh but it is that. Ye're too fuckin soft. All this hardman stuff but when it comes to it ye shite yerself.

Mmm.

Don't mmmm me. She's right in ma face wi the *mmmmmm.*

Wait an see how things go.

She blows her fringe. Fuck her.

You do it then, I goes.

She looks out the windie.

We'll get him on the beach. She says like she's in a dream, or a trance. *The seagulls'll be screamin. Get maself full of hate. You ride me all day – get me goin. Passion. Makes me bad if ye do it right. Fuck me up the arse an hurt me. Treat me like a hoor. Ma blood'll thicken an I won't give a fuck about nothin. The worse ye treat me the crueller I'll get.*

Fuck me I want to take her on the floor now. I lean forward an run ma hand up the inside of her leg. She slaps it away. She's talkin like she's drunk.

No take me down there an treat me bad. I want to feel so dirty ye'll suck pish out ma tits. I can see it now. They sky's black an Jimmy's tied up in the Windmill.

I think it turns you on.

She looks wi these glintin black eyes.

You liked me an that Scouse at it an doin him in. Ye were hard all through it.

Was I fuck!

Oh you're turned on wi it the same as me son.

She's facin me full on now an rubbin herself in wee circles an skimmin her tongue over her lips.

I know what ye want deep inside. What kind of man denies his own desires?

Every fuckin man! I goes. *Know somethin Carmen – I'd like to see ye if we were in the Windmill right now. I think* You're *all talk.*

You don't know me one bit.

Do I not?

Look – I've had a wane. Breast fed him right here.

She jerks a tit out.

See if it meant nothin comin up at me out the past I'd pull the wane's gums off ma tit an smash it off the nearest wall. So don't fuckin tell me what I would an wouldn't do.

There's this long silence. But it's black an thick like tar.

What if we get caught? Then we'll really be up shit creek.

Stick yer mouth shut an we'll never get caught. Froggy an the Edinburghslut're never away from McCann. We'll make it look like they done it.

How?

How the fuck do I know? Follow them out the Noggin an do Jimmy in soon as they're away.

She's holdin the door handle.

I'm away out.

Slam, an she's gone.

Day Trippers

It's the middle of the night an me an her in a knocked off
Escort. M6 near Preston. She's lyin in the back seat so it only
looks like there's me in the car. I've got a hat on an dark
glasses. We don't stop all the way to Blackpool. Word is
Jimmy McCann's back on the drink a fortnight. We're goin to
clear it up for once an for all. Who's goin to miss a jake like
McCann anyhow?

We park outside his digs. She found the address on a letter
he sent to Daz. Fuck all about us in it, thank Christ. We're
swiggin out this bottle of Voddy an there's no sign of Jimmy.
I'm paranoid as fuck in case some cunt phones the Polis. I
can hear the sea rushin in an out a street away. In ma head
there's a picture of the Scouse gettin washed up at the hoofs
of a donkey. Rollin over in the sand an fallin back wi the
retreatin wave. I keep thinkin about the donkey lickin his
chin an his puffed up mouth openin an shuttin like a
frightenin fish.

I know! says Carmen her face beamin, *I'll phone an kid on
it's from Scotland.*

Eh? I says without turnin round or indicatin in any way
she's lyin in the back seat.

Phone the landlord an ask for Jimmy. Then he won't see us.

But what if . . .?

He'll forget all about the call – I'll say I'm from Springburn.
She writes down the number from the sign.

I starts the engine up wi the screwdriver I hammered into the ignition. Most cunt's can hotwire a car but I always get it wrong. Took me ages to break the steerin lock. Off we pop down the front. The Windmill's sails're turnin slow in the wind. It's gettin dull. We whiiiiiiiiiiiiiiiiiiiiiiiiiiiiiiiiiiiiiiiiiiiiiiiiiiizz past an the water's splashin up from the road an the waves're splashin up from the sea. I feel cold an empty.

I pulls over to a phone box at Coral Island. I look through

all these lights an ding ding

click click an bodies blackened to

shadows by the nuclear ferocity of the Golden Mile. The arcade makes me wish it was as simple as when I worked there. All I had to worry about was an hour on the Yella Brick road an mibbi gettin the sack for stealin It's a big tragedy now an the way out's blacker than the way in. Ma head's about to explode. Everybody that passes I thinks is The Polis an Carmen looks that conspicuous in the phone box. Some cunt that knows us could pass any minute.

Carmen bounces back across the road. She's got a woollen tammy on wi her hair tucked up an she's got dark make up on. She looks nothin like herself.

Slam.

She's smilin.

She light up a fag. The match's like a welders torch. I dips ma head an she lies down on the back seat smokin.

He flung Jimmy out. No rent. Drunk all the time.

Yes! I says into maself. *Fuckin yes.*

All we need to do's find him.
Can't go in any pubs. I goes
Drive about an look for him.
*No. We'll stay on the one spot. Waterloo. McCann only ever
drinks in the Noggin or the Red Lion.*
Right enough. An she takes a swig out the bottle.

We get the car so we can see the Red Lion an the Noggin.
An we wait.

An we wait.

Carmen's in the front now. When anyone looks we start
winchin like day-trippers. It's night. It's late at night in fact
an all sorts're out on the streets wi

hats an hats that hold cans of beer an straws for walkin an
drinkin at the same time an all sorts of deely boppers that
light up. Tacky capital of Europe Blackpool is.

Every time I sees a Kiss Me Quick hat I think it says Kiss
me Quack an I think of her an the cleaver an the duck.

We can see the Windmill.

I looks at the big turnin sails tryin to dream somethin up.
She's still intent on doin Jimmy in. Fuck me! This leg comes
out the hole in the Windmill an then this body. I nudge
Carmen. It's Froggy. Next thing it's Froggy's burd. An
they're wavin as they walk along the sand. For a minute they
seem to be lookin right at us but it's just ma paranoia. This
arm throws out a big plastic bottle of Cider an me an
Carmen look at each other.

McCann! we say at the same time.

We're out the car like a shot an walkin up Waterloo. We
turn back at the Royal Oak cos people there might recognise
us. The sails of the Windmill're risin into the stars an fallin

back to the darkness of the sea. Risin an fallin. Risin an fallin.
Ma breathin's loud an raspin but she's calm. I'm justifyin it
in ma head – gives us a chance of a life thegether without
the threat of that Scouse hangin over us. He was a prick
anyhow. Deserved it. No cunt'll miss him. An then there's
Jimmy. Who'll miss an alky who lives in a toy Windmill in a
toy seaside resort for fucksake? A man that shites in pots.
He's overdue to die anyway the doctor says. Next drink's his
last.

We get nearly at the Noggin lane an who turns the corner
but Froggy an the Edinburghslut. They've went to the
Noggin an shouted up for a cargo. Carmen spins me to a
shop windie. Of all the windies in Blackpool, the Capo De
Monte shop. Lookin right at me's Jesus, Hands outspread an
that look of infinite compassion on his face an all the
Apostles lookin up in awe. Except Judas, he's lookin down
slightly. His head's hangin like mine. I want to smash the
windie an tear the heads off the Apostles.

Don't do it. Compassion my son. Find Jesus in everyone – even
Jimmy McCann. Jesus's sayin. All the Apostles're tut tutin
away but Judas's sayin, *get right in there kill the cunt. Get him*
before he gets you.

I want to break Jesus off an chuck him in the sea where he
can't see me.

Froggy an his burd're passin right by us an Carmen starts
winchin me an rubbin her bone off ma leg. Couples
practically shag in the main street in Blackpool so they do.
They walk on, don't even notice us. As they pass I looks
down an there's a cherry bowl. Who knows – mibbi the exact
same one Jimmy McCann stuffed down the couch. It's
cherries're glowin like blood in the orange streetlight.

C'mon! she goes, an grabs me an skips across the prom
holdin ma hand like we were two holidaymakers.

Oh My Jimmy Can Fly

I nips up to Raffles an ask a bouncer to get me a cargo. Tenner for hiself an thirty for the cargo. That's the usual procedure. No hesitation he comes up wi two bags of clankin bottles an stuffs eighty fags in ma pockets. I talk in a Belfast accent an stay out the light. I even crouch down so I'm wee'er an walk away limpin like I've been in some big accident before. I'm nothin like maself.

We move the car away up by Pontins an let Blackpool burn itself out for the night. We've three gram of whizz to stay alert. We do a line each on a cassette case. George Michael: *Faith*. We go over an over what to do an makin sure nothin's left to chance. Carmen remembers Jimmy can't swim. Make it look like an accident mibbi?

We park the car on wasteground across from the Noggin. There's no cunt about but just in case we hold each other like a winchin couple off down the beach for a shag. We stop every few feet for a right deep kiss an I slip the hand to make it authentic.

We get to the Windmill – quick glance an I shove her through the hole. The sails're spinnin slow an the mechanism's squeakin an clankin away. I glances round an it's silence except the sea. I hand her the carry out an heaves maself through the hole. We're in an the adrenaline's rushin through ma body wi the speed. I'm sharp as a winter star.

Inside the Windmill smells of pigeons an pish an stale drink. There's the smell of a candle just been snuffed out. It smells holy. Jimmy's sleepin up on his ledge. Ye can hear him snorin light an the Windmill turnin an the sea rushin up an recedin.

He's here, she whispers like a wane findin Santy Clause has been. I can see her face on this slice of light three inches thick comin through a crack in the wood.

I fumbles up an gets a candle. Jimmy gets them out St. Cuthbert's.

The place lights up like a Hammer House of Horror. Ye could be anywhere an our faces're grotesque in the upward light. We lights a fag each an crashes open a Super.

Kshhh.

Jimmy's up like a shot. His can detector's never switched off.

That you, Froggy? he goes an there's a trace of fear in his voice.

Carmen nudges me hard wi her elbow noddin furious for me to say aye.

Aye . . . aye, Jimmy, we're back.

Eh . . . is it the morra?

No, we got a cargo.

Jimmy's feet lower through the flickerin light. I hand him a Super an he crashes it. A couple of slugs an he's down on the sandy bottom. He's rubber out his head so he thinks it is Froggy an Edinburghslut.

D'ye, dy'e come back?

He's fallin about.

Carmen comes in wi this rough accent.

Haw Jimmy – I planked six cans out on South Pier want to go an get it?

Do do doo doo, says Jimmy an he's got one leg out the hole pointin a flattened palm at the sky like he's Superman. He gets his other hand curled round the edge of the openin an then falls back in on a moon beam. I hears the dull crack of his head on the edge of a timber. Hope he's dead.

Doo doo ra doo he shouts, like that mad colonel out *Chitty Chitty Bang Bang*, an makes for the hole again. This time he falls face first in the sand outside.

When we get out the moon's full an bright. It's low in the sky an Jimmy's wanderin across its spotlight like an escaped scarecrow. He's fallin an gettin up an throwin his arms up at the stars an shoutin the odds about fuck knows what. Then he starts flappin his arm like wings against the moon an shoutin over an over;

Oh my, Jimmy can fly. Oh oh my, Jimmy can fly, Jimmy can fly.

I must be sick. I laugh cos I think of him singin that as we fling him off the edge of South Pier. He's that happy It seems pointless killin him. He's got more happiness in one moment wanderin across the moon that we've had in our whole time thegether. I crushes the feelins in me right away.

They say God looks after children an drunk men but he's not doin Jimmy any favours the night. We don't even need to guide him his radar's sayin:

He's off over the sand an we're followin. I see the moon in

her eyes an her breath falls onto the expanse of sand. Ma heart's in ma throat an Jimmy's pirouettin an jumpin up an down like a ballet dancer all along the flat sand near the sea. The moon an South Pier an it's ghosts're gettin closer.

Jimmy's found a whole row of dance partners in the tubular iron columns that hold the structure up. He's windin round them first this way then that makin his way back towards the prom. I hear Carmen's heels stabbin the sand wi every step. She's sayin nothin. She's focused. She wants Jimmy dead. She's seen enough courtroom dramas to know he's the only real witness the night the Scouse got it.

As we get closer to the pier she gets closer to me. Breathes on ma neck. Her breath wraps itself round me like a strangle hold. She's chokin me.

Get him on the pier, she goes, through her teeth.

She starts to spike the sand quicker an harder. She'd changed recently. She's hard boiled through an through. Half of me's thinkin what the fuck I'm doin down here goin to kill some guy an the other half's completely under her spell an doin all she asks.

Yes, Carmen, no, Carmen, three bags full, Carmen, I'd be as well sayin in a Dalek voice.

Anyway. Jimmy thumps onto the wooden floor of the pier after fallin off the railins.

Whoooooooooooooooooooooooooooooooooooooooooooosh Carmen's over like a shot gettin him on his feet.

Are ye OK, Jimmy? she's goin, an she's got her arm round him an holdin him up. He makes to clamber over the fence again an what does she do. She bumps the gums right on him. I mean he's fuckin hackit teethless an wrinkly an she's winchin him. But that's not what she's doin. She's slowly turnin him wi a kiss – like a tug on a giant ship her kiss's turnin Jimmy round against gravity. When she knows he's facin out to sea along the length of the pier she slips the arm round him an starts walkin again. All the time she's wavin me up by swingin her arm past her thigh. I vaults the railins an jogs up.

The tide's turned an it comes in fast. It's pushin itself over our tracks. It's obliteratin Jimmy's intricate drunken moondance. It's shovin against an round the pillars. Pillar by pillar, sandbed by sandbed the water's takin over. It owns half the pier now an'll soon lie black an swirlin the length of it. There's no white out at the end of the pier. There's only the lap an slappin an deep rush of water. Jimmy's at the end an startin to sober up enough to wonder what the fuck he's doin here. Some car lights blur by an odd groups of people partyin silhouette on hotel lounge windies. But there's no sound. Blackpool's like a cinema screen wi no sound. No sound except the drownin noises of the sea an Jimmy startin to wonder what this's all about an Carmen's heels havin their last click at the floorboards an me wavin in the wind wi ma eyes fixed on Jimmy an the smell of danger – the scent of death. The hunt is now the kill.

I'm wonderin how I'm goin to do it. I've got a blade but I can't see me usin it.

Jimmy's lookin at me then Carmen.

Lift him up an tilt him in the sea? He'll never get out. Non swimmer. The wind's comin up an the sea's black an heavy. Carmen moves to ma side.

Jimmy looks – peerin through the sea drizzle. He's tryin to work somethin out. Ye can see it on his face. His eyebrows're bunchin an his top lip's liftin.

Kill him.

I can't move.

Fuckin kill him. We never came all the way down here for night time walks along the pier!

Still can't move.

Pressures on. Time's runnin out. Jimmy sees we're not Froggy an his burd.

C'mon.

Ma feet move scuffin along the planks. Jimmy's got a Puzzled look about him when I grabs his Wrangler jacket. His white hair's everywhere an close up I can see his eyes're blue. Definitely blue. Not only blue but the same blue as mine. An they're lookin. They're starin.

C'mon, she shouts through the dark. There's rain started an clouds've obscured the moon so it's a frightenin glow behind them. A circle of purple an crimson.

Where's Froggy?

I comes right round from ma waist wi this hook an smashes into the side of Jimmy's face. His head's that relaxed it hits his right shoulder. He's down an moanin.

Jump on him. Jump on him!
Are you goin to shut the fuck up. Leave me alone!

She fumbles about an tries to light a fag but the wind's too strong an her lighter's flick flick flickin.

Are you fuckin stupid or somethin? D'ye want the whole world to know that some cunt was out on South Pier tryin to light a fag the night Jimmy McCann gets done in?

Jimmy only weighs eight stone an as far as muscles go he's only got the ones ye need for bein a Jake an no more. I don't even consider he might put up resistance. But I'm forgettin one thing. Jimmy's from Springburn.

I remember he's from Springburn when he jumps up an starts flailin me wi punches an scrabs an bites. Fucksake! I'm on ma knees in seconds wi the shock an he's layin boots in ma head. I flings the arms round his waist an squeezes but he's diggin somethin in ma head – his tobacco tin it feels like.

Carmen's on his back scrabbin nails along his face. But Jimmy's fightin for his life an keeps diggin the tin in. He's got me by the hair wi his left hand. She's got her legs locked round him an shakin him about but he's not lettin go. He's got the strength of ten Jimmy McCanns. I gets the strength to stand up an he's whackin this thing in ma face. Golden Virginia. It's a blob of metal an blood an he's tryin to shove it in ma eye socket. Wi an unleashin of energy I springs the head right on him. I definitely break his nose. The crack's high an loud an Jimmy let's out a low moan an folds like a rubber doll in a bonfire. She wriggles out from underneath him.

Fuck fuck fuck, she's goin an spittin on Jimmy. She puts the boot in over an over as she's sayin it.

I gets ma act thegether an drags her off.

We're goin to get fuckin caught if ye don't screw the nut ya stupid cow.

She stands back starin mad an breathin heavy.

In the sea, she says. *Shove him in the fuckin sea NOW!!!*

An she lunges forwards an puts another boot in. Jimmy feels fuck all. He's not even movin an even though I don't want to do it I starts liftin him. Ever tried liftin a motionless body? Don't. I gets him stood up an his chin's on ma shoulder. I'm pressin him against the railins to keep him stood. He's startin to come to again an she moves back into the darkness.

I hook his arms over the railins an bring his hands thegether. It's not easy this either. Try it. I've got to hold his hands thegether wi one hand an work ma way between his legs keepin his head an shoulders over the railins. I gets between his legs an I can hear her breathin gettin faster in the shadows. I starts shovin him in little bursts till I've got him balanced halfway up the rib-cage. I let go of his hands an his fingertips dangle down at the ocean like sea anemones in reverse.

But yer man Jimmy McCann's made in Springburn an he springs right up again an gets an arm round ma neck. I'm expectin a battle again but that's not what happens. He stares in ma eyes an recognises me.

Mick – Mick – what the fuck're ye doin?

I hear that cow movin back further into the dark. I try shovin him but he springs up again soon as I let him go.

For fuck sake, Mick. It's me Jimmy – Jimmy McCann. Remember Blackpool.

I still don't say nothin cos he's still not sure what's goin on.

I lets him go an he stands wi his bloody nose against mine. I hear footsteps disappearin up the pier.

Mick're ye OK?

He looks about.

What the fuck're ye doin down here, Mick?

I starts greetin. Ma head goes down an I starts greetin. I lean over the edge an let the tears fall in the sea. Jimmy gets up behind me an locks into me. He cuddles me.

There there, he's goin. *It's the drink – it'll wear off.*

There's silence as he inspects his wounds.

Fuck me, Mick must've been some battle the night eh.

He slips the arm round ma waist again. I've not had that for who knows how long. Love. I'm tryin to do Jimmy in an the first thing he gives me's this body contact.

C'mon. I've got dope planked back at ma place.

We walk along the prom back to the Windmill cos the tide's in. I've not said a word so he thinks I'm out ma face an he's still pretty drunk. In the Windmill I wait till ma eyes're adjusted an fuck him on the side of the head again. He's holdin onto ma waist an I lay three rapid in right where the jaw pivots. He's out cold.

I leave The Windmill shiverin.

When I get to the car there's no car. She's fucked off. I manage to blag an aul Cortina an nurse it back to the Brig at fifty. All the way I'm hopin Jimmy'll think he's had a doin an the DTs. I'm glad I never done him in.

Here's Wolfie!

It's the end. Fuck – it's over. Any cunt can see that. After
Blackpool she's hardly talkin to me. *Fuckin shitebag!* is all she
can say.

Anythin good on the telly?

Fuckin shitebag!

That's a nice dress.

Fuckin shitebag!

Is the wane stayin at yer Maw's again?

Fuckin shitebag!

She's out all the time an I can't control the jealousy
anymore. I've wrecked the house don't know how many
times. I keeps hearin the Scouse whisperin out the sea. I can't
hear what he's sayin, only deadly whispers.

Big Slinky's left Don't. She's phoned me from Blackpool
sayin Carmen's the biggest Tart in Scotland. She's never
away from Daz. I don't want to believe it so I don't.

This night she's at the dancin again. It's three o clock an
she's still not in.

I'm drinkin.

It's half three an she's still not in.

I'm still drinkin.

It's four o clock an she' still not in.

I'm still drinkin.

It's half four an she' still not in.

I'm still drinkin.

It's quarter to five an the door handle turns.

I whips the door open an there she's swayin about wi her cousin. Her cousin's sixteen an she's got this white leather mini skirt on. I lets them in an they walk past me like they've just been to the van for fags. I sees dirt an grass on their arses.

Oh we had a great night fuckin shitebag! goes Carmen, testin the water.

I just looks.

Didn't we, Trish?

Mmm mmm, says Trish, all bright eyed an bushy tailed.

Trish's knees're covered in grass stains. Blow job. I check Carmen's legs. No grass stains but the seam of her tights at the front.

What time's it? I asks.

Half three, goes Carmen.

Half three? I says wi a threat in ma last syllable.

This silence falls.

Want tea, Trish? An they nearly kill each other tryin to get to the scullery.

I follows them in. They stop gigglin.

D'ye always wear yer tights the wrong way round?

Carmen looks down an they burst out laughin. The two of them gigglin away. Ma blood's already boilin.

I must've went out like that, She goes, an they go into fits again. I opens the fridge an crashes another can. Carmen's talkin to me that's how I know somethin's up. The kettles boils an clicks off. Nobody does nothin about it.

It's after five, I says.

Silence.

D'ye hear me?

They burst out laughin again.

Where the fuck've ye been?

Out.

To five in the mornin?

They slide back in the livin room.

I want to know where the fuck you've been to this time. Trish?

Trish panics an looks at Carmen.

Time ye get out the dancin it's three an we got somethin to eat an got talkin ye know yerself . . .

Oh I know all right.

They move closer thegether cos I'm movin out the scullery.

KERASH

I launches the can through the livin room windie an go for them wi this big knife. They scream an bolt up the stairs an lock theirselfs in the bog.

Up I goes.

Let me in let me in, I sings like a wolf in a fairy tale.

Silence.

Let me in little girlies . . . or ye might not like what ye see-ee. I'll chop ye's up in little bits little girly wirlies . . .

But they're not for lettin the Big Bad Wolf in so the Big Bad Wolf decides to let hiself in. But Wolfie's not interested in huffy puffy. No no. Wolfie wants to terrorise.

I pad to the end of the top landin an say,

Last chance saloon little girlies do ye let the Big Bad Wolf in or do ye wait an see what happens?

Oh what a big mouth Carmen has, she can't keep it shut.

If ye don't leave us alone I'll phone The Polis.

Not by the hair on ma my chinny chin chin, says the wolf.

They go quiet again. Ma turn to giggle but it's that eerie it frightens me. I thinks it's not me laughin but this cunt that's took over ma body. The Scouse mibbi? I stop before I have to run away from maself.

I hears the windie openin. They're tryin to escape even if it involves a leg breakin leap out the windie.

Girlies, girlies what big feet I have, I goes an runs the length of the landin an lands wi ma two back paws on the door.

The door comes off at the lock an hinges.

It flies through the air an I spies them standin up in the bath tryin to get behind each other.

The door breaks the toilet pan.

THUMP

I lands in the bog.

Heeeeeere's Wolfeeeeeeee, I goes like Jack Nicholson in *The Shinin* wi this big blade in ma hand.

AAAAAAAAAAAAAHHHHHHHHHH!!!!

They're crushin each other in the corner an I'm wavin the blade about wi these mad eyes. There's a tap drippin an the water's runnin down Trish leg.

I let them by me duckin an screamin an they shoot down the stairs an right out the door.

It's just a cold wind an me an the meaninless house.

I'm in the room when I hears deep voices mixed in wi the squeaky-fast voices of Carmen an Trish an then the dreaded crackle Oscar Charlie an all that shite.

Mick!? Carmen shouts nearly laughin wi glee, *the Polis're here. They want to see ye. Ye've to come down the stairs.*

Come down stairs? Come down the fuckin stairs? What? like it's ma Da down there an I'm suddenly a ten year old an our Angie's shoutin up cos she's grassed me for settin fire to her favourite doll or somethin? No fuckin way.

Tell them to get to fuck! I shouts.

Silence.

Crackle of radio.

Ye better come down . . . now.

If they don't get to fuck out ma house I'll come down an throw them out.

I can hear The Polis discussin tactics. Carmen's glad she's caused a bigger fuss than mine. That's what she always does if she gets caught at somethin – creates a mess ten times bigger than the original so as everybody forgets what she's done.

I hears big boots comin up the stairs. I can just tell she's down there wi her arms folded an a Club King Size at her lips.

He comes in the room an he's a big cunt. Like the Polis ye got years ago. Highlander. I've got this big blade stickin by its point in the floor. That's the first thing he notices. I'm waitin for him to make a dive at me an I'm goin for the blade. But he sits on the floor an crosses his legs. I don't say nothin.

There's this silence an I can feel ears down the stairs suckin in the airwaves. The only thing's the odd Charlie Oscar.

Wife at the dancin? In late? Think she's fuckin about?

He asks an looks right in ma eyes. An I know. He's no Polis. He's a real guy. An somethin else I know too – he's got a wife like mine. His heart's tore to fuckin bits too. Only thing holdin him up's his uniform. Take that off an he's mercury fallin through the cracks on the pavements where he walks.

I nod's an there's this tear in ma eye. I shuts ma eyes an hear him prisin the blade out the floor.

I'll shove this under the bed an say no more.

Listen we'll not lift ye. We'll take ye up the Lochs an ye can walk home – get a key so she can't lock ye out.

He stand's up an goes down the stairs.

On the way out I gets the back door key.

Out in the street the neighbours're twitchin their curtains an she's shoutin,

An don't come fuckin back ya bastard. I hope they lock ye up an throw the fuckin key away.

Even Trish shouts a few things at me as I'm gettin in the back of the car. Learnin I suppose.

So they take me up the lochs an I walk home. I've got a folded joint in ma sock so I smokes that. When I come to the canal I stand tryin to work up the courage to chuck maself in but I can't. I blow lines of smoke out over its still surface an wonder what the fuck it's all about. What the fuck's it all about anyway? When I get home she's gone. Only a matter of time now. It's only a matter of time.

Well! That's me right up to the week I flung her in the canal. I've already told ye about that so I'll move on.

There's not a lot to tell now really. Three things just:

1. How it finished.
2. How I got where I am now.
3. Jimmy McCann dies in the Victoria. Liver.

The Disappeared

It's months after the Here's Wolfie incident. An weeks after the night I flung Carmen in the canal. I'm in our Angies an the tears're varnishin ma face. It's mornin. I'm tryin to do the usual crack but she knows somethin's wrong so she does the automatic laughin.

Time ye got that fuckin grass cut. I can't see McGinty gettin her gear off at night for the height of it . . . the big bloomers an the wrap it round me dead tight belly flattener . . . an her wee stick-insect man's eyes bulgin at the monster she's turned into.

I shouts out the windie.

McGinty! Show's yer long black curly teeth. Show's yer long blonde tongue.

Laugh a minute, me. Jokes an patter.

I remember Gina. She wanted me to leave Carmen near the end. I spent a couple of nights wi her. Should've stayed.

It's ma birthday this day. She buys me a birthday cake an I greet all over it. Nearly ruin the fuckin thing. Nobody's bought me a cake an candles an a wee card before. She thinks I don't like the cake. I soaks it an kids on I'm shovin it in the tumble dryer.

Gina's on the verandah listenin to sirens. Saturday night.

An I've got the tumble dryer on kiddin on the cake's in
there. I goes out an holds her. She can't look me in the eye
cos I've been greetin so I holds her. Ma arms come round her
waist an they're tight an I says nothin – not a thing.

An at six in the mornin we're still there. I've got ma head
on her shoulder an holdin like it's a cliff edge an I'm fallin.
The stars're gone an birds're whistlin. Taxis're parked up an
milk floats're out.

I'm still at Angie's windie an I'm shakin. White as a fuckin
sheet.

Caught her in bed wi a guy the day, I goes.

Aye right, says Angie. But I looks up an like an iron rod
through the head, she believes me. I looks out the windie an
goes,

*Aye . . . I thought there was somethin up when I kept findin
shoes two sizes too wee for me at the bottom of the bed.*

She laughs quiet, sighs an lets me go on.

*I comes back just after nine an chaps the door. No answer. All
the blinds're shut . . . the blinds I paid a grand for . . . shut tight.
No answer an I'm shoutin. The house's that quiet ye know
there's two people not breathin up the stairs. I goes round an
tries the back door. Nothin. Next thing I knows I'm on the wee
roof an the windie's open. I starts climbin in an the blinds're
rattlin like fuck.*

*She appears in the room wi her arms folded in the sexy gear I
bought her. She wants to know what the fuck I think I'm playin
at. I crashes on the floor in ma workin gear an steelies. She tries
to block the path into the top landin. I hears some cunt movin
in the bed. Ye always know the sound of yer own bed so ye do.
She still wants to know who the fuck I think I am an what the
fuck am I doin in* her *house. She folds her arms tighter but one
look an she melts backwards prayin I'll only knock fuck out him
an not kill him. Anyway I walks in the room an she squirms
between me an him. He's lyin on the bed. An the first thing I*

*want to know's how good lookin he is. An it's that wee cunt
Daz!*

  Fuckin Daz!

  *Supposed to be yer mate an there he is shaggin ma wife – right
in there shaggin ma wife in the fuckin house that I'm out knockin
ma pan in to pay for. Bastard. Know what he's wearin? Black satin
boxer shorts. He's shakin uncontrollable. Black satin fuckin boxer
shorts. I'm thinking, need to get a pair of them. I looks at him. I
thinks, he's fuckin dead meat. He thinks he's fuckin dead meat.
Carmen thinks he's dead meat. He pisses his black satin boxer
shorts. There's no cunt more shocked than me when I don't kill
him. I starts feelin sorry for him. Fuck knows how? I just says well
I suppose that's that or somethin . . . I can't remember but there's
this big empty silence an I goes down the stairs an I don't know
where it comes from but I shouts up an asks if they want coffee
they must've swapped mad looks an they shout yes . . . fuckin YES
PLEASE in fact. I gets the kettle on – an this's the funny bit –
when I opens the spoon drawer the cutlery rattles an he's up the
stairs an he's thinkin . . .*

KNIFE
DRAWER
KNIFE
DRAWER . . . *man, he comes stumblin*

*down the stairs an he's strugglin wi the front door. He turns round
like a rabbit trapped in headlights an there's me sittin his coffee on
the table. I sparks up a fag an shouts her down the stairs. They
drink the coffee quick as fuck an off they go.*

  Angie gives me the *she was a tart anyway ye're better off
without her* routine an all that an off I pops.

  I leave Angie's house an become one of The Disappeared. I

Disappeared maself. I know enough about the seedy side of life to become some other cunt. I drink. I take anythin that gives me oblivion. I don't know how long passes – it could be weeks months or years. Time's shrivelled in ma brain now.

Time Bends

They thought I done maself in. Searched for me for years. No cunt ever found ma body. They dredged the Canal. The searched the Estate. They searched the Lochs. They searched the big house in Cairnhill. But the search slowed down. London. That's the place to get lost.

Don't know how long it is now. But I went back. Time bends when ye're down an out. Ye can never tell if life existed before. Or love. Is it real. Dream?

Glue sniffin. Done that when I was eleven an there's me in London – don't know what age – passin what might be five minutes or five years sniffin. Takin kickins. Drinkin. Takin abuse. Snortin. Takin men up ma arse. Smokin. Takin men in ma mouth. Vomitin. Then forgettin. Wipin out memories that make me feel shame. Ye've got to have another life to compare things to to feel shame. I mean one blow job's the same as the next. It's all relative. So if some poof's shovin it in ma mouth for three or four quid it means fuck all compared to yesterday's blow job. No shame. Nothin. But compared to walkin through the trees an the sun shinin an holdin Patrick's hand an Carmen up ahead movin, turnin, smilin, movin. Compared to that there's shame – infinite shame an degradation. So I wipe it clean. Ye've got to do that.

The doctor tells me I'm delusional. So fuck knows if what I'm going to tell you happened. One minute I've got some semi-hard cock in ma mouth on the Embankment an next thing I'm gettin off a train at Coatbridge Central. It's all changed. Fuckin Time Capsule. Spaceship. Kids playin. Could be mine some. I walk along the aul canal path an end up at the bridge. The one I told ye about when I flung Carmen in the canal.

I'm standin a minute or a week. I know it's Here. Like I should feel somethin about Here. But Here's all it is. Here. None of me exists in it any more. Skid row? What the fuck is it. Where the fuck is it? Any cunt ever seen it? No chance. Ye can touch it but it's nowhere. Ye can feel it but it's not solid. Ye can smell it but it's got no source. Ye can taste it but ye can't bite it. Ye can be in it before ye see it.

Skid Row's not a place, it's a state of mind. That's why when ye hit it ye're a goner. No turnin back. Who's goin to accept ye've hit Skid Row if ye're still doin ordinary things like workin an stuff? No cunt, that's who. Most cunts'll say ye've got a dose of the Poor Me's – that's all.

But ye've gave up an that's that. There's no energy in the statement, in fact there's no statement, there's only the acceptance of watchin the last drains of self-worth trickle out eyes that're finished. Ye've had enough; no point in whimperin.

It's more than yer existential dread . . . it's past the point of thinkin an feelin. It's wantin the temporary death of oblivion; too dead yerself to go to death so ye wait. An ye wait. I might get it crossin the road not lookin like I always do. Or the young team might do me a favour an stick me wi a blade or crush ma head wi a baseball bat. It's all irrelevant. It's nothin like the Poor Me's cos there ye're lookin for a perverted comfort; like a wane wi it's thumb in it's mouth. But this time there's no comfort wanted. It's blackness I

want; the engulfin nature I suppose death to be. The
paradox's that the spark, the tiny light needed to do maself
in, that wee bit of self propulsion's gone long time ago.

That's why I'm at the wall for the umpteenth time lookin
in the canal. Ten, mibbi twenty feet down. If I could climb
the wall (it's only five feet) I wouldn't need to jump. I'd just
topple easy over; keep the hands in the pockets an move ten
metres-a-second-squared into the flat black expanse. No way
I'd struggle. Even the breath'd be slow an rhythmical suckin
in two mibbi three gallons of water cold on the inside of the
lungs. I'd taste it wi indifference, bitter, an sink like all the
others that's flung theirselfs in.

I'd float up soon enough provided I never got snagged on
the weeds or an aul pram or an ASDA trolley or a burnt out
car in the murky water wi the current foldin in an out the
slow swingin doors. A wane mibbi, or some aul guy, might
find me an get a shock but what can I do about it? Ye're even
less in control after ye die.

I'm at the wall. Not back to the wall . . . not cliché's an
provokin statements . . . there's been enough of them over
the years. There's been all the drama an the violence an sex
an some success. Some success. Then the sting of failure after
failure an the ghostly tumble down till ye burst through
what ye thought was the bottom. Till nothin matterin doesn't
matter.

So I'm at the wall an if I was on the wall . . . on the copin
stone at the top . . . a wind could blow me over. If there was
stairs or somethin I could shuffle up them an over I go. If the
wall wasn't there mibbi? One step into the air'd do the trick.

But what if there's someone under there drinkin wine.
They'll see the splash an shout an get a fright. If it's the
young team they'll pretend not to be scared an shout abuse
an laugh as I die. They might even chuck a few bricks for
good measure.

Die ya aul cunt!

. . . they'll shout an call me Flipper an Kermit an all this stuff. But the laughter'll skite over the surface an scatter in the dark trees. Seein people die's easy. Laughin at them dyin's easy too . . . but livin wi it – that's the hard bit. That's the baggage that's too heavy. Aye yer muscles get strong cos ye're young an ye've got the hormones but what when they deteriorate an the weight ye've got to carry's still the same or heavier? What happens then? They won't think of that, the young team when they're hurlin bricks an laughin.

They'll only feel their future in that wee silent pause when they realise ye're dead. An what if some of them's cracked ma skull wi one of the bricks?

Murder case.

After the silent pause they'll laugh again but this laugh'll be different.

Empty.

Hollow.

Fear'll be stickin through like the spokes of bust bike wheel in a plastic poke.

If none of them get me wi a brick it'll be,

Get The Polis! Tell them some aul cunt's committed Sunnyside off the bridge.

If a brick gets me they'll shuffle away sayin the usual stuff that they say so that somethin can be said. They'll not say what they mean cos each an every man'll think that they're the only ones who know who done the murder an they can't deal wi it so it's all,

Some cunt else'll find him floatin by the farm or down Bargeddie way in the mornin. We weren't here the night. Right?

Off to the dancin an shaggin some bird they'll go. In the mornin when it starts to piece thegether they'll never be the same again. Oh they'll be silent an they'll drift away from each other but they won't forget. One day that weight'll take them to the same wall. Skid Row's not a place; it's a state of mind.

So I'm at the wall. Cars're rushin by. Mostly taxis. I can smell the young burds inside. Curly hair an shinin lips mean nothin. They're smilin at nothin an flickin their heads back an laughin. They don't even know me. Mines was another age, another set of dreams an, yet, the same aul wall an the same aul canal. There's a queue for this wall an the distance between the people is measured in time but it's still a queue. The last taxi had one that looked like Carmen an I remember a day.

Where're you goin? she shouts.

Where d'ye think I'm goin!

If you're goin where I think ye think ye're goin then ye're goin to end up where ye know ye'll end up so where the fuck do ye think ye're goin?

Where do you think I'm fuckin goin . . . ya bastard?

Fuckin go then – go, ye know what'll happen.

I might've no feelins now but I had them all then. I walked away from the door. The wane's peepin out the blinds. Fear – that's what I taught him, fuckin fear. I done the guilt bit over an over, now that's even gone.

It was the pub that night: there was a big cold through ma middle, a big fear an somehow I knew I wasn't right. My mind's not right.

Fuck knows how I got to here. It's all foggy now but down an down I went. I started in the hotel one night an ended up in the pop the next but that was years ago. Fuckin years. Where did I go? Everywhere that's where. The only thing different was the view. Blackpool, London, France, all them places where people like me go. But I could fight then. I was good at the fear game. I could roll in a ball when the boots were goin in an spring back up an lash out like a maniac. Basic survival. That went too – two, mibbi three years ago.

Or was it days, or was it months? It wasn't a bolt of lightenin or fireworks nor nothin. It was more like a gigantic sandglass that frittered away till there was none left. I was empty an the world could see right through me.

Oblivion.

Drink.

So I take a good slug of El Dee. The whites of ma eyes swivel an I wonder who's lookin at me. I can feel them behind but I don't turn round. So long as they don't want the wine. So long as they want anythin but the wine. They can have ma body. No problem. The young team'll reach that too, some of them. Some big hairy bastard'll shag them an they'll accept it. They'll fill up wi hate but they won't do nothin. They'll repress it all. They might do it for fear or they might do it for money.

The figure moves. It's some skinny cunt.

See's fuckin drink!

The knife's diggin in ma ribs an I laugh. More like a grunt. I laugh, so he laughs an I see his missin teeth. He's not in Skid Row yet cos he's got a knife an he's stickin it in ma ribs. That's how he's not in Skid Row. That's how I know. No cunt in Skid Row sticks some cunt wi a knife – ye need hormones for that. But he notices I've got no fear. In Skid Row the fear's gone. He takes the knife away an reaches inside ma coat. I let him take the bottle. I know he's comin to Skid Row an the knife's comin to his ribs so I laugh. He thinks I'm mad an takes a step away an laughs back wi big wide eyes swivellin between swigs.

I show no fear. He mistakes it for bravery an gives me the wine back. He grunts a cigarette under ma nose an scorches a match off the wall. In the hellish flame I recognise him. It's Daz – Don't Call Me Daz we used to call him. So what? He doesn't know I see who he once was so he lights ma fag, an his, an turns his face to the darkness.

He's a couple of steps closer to Skid Row now an he feels the jolt. I can feel his hand in ma pocket but that's nothing, nothin compared to the dead men's pockets I've searched. He moves to ma other side an I laugh again. He thinks I'm away wi the fairies an this time he stuffs his arm right in. He rifles all ma pockets. I'm not reactin. It's like sex assault. That's what I'm just thinkin when he pulls ma zip apart an gets his hand on ma dick.

I don't flinch. He starts wankin me. Hard ons I haven't had for a long time. No hormones. I let him fiddle an his breath's hot on ma neck. He's got it right out now an there's cars goin by but ma elbows're restin on the wall an I blow smoke into the cold air sittin above the canal. I imagine this's a wummin doin her stuff just to see what happens. But there's not a spark of arousal. He's obviously got the same idea an he's ticklin ma arse hopin that'll sort me out.

I flick the fag down, down, into the canal an out it hisses. He's carried away now an sticks another fag in ma mouth an gives me a light.

Ma trousers fall to ma ankles an there's cars goin by. No pants – shat them an threw them away two or mibbi three days ago. Or was it years? The canal's shovin it's way westwards an then he's on his knees an he's got it in his mouth an he's slobberin away there like a dog an there's cars goin by. Cars goin by. I can hear them an I can hear their brakes as some of them slow down to see what the fuck's goin on.

He slabberin away an goin,

Dy'e like it, Baby? D'ye love it, Darlin?

an it's floppin in an out his mouth an there's no reaction. That doesn't put him off,

Shag me, Baby!

he's goin now an he's grabbin ma hips an makin them sway

353

in an out. Cars're brakin as they go by. I know they're sayin, *Look at them, aul pervert,* an all that stuff but I let him carry on suckin. There's nothin else to do. He slaps ma arse quick an sharp.

Get fuckin hard ya bastard or I'll stick ye.

I notice that all this time he's been wankin hiself. He needs me to get hard for his own gratification so he stops wankin an works his finger up ma arse. I can feel his long nail on ma intestines. I don't react an he's shovin it in an out. A swan flies up the canal an then another. The fog's curlin up on the edges of their wings. An there's a noise. A woosh like angels wings used to make in the films. Woosh woosh an off to heaven. The swans're white. That's all they are – white.

I'm goin to shove it up yer hole tart . . . hear me tart – tart? he keeps sayin over an over. It's turnin him on to say *tart tart* all the time. He gets behind me an tries to force me to bend over a bit. I put ma forehead on the cold wall. He's tryin to get his semi up ma arse but it's not hard enough, his hormones're too low. He's gettin nearer Skid Row all the time. I suppose he knew he couldn't get solid an that's why he wanted me hard so I could shag him. He's far removed from ma reality if he thinks that. I sense him gettin angry an he spins me round.

Cars're goin by real slow. Their lights glitter on his knife.

He pushes the knife forward an, holdin ma cock like an elastic band, he cuts it off. That's it – he cuts off ma cock an the blood splashes out on the pavement. A passin car screams an I look at the blood. I decide that bleedin to death's OK. He laughs an throws the cock in the canal. Weird, I hear it's little splash an imagine a big pike snappin it up before it sinks to the bottom.

That act that'll take him to Skid Row. It's the rules of Hell: the more heinous the act the quicker ye get there. The look on his face I recognise. But somethin's happenin, I turn an by some miracle I want to try to climb the wall. The blood's drainin out fast but I try to swing a leg over the wall. He sees what I'm doin an does up his trousers. Wi his bloody hands he pushes me up.

Christ! I'm on the wall at last. I'm naked from the waist down like them dreams that used to embarrass me. Blood's runnin down both thighs an cars've piled up to watch. He throws the knife over an walks into the dark trees. I know he's goin to Skid Row but he doesn't. He still believes men can forget. The only thing they forget is that they can't forget. The blue light flashes in the distance. There's the drip drip of ma blood, oily, on the surface of the canal. A branch twitches. A slight wind catches me an I am fallin.

Fallin.

Fallin.

An on the way down the memories're pulsin in ma head. I've managed to keep them out. But I can't now. I'm too weak. Every vision flashes wi this noise like some cunt hammerin sheet steel in a big empty steelwork. It's ringin through ma body.

DEEEEEERIIIIIIIIIIIIIIIIIIIIIIIIIIIIIIIIIIIIIIIIIIIIIIIIIIIIIIIIIIIING

Ma wife's starin in ma face an greetin. Carmen's at the bottom of the close. *Are ye comin?* she's shoutin.

Don't don't, Caroline's goin.

DEEEEEERIIIIIIIIIIIIIIIIIIIIIIIIIIIIIIIIIIIIIIIIIIIIIIIIIIIIIIIIIIIING

It's three days before New Year. Caroline's been in the hospital havin our second wane an I'm fuckin about wi Carmen. Sixteen. Couldn't keep ma hands off her. I'm twenty-four. Fuck sake – see if ye could go back in time. What ye'll pay for one pair of knickers. Seem sleazy? It is.

At night I'm visitin the hospital an kissin Caroline an the

new wane wi the same lips that's been all over Carmen. I'm drunk every day.

Caroline gets out. Wummin always know. She comes right out an asks me. An what do I do? I goes an tells her *aye* an who it is. She sends me down for cans. I comes back an there's her an Carmen. I turn to mercury. I want to seep through the cracks in the floor. This sensible conversation starts an we agree it all over. Just a fling. Never see each other again. Well if only. Fuck!

Caroline pleads wi me not to leave her wi stretch marks like a map of the world. I holds her. Honest to Christ – I wished it never happened. Not cos I got caught – I wished it never happened cos of the way she was. Cos of what I'd done to her.

I'm fillin wi guilt rememberin squeezin into her oversize breasts. A black guilt thick as treacle, big as hell's, creepin up through the floorboards an seepin through the microscopic spaces between the glass on the windies. It's makin me shudder an this unexpected wind's tuggin at the roof. I'm sure it's goin to lift off. In the black pane all these faces're laughin. My head thinks the house has sunk into hell like the Amityville horror. There's lights flickerin out of sight below the windie. The faces know it's flames an they grin more. Their teeth're red an their eyes – their eyes're bright yella.

DEEEEEERIIIIIIIIIIIIIIIIIIIIIIIIIIIIIIIIIIIIIIIIIIIIIIIIIIIIIIIIIIIIIIING

Caroline's cryin her eyes out. I'm bubblin, promisin never ever to wrongdo her again. We can keep it quiet.

DEEEEEERIIIIIIIIIIIIIIIIIIIIIIIIIIIIIIIIIIIIIIIIIIIIIIIIIIIIIIIIIIIIIIIIIING

Hogmany. The house's brighter an the big impact of it all's fadin. It's all holdin the new wane an passin kisses an settin out drink an shortbread. About eleven the fiddle music's on an I crashes a can to watch. By the bells I'm a bit drunk. We kiss deep promisin to love for ever. The wanes're sleepin an the house's fillin wi neighbours. Caroline's tryin to be normal.

Where's Carmen? goes Caroline to some burd.

Mitchell's.

Oh!

I starts thinkin about her. I drinks two quick whiskeys but it's no use. Joe Mitchell comes up to me.

I thought Carmen was in your house? I goes

Aye she is. He winks an I'm tryin to decipher it. *She watchin the wanes.*

I'm tryin to not let him see I'm sighin wi relief when he goes, *Our Johnny's up – he's into her. Know what I mean?*

I laughs but ma insides're rippin. Rippin an I've only knew her a week. Ma promises to Caroline evaporate.

If I fell down dead that minute, that'd be a million times better.

I'm sneakin out an Caroline's tryin to keep an eye on me an another on the party so they'll not suspect. As I slips out the new wane starts screamin.

I pause . . .

I steps over the threshold. Fuck me! I'd never step back over that door in ma life. I slides in Mitchell's an click the livin room door open. They pull apart on the couch.

What's goin on here? I says

Carmen stutters like she's ma wife caught in bed wi another guy. She stands up. Red kimono an a white shirt underneath. She's walkin towards me an I hears this voice in the close.

Michael. Michael. Michael.

There's fear an anger in her voice. I'm terrified in case Carmen's Da appears. I steps out in the close an Caroline's leanin over the railin.

What the fuck're you up to? she says.

I . . . I . . .

Next thing Carmen comes out. Caroline goes ballistic.

Ya fuckin slut. Right that's it. I'm goin right in there an tellin yer mother an father. Everythin. The whole fuckin lot.

She's comin down the stairs. The wane's screamin in one arm an she's takin big swigs out this voddy bottle wi the other arm. Carmen's bolted to the bottom of the close shoutin on me. Caroline's outside Carmen's door. I looks in her eyes. She's dyin. If she walked back up the stairs I'dv'e went too. She never knew cos she reaches out an

flips

the letter box. I'm lookin at the flap in mid air about to come crashin down in an almighty way. I run like fuck. I'm out the close makin ma way across the grass before the second chap. I catches Carmen an we run in an out closes an over gardens till we're well lost an in a house where they're too drunk to notice us. I get the keys of an empty off this Burgh guy.

I wakes up next mornin. Know how it is. First thing's the hangover. Then the night before starts piecin thegether in ma head. I'm freezin in a single bed wrapped round Carmen. The bed starts spinnin an I feels sick.

I vomit on the bed. It stinks. There's some on ma leg an long slavers hangin off ma face. I'm gaspin for breath at what I done. Next minute there's this music comin from somewhere. Talkin Heads's playin in the wardrobe. 'Once in a Lifetime'.

The words're a voice in ma head. Then I realises it's me – me talkin to me. It's a bit of me I never knew I had surfacin like a black shark an it's talkin. Fuckin freaky. That was the start. That was the start.

SPLASH

I HIT THE CANAL

Hartwood

So that's the story. They fished me out the canal an stuck me in here. Never found ma dick – probably swallowed by a big pike right enough. They keep telling me the canal/dick stuff is a figment of my illness. That it never happened. But it did – even if it didn't.

Been in here five – ten – fifteen years – or it could be days. Who the fuck knows. No cunt comes an no cunt leaves. No cunt even dies. It's always the same people. Same doctors. Same nurses. They have the meals at different times every day but they change the clocks so it looks like the same time. I've got these cunts sussed.

There's always pish in the air. They spray it. I've seen them. They collect bed bottles an put it in scooshers an walk about sprayin it in the air an on the plants. It's the smell of the place. A long long corridor disappears to the other worlds. I used to go there but this world's safer. This one white room. I like here. I like the size of this universe.

They don't spray the pish squirts in here. The food comes up the corridor floatin on it's own mist. They mix shite in wi the food. No-cunt knows they do that but I know. Next time ye're here smell the food. Turn off yer pish nose an turn on yer food nose an ye'll smell the shite. I throw the bits away that smell like shite. They just think I don't like some of the food.

Other people that left life an never died're here too. They creep in nooks an crannies like spiders. After lights out they switch off the electricity. There's a lot of different electricity. After they've switched off the stuff that burns in the lights they switch off the stuff that works us. But I'm fly as fuck. Exactly twenty minutes an thirty-three seconds after the lights go out they switch off the electric that works us. I know about electricity – I used to fix fruit machines. I jump up an down so as to insulate maself an they can't switch me off. I keep ma mind to think in the long nights when silence presses on me from all angles tryin to make me not breathe.

In the mornins laughin twists an echoes out shadows. Eyebrows lift. Eye whites show. Faces creak to nurses holy whispers. Plenty missin teeth – Tombstone City. Loppin tongues squeak over gums. I can hear it all cos I've been thinkin all night an ma ears're tuned wi ma head. Slidin slippers next then heads poke out secret caves of darkness. The noise goes up wi the voltage. The nurse in the wee room has this big round control. She's got to turn it wi two hands an as the brightness goes up so does the shufflin an mutterin in tongues an gums an slobbered lips. In the thesaurus it describes them:

Idiots, **eejits,** **dafties,** lunatics, *mentally disordered,* **insane,** **mad,** **lunatic,** *moonstruck, of unsound mind, not in one's right mind, non compos mentis, deprived of one's wits, deranged,* **demented,** *certifiable,* **mental,** **abnormal,** **psychologically abnormal,** *sick, mentally disturbed, mentally ill, of* diseased or disordered or distempered mind, *unbalanced,* brain-damaged, *ravin mad, stark ravin mad, mad as a hatter, mad as a March hare, off one's rocker,* **gaga,** *loony, declared insane,* **certified,** *mental . . .*

I see them pass ma door. If they look they only look once. Ma eyes penetrate them an they're wounded wi ma wounds an they can't take it. They walk on.

Every mornin the pish nurse comes in ma silent room. She wants me to pish. But I've got no dick. She waves a pencil where ma dick used to be an goes,

What's this, Mickey – here's yer dickey. We sewed it back.

But I haven't got a dick. I haven't pished in years. Yet she always goes away wi a full pish bottle. Witchcraft.

Out ma windie I can see everythin. In the far universe high angels sing me to sleep. In the sky one star shines. The moon rolls over the trees. On a twig near the windie a robin lands an peels an unpeels its eye in one long slow wink. I remember Carmen that day she asked me to marry her. The robin flies off shudderin rain from the twig. Waterdrops're fallin.

Fallin.